Emerald Thorn

Irene Martin

Hearthstone Publishing Ltd.
P.O. Box 815 · Oklahoma City, Ok 73101

A Division Of
Southwest Radio Church Of The Air

All scripture references are from the King James Version unless otherwise stated.

Printed in the United States of America

Published by:
Hearthstone Publishing
P.O. Box 815
Oklahoma City, OK 73101
(405) 235-5396 • WATS 1-800-652-1144
FAX (405) 236-4634

ISBN 1-879366-20-7

Table Of Contents

Chapter One

Bed And Breakfast

"The last match," Emerald spoke to herself as she struck the sulphured top against the cement wall. Torn paper and rags, resembling petticoat ruffles, ignited in brilliant coral. The flash subsided as quickly as it appeared, leaving a struggling glimmer of fire. Frail hands bent and pulled at a scrap of discarded wall paneling until it lay in a splintered heap upon the fragile campfire. When the wood slivers became a healthy flame, Emerald placed upon it a tin can of water.

Several slugs were added to the liquid, most dying instantly. The woman waited for her supper to boil. A carrot or potato might make a tolerable soup, she thought. I guess I can rule out ever seeing spices again. Occasionally she tapped the can to knock a slug from the can's side. She could not afford to have any of the slimy delicacies become escapees.

This time last year, Emerald wouldn't have been eagerly awaiting a supper of boiled slugs. But much had changed in one year. Everything had changed, in fact. How often in her life she had made wrong choices, and scolded herself later. If I'd only known then, she thought, what I know now. But no amount of remorse could change her present situation. She cried anyway.

Emerald wept for her loneliness. She couldn't bear

the void left by her best friend's absence. Her best friend? Yes, Emerald had to confess that Rose had been her best friend and she loved her. But Emerald acknowledged that her own arrogance had prevented her admitting the truth, until now. Her destitute state also received a fair share of tears.

Never had Emerald been without a bed in which to sleep. The way I lived, she reflected, I must have thought I was queen of the world. Her hand reached into her jacket pocket to retrieve her handkerchief. But it wasn't there, as she knew it wouldn't be. I must have left it at home. At home. She flinched at the thought. I can't think about home. Tears streamed once again. She wiped her eyes with her jacket sleeve. "Wow," she squealed with amazement. "That's something I never thought I would do."

Steam rising from the makeshift stewpot smelled of the waste water which had always repulsed her as she passed the wharf. If only I had some salt, she wished. Maybe tomorrow.

At that moment, a slug fell from an overhanging rafter, suctioning itself to Emerald's pale hand. She scraped it into the brew and chuckled.

"Last year you would have made me faint, but sorry, fella, tonight you're supper."

With a silver fork she drew from a soiled silk purse, Emerald stabbed the slugs, one by one. As she ate them, her past crept before her again. Attempts to push her thoughts away were unsuccessful. The days, weeks, and months had taken too great a toll on her. She knew the worst was yet to come. Had it really been a year ago? It felt like ten. Emerald tried to organize her fragmented flashbacks. The nineteen-nineties. They had started out so peacefully. When did this nightmare start? Nineteen ninety-what? She couldn't remember; but last year, sometime, the world changed.

A delicate patent leather shoe stepped over a slug which stretched and pulled its way across the cedar plankway. Emerald recognized the image as herself. She was back at the home she so dearly loved. Other feet followed hers, making their entrance into the dark room. The patent shoes clink-clinked across the hardwood floor to a window. When she drew the draperies, the weary faces of the guests burst into ecstatic smiles.

"It's enchanting! Oh Harold, look at that fireplace," said the burly woman from deep within her silver fox jacket. It was obvious that Harold saw nothing as he struggled across the room with overnight bags, suitcases, camera, and heavy parka.

"Let me help you, Mr. Higgins." Emerald Thorn, the proprietor of the establishment, tapped her noisy heels as she backtracked, taking hold of the articles that didn't appear to be permanently attached to Mr. Higgins. His wife, oblivious to the scene, gazed out the window onto the water below. A rosemoss carpet lined the footpath steeply leading down the hillside. At the bottom, crystal waves coyly slapped the grassy shore.

"We pride ourselves on our view," said Emerald.

"It's heavenly. Beautiful. Magnificent. What mountain range is it?" marveled Mrs. Higgins. Her husband blundered about the room, reluctant to mess the meticulously kept room by depositing any of his parcels.

"Sir, let me take those, also. We have a nice, big wardrobe to accommodate your clothing and luggage." Emerald stowed the belongings and continued. "Those mountains are part of the Olympics."

Mr. Higgins stared at the wardrobe. His eyes followed its height to the ten foot ceiling.

"We've tried to make your room as comfortable and convenient as possible. You are as isolated as you want to be. You don't have to come around to the main house, or come as often as you like. Whatever you prefer. There are spare blankets right in here. A lot of folks don't anticipate our cool temperatures and moisture. With Port Orchard being on the tip of the peninsula, we get rain everyday. Therefore, we keep little rain bonnets, slickers, and galoshes on this shelf. There are towels in the bathroom, but extras are in this compartment." Pointing to each niche as she mentioned it, she continued the presentation she had delivered hundreds of times.

By now, Mr. Higgins had arranged the belongings and closed the massive hardwood door. Both he and Mrs. Higgins stood quietly surveying each corner of the room that would be their home for the next week. Emerald gave a brief history of the house and town that lay around it. It always made the guests feel they were getting their money's worth for Emerald to recite the entire speech.

"The Seattle area first received settlers after the Civil War. This mansion was built by a gentleman, Greyson Hansen, who had previously been a plantation owner in Atlanta, Georgia. They say that this house is a replica of the home he and his wife, Doreen, loved so much. They were in Atlanta until the lumber business brought Mr. Hansen out West. Every detail was carefully duplicated to be exact and true to the colonial architecture of the pre-Civil War era. Hansen personally selected each piece of furniture in the entire house."

Mrs. Higgins' face showed delight at the story. "You love this house, don't you?" she smiled as if knowing the answer already.

"Immensely. This home was a wedding gift to me twenty-five years ago from my late husband."

"You appear to be part of the fixtures. Even your accent is from the South. Am I correct?" beamed Mrs. Higgins, once again knowing herself to be right.

"Certainly. My family was from Atlanta. I maintain my heritage through this lovely home. Raylon, who was my husband, would be delighted that I've not changed a thing since his demise. I don't believe I will ever change even one teeny thing or ever leave this place."

Mrs. Thorn turned to glance out the window. How could she leave, she thought. Sunlight tiptoed across the bay's slowly pulsing waves, transforming the huge window into a watercolor of corals and grays. She thought that in as many times as she had looked out this window, she had never seen the same seascape twice. She was the owner of the most extensive private collection of mental paintings in existence. They could not be bought or sold, but were part of her being, ingredients of her soul. Her fragile lips revealed a quivering smile, and her eyes grew less distant as Mr. Higgins' stomach roared.

"Excuse me, won't you, please? Supper is always served at seven p.m. Breakfast is promptly at nine in the dining room of the house. However, if you would prefer to stay in the guest chambers, a tray can be brought to you. Which may I expect?"

Mr. Higgins shrugged. He moved to investigate the morning nook and bathroom again. "Makes no difference," he said. His wife cast an impatient look at Mr.

Higgins.

"We'll be eating in the dining room, then," she voiced.

"Wonderful," said Emerald. "Then we will see you at supper in an hour or so." She strolled, as a southern belle might, in her calf-length silk dress. Mrs. Higgins watched each graceful step. Emerald appeared to maneuver a hooped, ruffled gown across the room. Waving her hankie, she said, "Most of our guests appreciate the seclusion here. You have no phone in the room. But you may use the parlor phone whenever you would like to. If you want to venture down the hill, you will find a hidden cave. Watch closely or you'll miss it. It is concealed by English ivy and evergreen ground cover."

"How romantic," squealed Mrs. Higgins.

Emerald stepped carefully over the door facing onto the plankway and added, "The Emerald Thorn property extends a mile in three directions, then down the hillside to the water. Enjoy it all, please. See you at supper."

"How gracious of you," said Mrs. Higgins, waving in imitation of Emerald.

Emerald sauntered along the damp planks, carefully positioning her slender spike heels to avoid the empty spaces between them. Glistening, viscuous trails bore witness that slugs had preceded her by only moments. The deliberate manner in which snails and slugs travel fascinated Emerald, but the thought of their slippery flesh coming in contact with her skin made her every pore tense. At that moment a slug dropped from the overhanging porch, plopping onto her arm. She screamed and flailed her arms wildly as she ran for the front door. Emerald felt herself hyperventilating, but the slimy predator clung tightly as its hysterical host beat herself and shrieked.

"What happened?" she asked, as she felt a cool cloth dabbing at her face. She looked around to find herself on the sofa in her parlor.

"Mr. Higgins heard you scream and heard stomping on the walkway. He found you collapsed on the walk; you must have tripped. Your shoe heel was stuck between the planks," explained Rose, sympathetically.

"I remember a slug slapping down on my arm. It must have fallen from the overhang. It was awful. Cold! Slippery, horrible. The adhesive varmint clung to me. I couldn't get it off." Emerald breathed faster as she recounted the episode.

"You could have hurt yourself," said Mr. Higgins.

"Oh, I'm fine, now," said Emerald sitting upright. "Our guests deserve some peace and quiet. And supper. What about supper? What time is it?" She patted her hair, straightened her dress, and took a deep breath, exhaling deliberately.

"See?" she said. "I'm okay, now. Come on, Rose, we must set the table. What have you planned for dinner tonight?"

It would have been easy for Rose to say escargot. Emerald knew her wise-cracking sister-in-law would not miss the opportunity to harrass her for her delicacy. But to Emerald's surprise, Rose answered in a kind, comforting tone.

"Baked salmon," she said. She walked with her arm around Emerald's waist to steady her on her walk to the kitchen.

"Local salmon?" Mr. Higgins followed the ladies into the kitchen with its glass cabinet doors displaying extremely organized dishes, containers, and delicate tea cups.

"Yes, Mr. Higgins, local salmon. I am sorry you had to witness such an unladylike exhibition. But, I assure you, I am quite fine. Please rest a bit and bring your wife to supper at seven." Emerald shooed at Mr. Higgins.

The tall man stood silent, nodded, and turned to leave. "If you say so, ma'am."

When the women were alone, Rose laughed. "Remember," she said, "when I arranged for the two of us to get away from the inn on a little vacation? Sun Meadow Health Spa?"

"That place in Canada? How could I forget. I almost died there."

"Admit it, Emerald. You loved it. Those full-body massages, relaxing wraps in towels freshly warmed under heat lamps . . ."

"That horrible, sticky eucalyptus masque," interrupted Emerald. "It was cold and slippery. I nearly suffocated beneath that deadly goo!"

"The beauty technician and I, both, told you to relax and enjoy it. You panicked."

"Panicked? I couldn't breathe, I tell you."

"That was no excuse for plunging into the swimming pool, especially when you can't swim a stroke."

Emerald pivoted, angrily slinging a pan of bread into the oven. "But you could, I remember. And you rescued me. So there! I told you thanks back then. What more do you want? I'll owe you forever. Is that what you want?"

"No. I just meant," said Rose, walking to Emerald's side, "you haven't changed. You are still the squeamish, southern belle type you were so long ago."

Emerald's face beamed with delight that Rose could see the obvious resemblance between her own mannerisms and those of her ancestors.

"But face it. It's all part of the show. You are acting out the role of plantation mistress. You are no more southern belle than I am."

"I'm more southern belle than the nineteen ninties have ever seen. You're jealous, that's all."

"You need to develop a thicker skin, Emerald. It's okay to play the game with the guests. But if you ever had to take care of yourself, the role of delicate flower is not practical. You would never make it alone, in the real world."

The women faced one another. "Is that what you really think, Rose?" blurted Emerald.

"Sure. Why do you think I stayed on after my brother's memorial service over twenty years ago? I didn't think the grieving widow would hold up. You still can't."

"That does it," shouted Emerald. "If you weren't half owner in this bed-and-breakfast inn, I'd kick you right out of here. You could go back to your precious Oklahoma. I don't need a babysitter." She drew back her hand as though she might slap Rose. But instead, she reached for a dish towel and meticulousy, frantically wiped water from the spigot and sink. "When Raylon comes back, we'll buy you out and you can go back home!" she screamed.

"Emerald, admit it. Raylon's body was never recovered from the submarine accident. Probably never will be. Sharks most likely got it."

"Oh, God!" Emerald stared nervously toward the ceiling. "Never say that again," she said avoiding the sympathetic gaze of Rose. "Ray is safe somewhere and unable to get back to me. But someday . . ."

"Someday," comforted Rose in a hushed tone, "you'll work it out, putting Raylon's death into perspective."

Emerald shook beneath Rose's embrace. Sobbing, she reached for her handkerchief in her apron pocket. Dabbing at her eyes, she said, "You are wrong. And in the end, you'll know it."

"For your sake, I hope so. But I doubt it, Emerald."

The table was set with no further talk between the women. Each worked mechanically, as though they could arrange a buffet in their sleep. The Higgins came for supper, Emerald remembered, but she couldn't recall the conversation. She hoped she had been her usual, cordial hostess self. Somewhere, alone in the Pacific, Raylon needed her. Emerald knew it because she felt his presence strangely with her, day and night. Emerald also knew that, somehow, she would find him.

Chapter Two

Fantasy Recluse

Newspaper hung over the edge of the breakfast table, as Rose peered through her red-framed glasses. She announced, "Today Rusty Lively writes that AZT could cost between eight and twelve thousand dollars per year for each person receiving the medication to treat the symptoms of AIDS. The state of California has listed this drug among those available at no charge to recipients of AIDS programs who are unable to afford the drug treatment."

"Well, there you have it! That's probably eighty percent of the homosexual population of California. I swear. And who, routinely, has twelve thousand dollars excess for such expensive treatment? They'll all be signing up," said Emerald harshly.

"Emerald, take hold of yourself," mused Rose, glancing up from her reading. "Not all eighty percent are eligible, only those who are in the final stages of the disease qualify to receive the drug."

"Just wait. The hungry and poor will be doing without while the California state government spends millions of dollars each year keeping these guys going." Emerald pounded the biscuit dough she was working, sending a cloud of flour, with most of it attaching to her shoes.

"These guys, as you call them, only have one to two years to live after diagnosis with the drug. Many aren't gay men, but are heterosexuals, and then there are the kids who contracted the disease through blood transfusions." Rose neatly folded the newspaper and continued. "It's not a cure. It just lessens the discomfort and prolongs their lives a short while."

"Yes, long enough to run up a healthy tab of five or six years worth of AZT, calculated at twelve thousand dollars per year."

"Which is still less expensive than treating the patient without the use of AZT; hospitalization, pain killers, antibiotics, long-term care. It all adds up."

"Yes. It adds up and at taxpayers' expense!"

Rose neared the counter where Emerald rolled out thick dough on the cutting board. As she cut out large biscuits with the open end of a drinking glass, she commanded, "Grease that pan! I'd like to give that Rusty Lively a piece of my mind. I hope you plan to counter that column with some sensible suggestions."

Doing as she was instructed, Rose opened a cabinet door, retrieved the shortening, and carefully inched the door shut. Each panel had a glass pane, making the contents of the shelves visible. Rose thought the glass was used deliberately by the original owner as a means of assuring that his wife kept a tidy kitchen. Rose personally enjoyed a little clutter to remind herself that the house was lived in. Emerald, on the other hand, loved the clear panes, kept them sparkling clean; and each item behind them had a designated spot on the shelf.

"Emmy," proceeded Rose, while Emerald plopped the huge raw biscuits onto the greased cookie sheet, "why are you getting so up-in-the-air? That's California, not Washington State."

"Oh really? And how far do you think California is from here? Seattle is practically the homosexual capitol of the world." She shoved the biscuits into the hot oven and stoked the fire with another slender strip of wood. "Another year or two and legislation will have passed here. We'll be taking money from the Keep-Washington-Green fund and handing it right over . . ." She removed her apron and dusted the flour from her shoes with its dangling tie. "Right over, I tell you, to the gays to pay for their AZT." Emerald sashayed out of the kitchen to the dining room, nodding one last approval at the flower arrangement and vast array of fresh, sliced peaches and tomatoes. "I'll not say another word about it, lest I lose my appetite. We have guests arriving any moment." Scurrying about the room, she arranged and rearranged magazines into little fans beneath the smoking stands.

Filling her coffee cup, Rose thought she had time to dash upstairs and jot down the bits of inspiration gleaned from Emerald's reaction to Rusty Lively's column. As she turned toward the staircase, the orange beauty of her roses captured her attention through the bay window. She lowered her body to the window seat. Drawing her leg up beneath her, she sat facing the lawn.

"Oh, Emerald. I've got twelve, thirteen, fourteen, no . . . so many new buds. They'll soon be blooming. The weather this year, I suppose. No last minute cold snap at Easter. They are so lovely. I think I'll cut some and walk over to Tracy's house after breakfast."

But a knock at the door brought Rose back to the parlor as Emerald rushed past her in a blur. "Hello, come in. Rose, it's the Higgins, here for breakfast." Meeting them in the entry hall, Emerald took their sweaters. Hanging them on the hall tree, she announced, "We have just enough time for a quick downstairs tour while we wait for the biscuits to brown."

The smell of bacon and eggs slapped Mr. Higgins' nostrils, fully awakening his countenance. His feet followed the tour group, but his gestures showed his mind was back at the dining room table.

"The kitchen has all the original furniture and appliances: wood cookstove, ice box, and pie safes." Emerald's eyes gleamed as she showed off her favorite room.

"You really don't use them, do you?" marveled Mrs. Higgins.

"I surely do," assured Emerald, "each and every day. I bake homemade bread for the noon meal and supper, and also . . . " she donned her padded oven mitts, retrieving the steaming pan of biscuits from the oven, "biscuits!"

"Delicious. Mr. Higgins has never eaten a real breakfast, at least not that I am aware of."

The women laughed as they paraded single file to the dining room. Emptying the bread into the warming basket, Emerald removed her mitts, reached for the coffee pot, and as all were seated, filled dainty china cups with the brew. "Please, don't wait another minute. Help yourselves to this breakfast while it's still hot."

Mr. Higgins spoke out, "Well, I just got my money's worth, that's for sure. Biscuits, gravy, eggs, whoa!"

"Don't forget," said Rose as she passed the meat platter to her left, "your choice of bacon, ham, or sausage."

"Hold up here, is this for real?" he asked, forking a slice of each of the meats.

"And may I add, that is not just *any* gravy, sir. That is Emerald's special sawmill gravy."

Mrs. Higgins cried, "The sausage is out of this world."

"I'm from the South and sausage here just doesn't taste quite the same as back home. I have a favorite brand that I add a few spices to."

"And lots of sage," Rose finished the statement for her sister-in-law. "I eat it day after day and never tire of it. Never gain an ounce, either," she laughed.

"Neither would I," said the male guest, guiding an entire fried egg, on the end of his fork, into his mouth. The ladies watched him, each puzzled over what he was trying to say. He shook his head, managed a mouthful-of-food smile, garbled a statement, then swallowed. "Yes, siree, that's good."

The innkeepers glanced at one another, both thinking this would be one couple to add to their list of guests to remember. After Mr. Higgins had eaten every crumb within his reach, the group moved to the parlor where they finished the pot of coffee. Seating themselves on the low, claw-footed sofa, they soon were amidst dozens of brochures and maps of tourist attractions. The Higgins desired to travel along the coast of Canada.

"Ferries leave from Bremerton regularly. You can drive your car onto the ferry which docks at Seattle," said Rose, handing Mrs. Higgins a ferry schedule. "Or, if you'd prefer to leave your car here, my sister-in-law would be at your service to drive you down the hill to the foot ferry. That ferry connects with the larger ferry to Bremerton."

"Perhaps we will relax until tomorrow morning. We can leave here after breakfast, and still have time to drive to Bremerton to catch the ferry. Right, honey?" asked Mrs. Higgins.

"Sure," answered the husband, "as long as we get one more stab at breakfast, Mrs. Thorn."

The laughter subsided, the atmosphere becoming sedate. Rose had errands to run, yet her obligation to entertain the guests as long as they cared to sit and visit was part of the services offered at the Emerald Thorn Inn.

Mrs. Higgins' eyes wandered from Emerald to Rose. Both women stood scantly taller than five feet, five inches, and had slight frames. Rose's strawberry blond gleamed lighter in color than Emerald's auburn hair. At a glance it wasn't obvious whether the difference was due to more activity in the sun, or a chemical highlighter.

"Which of you sisters has the true hair color?" began Mrs. Higgins.

"Oh, we aren't sisters," giggled Emerald. "Rose is the sister of my late husband."

"I'm sorry. I remember you calling her your sister-in-law. But the resemblance is more than slight. Isn't it, dear?"

But Mr. Higgins, having consumed far too many portions of everything at breakfast, was dozing on the deacon's bench.

It didn't seem to bother Emerald that she was mistaken for Rose on occasion; she was an only child and enjoyed having a companion she could consider a sister, too. But she knew Rose pictured herself younger at heart, more attractive than Emerald, and resented people thinking she might even remotely resemble a southern belle.

In fact, Emerald recalled that she and Rose had their

first argument, which would set into motion a twenty-year chain of disagreements, after seeing the moving *Gone With The Wind.* They had driven into town to the theater, shortly after Raylon's memorial service.

"This has to be my favorite picture of all time," said Emerald as she stood in line to get popcorn and an RC. "Let's sit down front so we will feel like we are right at Twelve Oaks." As the big barbeque unfolded, Emerald's eyes seemed to defocus. She had cried as Atlanta burned and laughed as she flirted with Rhett; she was totally absorbed into the screen.

Emerald also remembered that during the drive home, she came back into control of herself and recounted the movie's sequence. "Rose, I just love that film. I'd give anything to have lived on a lovely plantation. My ancestors did. They had a plantation near Atlanta, one of the first to be destroyed by those . . . those Yankees. Sometimes I have this overpowering feeling. I sense that I actually did live in those days. I know it sounds silly, but I feel that I am remembering the lifestyle. You know? Like I had actually lived it?"

"Emerald," Rose answered, "you deserve to be back in the Civil War era. What a name. I suppose in this past life your servants called you Miss Emerald?"

"Don't tease. Just picture yourself in one of those beautiful, hooped dresses. Wouldn't it have been romantic?"

"No, I'm sorry. These are the good, old days, Emerald. I wouldn't have wanted to be alive back then."

"Don't you think their attire and lifestyles were elegant?"

"They looked fine on screen, but be real, Emerald.

Do you think it was very romantic getting all those skirts and hoops hiked up to go to the outhouse?"

"The elite had maids like Mammy who took care of emptying chamber pots. So they didn't have to go outdoors to some uncouth out-building."

"Thank goodness for that. I can see Scarlett O'Hara dragging yards of taffeta and lace through the dirt, then wrestling it around to just get the toilet door shut. There were no lights in outhouses, either. How would she see to get all that taffeta up over her head and get those pantalettes pulled down? I don't know that they even had toilet paper then, let alone feminine hygiene products. How romantic that must have been, ripping up old rags for use as sanitary napkins. No ma'am, Miss Emerald, I will take today over the plantation of Tara, anyday."

Instantly Emerald sensed her delicate, ivory cheeks reddening as a blush of anger flooded her countenance. Her neck and face muscles drew tighter until her jaw felt welded shut. The silence of the drive home was broken only on occasion by Rose's attempts at reconciliation.

"I said I didn't mean those things. The whole film was breathtakingly done. And you're probably justified in thinking that would have been a glamorous era to have lived in. That is the aura they wanted to create when they made the film. There are different ways to view any situation. Take, for instance, the slavery issue. Slaves were those servants who attended the elite. I'm sure they didn't feel it was a romantic period of history. It's over and we needn't fight over it. We just don't see eye-to-eye on this particular issue. Truce?"

But a truce it was not. Emerald wheeled Raylon's classic 1952 Chevy into the drive, scattering gravel as she stopped short of a collision with the smokehouse.

Emerald stomped up the stairs to her room. She had been there for two hours before Rose gathered the courage to enter and attempt an apology. Emerald had watched Rose's shadow against the light oozing through the crack beneath her bedroom door.

"May I come in?" Rose turned the crystal knob and cautiously entered the darkened room. She flinched as though anticipating an object being hurled in her direction. But no airborne brushes or shoes came her way. Emerald was too distraught. She sat on the floor beside the bed. Rose crossed the room and knelt beside her.

"Truce?"

"No!" she insisted. "You come into *my* home, at a time when I've just lost my darling husband; a time of extreme sorrow. And you attack all that I believe to be warm and wonderful. A dream, the only thing that I have to comfort me since Raylon departed."

The chandelier reflected a silvery lake onto the tears that had sloshed onto a photo of the mourned Raylon Thorn. As Raylon's wet features smeared into a gray puddle, they slid from the picture. Emerald's sobs turned to soft sniffles, and soon subsided as she drew a long, deliberate breath.

"Listen to me, Emmy," Rose comforted. She pulled Emerald to her side. "He was my brother. I miss him, too. My heart is breaking along with yours. Again, I am really sorry. I should have shut my mouth about your love for Scarlett and Rhett. I promise to never say another word to you to cast shadows on those days you want to remember as charming. Perhaps since your family was from the South, you have a genuine right to feel so strongly a part of it. Forgive me and let's be friends. Sisters?"

From somewhere in her bodice, Emerald pulled a silky handkerchief. She dabbed gingerly at her nostril. Rose appeared to resist the intense urge to laugh, as she leaned the sniffling Emerald Thorn toward herself and hugged her.

"Okay, Sister Rose."

Thus, for years this pair of mismatched females had arrived at thousands of standoffs. For years they had been considering a vacation, but failing to arrive at an agreement as to *where* to go, the trip had been postponed. Neither, it appeared, wanted to accommodate the other. Rose was voicing the need to "air out," as she called it. But Emerald felt more and more settled into her duties at the inn. Would Raylon forgive her for abandoning her obligations, even temporarily? Emerald had never felt that release in her inner being that would allow her the freedom to do so. Daily talks with Raylon had resulted in one-sided, frustrating conversations, with no direction being revealed.

"Harold, please wake up. How embarrassing. Falling asleep in the presence of our hostesses." Mrs. Higgins swatted her husband's knee with a pamphlet. The overeater and his wife stood and ambled through the entryway, donning their sweaters. The cool breeze swept in as Emerald held the door open for her guests. Stepping onto the front porch, Mrs. Higgins announced, "On second thought, we won't be back for supper. I believe Harold has had enough to eat for the remainder of our holiday."

The ladies tittered as they watched Harold stretch in

the damp, mid-morning mist.

"Will you spend the day in Seattle? Should Rose or I drive you over to the foot ferry?"

"No, thank you, though," Mrs. Higgins responded to Emerald's offer. "Harold and I will pack a change of clothes and drive over to Bremerton. With the maps and wonderful directions, I'm sure we can make it to Seattle quite well."

"Can we plan on you for breakfast, then, in the morning?" queried Rose.

"I really hate to spend our vacation eating. And I seriously doubt if poor Harold could handle another home-cooked breakfast. You know, since it's the first he's had, to my knowledge. But now you ladies have been wonderful. We may stay overnight in Seattle and find a pancake house or fast-food chain in the morning to have a quick brunch. That will give you two a break from houseguests."

"But's that's what we are here for," insisted Emerald.

"Oh, you aren't permanently rid of us. Count on us tomorrow for supper. Harold's stomach will be craving your cooking by then."

Even Harold laughed as he pried at a fragment of trapped bacon with a toothpick.

Rose hummed as she packed a wooden picnic basket for the Higgins to carry with them. "Tomato, cheese, ham, and bread," she chanted as she singlehandedly operated the sandwich assembly-line. "Mayo, lettuce, tomato, cheese. Mayo, lettuce, tomato, cheese."

Tinkling dishes, stacked a foot high, indicated that Emerald was clearing the dining table. Lowering her load into the sink she began, "What do you do at Tracy's? Is her foot doing better?"

"Pretty much healed, now. I just read to her. And we talk. She's not supposed to put any weight on her ankle for another week."

"How silly for a grown woman to be traipsing about in a clown costume," smirked Emerald. "And to break an ankle breakdancing, whatever that is."

"Tracy loves clowning. Not only is it an excellent stress reducer for Tracy, but she feels it is a way she can serve her fellow human being — cause someone to laugh."

"She certainly did that. The whole children's ward. Lucky for her she was already at the hospital. She'll do anything to get attention."

"Having never done anything outside of operating the inn, you can't possibly imagine, can you, having an interest in the real world. There are other people out there, Em. People that live totally different lives than ours. The only people you see are our guests — rich people on vacation. Occasionally you go down to the market to shop for fish and vegetables. And, let's not forget the grocery boy who delivers the edibles. There's more to life than this bed-and-breakfast. Tracy enjoys entertaining and ministering to others. It's good, clean fun. Leave her alone."

"You are wrong about my not knowing about the real world. I read the papers. I'm not an idiot, just because I choose to devote myself to the inn." She spun around and marched back to the dining room to gather the remainder of the dishes. "And besides, I love this inn," she screamed from the dining room. She saw the Higgins backing out of the driveway. Rushing to the kitchen, she grabbed the basket handles and tap-tapped out onto the kitchen porch. "You! Higgins, hold up!" she waved.

"Sure, take credit for making the picnic lunch," mumbled Rose as she viewed Emerald through the ivy-framed window. Mrs. Higgins thanked Emerald for the lunch and Mr. Higgins thanked her, once more, for breakfast.

As the car drove down the gravel road, Emerald felt a raindrop slap her hand. Two, three, then scores of drops rushed from the clouds showing through the openings in the tall, leafy ceiling. Head down, Emerald trotted toward the porch. Remembering the last words she had spoken, she wiped the rain from her cheek with her handkerchief and continued. "Besides, the elegance and charm are all part of this business of Emerald Thorn. I have to be here, baking breads, preparing fresh meals, and taking care of our guests. Otherwise, we would go out of business."

"Emerald, don't you see, you've worked so hard at it? You're a success, but you have to take a break sooner or later. This place is an obsession with you. You've become obsessed with the place and the fantasy of the place. Emerald Thorn. The place is a bed-and-breakfast. The woman is a fantasy recluse."

"Dry!" snapped Emerald, pitching a cup towel to Rose.

"You need to get out more, for longer than an hour. Take a day off."

"By all means. An excellent idea. Sorry I didn't think of it. And the Little Red Hen will bake the bread?"

"I could bake the bread. Or we could buy a loaf."

"All you can do is make canned biscuits and read books. When you aren't doing that, you are writing for that Everett newspaper. We don't think alike. The inn has a reputation to maintain. Store-bought bread? One day with you as hostess and the business would crumble."

"What makes you think that I couldn't handle it for one day?"

"Who, pray tell me, would write your column while you so nobly hold down the fort? The fort vacated because I half-wittedly gallavant around the state sweeping cobwebs from my dusty mind?"

All was silent as Rose's frustrated jaw loosened slightly. "The Higgins will not be back until supper tomorrow. True?"

"How journalistically observant of you."

Deciding to ignore Emerald's sarcasm, Rose continued. "Tomorrow I plan to drive over to Everett to drop off a story. Come with me. If we leave early, we'll have time to shop at that lovely fruitstand on Broadway."

"We would have to leave too early. And I don't enjoy that long ferry ride."

"Why not drive through Tacoma and up through Seattle? We would be there in less than two hours, and we can eat Chinese food while we are in town. You know how you love Chinese."

"I have a good recipe for chop suey, if that's what I have a hunger for."

"Emerald, don't be cantankerous. I'll gas the car up this afternoon. We'll leave after breakfast."

"Don't volunteer to fix breakfast. I couldn't stand the surprise."

"You fix breakfast. I'll spring for lunch in Everett. Fair enough?"

Emerald dried her hands on her apron as she carefully folded it. Without further words she stepped onto the wet porch and tested the air. With no rain at this moment, she strode over to the three-tiered bed of marigolds. Snapping the stems of several, Emerald gathered them into her large skirt pockets and started down the narrow footpath to the ocean.

For more than an hour she sat on the flat stone. Sudsy, cold water sneaked over her toes, then raced back to sea.

"Darling, you'd love the way the inn is thriving. We have guests every night, just about. The Higgins are great. Most of the guests are. They are all hungry for a unique experience to boast of upon their return home. I've been so busy creating experiences for others, I have had none of my own. I look into the mirror, Raylon, not the same lass you deserted so long ago. But a woman, almost fifty. I've never experienced anything, except the fulfillment of having my charm and culinaries complimented over meals."

Emerald grew sick for a moment. There has to be more to life than this constant waiting, she thought. The worst part was not knowing what she was waiting for. Her spirit seemed to be waiting for some secret, anticipated experience.

"Tell me, Ray. Where are you now? Are you happy? Are you trying to tell me something?" The slapping sound of the water, hypnotic and calling, beckoned her to join Raylon. Tranquilly she swayed with the rhythm of the tide. "Where am I? I read of women who suffer from Empty Nest Syndrome. They raise their children, then find they've lost themselves during the process. I've lost my husband and have nothing to show for my years of living. Living, waiting . . . living, waiting."

Emerald threw a flower into the water and counted the ripples it made — ripples which were soon consumed into the froth. "If only I knew, Ray, what it is I am waiting for. Still waiting. Time passes. They never found your body. And I wonder. I feel you are still here, yet gone. Raylon Thorn has sailed deeply away into a tiny dot in this seascape. My whole life is a painting. It isn't real. I'm not real. I've sailed away, never to be recovered."

She leaned back onto the spongy moss which upholstered the incline. The sun struggled to be seen through the shadowing clouds. When it managed to steal a moment, it glistened in Emerald's hair. Too soon, its brilliance was imprisoned by cloudy captors. A similar struggle burned within Emerald. She placed the marigolds over her bare feet. Reflectively she watched waves stealing them, one by one, as Ray had stolen her days and life.

Chapter Three

Year Of The Goat

"Come on back. Yup. Yup. Back. That's got it." The flannel-shirted arm signaled the driver of the eighteen wheeler to stop. "Smitty. Glenn. Get out here, fellas. We've got six tons of melons to unload."

"Where's Perry?" chimed the two teenagers. "He always gets out of stacking melons."

"Here I am. Uncle Ted said I am to count melons as they are thrown from the truck. You guys stack."

"Forget it," Smitty jumped from his post atop the mountain of gunny-sacked potatoes. The skinny arms flailed wildly at his cousin's face which was grinning arrogantly.

"Cut it out, Smitty. You're making a fool of yourself." Perry bravely dodged the attacker's swinging limbs as Glenn held his scrawny cousin by the collar of his black leather jacket. "Settle down. Perry's going to work, too. Ted has him scheduled to work the stand, instead of stacking melons. You know it never works out with the two of you on the same job."

"The sissy better stay out of my way today," Smitty threatened Perry, adjusting his horn-rimmed glasses.

"Stackers. Where are you? Six tons of melons won't stack themselves," called Ted from inside the green-filled trailer.

"Umpf!" Smitty stumbled as he caught the first melon of the day and systematically pitched it to Glenn.

"Good job, Smith," called Glenn. "Last month you couldn't handle a ten-pounder. That Cobb Gem was forty pounds." Quickly the two stackers molded melons into large pyramids. The remainder of the load was stored in the cooler where Smitty stayed for a few minutes out of Uncle Ted's sight.

"Smith, you're in the stand today," Ted's voice found him.

"Aw, Ted. I thought you wouldn't need me till the produce truck rolls in this afternoon. Me and Glenn were going down to the wharf to grab a crab burger."

"Wrong. We need you. Your Aunt Jo is hauling a load of garbage to the dump today. Glenn will ride over with her to help her shovel out. That's one less hand around here, unless you want to go with Jo and let Glenn work the stand. Otherwise, grab your fruit knife and head to the stand."

Overripe fruit had been pitched into crates, stashed behind the stand, and when a load was accumulated, Jo went to the dump with it. At the dump, sea gulls scavenged the heaps for anything edible, leaving their own waste, adding to the sickening stench. So not only did Smitty know he would be in for hard work shoveling the bad load, he did not want to repeat the embarrassment of throwing up like last time. Accepting his assignment, Smitty dragged his feet toward the back entrance of the fruitstand.

Instantly, his nose caught the aroma of the combination of every fruit and vegetable on the premises. His spirits lifted, realizing he might not dread this as much as he had thought. For him, no fragrance could equal the magnificence of this giant fruit cocktail. He breathed a long hit of the drugging, vine-ripe incense and peeled a banana.

"Here comes a customer, Smith. Little old ladies," grinned Perry. "My speciality. I'll whistle if I need you."

Emerald opened her car door, stepping onto the pavement made warm by the late morning sun. Smitty adjusted the large umbrella which shaded the strawberries, turning it slightly more toward the sun. He twisted the green cap of leaves off a large berry and popped it into his mouth.

"What an ingenious way to protect your produce, and lovely colors, too," said Emerald, removing her white gloves.

"Yep," said Smitty, "just trying to keep from having fruit soup at the end of the day." He scanned the flats for a handful of the most delicious-looking berries. Pocketing an apple, sacking a dozen apricots, Smitty stood back to watch Perry at work.

"May I say, you ladies look lovely today?" Perry opened his fruitknife and halved a canteloupe, scraping its seeds into a small bucket. Peeling a small sliver of the golden melon, he offered it to Rose. "Please sample our tasty canteloupe. They are four-for-a-dollar, today and every day." He continued to look Rose in the eye until she accepted the dripping offering.

"Oh, Emmy, this is wonderful. Sweet, too," said Rose, licking her fingers. "Try a slice of this."

"Not me," said Emerald, not wanting to get her hands sticky. "I can smell how sweet they are. Very aromatic. Let's take about twelve of those." She wandered toward the watermelon stacks. How long it had been since she had a slice of watermelon. As a child, she remembered, she'd heavily salted it and eaten it with her hands.

"How about a sample of our ripe watermelon? We've got both, yellow and red meat."

"Yellow?" She hesitated. "I had forgotten there was such a thing as yellow-meated melon. But I couldn't trouble you for a sample."

"No trouble. I think they broke one while unloading the truck this morning. Mr. Smith!" yelled Perry, "don't you have a yellow melon handy?" Smitty climbed off the stack of potatoes and ran to the cooler. He reached for a melon, held it a foot from the floor and let go.

"One yellow melon coming up!" He cradled the two pieces in his arms, leaving one on the potato mountain as he passed through the stand.

"Look at this, ladies," said Perry, slicing a healthy section from the melon's heart. Stabbing it with a blade glistening with juice, he held it in front of Emerald. "Check that out. I even have salt." Emerald nodded in acceptance.

Perry produced a shaker and salted all sides of the orange cube. Emerald's mouth watered and she could practically taste the melon in its powerful odor. Without further coaxing or concern over soiled hands, she delicately nibbled the sample. The slender woman felt as though she'd melted into the pavement as the melon disappeared within her mouth, her eyes tightly shut.

"I'll take two," she garbled. "This is wonderful."

Rose stopped sacking up tomatoes, watching as Perry demonstrated his ability to select perfectly ripe specimens by thumping them all.

"Mr. Smith, carryout!" he announced, weighing and marking the melons' prices on their deep, emerald rinds. Smitty wiped watermelon juice from his face with his shirttail. He loaded the watermelon into the floorboard of the Thorn's car and retreated to scrape his melon rind clean.

Emerald felt herself having fun, exchanging flirtations and niceties with this sample-wielding salesboy. "Son, where are you from? You have an accent that I feel I recognize."

"Ma'am, I'm from Allen, Oklahoma. Have you heard of it?"

"Allen, no. But Oklahoma, certainly." Emerald glowed as she announced to Rose, "This boy is from Oklahoma."

Rose peered over the mound of navel oranges, carefully watching the ecstatic look on her companion's face. "I know where Allen is. I have folks from Oklahoma." She joined the chatter, asking what Perry was doing so far from Oklahoma, and inquiring if he was here alone.

"My folks and brother are here, too. We came up for summer vacation and my Uncle Ted put us to work. The carryout boy . . . hey, Smitty, that's my cousin. We picked him up on our way through New Mexico. His mom thought he needed a break from cactus and deserts. We're trying to fatten him up. He's sort of from Oklahoma, since all our relatives are from there."

Smitty did not respond, for he had drifted to sleep after partaking of a dozen assorted fruits and vegetables. Other customers had come and gone, and Perry meticulously followed his system of offering samples, flattering, and totalling their bills. The Thorns browsed among the canopied racks and visited with the boy between customers.

Emerald laughed and blushed as Perry complimented her on her striking hat and soft, jersey dress. "So feminine," he said. "And could not be worn by a more lovely lady." When Perry learned that she was the owner of the Emerald Thorn Inn, the dramatic fruit peddler finished his performance with the ultimate compliment. "May I please remember your name to our other customers? I would love to boast that the Emerald Thorn Inn endorses our fruit and produce market."

"Feel free to use my name. I've enjoyed our visit, and am positive our guests will love all this lovely produce."

Perry kissed Emerald's hand and bid the women goodbye. He grinned widely as he said, "Okay, Mr. Smith. Top that sale for the day; forty-two dollars and fifty-nine cents and a five dollar tip."

As Rose drove south on Broadway, Emerald checked herself as she refrained from reminding Rose to fasten her seat belt. Since the law had gone into effect, requiring all occupants of a car to wear seat belts, Emerald became furious each time she rode or drove anywhere. Rose had forgotten, this time, to buckle up, and Emerald was not about to bring up the subject. Studies Emerald had read, conducted by who-knows-who, indicated that use of seat belts saves lives. The laws regarding just about everything were so numerous, Emerald thought, America's freedom of choice was a vapor of smoke. "Why don't they treat citizens like they have the capacity to make decisions on their own?" she blurted.

"What decisions are you talking about, Emerald? And who is this *they*? What are you talking about?"

"The legislators, the government, the state, the Feds, the coalitions. All those people telling me I have to fasten my seat belt."

"Oh my! Buckle up!" said Rose, swerving as she secured her own shoulder harness. "Thanks for reminding me."

"Look how puppetlike you obeyed the law. Just because the law told you to do it. I won't buckle up."

"It's a hundred dollar fine for not doing it, Em."

"A loss of freedom is what it is. Whether you put on your harness or not, turn left here, does not affect anyone else's safety. So what right does the government have to dictate what decisions we make regarding an act that may or may not affect our own safety?"

"That could apply to euthanasia, the right to abortion . . ."

"No, those are both murder. They directly affect other lives. Don't try to get me sidetracked or confused."

As Rose guided the car into a parking space, she anticipated her next words. Not wanting to ruin their lunch, yet not anxious to let Emerald have the last word, she mustered the courage to utter, "You, Emerald, are overreacting, as usual. It's not that big a deal."

"And, you, Rose Thorn, will be among the first people to lose all your basic freedoms as an American. You won't even know when they are all gone. You will submit to one law after another, until you are a slave of the government." The killing of the engine caught the car and its occupants quiet.

"Do we want to eat or drive home?" asked a sarcastic Rose.

"I may not enjoy wearing a shoulder harness, but my

stomach has been set for this since yesterday. You won't get the satisfaction of saying that I spoiled your trip to town." Emerald bailed out of the car and was standing at the restaurant entrance before Rose could unhitch her seatbelt.

Inside the door, Emerald awaited Rose. An Oriental hostess inched toward her, smiling. Without dropping her jaw, the china doll face uttered, "Table for one?"

"Two, please. Here she comes." Emerald waved to her companion.

"This way, please." The tiny feet took endless seconds to reach a booth in a dimly lit corner. The ladies smiled at the hostess and squared off at opposite sides of the table.

"The special today is chicken subgum and egg roll, three dollars and forty-nine cents. I be back one moment with you water." She lowered the upper half of her body, and inched backward into the kitchen. From an origin somewhere above their heads, a cool breeze drifted across the ceiling, tinkling dozens of cut glass windchimes. The pungent aroma of sweet and sour sauce stung Rose's nostrils.

"Mm, I didn't realize I was so hungry until I sat down."

The ladies perused the menus several times until final choices were registered with the girl with the immovable jaw. Rose sipped her green tea, trying to see through the thick dimness to the artwork on the wall beyond Emerald. Jade and coral pieces had been intricately sculpted into flowers and animals, each depicting a scene from Chinese legend.

Paper placemats displayed the Chinese zodiac, with colorful animals as symbols of the twelve-year cycles.

"Let's find our birth year on the calendar and read our personality traits," said Emerald, relaxing after her most recent disagreement with Rose.

"Naw, I don't believe in that zodiac stuff. I won't even read the astrology section of the newspaper." Rose's eyes strolled to a huge fan, ornately carved from ivory strips, bound together with delicate grasses.

"You wouldn't," accused Emerald. "I don't believe it, either. It's just innocent fun, something to pass the time until our egg rolls get here." She read the placemat, then announced, "Here you are. Born in the Year of the Goat. No wonder you are so stubborn, you old goat," she laughed. "Except for the knack of always getting off on the wrong foot with people . . ." Emerald laughed and continued reading, "the Goat can be charming company. You are elegant and artistic, but the first to complain about things. Put aside your pessimism and worry and try to be less dependent on material comforts. You would be best as an actor, gardener, or beachcomber."

Emerald glanced up at Rose, who stared angrily past her. "Did you hear that, Rose? Beachcomber. Lucky for you we live on the coast." Her titters became a roaring burst of laughter, which abruptly ended as Emerald felt self-conscious at her own undignified behavior.

Rose did not laugh, but flung her fork onto the placemat. "I said I did not want to hear it. If you're determined to read, do so silently. Those traits could describe any number of people, and all *coincidentally*, at that." Rose lowered her voice as she caught sight of the waitress approaching with their egg rolls. "You shouldn't waste your mental energies even reading that junk. Before long you will believe it."

"Egg roll. You want sweet sour sauce? Hot mustard?" grinned the waitress as she spoke. She set down a container of each and backed away.

"Good grief. I had no idea you felt so strongly about something so harmless."

"Pass that sauce and hush," she emphasized, "please!"

Throughout lunch, Rose avoided Emerald's eyes, as if to make contact would mean compromising her views. Each crunch of the crispy egg roll crust echoed through her sinuses — the noise rescued her from the screaming silence.

She recalled a high school friend inviting her over one afternoon to play records. Rose followed Kara into her dining room, where her father, grandparents, and three sisters were hunched, empty-eyed, over the dining table. Rose felt a sinister icyness glide over her skin as Kara's older sister said, "Mother doesn't want you here."

"What?" Rose modestly asked.

All faces turned to Rose as Christen continued, "She says you don't approve of this. You don't believe in her. You have brought an unwelcome spirit with you. Mother wants you to leave." Christen's head tilted toward the table, then nodded in the direction of the door. The table was cleared, except for a Ouija board. Christen's nod indicated she was expected to leave as quickly as, and in the same direction from whence, she had entered.

Rose did not hesitate, yet disliked the idea of a dead woman telling her what to do. A feeling of nausea gripped her as she followed Kara back outside. The two girls sat down on the sidewalk and Kara explained.

"It's my fault. I'm sorry about what just happened. We always talk to Mom on Saturday afternoons. I lost track of the time."

Rose didn't know how that was possible. When

you're dead, you are just dead. Kara's mother had died in an accident when Kara was three years old. That cold, sickening feeling lifted away in the sunlight as Rose picked grass from the cracks in the sidewalk. She hadn't even thought of that afternoon in years.

But the sensation of cold and nausea had returned to her memory as vividly and unexpectedly as it had over thirty years ago. This insistence of Emerald to entertain herself with the reading of Rose's personality traits felt as wrong as Kara's family consulting their dead loved one.

She dragged a fork through her chow mein and thought that the chicken did not taste fresh. She wanted to go home. Emerald had said nothing since Rose told her to hush. At times she must appear very ungrateful to Emerald for letting her remain at the inn. She paid no room and board, but did pay half the utility and grocery expenses. They tolerated each other more than anything else. The inn was home and office to both women.

Rose's office adjoined her bedroom at the center of the upstairs hallway. A back entrance allowed her to come and go without disturbing Emerald. The outside stairwell branched off, emptying onto the side lawn near the car house and the kitchen's back porch. The layout had provided easy access for servants in days past. They could enter the house to clean and cook without bothering the occupants. It had always worked out well when one or both of the current residents needed their privacy.

Being a freelance writer who had created a discussion column in a Snohomish County newspaper, Rose was also a ghostwriter for a rival column in which she disputed her own original story. Late hours of research and organizing of separate journals and record keeping systems were required to keep the columns separate and distinct. And much self-control was required to keep the double life a secret. Emerald never fully agreed with Rose's column, but defended it whole-heartedly against her rival, Rusty Lively.

If Rose wrote it, Emerald defended it. Even if she didn't actually verbalize her agreement, Emerald was a good sounding board for Rose's opinions. If she had only been less abrupt in telling Emmy to be quiet, she'd be chattering about some trivial fact of life. Rose got numerous ideas for columns from complaints Emerald had about one thing or another. She dug her hand to the bottom of her purse to find an ink pen. Upon her napkin Rose scribbled *seatbelt*. As she twisted the pen to retract the point, Emerald squealed from across the table.

"What is it, Em?"

"Bone!"

"A bone? In your dinner?"

The waitress was promptly at the table whisking Emerald's plate away to the kitchen. Other diners watched the choking woman, without action.

"Are you okay?" asked Rose, ready to assist if she only knew how.

Emerald shook her head. She coughed, then fingered the roof of her mouth to retrieve the foreign object. "Glass! It's a little piece of glass," she whispered.

The manager was soon by her side. "I'm so sorry. I don't know where this could have come from," he apologized, placing the fragment in his palm. "What can I do to assure you of my sincere wish to set this situation right?"

"We won't be paying for this meal," said Emerald sternly as she rose to her feet. "And you may keep the glass as a souvenir. Or shall I take it to the Health Department?"

"Let me give you a credit voucher, please." The manager whisked away and was back instantly with a slip of paper. "This is good for free meals anytime you want them. I have written the expiration as *never expires*. Please accept it with my apology."

"Thank you and good day," snapped Emerald, prissing out the door into the sunshine.

"Please, I beg your consideration." The manager's necktie appeared to be tightening about his neck, reddening further an embarrassed face. Rose nodded, then hurried to fold her napkin and tuck it into her handbag. She knew Emerald could not leave without her, yet she clumsily prowled for her keys.

"I'm sure it was an accident," she said. "What's done is done. Don't worry about it." Her keys surfaced and she dashed to unlock the door for Emerald, who already appeared to have forgotten the incident.

"Hurry, Rose. You've still got to drop off your story." In defiance, Emerald sat on the seatbelt with the fastener clasped to keep the warning buzzer from demanding she buckle up. Rose inserted the key and instinctively reached for her harness. Gazing out the window, Emerald spoke softly, "I'll risk it."

The newspaper office was just blocks from the restaurant. The drive took only moments. It seemed hardly worth the trouble of fastening her seatbelt, for Rose was now releasing the latch to slide out of the car.

"Come in, won't you? Meet the editor, Em," smiled Rose, as she leaned into the back. Her briefcase was heavy and difficult to hoist over the seat, but she managed with a push from Emerald.

"I'll rest. I have no desire to meet your writer buddies. Hurry up, though. Don't take all day." Rose nudged the dusty door with her hip and proceeded up the concrete steps into the old house that had been converted to an independent newspaper office. The paper was supported solely by subscribers, community-service oriented advertising, and private donations. Most of the writers on staff were freelancers with their livelihoods being in fiction or technical writing. But Rose got paid well for authoring the sister columns.

She had conceived the idea three years ago as a result of deciding where she stood on the right-to-abortion issue. She had strong inclinations toward both — pro-choice and pro-life. Therefore, she wrote two articles, hoping that by reading her written thoughts, she might be swayed in either direction. She presented them to her editor for approval. The columns had been a success from the first run. Ever since, Rose had given careful consideration to every current issue. Anything that could remotely supply controversy, she had gleaned for an item to keep up the facade. She loved the dual role and her success.

The upstairs office door was locked. She placed her face near the opaque glass, making out the darkness of two figures beyond. Setting down her satchel, Rose tapped on the glass. "Hello, are you in there?"

The door swung open and her editor leaned sideways into the hall. He grabbed Rose's arm and briefcase, giving her a gentle tug into the room and pushed the door shut with his foot. Rose winced as always, fearing the glass panel would shatter into a heap of splintery flakes at her feet.

"Rusty! It's great to see you. Where in this wide universe have you been? The last two months you've been mailing in stuff. I had nearly forgotten what you look like." Still holding to her arm he pulled her closer, molding his arm around her shoulder. "I take that back. I can't forget that face. I've memorized each freckle." The couple walked the few feet to the editing desk and the robust man sat atop a stack of papers.

"It's so quiet today. Where is everybody? Hi, Fred," Rose nodded to the assistant editor across the room.

"Rusty," he waved a sandwich at her and saluted her with a can of pop, "it's Sunday. Did you forget? No one's here on Sunday except me and hard-at-work Fred. We two loyal staff members never go home," he mused, gazing at a strand of hair that had gone its own way on Rose's crown. "Gone punk these days?" He pretended to spit on his fingers and attempted to stroke the wild hairs into place.

"Forget it, it's the humidity." Rose stopped the stroking hand and held it firmly, pulling Sven's elbow under her own against her side.

"You are used to seeing all the busy bees at work, but you usually drop by on a weekday. Really, what's up?"

"Nothing is up, you crazy Svede." She loved the sound of Sven's name, and the play on the *w* she used on every word she could work it into. They laughed and hugged quickly, remembering Fred (who grinned with mayonnaise dripping onto his chin). "I had occasion to be in town today, rather than some other day. So here I am." Dropping Sven's hand, Rose reached for her briefcase, tugged at it. It did not budge. Sven lifted the case onto his lap with ease and clicked the latch.

Opening the case, he flinched. "All this?!"

"No, just this stack," Rose said, moving aside notebooks and magazines. She lifted two rubber-banded manuscripts, "And this. There are a total of six articles. Enough for the rest of the month."

"That sounds as though I won't see you again for weeks." Sven stood to his feet and retrieved his jacket from the back of his chair. He stood much taller than Rose. She felt a sudden inclination to look away from his questioning eyes. "Babe, I haven't seen you in ages. I've tried to call, but your sister-in-law said you were out on errands or clipping rose bushes. Always some nonsense." He slid his desk drawer open and produced three neckties. "Take your pick," he said.

"The gray one," Rose answered with her back turned. "It looks so good with your eyes." His tie in place, he touched her shoulders and pivoted her to face him.

"Still avoiding me?" Rose's eyes skimmed the straw-colored head of curls which always looked as if each hair had been airbrushed into place. She reached for the one curl that had hidden itself down the collar of the mauve shirt.

"I've not gotten any of your messages. No kidding, Sven. I have never avoided you. Neither of us knows what we want out of this relationship. Thinking things over is what I've been doing, not avoiding you."

"I was just knocking off for the day, Rusty. Let's go get a bite to eat and catch up on these things you've been thinking over."

"Emerald is downstairs; we just ate Chinese food." She could no longer avoid his eyes, and knew what was coming next. Glancing into his face, she flowed into his arms. For several moments she listened to the heartbeat within his chest and as slowly as she had melted her arms around him, collected herself and pulled away, reaching for her briefcase.

Sven responded quickly to her coolness. "We won't let this end, Rusty. Set a date and time, right now, while you are here. We'll meet on neutral ground, have dinner, and talk about it. Okay?"

"An empasse was reached last time, remember?" She sighed as they walked toward the door.

"Fred!" called Sven, "see you early tomorrow, right?" Fred still chewed. He waved an affirmation. "I'll walk you down. Next Friday, got it? You run by here. We'll walk over to the wharf and I'll buy your lunch. I'm even willing to meet in broad daylight. How much more open can I get?" He was laughing, but his mellow voice was powerfully insistent. He walked slower to give Rose's thoughts and will time to agree. "Friday. Just say yes." He stopped near the car and smiled to Emerald through the windshield. "Give me a chance. The religion stuff scares me. I don't understand where you're coming from, but it can be worked through. Let's talk, okay? Just talk."

"Sure, Friday. I'll be here. No goodbye kiss, though. Emerald, you know?"

"Bye," Sven waved and sauntered toward the wharf. He became a pale spot, disappearing against the threatening clouds beyond sails and fishing boats.

Inside the car, Rose adjusted her skirt which had become twisted while sliding onto the seat. As she started the car, she asked, "Why didn't you tell me Sven had been trying to reach me?"

"Actually, it slipped my mind, Rose. You get mail

from the office every day. I suppose he can't slip a note into some of that correspondence. It would save him a long-distance call." Emerald rubbed her eyes as though she'd been dozing.

"He had special projects for me, which we needed to discuss at length."

"Which is all the more reason to communicate via mail. Those at-length discussions can add up to a phone bill."

"Thanks for the concern, but the call would come off the paper's business expenses. Do not hesitate to call me to the phone if he calls again. If I happen to be out, please leave me a note. Will it be any trouble?"

"Not at all."

"We should get right home and get these vegetables refrigerated or the whole batch will go bad."

"Rose, do I need to remind you that you are nearly fifty years old?"

Rose felt she knew what Emerald was alluding to. "If you are concerned about Sven being interested in me, you shouldn't be. Sven has been a dear friend for over ten years."

"Yes, I know. Ever since you worked together on that river dam project. Turn here. I'd like to drive the old highway home."

"It will take longer."

"If we have time to stop and see Gregory Svenson, we've got time to drive the old highway. He likes you."

The buildings were disappearing and evergreens lined the highway. The threatening clouds had followed through with rain which had washed dust from the air, sky, and road, giving the scenery a look of fresh color. The constant hum of the engine and vibration of the car had lulled the passenger to sleep again. She was accustomed to resting for an hour or so each afternoon. Somehow, the absence of Emmy's chatter was disturbing to Rose's soul.

"Let's talk, Rusty, just talk, he says," Rose repeated Sven's words as they played in her head. She couldn't talk to Sven about how she felt. The things which were keeping her from making a total commitment to him were not tangible. They were feelings, instincts, and convictions she herself could not understand.

For months, every ethical, moral, religious conviction she had ever experienced had come back to haunt her. Even those watered-down Koolaid days in Vacation Bible School came back to her.

And what had Emerald meant by having to remind her of her age? Her spirit didn't seem to be aging. She was still the same spirit as that ten-year-old at Bible school. She felt no older than when she and Sven met ten years ago. She simply couldn't perceive growing old in spirit, just wiser — or perhaps less wise, but she was an eternal, constant age.

Rose felt she had always loved Sven, yet at this moment she felt further away from him than ever. At times when she drew extremely close to him, something within her withdrew suddenly. "I can't figure myself out, Sven," she whispered as she turned the radio to their favorite mood music station. The Mystic Moods played *Autumn Leaves*. It was beautiful; they had danced to it. She continued to drive, disquieted by the memories of the music and the wet afternoon.

"God, this is confusing. Help me figure out what's going on with me." A sensation of panic shifted her stomach. Had she just asked God to help her get her head straightened out? It had been a long time since she had prayed. She wasn't sure that's what she had done, but felt from within herself that it was what she had intended. "I know you are there, God, after all this time." She could say no more.

Chapter Four

The Search Initiated

As Rose sat on the deep, cushioned sofa in the doctor's waiting room, she thumbed through a once-familiar magazine. The only semblance it now had to issues she remembered from her early womanhood was page-after-page of recipes and mouth-watering food pictures. Before her, cluttering the pages, were articles entitled, "How To Have An Emotional Affair" and "Coping With Sexual Discrimination On The Job." Whatever happened to "Thirty-nine Ways To Organize Your Kitchen Cabinets"? What had happened, she knew, was that more women were in the work force than in the kitchen. Actually most were in both places. Someone must be reading modern women's magazines, or they wouldn't be so plentiful. The change in lifestyles, no doubt, had led to this evolution of reading material.

Rose reached for another magazine when the alluring eyes of a pouty blonde captured her glance. A dazzling, sequined pullover sweater, cut to the naval, revealed only the slightest amount of cleavage. With hair teased and moussed in several directions, this vampish youth's smile appeared tantalizing and innocently perplexed. The cover story revealed that sixteen-year-old Shelly Stanton was wearing makeup by Eric, hairstyle by Simone, and sweater by Jacqua. This baby had been powdered, pampered, and dressed up to imitate a sex symbol in order to sell magazines that amounted to little more than a stack of dish packing, as far as social values go.

The women's movement, which Rose so heartily supported just fifteen years ago, now seemed a two-headed dragon. Her mother's generation, who had been trained to stay home and happily nurture their families on a household stage, were now adjusting to the entrapment of the freedoms wrought by liberated lifestyles. Freedom to be your independent self, freedom to work outside the home, and right to equal pay had molded women into less-than-fulfilled actresses of a different nature. Women of all age groups were now encouraged, through these very magazines, that they are equal to or better than men; they stand up to their husbands, demand to join the work force, and compete, using the threat of discrimination suits if necessary, to become true equals.

Once in the work force, these newly evolved free women join men in all areas. Women smoke and drink more. With female heart disease and stress-related illnesses on the rise, women too have staked legitimate claims to burnout, and by all means, have just as much right as their male counterparts to carry on affairs. After all, thought Rose, men need someone to carry on with. Where are the morals this country was founded upon, she wondered. Hadn't one church in the eastern part of the country even changed the sex of Christ on the crucifix in order to keep from being labeled *behind the times* or *sexist*? The women's movement had backfired, as far as Rose was concerned. Her involvement in and approval of it had dwindled. Her own views had changed slowly and now resembled her mother's. She would never have thought she would boast of old-fashioned values.

Her changes in attitude had caused most of her friends to drift politely away as she maneuvered a course through oceans of difficult issues and decisions. She knew, for a fact, that whatever else she believed, a female God was not viable. Perhaps that was when her search for God had really begun. As she explored her feelings, questions had presented themselves. She had always been independent, knowing that she could rely on nobody but herself. But the Bible teaching, she remembered, insisted that she rely on God, not on her own abilities and understanding. She couldn't handle that. Intellectually, that made no sense.

The more answers she sought, the more friends she alienated. Rose discovered that her generation is living happy, successful lives in appearance only. However, when unanticipated problems arise, there is no script to follow. To confide in friends would be to admit that the perfect life is a dream. Therefore, the troubled withdraw from their friends, if friends haven't already withdrawn. They struggle with crises and turmoil alone. Each new surprise encounter confirms that fate is unfair and that somehow they've done something wrong to have been dealt this hand of destiny. Not knowing the exact mistake or moment in time when their futures negatively turned, they strut hopelessly, led as Shakespeare's poor player upon the stage by whatever current forces direct the era. The script has been written and is merely played until the final curtain falls. They live day-by-day according to the current social crazes, never knowing what they think or believe, just keeping up appearances.

Plastic people, Sven called them. Not real, but ticky-tacky. For all the years Rose had known Sven, he was the most real person she had known. Emerald, in her make-believe southern plantation on a Washington State peninsula, was living out what was expected of her as an actress in a series of sequels. Many nights Rose had escaped to Sven's realism rather than have to face the continuing saga of Emerald Thorn. Sven had been a free spirit since beatniks were expressing themselves. Rose hadn't known him then, but since had spent numerous hours at his feet as he chanted his repertoire of poetry written in favor of love and opposition to war. His loft apartment, overlooking Puget Sound, sported pictures of long-haired, barefooted people sitting cross-legged on a floor with Sven seated on a tall stool. He wore dark shades and his shoulder-length blond hair haloed his face.

More photos were set at university campuses across the country where thousands of students gathered to hear their favorite peace singers, the Kingston Trio and Christy Minstrels. The faces in the audience were so young, practically babies. They clapped their hands and hummed softly as they learned of the demise of all the flowers, a direct result of war, through the harmonization of Peter, Paul, and Mary.

They were beautiful times, Rose remembered Sven saying. So much love and genuine caring for one another. Sven still loved espresso coffee and brought a cup to Rose as she lay across a large pillow on the hardwood floor. The fireplace flames curled and flickered, appearing as characters reenacting Sven's lovely memories of his beatnick experience.

"There were coffee houses in most major cities where the groups met and sang for enough money — bread we called it — to get on to the next town. And I did poetry reading, sold handwritten copies of some of my pieces, and just followed the brothers and sisters from one hootenanny to another."

"Concerts?"

"No, hootenannies. Concerts are musical shows, but they're strictly squaresville." Rose loved how Sven regressed into his beatnik self for the purpose of entertaining her curiosity about a life she herself had stayed safely away from.

"Okay, get that banjo and sing me a tune, daddyo."

"You don't have to ask twice." Sven crossed the room and retrieved the instrument which he kept hanging among his past life memorabilia and motioned to the spot beside the fireplace where the bongo drums proudly stood sentry over the hearth.

"I've never played bongos."

"And I've never played banjo, so we're even. What'll it be?"

"I love them all, Sven. Sing your favorite."

"Okay, are you tuned in?" He laughed at Rose as she sat, bongos between her knees, hands awkwardly suspended above the drum skins. "Rest the heels of your hands on the very rims and let your fingers and palms lay on the surface, as if tap dancing. Take off. One, two, three . . .If I had a ham-mer, I'd hammer in the mor-or-ning, I'd hammer in the eeev-ning, all over this world. I'd hammer out dan-ger, I'd hammer out war-ning, I'd hammer out the love between my brothers and sisters, ah-ah-ah-all over the land, ooh."

The banjo sounded like liquid ice crystals slipping over a waterfall. "If I had a bell, I'd ring it in the mor-or-ning . . ." Sven continued. Rose felt the electricity Sven generated as he sang this song he still believed in. His collar-length curls shook as his message intensified. He approached the tune's end. His eyes, which had been shut throughout the performance, squenched even tighter, showing his laugh lines to be highways on an atlas. They no doubt had been there when he sang so seriously for a meal and a little *bread* in some espresso shop in Albuquerque or Maine. The tune slowed in speed but intensified in volume and vibration, as Sven belted out, "It's the hammer of juh-us-tice, it's the bell of free-eee-dom, it's the song about the love between my brothers and my sisters, ah-ah-ah-all over this la-a-and!"

He played a fancy lick and stomped his foot as he jumped from his perch atop the sofa back, landing just inches from Rose. He bowed low several times as he enjoyed the imaginary applause. Reaching for Rose's hand, he helped her to her feet. Holding hands, they bowed several more times in all directions until the cheers subsided.

"Mr. Svenson, sir, daddyo. May we hear one of your famous readings?" The crowd fell silent as Sven returned to his perch. Rose curled up once more amid the fuzzy pillows and sipped her rapidly cooling espresso. The shades had not yet been closed; dusk concealed itself in blackness, unnoticed. Stars now signalled an S-O-S across the sky as the moon's orange light mirrored rays of enchantment from the ocean waves onto the slowly bobbing houseboats at the wharf below. "What is the name of this poem, Sven?"

"It doesn't have a name, but the feeling is 'Death, You Have Killed Me.' "

A shiver went through her body as Rose snuggled deeper into the cushiony refuge. The private reading began. Sven's eyes defocused. He seemed to transport himself to a time and place other than the present. Turning his face toward the fireplace, the stars and moon assisted the flames in spotlighting his features. Slowly, softly, he snapped his fingers in rhythm with his heartbeat. His expression grew solemn and fuzzy caterpillar eyebrows stretched toward one another. His lips trembled as he read from memory.

My spirit of electricity and vapor
forced itself into this jar
to be born among amarylus and
oceans and writhing pain.
Its song was ever let me be free
to sing and dance and love and I was
yet, that man tells me to be free I
must fight as never before and I have not.
I know but to laugh and hold and express
myself in joy
for I'm part of a universe of belonging to love
we'll teach you how, we must conquer those
that do not believe in freedom, but I do.
Yet in conquering those my soul cries out
that I conquer and wound myself
cannot this jar be trusted to contain
the very composition of the universe, of god?
Slashing of vessels and firing angry cannons
the pantry empties of all vases and
pottery and jars and wineskins
so different, but capable of containing.

Though mortal wound, I have not
my spirit pours from my mouth
as doing unto others they have done unto me
Death! you have killed me.

The last finger snap coincided exactly with the last syllable. Then the poet's lips and hands fell silent. Several seconds, more like minutes, passed as Rose waited for Sven to move. With only a slight drop of the jaw he spoke softly, head still bowed and eyes closed, "What, no applause?"

Rose, fearful of destroying the newly created atmosphere, lightly patted her hands together. "It was wonderful," she whispered.

"No," said Sven, concealing a smile, "that's not hip." He snapped his fingers and nodded for Rose to do likewise. She did, and Sven chanted, "Cool, way-out daddyo." Rose repeated and they both exploded into an electrically contagious laugh. The laughing subsided into giggles, then Rose realized she was still in the doctor's office waiting room. How long had she daydreamed? Embarrassment overcame her.

Two ladies, sitting adjacent to her on the long sofa, were laughing while a woman and her small son watched Rose's ankles curiously. Feeling much like a new strain of virus under a microscope, Rose wanted to be let in on the joke. She felt, though, that somehow she was the joke. She crossed her legs and nervously began rocking her leg to and fro.

A tiny nylon banner waved proudly from her jeans hem. She remembered having pulled off both jeans and pantyhose last time this particular pair was worn, and throwing them into the laundry basket. She almost always found panties or hose inside slacks as she sorted laundry. Obviously, this pair had eluded her inspection and the taupe flag now taunted her. How to correct this error was the question Rose puzzled over as Tracy stepped from the inner office.

"All set, Rose?" Tracy's cast was gone and her sandled foot looked slightly smaller than its counterpart. "I'll buy you lunch for being such a good taxi driver today," she said as they walked from the waiting room and into the hall of the medical building.

"Until I fix this," said Rose, stretching her leg straight out to show Tracy the dangling menace, "I'm not going anywhere."

"How did that happen? Let me help. It'll probably come right out." Tracy stooped to grab the fragment of nylon. She tugged and Rose lost her balance.

Stumbling to the wall, Rose leaned against it. "I can get it; hand me that end."

"No, I've got it. Just steady yourself," insisted Tracy. As a magician revealing lengths of colored silks, she pulled and pulled. The undergarment was trapped inside the jeans, held tightly in place by Rose's firm hip. It stretched, but did not exit the jeans' leg. "Guess you should have stepped into the ladies room and dropped your drawers to do this." Tracy began the tug-of-war again and stretched the springy rope three feet with Rose's leg extended into the center of the vacant hallway.

Out of the doctor's office stepped a man with a cane followed by his petite wife. The gentleman tapped his cane along the baseboard, hitting Tracy's ankle before she could announce her presence.

"Ow!" she squealed, still hanging on to the pantyhose

and their wearer.

"Excuse me, my fault," and the man attempted to proceed, stopped by the elastic barricade.

"One moment, please, sir." Tracy limpingly joined Rose on the opposite side of the hall, allowing the elderly couple to pass. The tiny wife squinted and frowned at the two ladies as she passed.

"What is it, Mama?" the blind man inquired

"Perverts, Barney. Here's the elevator, dear." They stopped and Rose proceeded with her strongest pull to disengage the trapped garment. She felt the bulk of material sliding from the seat of her pants, and escaping into the leg of her jeans. The other leg of the pantyhose followed and with great ease fell onto the floor.

Rose quickly wadded the stockings, cramming them into her handbag. The two ladies, hearing the elevator bell, stepped gingerly down the hall and into the elevator. Silently, the old man and woman rode the five stories to the lobby while the icy blue eyes of the woman kept watch on Rose and Tracy. As the elevator door opened, the couple made a speedy exit. Outside the building the prissy wife looked back every few steps to make sure that she and Barney were not being followed.

Tracy surveyed the traffic and agreed that this time of the day luncheonettes would be too crowded for them to enjoy a quiet lunch together.

"I'll get the car. You should stay off that ankle for a few days," she instructed.

"Dr. Franklin said I'm fine."

"That was before that old geezer whacked you with his cane."

"No argument from me. I'll sit on this planter until

you bring the limo around." She smiled and with her hand dusted the place where she would sit. The sky was overcast; a shower was inevitable. Tracy spread her sweater over her legs and leaned against the building to wait.

Rose walked the two blocks to the car. Her eye caught a glimpse of a familiar floral pattern. A woman, walking briskly, crossed the street in the next block. Could it be Emerald? She so rarely ventured out of the inn without being coaxed. But that dress. Bright red jersey with miniature turquoise flowers? She was too far away to make out the print or the woman's face, but Rose felt certain that was Emerald's dress.

She fumbled in her bag for Tracy's car keys. Once found, none of the keys unlocked the door on the first try. Driving another's car was always an inconvenience. Nothing was ever in the proper place. The ignition was stuck oddly on the steering column instead of on the gauge panel. She wondered if all newer cars had the instrumentation scrambled. Trying to keep an eye on the red dress, she careened out of the parking lot and into the traffic. As she neared the corner where the dress had been spotted, the woman wearing it glided through a shop door.

Rose did not recognize the shop. Driving as quickly as traffic allowed, she made a U-turn at the next corner and slowly drove past the shop. Its windows had been darkened completely with a smoky film and a sign above the door read: "Answer In The Wind — A New Age Shopping Experience." Rose wondered what type of merchandise could be purchased in such a shop. She could not think of what Emerald would be doing concerning herself with anything other than culinary supplies and ingredients for recipes. She certainly would not be into any New Age. It didn't sound old-fashioned enough.

Sven had once urged the newspaper staff to attend a New Age thinking workshop as part of some goal setting, self-improvement article he was putting together. Time had been a problem and Rose had not made it to the seminar. However, her interest had suddenly been piqued. What lay beyond those darkened windows compelled her to investigate. But she had to get back to Tracy.

Letting flashes of sunlight close her eyes, Tracy was startled when Rose tooted her car horn. She staggered to her feet, feeling slightly older than a moment ago. But she smiled when realizing again that her cast was finally gone.

"How about a club sandwich?" asked Tracy, unloading the refrigerator onto the kitchen table. "Turkey, ham, I could fry some bacon for BLT's. What's your pleasure?"

"I could go for a turkey, lettuce, and tomato on toast."

"You've got it. Sit down. I'll fix them. It's the least I can do to repay you for the chauffeuring you did today."

"I would have driven, anyway. I only wish I had checked my pants for dangling hosiery before I put them on this morning." The ladies cackled again about the doctor's office scene.

"And that poor blind man. He sure came to a sudden halt," laughed Rose.

"How about iced tea?" Tracy smiled, trying to catch her breath. "Or club soda and lime?"

"Mm, that sounds good. Let me fix the drinks while you finish the sandwiches. Where's your lime squeezer?"

"There's a reamer in the cabinet." Tracy pointed with a knife. Tracy sliced the turkey paper thin. Heaping the toast slices two inches high with meat and condiments, she salted, peppered, and topped the sandwiches with their toast lids. The ladies consumed their lunch without speaking, then cleared the table.

"Shall I drive you home?" offered Tracy.

"Are you kidding? It's half a mile, as the crow flies. I can be there in a jiffy."

"But it is raining now."

"And not enough to melt me." As Rose spoke, the rumble of a car and crunching of tires on the gravel road disturbed the mood of the somber afternoon. Rose looked out the kitchen window as she donned her hooded sweatshirt. Emerald's Chevrolet barreled down the road as if on its way to a fire.

"What do you know about New Age stuff?" Rose asked.

"You aren't involved in the New Age, are you?" Tracy's face showed surprise.

"Well, not directly. But what do you know about it?"

Diagonal slices of a waterfall appeared to rain from the sky. "I've got a couple of books I could loan you, if you're interested in reading up. Want to take them with you now?"

"Not now. Gotta get home."

"Don't get involved, that's all I can tell you off hand. The New Age movement is a tangled web of death." Tracy pushed Rose toward the door and laughed. "Don't get wet."

Rose fairly trotted through the woods. The overhanging branches were an umbrella against the falling torrents. As she reached the clearing, she crossed over to the car house. The car radiated a vapor from the hood where cool drops of rain had met the hot metal.

Emerald's trip from town must have been made at great speed in order to heat the car so. Back out into the rain she darted. The heavy drops were easing a bit. She wondered how she would confront Emerald about her trip to town. Emerald had made such a deal out of not driving into town with Tracy and herself. And what about that shop? Was it Emerald she had seen there? After supper would be a good time to find out. Emerald would sit in the parlor sipping tea. Rose would ask her, "Was that you I saw going into Answer In The Wind?" Or maybe Emerald would just volunteer, "Hey, guess where I went today?"

Her wet sweatshirt felt heavy and uncomfortable as she pulled it from her arms. A warm shower was in order to keep away a chill. Halfway up the stairs she met Emerald. Dry Emerald, looking as if she'd been in her cozy kitchen all day.

"My, my. You should get out of those wet things and get into a hot tub. I'll fix you a hot cider." Down the stairs she bounded, virtually gliding. There was a lilt to her step which Rose had not seen lately.

"What did you do today, Emmy?" called Rose as she peeled wet jeans and pantyhose from her cold rear end.

"We have a new couple joining us for a few days. They will be here for supper," Emerald answered.

"So, what have you been doing all day?"

Emerald appeared at the bottom of the staircase. Her voice wafted up to Rose. "Why, Rose, I've been preparing for our company. I've got hot bread and baked chicken with dumplings. There's work to be done before guests arrive. You know that. Unlike you, I have obligations. I can't go traipsing around the countryside all day."

The comment didn't deserve an answer. Rose crossed the hall to the bathroom. She dropped her robe to the floor and climbed into the clawfooted tub, closing the curtain behind herself. As hot water plastered her hair to her head, Rose wondered why Emerald had lied. The car was still hot. Emerald couldn't have beaten Rose into the house by more than fifteen minutes. Yet she appeared dry and fresh. Rose knew Emerald did not always agree with her, but Rose didn't feel that her sister-in-law had ever outright lied to her.

Drying quickly to warm herself against the cool draft, Rose wrapped herself in her bathsheet and sat down on the toilet seat. When she was quite warm, she donned her robe and opened the hamper to discard her bathsheet.

Inside, crumpled beneath a towel, lay Emerald's red and turquoise dress. The woman in town was absolutely Emerald. How unlike her to put a jersey dress in among wet towels. It would shrink. It must have been done in haste. Emerald did not want Rose to know she had been away, nor did she want to explain where she had been. Why? Rose determined to find out, if it took her an entire evening of interrogation.

The Standfords were a couple from Sparks, Nevada. As of yet, they had no children, but Neva Standford was pregnant. This would be their last vacation as a childless couple. Probably their last, according to Mrs. Standford, until this child is shipped away to college.

This was not Emerald's best meal, either. Oh, it was certainly edible, Rose thought. But Rose had tasted better. The rolls were hard. Maybe Rose was critical since she was not really hungry after eating the sandwich at Tracy's. Although everything was fresh, it tasted like leftovers.

Rose listened with conjured concern to the long story of Neva Standford's pregnancy. She had practically documented the exact moment of conception and had kept a detailed diary, including dates and times of each incident of vomiting pertaining to morning sickness. Neva had written down every food she could or could not keep on her stomach. She had not, according to her oratory, been relieved of the sickness for an entire day during the six months of her condition. That is, until last week, with the aid of rectal suppositories, which she insisted on at her last checkup. "How can I enjoy my last vacation if I'm going to be puking my guts out, I told my doctor," said Mrs. Standford, getting the attention of all present at the supper table. "Of course, they make me extremely drowsy, and I've slept practically every minute of the drive up here. But it's worth it, you know? 'Cause when I didn't have something on my stomach, I just had the dry heaves."

The distasteful conversation had not affected Mr. Standford's appetite. He hungrily mopped his plate clean with a dinner roll and popped it into his mouth.

Normally Rose would have entertained the guests with Emerald. She did not feel up to it tonight. Therefore, she excused herself, told the Standfords goodnight, and made her way upstairs.

Rose slipped a nightshirt over her head and flipped

the light switch off. As she reviewed the events of the day, she thought of Emmy's good jersey dress shrinking in the damp heap of towels. Quietly, she slipped from her bed and looked into the hallway. Emerald was also bidding good evening to the Standfords. Without being noticed, Rose hurried across the hall and shut the bathroom door behind herself. After searching the hamper, she replaced all the damp towels. No dress was to be found. Tomorrow Emerald would empty the hamper, do laundry, and make no mention of the dress.

The rain softly slapped the French door panes in a bongo beat as Rose heard from the guest quarters below the muffled tone of Neva Standford puking her guts out.

Chapter Five

Kamikazes

"Rose," softly came Emerald's voice at the door, "are you awake? I'm coming in."

Surely, I'm awake, thought Rose. But focusing her gaze on the hands of the clock, she realized she'd not just dozed off. She had not stirred for almost twelve hours. The slow, slapping rain of last evening had transformed her last thoughts into fathomless oceans of churning, comforting dreams, dreams forgotten upon opening her eyes. The rain had not completely ceased. It hovered heavily over the grounds as a spider web saturated in morning dew. "What is it? Come in, Em."

"The Standfords have already left," she said, setting a breakfast tray on the table beside Rose's bed. "I think that Mrs. Standford was feeling under-the-weather. Didn't sleep well. She couldn't handle any breakfast."

"So what's-his-name ate alone?" Rose climbed from her bed and stood quietly for a moment to steady her aching bones before stepping into her fuzzy, purple slippers.

"No, Mr. Standford knocked at four a.m. and said they'd get breakfast down the road." Emerald poured a steaming waterfall of tea into a translucent china cup as she continued. "I couldn't have them go off without something to eat, so I sacked up a dozen orange rolls and a quart of milk. By now, that will have eased Mrs. Standford's tummy."

"Em, I'm sorry, but I'd rather not hear anymore about that constant morning sickness. The last thing I heard last night and the first report of this morning. That's enough." Emerald had already turned to leave when Rose realized that she had never had breakfast brought up to her room. "Why the breakfast in bed, Em?"

"It's not breakfast in bed. Just threw an orange roll and teapot onto a tray and . . ." she hesitated as if going to make an announcement, then released the preparatory breath, "I felt guilty I guess for not cooking a full meal. I'm so used to having guests, I really don't know what to do with time on my hands."

"Let's both have tea. Out on the terrace. There's no reason for you to wait on me hand and foot. I live here, I'm not a guest." Rose opened the French doors and walked onto the terrace. The cool air rushed onto her face, transforming her to a delicate fern being gently misted. Stretching toward the clouds, she turned back toward the room to find Emerald gone.

Rose crossed the room and straightened the covers on her bed. Emerald still had not returned. She must have gone downstairs for a second teacup and breakfast roll. Rose slid her arms into the sleeves of her duster and carried the tray to the terrace. Having placed it onto the table, she leaned far out over the railing to see onto the yard. There among her lovely roses, a figure was stooped. "Emmy, is that you?"

Emerald waved back through the thick mist with garden shears in hand. Seconds later she joined Rose on the terrace. She quickly arranged the sunrise-colored roses in a deep, crystal bowl of water and poured herself a cup of tea. She must have been up for hours; her makeup did not appear to be fresh.

Gazing into Emerald's tired face, Rose felt a twinge of guilt for having slept so long and so well. The guilt passed as quickly as it had attacked. "Couldn't get back to sleep after the Standfords left, huh?"

"I wasn't asleep when they knocked." Emerald sipped her tea and placed the cup back onto the saucer. She dipped a finger into the bowl of flowers, swirling the water until the roses followed each other round and round in a hypnotic merry-go-round.

Rose again felt that Emerald was getting ready to say something. The jersey dress had not been mentioned. Perhaps Emerald would admit she had been in Everett the previous day. She would tell Rose why she had lied about not having been away from the house. Microwaved. That's it. The rolls at supper had been microwaved. Emerald had always steered clear of that modern-day appliance. Too unnatural, she always insisted. Maybe Emerald would explain this mystery.

"Perhaps," she began, "I had too much dessert at supper. Anyway, something kept me awake. The rain? I don't know."

"Rain helps me sleep. I love it," announced Rose. "As long as it's not storming. Remember those terrible Oklahoma tornadoes?"

"Well, not me. Rain usually keeps me awake. I was lonely. After so long, I still miss Raylon. Can you believe it?"

"I can believe it. Did you ever consider that if you had sold the inn and gone away from Washington that your loneliness for Ray might not be so great after all this time?"

"But, leaving?" Emerald's eyes closed and tiny crow's feet, lines Rose had not noticed until now, stretched toward her temples. Silver streaks seemed painted onto two strands of hair, pulled smoothly upward and secured with amber combs. "Raylon would not want me to leave. I feel him here, but it's an aggravating, disturbing presence. Not at all the Raylon I loved."

"You have stayed all these years, not because you loved the inn, but for Ray?"

"You know I love this place. I'm part of it. I belong here, doing this."

"Doing what? What is it exactly that you do here?"

Emerald felt like a child being reprimanded for some elusive crime. "Ray gave me this place. So, it's up to me to keep it up. To invite guests to enjoy what I love and have worked for."

"Emmy, you've done a wonderful job. The inn is known all over the country."

"Rose, I feel like there's more, something that I'm supposed to be doing. I'm afraid."

"Are you afraid of something in particular, or afraid of not knowing what that something is?" Rose waited for Emerald to answer and watched her eyes, which focused into the distance.

"Afraid I'll get to the end of all this and discover I've done it all wrong." Beyond the mist, sunlight struggled to be seen. Glimmers of gold flashed periodically through the veil of seaspray blowing up over the hillside. "Where to go, what to do, how to do it. I don't know. I feel so out of control. Out of control, as if . . . as if I can either do it right or mess it up real bad."

"Join the club. Do you think I can tell you how and what? Emmy, do you think I or anybody knows what they are doing in this rattrap maze?"

Emerald stood and walked to the railing. She stared toward the ocean just being revealed beneath a large cloud canopy. "You always know what you're doing. You always know what you want. Do you think I don't know you lived with that Mr. Svenson, that you were lovers all those months you told me you had an apartment in Everett? Nobody to hold you down. No real obligations. You love life. Life loves you. You go after whatever you want. I wish I had that freedom, and I hate it that you have it. Selfish, right?"

Nausea began as a twinge of movement in Emmy's stomach. She moved through the French doors and sat on Rose's bed. "Even if I live to be a hundred years old," she said, standing before the dressing table, "I'm halfway finished with my life." Emerald seated herself and gazed into the mirror. "And God knows I'll never make it to be a hundred." She searched the mirror for the Emmy she knew. "She's gone, that young girl. She's dying, slowly, day by day. Each day swirls around and around in space, chasing the day before and being chased by the one to follow. And for what?" Rose quickly crossed the terrace and stood behind Emerald. Watching Emmy's reflection, Rose sought the words to console her. But the words forming in her head resisted being spoken.

"Emerald, listen to me," Rose finally spoke. "I feel the same way. It will end, someday. We just don't know how long any of us has on this earth."

"But how are we supposed to know what comes next,

if anything? Sometimes I can't stand it. I keep seeing those channelers on talk shows. I need something like that to tell me what Emerald Thorn is supposed to be doing." The sickening feeling was hot tentacles of adrenalin creeping through her veins. Her skin grew cold. Emerald's head suddenly felt as though it were too heavy for her shoulders. She leaned into the mirror and saw nothing but fog as she laid her head onto the table.

"What about God? He's got all this figured out."

"God, is it? I've never heard you talk about God. For all I know, you're an atheist or something!" screamed Emerald.

"Oh, good grief." Rose knew the subject was much too serious to be taken lightly, but she wanted to laugh at this scenario. Hadn't she herself been in a similar state of desperation these past few months? "You know I believe in God."

"You never said so. Never once have you just right out said, 'Emerald, I believe in God.' Why do you believe in God? Why didn't you ever say so? What good does it do you to believe? I feel hopeless, like something is ripping my insides out. Like we could die and just be disintegrated into nothing. I can't even comprehend being just nothing." She sobbed hysterically.

Rose knew Emerald was tired. She'd probably been awake all night crying over Ray's photo. Ray was special to them both, but Emmy had never adjusted to his being gone. Staying in the past and present only for Ray's sake, she'd hidden in this inn, sheltered from the real world, never nurturing her own identity. What will we both do? thought Rose. Two aging women, searching for themselves. "It's hope," she said, "to have a belief in God. It's the only hope we have. We just go on and hope it's okay in the end, I guess. It makes more sense than what some people think; just swirling spirits waiting to reincarnate."

"What if it's not true and there is more, something else, and we missed it?"

Rose helped Emerald up from the dressing stool and wrapped her arm around her waist. Moving toward the door, she announced, "We'll work on this together, Em. We are not the only people to pose these questions. It would be nice if it were all written down and we knew what comes next. But life is not a novel, Emerald. If it were, you could skim the last chapter, like you do all books. Don't pretend that you don't do that, either. I've seen you. What you need is some sleep. To your room and don't argue with me. You are going to take a nap."

"If life were a novel, I'd do just that. I'd read the last chapter. Just to make sure I could handle the whole story. If I couldn't, I'd get out. If I know what happens, I can tolerate anything between front and back covers."

"You are exhausted. I'll work on the bills and supper. Rest," said Rose, as she slipped Emerald's shoes off. She pulled the comforter up over Em's legs and drew the heavy tapestry draperies shut.

As she turned to leave the room, she heard Emerald faintly speak before lapsing into sleep, "I have to know about Ray. Yesterday I learned of a man who can help me."

"Help you what, Em?"

"Find out about Ray. He's still alive; I feel it."

An icy coldness fell over Rose. "Raylon is gone. D-e-a-d." But Emerald was gone also, into a deep sleep. Rose closed the door. Descending the stairs, she marveled at the strange magic fatigue has on the human body and mind. Emerald is usually so energetic and tends to be of the same headstrong, go-getter personality of which she had accused Rose. Had fatigue caused her to temporarily lose her senses? Or had she just come to them?

Rose sat on the window seat and suddenly became embarrassed about being in her duster long past noon. The day was half over and she had things to do. But those priorities eluded her mental list as she thought quietly about Emerald's questions. These two women had lived together, but had rarely talked about controversial matters; to do so would have caused an argument. Religion was among one of the topics avoided. Rose had just assumed that Emerald believed in God. Just as Emerald had supposed that Rose did not.

There is a God. I know it; otherwise, what hope would there be? she wondered. But to imagine an eternity in a heaven she had learned of in Sunday school was a thought she could not fathom. "What if there's really no eternity, and when we die, that's that?" she asked herself. I can't imagine *not* being alive, just as Emerald couldn't comprehend the possibility of not existing in some form. But if there is an eternity, what's to keep God from deciding to change his eternal life plan for mankind and just zap us. We'd be gone, period. Rose's skin prickled on the back of her neck and her scalp felt as though tiny ants were marching through the forest of hair. Her chest cavity felt empty, yet her heart raced wildly to know the answer to this mystery.

No, Emerald, she thought. We cannot turn to the final chapter to ease our curiosity and satisfy our seeking souls. God, you're real and you must have it under control, right? Well, don't you?

She stood and dashed to the kitchen to escape her anxiety. "I'll eat first," she said, "and go work in the garden." She opened the refrigerator door, and as she reached for the carton of milk, she sensed words resonating within her. Words which felt like "I am your God and I am with you always," echoed throughout her body. The sickening nausea was sucked out the top of her head as the empty chest filled with a peaceful warmth. The fear that had gripped her just moments before was now a memory. Hurriedly, she constructed a sandwich. She still didn't know the answers, but it no longer bothered her that she didn't.

How could she explain this sudden peace to Emerald? "I am with you always," she repeated. She wanted to remember those words. She dashed upstairs, taking her lunch with her. Placing the sandwich and milk on the nightstand, she found a slip of paper and jotted down the words, reading them several times before folding the paper and sliding it into the drawer.

The conversation with Emerald was vaguely reminiscent of one she'd had with Sven just days before she moved out of his apartment. The terrace still dripped a steady patter as overhanging trees released the captured drops of last evening's rain.

It had been after midnight and sleep was elusive. Rose remembered stepping out onto the terrace into the navy blue night. Brushing the wet layer of snow from the canvas, she lifted the tarp covering the firewood. Two ought to do it. Sven would be here soon. She shook the snow from her feet and hoped, in these early morning hours, that no neighbors had seen her slip outside barelegged. Kneeling upon the warm stone hearth, she fed the small logs to the subsiding flames and briskly rubbed her toes. She then propped her feet upon a pillow. A knock at the door startled Rose, who darted to and fro, looking for her jeans to pull on beneath her oversized sweatshirt.

Thud, thud. The knocking became a kick, and Rose realized it was Sven. Probably he was unable to get to his key. He had mentioned picking up a late night snack on his way home. "Hello in there. If you want Chinese, you'll open up," he said quietly. Rose cautiously opened the door, avoiding the drafty frozen air on her legs, and stayed behind the wooden barricade.

The guy in the adjoining apartment was a pro football player who spent most of his time away from Everett. He had just returned and must have gone right to bed, for Rose had not heard a sign of life from that apartment since the cab had dropped him off an hour ago. He was a quiet man and his presence was rarely noticed. Rose loved that. Sven's place was a sanctuary, a place to recover when deadlines and decisions pressed in on her.

The couple spread their midnight picnic upon the hardwood floor before the open draperies of the terrace. As they shared chow mein from the same carton, large flakes of snow drifted onto the terrace, silently slamming into the glass door. They appeared to be fragile crystal, flitting and twirling to the mystical, twinkling sounds of Ion Jazz emanating from the stereo system.

"When I was younger," Rose said, "I used to buy goldfish at the dime store."

"And did they actually cost a dime?" Sven mused.

"More or less."

"And what about the dime store goldfish?"

"The pet department clerk put them into little cartons like these, that's all."

"Ooh! What if we get to the bottom of this chow mein and there's a goldfish there?" Rose bumped against Sven in reprimand. "I've only seen them packaged in little sandwich baggies with bread sack twisties. What happened to your fish?"

"They died. All of them died. I probably bought twenty over the years."

"And flushed them down the toilet when they expired?"

"Sure, or threw them out back for the cats to get." She laughed and rolled onto her back. With her head tilted back, Rose got the sensation of being a part of the snowfall. She could see the unusually clear sky throwing snow which seemed to blow past her, never landing.

"I hope you didn't really feed them to cats. What bad karma. I'd love to think of them floating around in that big fish pond in the sky."

"Cut it out. They were just little fish. Dead is dead, for animals at least. No souls, you know."

Sven leaned over Rose's face and looked deeply into her eyes. He whispered, "I see the snow falling into your eyes. Here it comes. Falling, falling, splat!" He laughed and stood up. "Let's dance. On your feet, please."

They danced, swaying in each other's arms for what seemed endless time. The embers in the fireplace glimmered and sparked as Sven looked full into Rose's face. "We're nearly finished with the Mount St. Helen's study. Two days maybe. I think we can get it into press and in Sunday's edition."

"Mm, good."

"No, not so good. I mean, I'm getting accustomed to your being around on these special projects. I love it."

"The snow will melt, probably sooner than later."

"Rusty," he enveloped her chin between his hands and said, "don't faint; just say you'll move in. Long term."

She stood still, but rested her head against Sven's shoulder. "I can't, you know that." All her life Rose had wanted to be unattached, to take care of herself. Just doing what made her feel free was her desire. Those goldfish. Every time she needed to be away from home longer than usual someone else had to be relied upon to feed them. Dogs, cats, roommates, and lovers. They were all the same. Demanding something. An obligation to have to come home to and feel saddled by.

"Rusty, don't say no. Look at me."

"Sven, this is all wrong. You and I don't have any business getting into anything long term."

"Come on and look at me; I mean it."

Rose slowly turned her face toward Sven's and saw the puzzlement and hurt in his eyes. "What's wrong with your living here?" he said. "Us, together. Sounds perfect."

"Good night, Sven. I can't believe all this. Take a good look at me. I must be going through a second childhood. Playing these games. Having an affair at my age. . . ."

Sven laughed loudly and plopped onto the sofa, pulling her to his side. "An affair? You're kidding! Anyone can have an affair. You and I are something more than that. This was destined to be. It was supposed to happen. Someday I'll be capable of putting my feelings down on paper and I'll share them with you. For now, trust me that we have a sexual, spiritual union made in the heavens. And why bring up your age? I'm as old, or should I say young, as you?"

"I didn't mean I'm old. I just wonder, why now? Why not thirty years ago? Fun and freedom is all I've wanted for a long time. I never wanted anything permanent. Not even a quasi-permanent setup like we've had for the past few months."

"You are afraid of commitment. Think back, Rusty. You made a commitment the moment you were attracted to me. The first night you accepted my invitation to stay over. Admit it. Do you love me?" Sven didn't wait for an answer, but stood up and crossed the room. The window facing the bay had accumulated a thin film of frost. "You don't feel guilty for our being together, do you?"

"Oh sure, all I have to say is that everything's fine. No guilt here. That let's you off the hook, right?"

"Off the hook with who?"

"Your conscience or God. I don't know."

"God? How did we get onto that subject? Is that what this is about?"

"Maybe. I've tried not to think of it anymore than I have to. I was raised in a Christian home, knowing that this type of relationship is wrong. I've stayed here, having the most wonderful times of my life and regretting every single minute. I do love you, but I can't stand this guilt anymore. I can't move in."

"God doesn't intend for you to feel guilty," said Sven. "Society used to. Even that is changing now." He wrapped his arms tightly around her shoulders and whispered, "God, if that's what we are calling it, wants good for everyone. He wants you to have fun. He wants me to have fun. By loving and experiencing others, and that includes sexually, we are expressing our spirituality."

"Oh come on, Sven. What you and I consider spirituality are two different concepts."

"Yes, they're different in that you look at everything in black and white, like your two columns. Right or wrong, nothing in between."

"You don't have any absolute religious convictions then, do you Sven? I mean, everything is a matter of opinion. Opinions are all correct; no one's opinion is wrong."

"Basically, yes. Everything we do, in love or in life, works to develop our character and advances our growth toward the self we are meant to be. You believe it too."

"No. I admire your freedom and spirit, but it bothers me that we just go through these motions of living and loving. I really don't know where we are going. I only know it doesn't feel right. I can't move in with you."

"Okay, babe. I'm sorry I brought it up. I've never asked anyone to move in, or even spend more than a few hours with me."

"But I feel your invitation is untimely. We are playing a game, a game that supposes we are two consenting adults moving around a game board. But beyond right now, there are no rules. I have to decide what I believe and what I want out of this short life. Those things can't be decided instantly. You are too strong an influence on me. I have to go home and think. I have too much going on mentally to think clearly, especially with you so strongly believing whatever it is you really believe."

"It's that religious upbringing of yours. If you would stop whipping yourself with the guilt and accept what each day brings you, it would all fit into place. There is no God.

At least not the way you think of him! He's energy within you, within me. He *is* you and me because we are part of the same cosmic force that makes up God. God is us; we are God. Do you see that? You must give yourself permission to be yourself. There can be no condemnation in that."

"Go with the flow? If it feels good, do it? What other clichés apply?"

"Rusty, you are twisting what I've said. No religion or philosophy has the whole truth. But we have it within ourselves. Trust yourself, not some doctrine crammed down your throat at the First National Church of whatever it was. I don't guess this would be a good time to change the proposition to marriage as oppposed to fornication?"

Rose smiled, but quickly saw the hurt in Sven's gray eyes as she turned toward him. His hair needed combing. She twisted a forelock around her finger and pulled his face toward her own. "You are the only one I want. I just need time to think about all this. Surely I can make a place in my mind for it all. You know what you want. You always have. Sven, the beatnik, turned hippie, turned whatever you are now."

"Member of mankind, Rusty. Cosmic New Ager. Traveler through time. I'm just following my own map like everybody else. All those snowflakes are unique, like fingerprints. Yet to us, they look alike. Watch them falling, spreadeagle, to their destinations. They don't question where they came from or what they are to do here. They glide and bank against the wind and plant themselves firmly wherever they land. They become a foundation for others who follow, each becoming interlocked with those who fell before and those to come. An icy blanket they weave. A coverlet whose beauty others will enjoy until the warmth of the sun gently heats the coverlet into fluid that will flow back to the ocean, there remaining until new and distinct droplets are called upon to become mist or rain or snow. Those exact flakes will never be again exactly as they are. But they've been extracted from, interacted with, and will return to their source, always having a distinct place in this universe."

"Whew. That's pretty heavy. It's two in the morning. No wonder we're still awake, talking about the secrets of the universe. We're delirious with fatigue." She stared at the terrace made wet by kamikaze snowflakes. She knew there was no connection between the cycling of moisture and souls, but it proved there had to be at least some correlation between fatigue and delirium.

Emerald was still asleep as Rose came back to the present. She looked into Emmy's bedroom on the way to the garden. Working in the dirt with her bare hands always helped Rose put things into perspective. Silently God had assured her that he did have her best interests at heart, whatever the outcome. I am with you always; she reflected on the idea as she stepped onto the back porch and breathed in the rejuvenating moist ocean air.

Chapter Six

Answer In The Wind

The humming was a simple tune as it neared the house. Tracy recognized it as being the only song Geneva ever whistled, hummed, or sang. Occasionally the four notes within Geneva's range were actually recognizable as those of "Put On Your Sunday Clothes" from the musical, *Hello Dolly*. Geneva only orchestrated the tune when, in her own words, "The most wonderful thing has happened."

"We're out back," Tracy hollered lazily from her hammock. Geneva swung open the wooden gate, startling the hen where she was sitting on eggs. Black feathers and dried leaves flew as she batted her wings in warning to Geneva from beneath the hollyhock bush.

"The most wonderful thing has happened," she began as she sat on a redwood bench opposite Rose. "The most wonderful thing in my whole life."

As Rose brushed Tracy's cat off her lap, she thought how unusual that the most wonderful thing happened so frequently to the same woman. She meticulously picked black and white cat hairs from her dark jeans and forced a smile. "What in the world could have happened this time?"

The bearer of glad tidings stretched her dress over her knees, combed through her crisply dyed black hair with her nude fingernails and announced, "Duncan has asked me to marry him."

"Again?" mused Rose. "Oh, I don't mean again Duncan, but again? You are going to marry again?" She thought of the only semi-serious proposal of marriage she had received back in the winter months. It had been six months ago, yet Rose could not solidify any thoughts that might lead to a definite *yes* to any permanent relationship. But here sat a woman who had been married no fewer than five times. That was just in the seven or so years that Geneva had lived across the road from Tracy.

"Well, yes. My divorce from Ledford will be final Friday. And, well, Duncan and I are driving up to Marysville on Saturday to tie the knot." She giggled timidly as if she were to be a first-time bride, embarrassed at the puzzlement of the yet-to-come honeymoon night.

Tracy turned her face toward the other ladies without opening her eyes. "We didn't know Duncan had a home of his own to move a wife into. I don't remember even hearing you mention what he does for a living. Maybe you'd better clue us in on some details if he is going to be a neighbor."

"Uncanny that you should say neighbor, because Duncan will be moving into my house after the wedding and all, but only until we can look at houses and find just what the two of us want." She blushed one last time, then became more aware of her surroundings.

Other than Emerald, Geneva was the second person whose presence Rose found intolerable for long intervals. A fleeting shower of rainwater was released onto her neck from the overhanging arbor. "And what does he do for a living?" Rose quizzed.

"Actually, he's retired."

"From where?"

"From the paper company. He has a nice, healthy pension."

Rose was only slightly concerned over her friend's imminent mistake, yet felt that these questions should be posed in the event Geneva had not thought this thing through, as Rose suspected she had not. "So, why doesn't he own a home of his own?"

"He's paying alimony to his last wife." Geneva looked to Tracy to come to her aid, but the hammock had stopped all swinging motion and Tracy had succumbed to sleep.

"His last wife? How many wives has he had?"

"Only two. Are you going to judge him by his having been married more than once? Maybe you begrudge him having been married at all." She drove the final words in, giving them a twist.

But Rose ignored the stab and continued the questioning. After all, it was in her friend's best interest. "So he'll move in. You'll live on his pension, what there is left after alimony to wife 'X'. Then there is your savings, right? Will that be enough?"

"I didn't mention, Rose, but he has some furniture and a deep freeze full of meat. Well, not full, but he has thirty-eight chickens in the freezer and some pot pies."

A suspicious tingle began as a butterfly in Rose's stomach and suddenly erupted in a blast of laughter as she pondered all the possible menus Geneva would be planning. Chicken and dumplings. Chicken *a la* king. Fried. Baked. Broiled and fricasseed. Chicken and rice. Her laughter became short explosions and gasps for air as she voiced, "When you eat all the chickens, you can start on the pot pies. I hope they are *chicken* pot pies!" Tears of delight had melted her mascara into a black river of sludge, leaving trails on her cheeks.

Rose wiped at her face with the back of her hand. But the mascara caused her eyes to sting and she was now unable to open them. The more she cried, the more her eyes smarted. Her laughter ceased and Geneva's began. "You could go get me a kleenex or napkin. A tea towel, toilet paper, something. I can't see."

"Serves you right for making fun of my man friend and his thirty-eight chickens," said Geneva as she sauntered toward the house. Rose knew it was no use opening her eyes now, as all she could see was swirling, black whirlpools. She tightly squenched, hoping to keep the stinging fluids from further seepage. Propping her elbows upon the picnic table, she rested her chin on her interlocked fingers to await rescue.

Far away she heard Tracy's steers lowing faintly in the meadow behind the barn. Clucking chickens, quacking ducks, and crafty cats had the run of this "ranch" as Tracy called it. It was no wonder Tracy had dozed off so quickly, totally enveloped in the caress of the serene setting; no traffic or city sounds could invade the privacy of this valley hideaway. The afternoon sun stepped from behind a cloud and Rose's dimmed eyelids allowed her to see a bright yellow film.

Then sudden shooting pain ripped through her neck and head as she jumped to her feet screaming, "Oh God!" She knew not from what she fled, only that something had attached itself to her shoulders and clung tightly with piercing claws. She ran blindly. Her eyes no longer stung, neither would they focus through the smoky glaze.

Following her mental map of the yard's layout, she made straight for the back porch. Forgetting the hollyhocks and sitting hen, Rose careened into the bush, sending feathers and cat hair into a flurry.

Her mouth was filled with grass. The pain had eased in her neck but throbbed in her chest. She wondered if any ribs were broken. Forcing one eye open, she caught a glimpse of the black and white cat skidding into the barn. From across the driveway, Geneva strolled back with a very smug grin adorning her pale face. "Here's a towel. You nearly scared little Mickey to death, taking off like that. He just wanted a little piggyback ride," she laughed.

Rose twisted carefully onto her back and stared at the sky. The bold cartoon clouds were a perfect backdrop for the afternoon's events.

Tracy, awakened by Geneva's laughter, stumbled to her feet. She rushed to Rose's side and gazed down at the raccoon eyes which hypnotically stared upward. "Is she alive?" She smiled, puzzled, and knelt. "Want some help?"

Recovery was speedy. A little peroxide on her scraped hands and chin was the only medical attention warranted. "I can finally breathe without feeling the sharp pains in my chest. Nothing must be broken."

"Guess you'll be sore tomorrow, though. That's the way it usually ends up. Let me fix you some hot tea. Geneva, hot tea for you, too?"

"I'd rather have coffee if you have any made."

"It's on my grocery list, but I don't have a ground in the house right now," announced Tracy.

"Then tea is fine." The ladies continued the lazy pace set earlier in the yard by quietly drinking cup after cup of tea. They hardly spoke; when they did, it was about the simple wedding Geneva and Duncan would have. They would both be wearing beige, spend a couple of days at the Best Western in Mt. Vernon, then on Tuesday they would meet the moving van that would deliver Duncan's chickens. As Tracy used the last tea bag, she added the item to her grocery list and saw Geneva out the door.

"I need to leave soon, myself," said Rose. "Work is caught up for the moment, but there are a couple of thoughts I need to think out and get written up for the paper. Columns don't write themselves. Thanks for the tea and conversation. Many more calms days like these, I won't be fit for anything. Busy, busy, busy. I've got to get back into the swing of work."

"If you don't mind my saying so, Rose, you were looking a little worn from the work. Something about you is different lately. I can't really decide what it is, but you look more rested and at peace."

Peace? Rose thought it probably was not solely peace, but she had experienced that strange confirmation that she was important and not alone, for God was with her. She wanted to tell Tracy about the voice ringing from within her, but she felt her common sense check her. If you mention that, she thought, Tracy will think you are crazy, especially if you say it was God.

Rose wanted to assure Emerald that God cared about them both, and longed to share the consolation that he is with them always. But what words could she use? She had nothing tangible as proof, just feelings. Her feelings had deceived her in the past. Why should these feelings be any different? But they were. The problem was that feelings could not be easily translated or described; therefore, she felt inadequately equipped to do anything further where this strange revelation was concerned. But she could not go back to the time when she wondered about the existence of God, nor could she go forward as she did not know what to do next. Lifting her gaze from the terra cotta floor, Rose turned to say goodbye. She was stopped by the look of total understanding on Tracy's face.

"Rose, the Lord God wants to tell you something," she began. "He says you are careful and troubled about many things. But one things is needful, and Mary hath chosen that good part, which shall not be taken away from her. That's a scripture, Luke 10:41-42. Lo, I am with you always, even unto the end of the world. That verse comes from Matthew 28:20."

Tracy wrapped her arms around Rose's shoulders. The conversations with Sven and Emerald flowed from Rose's mouth and heart as if a floodgate had been opened. And as she told of the warmness that had filled her chest where cold emptiness had gripped her, she recounted the words that God had spoken to her at that moment; the same words Tracy had just quoted her.

"I am with you always. It must be God. How else could you have known. I haven't told anyone, not even Emmy, about those words." The same warmth filled the room and Rose felt at peace. Then a twinge of panic struck. "You aren't channeling some spirit are you?"

Tracy smiled and hugged her. "Sit over here and let me show you something." Taking her Bible from the arm of her favorite chair, she swiftly turned the fragile pages.

Rose sat quietly, anticipating the unknown. Tracy said, "You didn't come here by accident today. The Holy Spirit led you here. You've been searching for the truth, haven't you? Everyone wants to know the truth. Some people are too open-minded to accept something as limited as the Bible. Therefore, they spend years in meditation and searching to find truth. The truth never was any further away than this book. So it can't be that hard to find for those who are really seeking the truth — God's truth. Lo, I am with you always. It's right here in Matthew 28:20. Jesus said it. He is the truth. It says that, too, right over here." She pointed to the verse. "And Jesus said to me, I am the way, the truth, and the life; No man comes to the father, but by me," read Tracy. "That is John 14:6."

"I believe it, even though I never heard it before," said Rose, spellbound.

"Rose," said Tracy slowly as she reclined against the back of the sofa, "the truth is that Jesus is the Son of God. He died on the cross to pay for the sins of the world. You accept that as the truth and you inherit everlasting life. Life to live forever with God, the creator of the universe. If you don't believe it and accept it, there is no life after this. Only death, both physically and spiritually."

Tracy leafed through more pages and said, "The two sisters, Mary and Martha, were preparing dinner for their friend, Jesus. Martha came tattling to Jesus that Mary was not doing her share of the mealtime preparation. All she wanted to do was to sit at the feet of Jesus. 'Make her help me,' said Martha. And Jesus said, 'Martha, Martha, thou art careful and troubled about many things. But one thing is needful. And Mary hath chosen that good part, which shall not be taken away from her.' Do you see?" asked Tracy.

"God has laid your concerns upon my heart," continued Tracy, "and as the Holy Spirit led me, I spoke the words he wanted to confirm to you. Jesus loves you and wants to end your confusion and lead you to the father, God. No channeler would do that. Satan is the author of confusion. God wants to restore you, along with all mankind, to the glory of God. Do you want to accept Jesus as the way, the truth, and the life?" She laid her Bible on the sofa between them and took Rose's hand in her own.

Not knowing what to do, but knowing that if this was really God, she wanted whatever comes next; she timidly nodded her head.

"Then it's easy. Just repeat this prayer with me. Jesus, I ask you to forgive me of my sins," Tracy whispered. Rose's lips became thick and her throat threatened to close completely. She could not admit she was a sinner. Was she?

Rose had not used her discretion in a lot of matters, but she suddenly realized why Sven had protested at the thought that they had committed any sin. "We are all born into sin," Tracy continued, "whether or not we do evil intentionally. We are sinners until Jesus takes that sin from us at our request. Jesus died for it already. It's sin, no matter what we call it. You just have to acknowledge that it is present and accept forgiveness for it."

"Okay." Rose closed her eyes and repeated after Tracy. "Jesus, I ask you to forgive me of my sins, to come into my life, leading me in the paths you have prepared for me. I give to you my whole being: spirit, soul, and body. Thank you, Jesus. Amen." She felt surrounded by warmth and sensed that the confusion had lifted from about her head. She laughed, not sensing anything particularly funny. Yet, she felt new and happy. "That's it?"

"Yes, does it feel like that's it?"

"Yeah, I mean, I feel changed, different, glad of something."

"If you could see into the heavens, Rose, an angel has just written your name into a registry of people who are worthy to enter heaven — the Lamb's Book of Life."

Rose recalled the words of a hymn her mother sang as she flitted about doing her housework. "There's a new name written down in Glory. This is what she meant, isn't it?"

"Do you know the song?"

"Just parts."

"It goes like this. There's a new name written down in Glory, and it's mine, oh yes, it's mine. And the white-robed angels tell the story, a sinner has come home. There's a new name written down in Glory, and it's mine, oh yes, it's mine. With my sins forgiven, I am bound for Heaven, never more to roam."

The two sang the song over and over as tears washed Rose's face. If Rose's mother had felt like this as she sang through her chores, it was no wonder her jobs were done so quickly.

Rose felt a supernatural high as she again began laughing. Laughter seemed the only form of expression appropriate for the well of life which had sprung from her spirit.

Tracy joined Rose on the floor and they sat quietly against the sofa front. Rose felt that electricity had penetrated every cell of her body and she wanted to continue in that moment of time forever. All the work she had planned to do today became of no importance as she realized that she had been transformed from Martha, the busy sister, to Mary, who wanted nothing more than to sit at the feet of Jesus, for in His presence she felt a restful freshness that filled all her senses, as though she were breathing in the healing, fragrant mist of a cleansing spring rain.

"Do you have a Bible at home?"

"Somewhere. Maybe in the cedar chest."

"I've got a spare, never know when I'll need to look up something quick as a flash. I'll be right back." She left through her bedroom door and reappeared with a Bible and several bookmarks.

"You'll find," she said, "you will grow so fast in the knowledge of God, things you never could have thought of, if you'll stay in God's presence and read His Word every day." She marked several pages with the bookmarks and handed the Bible to Rose.

Tracy stepped into the kitchen and brought back two glasses of water. As she handed one to Rose she seated herself in her favorite chair. "I spend as much time as I can praying, right here in this chair. Then anytime I feel an attack of Satan, I pray. Satan will give you a hard time because of this commitment to Jesus Christ. But the Holy Spirit knows when you're in need of rescue, and he will intercede in your behalf and help you stand strong. Be sensitive to his presence. No problem can remain unsolved if you rely on the Spirit to help out. Use the Holy Spirit to edify your spirit."

It was still early afternoon and though she had much to do, Rose wished to get home and start reading the scriptures Tracy had flagged.

"I appreciate this, Tracy. I knew you were a special friend, but never knew how special until now."

"Not just a friend, a sister in Christ. You're family to me now. I love you in the Lord, Rose." The women hugged and said goodbye. Rose's lilt was the result of a new, life-giving energy. She was home in moments. Emerald had to hear about this. Rose could not wait to share Jesus with Emerald, whom she knew was as actively searching for truth as she herself had been until now. But Emerald was not home. Puzzled, Rose read the note:

> *Dear Rose, I've gone into town to see that man I told you about, the one who will help me find Ray. Left some lunch for you on top of the stove. Be back before supper. Love, Em.*

When she laid the note upon the dining table, a pang of fear rushed through her body. Immediately Rose felt the inclination to pray. As she climbed the stairs, crying out to God, a washing of calm overtook her before she reached her room. For what seemed an eternity, Rose prayed, becoming acquainted with her new-found Savior.

Slender fingers hesitantly pushed down on the oblong brass handle and Emerald stepped into the darkened building. Her head was instantly filled with a mysterious odor and delicate tinkling sounds and singing as faint wind coursed over her head. The wind chimes and musical instruments playing were oddly familiar as if something from a dream were recurring to her. Harps and sitars created a mystical, magical effect. Emerald fairly glided to a huge glass counter.

Breathlessly she appraised each piece of jewelry,

most of which was unusually designed with various gems and symbols engraved in gold. Mirrors and lights within the showcase reflected the brilliance of flawless crystal, prisms, and statuettes of colorful gemstones. From nowhere, silently, stepped a tall young woman, dressed neatly but reminiscent of those love children of the nineteen sixties, her gauze blouse as pale as her cream-colored skin.

"May I help you find something?" Her smile was lovely against flawless skin, wearing no makeup, that emitted a beauty Emerald had not seen outside a book of fairytales. The woman's eyes were a lighter blue than gray doves and compelled Emerald to come closer. Emerald thought she should whisper a response. She leaned over the counter to answer.

"I have an appointment with Grant Sands." She was mesmerized by the length of burgundy hair cascading from behind this lady, hair which waved and swayed about her shoulders and waist. She gingerly smiled and either nodded or mentally motioned for Emerald to follow her. This Emerald did, passing a medley of crystal balls.

Emerald was shocked at the range of prices, as varied as the sizes available. Smaller orbs, priced at twenty-five dollars, were out-brillianced by one a foot in diameter. She tiptoed up to view its price card. Whew, six hundred and fifty dollars, she thought, carefully stepping around it.

To a room at the rear of the store she was led. There, hundreds of little ornaments of crystal were meticulously displayed behind a streakless glass. And over her head hung ceramic and porcelain masks — some of beautifully painted features resembling fairies and elves; others were hideous and frightening, exhibiting evil eyes and blood-stained fangs.

She felt awkward, standing beside this attractive woman facing a shiny black wall. But suddenly the barrier she thought to be a wall opened to one side. The sales clerk had neither rang a buzzer nor knocked, yet this door, now a gaping hole amid the dazzling crystal, was bidding her to enter.

Once she was over the threshold, Emerald realized the door to be a smoke-colored one-way glass. The man seated at a small table had obviously seen their approach and flipped some sort of switch to allow them entrance. Emerald felt a bit more comfortable with this speculation.

"Thank you, Sanguine," he said, standing to shake Emerald's hand. "Please take a seat." The chair was plush and Emerald felt as though she had sunk to her chest in its comfort. She could not discern the color of the chair, or of anything else in the room for that matter.

Her surroundings were lit only by thin pink and green neon strips bordering the walls at the ceiling. The mystical scent, she decided, must be incense. It was much stronger in here than in the outer shop. Her head filled with the powerful fragrance of a flower-laden funeral home and she felt faint. Yet the wind and tinkling glass sounds had followed her into this enchanting hidden room. "Just get comfortable while I get a few preliminaries out of the way," he said, securing an ink pen from his inside coat pocket. Placing an index card on the table before him, he continued, "Give me your full name again, if you don't mind. I know you told me over the phone, but . . ."

"Emerald Thorn. No middle initial."

"Fine." He wrote as he queried, "How was it you got

my phone number?"

"I saw the ad for the Psychic Fair in the newspaper. It listed the dates and times for the fair. I couldn't envision myself attending something like that. So I called the number for Dial-a-Psychic at the bottom of the ad. I must admit," Emerald squirmed in her seat, "I felt a little awkward calling. I never would even call Dial-a-Prayer before. It is a little weird having a tape pray and all, so I certainly couldn't imagine a tape recording doing anything psychic."

"But it wasn't a tape after all, was it? Aren't you glad you called? We've tried to develop a comprehensive clearinghouse of psychic resources to help with any problems a person might encounter." Having put Emerald somewhat at ease, he said, "You came into the shop once before but did not keep your appointment. Can you tell my why?"

"I was slightly taken aback by the eeriness of the shop. And perhaps I was a dab frightened, having never gone to a psychic."

"You made a purchase that day, did you not?"

"Well, yes. But I only shopped in the card and book sections. I bought some birthday cards and bookmarks. Everything here is so mystical, fantasy, fairytale looking. Do you know what I mean?"

"Yes," smiled Mr. Sands, "I know exactly what you mean."

"I must tell you that my curiosity caused me to reschedule my appointment."

"And do you still find us eerie, as you say?"

"Oh no," she lied. "More like enchanting than eerie."

"Good. I'm glad the first impression was not lasting."

Mr. Sands placed both hands on the table and said, "You have come here to look for your husband. Is that correct?"

"Yes," said Emerald, gazing into his greenish face.

"Don't be surprised that I seem to know so much. You feel he is not dead, as you were told. He was in an accident?"

"Yes, a naval accident."

"He has been released from his body, but still lives at your home, Mrs. Thorn." A piercing, cold draft caused Emerald to shiver as Mr. Sands confirmed what she had felt for years. "Would you like to speak to him? He has come here with you today." Emerald hesitated. How many times she had pleaded for Raylon to answer her, to tell her what to do. And he had not. Now she could not bring herself to utter his name.

"I, uh, I don't want to talk to him, per se. I only want to know what he wants me to do. With the inn, that is." She lowered her eyes and waited humbly for the answer.

"Mr. Thorn wants to be near you. He laughs and says you always did want to know the future and be assured of the outcome of situations. Also, he mentions that you read the last chapter before beginning new books."

Emerald's face flushed; she became dizzy as though she would faint. Raylon must be here. How else could this stranger have known that secret about her. "What I have to know is this: does Raylon want me to sell the inn or stay there? I want to do what I'm supposed to do."

"Raylon has been speaking to you, but you have not listened. He is in another place. A place that you too can journey when the time is right. You must, however, be patient and not be afraid to talk to him."

"I'll try. That doesn't answer my question, though. Won't you tell me about the inn?"

"He is no longer here. I sense that you could discern the future and learn those truths for yourself. You don't have the confidence in your own ability; therefore, you seek the answers from others. You have the answers within you. There is a wind that is part of the total cosmos. That wind is inherent in everything. Learn to listen to the elements of nature — the stars, the sun, the rain, and the wind. The elements are part of you. Listen. Know your own future."

"Tell the future? Me? How, I mean? I don't understand. I'm sorry, I just don't know how I could possibly know the future."

"There are as many ways of knowing the truth, which includes the future, as there are souls in this universe. You just need to think positively about yourself and know that you are worthy to receive that truth. You'll discover the best vehicle for yourself, eventually. The girl who showed you in today, Sanguine, is a practitioner of the craft — witch to you — among other things. I see you are surprised. She is very skilled at doing life readings. You could visit with her and give her some information. Your charts can help you in the direction you are to go in life."

"There is definitely something unsettling about someone, even as lovely as she is, drawing up a plan for me to follow. I mean, things change from day to day. The chart wouldn't."

"You are right about that. It would stay the same. But it is general enough to accommodate change. But your destiny as well as your overall goals will stay the same. It would be a tremendous help. It is only one option, Mrs. Thorn."

"Except, I just want to know a couple of things. Like does Ray want me to sell the inn? Should I close up and go on vacation? Stuff like that."

"Let me escort you to the book room, and I will see if I can assist you in making a selection. Perhaps if you would read up on options in the New Age menu, you would be more comfortable than if a stranger, like myself, imposes suggestions on you."

"Thanks. But what do I owe you for your help today?"

"Whatever this information is worth to you. As little or as much as you feel comfortable with. This is primarily a service I provide."

Emerald folded a twenty and a five dollar bill, placing them on the table. Mr. Sands pressed the door release and the door slowly opened. Once into the outer shop, Emerald made her way to the bookshelves catalogued *fortunetelling*.

Mr. Sands' face was no longer green. He quietly explained, "Futures may be read by use of tarot cards, studying the lines on the palms and wrists, meditating with the aid of a crystal, interpreting images in tea leaves . . . "

"What about tea leaves?"

Mr. Sands scanned the shelves, picking out one, then two thin books. "Tea leaves can be interpreted daily for insight into what will occur that particular day. Nothing long term, however. You can learn to read your own future, as well as those of friends and acquaintances."

"And besides," said Emerald, "I love tea." She thumbed through the colorful pages of the books.

"Very good then," said Mr. Sands. "It sounds like tea is your cup of tea." The pair laughed and Mr. Sands recovered his somber countenance quickly. "At least it is an excellent place for you to start. One thing leads to another. I doubt if you will be satisfied with this method, once you have gotten a taste of the power that comes with knowing the future before the fact. There will come a time that you will want to expand your abilities in the arena of controlling your own future. But this method is quite simple. These two books are wonderful in helping beginners interpret the images they discern in the teacup. But the word *discern* is the key. You are the discerner. The tea residue is merely the vehicle."

"Will I need special tea?"

"Oh no. We do sell special blends here, but whatever you enjoy at home is best. As long as it is loose leaf, no bags. And real china cups are conducive to accurate readings. No Tupperware mugs. But you don't strike me as a woman whose lips have touched plastic, so that's an aside. You can study these books at your leisure and find out the details. They are excellent at teaching the basic techniques."

"Thank you so much. You have been a world of help."

"The main thing is that my help is only a beginning. And, Mrs. Thorn, on these books?" He smiled, then recovered instantly, "Don't read the last chapters first." He chuckled without smiling and disappeared through his black glossy wall.

As she waited for her change, Emerald puzzled over whether Sanguine's hair was really oxblood red, or if the color was a result of candles and the effects of pink and green neon.

"Thank you for visiting Answer In The Wind. Here's your change," said Sanguine's delicate heart-shaped lips. "And please come back." Her dove-blue eyes bid Emerald farewell. Somehow, Emerald knew she would return.

Chapter Seven

Riversong

The screaming phone pierced the dawn like a distant tolling bell. Emerald's voice was equally obtrusive as she announced that Mr. Svenson had just called. "He'll drop by for you about eight. Be ready or he will take his presence elsewhere, he told me."

"Really? I mean, I remember telling him I would see him Friday, but . . ." Rose thought she and Sven would meet for dinner in Everett. "Neutral territory, he told me. I can't be ready at eight. It's not even time for breakfast, yet."

"I was going to call you down to breakfast directly, so slip on your robe and ease downstairs, dear."

As Rose drew a foot up under herself, she arranged the chenille housecoat into a blanket over her bare legs. Steam from the deliciously tempting cup of tea teased her tastebuds when Rose leaned over it. Each tiny vapor particle sought out and clung to a sleepy pore, coaxing her skin to awaken. As she drew her face away from the cup, the moist skin chilled in the morning air. It tingled and shouted that it was alive.

Something about this morning made her feel brand new. Maybe the huge omelet with its fresh mushrooms and tomatoes, or the briskness of the air were the cause. After all, it was the immaculately clean blend of cold mountain air and salty ocean spray that kept her rejuvenated and loving the peninsula.

Rose had given little thought to how she would tell Sven about Wednesday afternoon at Tracy's. She could not anticipate how he might accept her experience of being born again. She had practiced various opening phrases the previous day. There's something I think I should tell you, Sven, she led off mentally. My life has changed. Let me tell you what has happened. How's this? Sven, I've been so confused about my purpose here on this earth, this space and time in history. My confusion has been dispelled. I know what life is about now. May I share it with you? It all sounded unnatural. Forced. Somehow the words would just have to come when the time was right. She would convince Sven that she had found the truth. He too would find it. A twinge of excitement struck. She contemplated what it would be like if Sven would accept Christ as she had. Would Rose accept that proposal of marriage, that is if Sven offered again? She finished her breakfast and sipped her tea as she further contemplated.

Surely no relationship, with any man, could be more perfect than if both were born-again Christians. She suddenly realized that bonds of love could only be strengthened when bonded spiritually. That's what Sven had been saying all along; their friendship was as much spiritual as it was physical. But it hadn't felt right, even if that was what he had meant. The spiritual force had to be from the same source. And although Rose knew her own spiritual source, she was not at all sure about Sven's.

Now that she had been forgiven of her past, she could embark on her new life, which she hoped would include Sven in a spiritual union of matrimony.

"Rose," interrupted Emerald who had been carefully watching her sister-in-law's facial expression. Rose felt Em had read her thoughts. Her countenance colored to match her name. "I didn't mean to startle you, but your tea, dear. It is almost gone and it has gotten cold."

"I'll warm it."

"No, let me," said Emerald, and she dashed off to the kitchen. "I'll bring it upstairs to you. Go ahead and get dressed for your outing." Emerald had never shown as much enthusiasm about Sven's presence.

The only thing predictable about that woman is her unpredictability, thought Rose. She sat at her dressing table, silently praying that God would strengthen her new-found faith and give her courage to speak to her loved ones about the joy she had found in Christ. This new subject was definitely out of her normal purview. She felt inadequate yet desperate to share her experience.

Downstairs, Emerald held Rose's teacup firmly in hand, swirled the liquid three times to the left, and turned its contents swiftly into a saucer. "I know she is supposed to do this step herself, but maybe it will still work. I need the practice."

She peered inside the cup and blankly surveyed the composition of tea leaves clinging to the sides of the bell-shaped china cup. "Hm, maybe a ring. Yes, it's a ring. A wedding ring? Could be." She rinsed away the residue and poured Rose a fresh cup of the predictive brew. Having set the cup and saucer upon the bureau, she wiped her damp hands on her apron. "Do you think Mr. Svenson is leading up to a marriage proposal?"

Once again, Rose felt her secrets were being announced telepathically. "What would make you say something like that?"

"I just wondered. I know he likes you. And you did live together for a while, after all."

"Em, sit down a minute, right there." She pointed to the foot of the bed. "I've wanted to tell you this since the other day, but haven't had time. Didn't know how, exactly." She felt this would be good practice for telling Sven the news. "Remember when we were talking about needing to know the truth about why we're here and what we are supposed to be doing? In life, I mean?"

Emerald flinched. Could Rose know about the tea leaf reading? But Em felt she had nothing to justify to Rose.

"I now know the truth," Rose continued.

"You do?" Emerald looked amazed and was not sure what to say next. How could Rose know what she had been about?

"Yes, I know the truth. Tracy prayed with me and showed me some scriptures from the Bible. Here, look." Rose stood and moved toward Emerald with her Bible. "Jesus says right here that he is the way, the truth, and the life. He's the answer. It's his love we've been needing and struggling to find."

"What on earth are you talking about? The subject was Gregory Svenson."

"I am talking about Sven. What Sven and I had, at that time, was wrong. But God has forgiven that wrongful relationship and has made me a brand-new person."

"Snap out of it, Rose. You sound like one of those testimonials we hear on that Christian television network. It's sickening. And if that relationship was all wrong, why are you going with Sven today?"

"To share with him what's happened to me. Em, it

was great. I have to describe it to you."

"Rose, collect yourself. What dress are you going to wear? I'll lay it out for you," she said, crossing the room to the closet. Nervously she slid hangers back and forth along the long metal bar. "Here, this lavender is lovely."

"I'm not wearing a dress, just jeans. Why are you avoiding me?" Rose stood behind Emerald, blocking her exit from the walk-in closet.

"It is beyond me why any real woman would want to wear jeans instead of a nice, feminine dress. And avoidance, as you say, is not in my vocabulary. It's just that I don't understand what you are talking about, nor can I believe this strange behavior of yours. You've always been so liberal. Now this tunnel vision toward Christianity?"

Emerald was relieved that Rose had not discovered her tea leaf secret. Practice would enable her to discern the patterns of the loose leaves and their meanings quickly and with ease. Only after many successful predictions would she share her new hobby with Rose. She knew that the investigative reporter in Rose would insist on statistical data to back up the accuracy of the readings. Rose was a firm believer in facts. She was a natural-born skeptic, too logical for her own good, Em felt.

"Em, have you been born again?"

"I don't know what you mean by born again." Her relief was forgotten and she felt an uneasiness in her chest. "Besides, your date will be here soon. I poured out one good cup of tea and you've let a second get cold."

Rose found herself alone. Emerald had vacated the room, teacup in hand. Rose dressed quickly and was in the garden cutting fresh flowers when a smear of white invaded the lovely summer landscape. The smear focused and revealed itself to be Sven's car as he slowed and turned into the inn's driveway. The Jaguar's horn called. From deep within she felt a calm reassurance that her experience was important and that she was to share it with Sven.

But how would she tell him? She could not erase past intimacies from Sven's memory as simply as God had removed them from her list of transgressions. "Tell him the truth. I'll give you the words." The thought formed in her spirit and Rose knew then that the same God who had given her the task would help in its fulfillment.

The entry door was ajar. Emerald had stepped outside to greet Sven. She hoisted a picnic basket into the backseat as she assured the driver that his charge need not be home at any particular time. Visitors were not scheduled until late Saturday morning. "Keep her out all day, if you'd like. Bye now. You two kids have a great little drive." Emerald waved her white hankie in the air.

That's so unlike Emerald to go out of her way to even talk to Sven, thought Rose. Let alone fix a picnic lunch. She felt amazingly like a teenager, though, on her first real date. Emerald played the parental role of checking out the boy and bidding them farewell. First dates were usually frighteningly wonderful, with each member of the couple nervously anticipating what the other would say or do, yet not knowing what they themselves would say or do.

Rose's hair flew in many directions as she became part of the speeding blur of the white sports car. En route to a higher altitude, she had always wondered why, when riding in a convertible, one's hair is never pulled straight back with the wind but seems parted down the middle and sucked forward into the windshield. She laughed and thought about asking Sven. But the air, slapping rapidly against her ears, would have made it impossible for her to hear his respone. She sat and smiled, occasionally brushing at the hair flying erratically about her face.

The deeper into the forest they drove, the taller the evergreens. Cooler became the air and Rose wrestled into her jacket sleeves. The steep winding road was soon reduced to a trickle and turned into nothing more than a cow trail. Finally able to hear herself speak, she inquired, "Where are we. We've never been here have we?"

"No, I don't recall even seeing this spot on my map. The road must still be used, though. It's beaten out pretty well."

A rumble shook the small car and Sven's face showed a grimace of concern. He slowed to a stop and killed the engine. "An earthquake? Eruption of Mt. St. Helen's?" were Rose's wavering words.

"Worse," yelled Sven. In what seemed to have taken a never ending instant, he started the engine, crammed the transmission into reverse, and accelerated. The compact car slid into a clearing between two huge aspens just as a loaded logging truck barreled past. "Yep," he said, "this road is still used." He reached for Rose's hand anchored to the dashboard.

"It's passed," he said, "just a load of toothpicks."

Rose marveled at Sven's calmness. He laughed at her still wide-eyed expression and bolted from the car, taking the lunch prepared by Emerald. "All out!" Sven rubbed his knees which suffered numbness; whether from the long drive or the realization of the recent past danger, he was a bit shaky. Upon inspection of the surrounding area, he observed less than two inches of space bordering either side of the car. It appeared to have been literally picked up and lowered into the clearing. The only clearing for miles now sported picnickers. "If I believed in them, I'd say this was a miracle. Or some really good karma."

The sudden rise and fall of adrenaline had left the couple ravenous. They soon devoured boiled egg sandwiches and still-warm fried apple pies, washing down the welcome nourishment with a thermos of hot cider.

Scenery seductively and completely inhabited Rose's senses. Her lungs were awakened with the cool air. A faint mist of breath escaped from her mouth, stretching in every direction. Its ghostly appearance dissipated, joining unseen elements of the ecosystem. It would soon be captured by the greenness of this mountainside, be cleansed, and released back into passing air to be once again breathed at a future time by another being unaware of its previous transformation.

Rose thought about one breath travelling across the Pacific, being breathed in Hawaii, then on to Hong Kong, gliding through the Philippine Islands, moving down to Australia, and winding up back in the icy freshness of this picnic spot. She leaned against a boulder decorated with velvety green moss. All the beauty of the moment, of eternity, was now hers in a way she had never known. Though in years past she had enjoyed each day for its own uniqueness, she had observed these past few days that all her surroundings seemed as young as they were beautiful.

"My lovely, lovely lady," Sven flattered. "A penny I would flitter for your thoughts to be revealed; however, with inflation as it is, it would doubtless earn me very little."

"Gregory Svenson, you are the only person I know who can produce such poetic nothings for all occasions."

"Thank you," he tipped his head. "Now, may I ask in

seriousness, what were you contemplating so?"

She grabbed at the sky and said, "Just wondering how long it would take for this handful of air to make it around the world."

"You weren't either. You were thinking of how handsome I am. How irresistible. How you'd like to inch your way toward me and sit by my side, sharing this soggy moss patch. I know the truth, so get over here."

Rose felt a flash of embarrassment flood her being. "Not on your life. You are the least thing on my mind today, Sven." She diverted her eyes as if she could not see Sven through the foliage and thick mountain air.

"And," Sven continued his mind-reading act, "you can't imagine why I haven't given you your present." He produced a small, cube-shaped box.

"Right, you're so forgetful," Rose whispered, trying to continue the matter-of-fact flow of teasing. Masking her surprise and delight, she meticulously peeled away the gray ribbon and opened the parcel. Its contents snatched the midday light, transforming it to a sparkling globe strobe as she lifted the necklace from its box. "I can't believe it. Why did you do this?"

"Is it so hard to guess? I love you. And I have missed you. Besides, it was on sale. Half price. I know you would have hated for me to miss a half-price sale on anything."

"Right. I'd hate for anyone to miss a bargain."

"Scoot on around here. I'll help you with the latch."

"What is it, Sven? I've never seen anything like it."

"Well, it isn't a diamond, but it still could be your best friend."

"Is it some sort of gem or glass?"

"Crystal. Quartz to be specific."

"It's much too beautiful to be worn with this old sweatshirt," Rose said.

"Look closely," said Sven. "It is a teacher stone." Sven held the crystal in his hand. "Crystals are among the popularly used power objects these days. They are alive, unlike glass and gems. They have the ability to focus energy and amplify effects of your normal meditations and other pursuits. Once they've been cleansed, the owner can program them with positive energy and receive some profound enlightenment."

"That's weird. I don't feel a thing."

"Very funny. You wouldn't; not sensitive enough."

"No really, Sven," Rose replied, "what's the deal? It is beautiful, but it's somehow occultic sounding."

"I'm serious about the energy. It gives off vibrations. After it is programmed, it can be used to help you learn. After all, it is a mineral. It has been part of the universe forever. Since the beginning of time, it has been vibrating with the energy of the cosmos."

Rose perceived a familiar topic of past conversations looming as Sven continued. "After all, all things are composed of the same cosmic matter, and if you can clear your mind of daily concerns and past garbage, focusing on the stone, after practice you begin picking up some pretty profound truths."

"Thanks. The thought is appreciated, but I can't accept this gift." Rose began to unclasp the chain when Sven's arms encircled her.

"Now, now, take it easy. I know what you're thinking, Rusty. You think that we are once again speeding down the road which once led us to reach an impasse due to our differences."

"You're right this time."

"No, let's stop and work this out. All kidding aside. If each can understand where the other is coming from, I believe an understanding, a compromise can be reached."

"And all will live happily ever after, right?"

"You're laughing at me now. Compromises on each side can enable us to work this out. I've thought of you each day of my life. Since the day I first met you, you've been an integral part of my life. I can't live without you. It's like those crazy perfume commercials. I am obsessed with you. Sounds impractical, I know, for someone as independent as myself to rely so heavily on one person, but I'm leaning toward the old-fashioned lately."

"What you believe about life and existence is not what I believe. Holders of two opposite world views can't possibly continue on eternal parallel courses and expect them to intersect. It's not possible."

"Rusty, don't you think education can play a part in curving one or both of those lines?"

"Oh, I see. Sacrificing one set of beliefs for the sake of our relationship."

"Sacrificing? Never. Merely learning about, even tolerating if you can't fully come around."

"And I *am* the one who would be coming around to your way of thinking?"

"You're the one who keeps bringing all this up. We used to be ignorantly blissful in one another's company. I enjoyed you. You enjoyed me. At least I thought all that was real."

"I did, and I still do enjoy you. You're the only person exactly like you."

Sven studied Rose's face before continuing, but now

his voice held a new earnestness. "Maybe you thought I was insincere for moving so slowly toward a commitment, but to move quickly, I assumed, would frighten you into bailing out."

"At that time, Sven, I didn't want a commitment. You sensed that accurately. I only wanted to experience each day for what it could offer me."

"That's the Rusty I love. Fun loving. Serious. Competent and selfish."

Rose laughed at the analogy, "You were so free. That's the element I wanted to be around. By enjoying it in you, I thought I could get it, too."

"But you changed, midstream? People don't just change like that," said Sven.

"Then I must have been pretending I wanted the freedom. No commitment. No obligations. Just pleasure. That must not have been me you were with, but my alter ego."

"It was you. I just messed up by asking you for something long term."

"Sven, you didn't mess up. It was me that was the problem. I was looking for who I really was. I had been Rusty Lively for so long, I didn't remember all the things that Rose Thorn was running from. I know now they were things like convictions, a sense of purpose, a mission."

"Well then, let me put your mind at ease. There is no mission. No purpose to life other than to live and enjoy. Let's do that. Live and enjoy each other. Let's start over and not question."

"I can't do that." Rose wondered how the conversation had gotten so far from the news she had expected to share today. If she didn't say it now, she couldn't. She would not know how. "Sven, I've had a spiritual experience. You need to know, I suppose, what has happened."

"First, let's make a deal. Here and now. You talk; I'll listen objectively. Then, when you're finished, I'll tell you as nearly as possible what I think of it all. Fair?"

"Then debate?"

"No debate. Just objective communication and logical analysis of the situation. This is something that can be worked through. I want very much for you to share with me this spiritual experience." He stood up, brushed loose moss from his jeans, and looked upward through the tree-lined sky.

"Well, that's full attention if I ever saw it," Rose voiced and shook her head.

"Over there," said Sven, "I hear water. Must be the river. Let's find a spot to watch it from." He helped Rose to her feet and they created their path, hiking deeper into the forest until they saw the river. Statuesque trees formed a dense canopy overhead, preventing sunlight's penetration; no undergrowth existed, but a thick, spongy layer of moss and fallen pine needles created a carpet which silently absorbed the impact of water droplets journeying from the canopy to the earth. A fallen tree provided a bench on which to monitor the coursing rapids.

Rose expressed, as well as she could, the chain of thoughts and events she had experienced since last she had seen Sven. Each word was contemplated and knitted into a picture which she prayed would be perceived and accepted by Sven. He watched the facial gestures of concern and elation of the storyteller. The small audience showed no expression by which Rose could gauge her success.

She sensed the presence of the Holy Spirit and Rose became more excited. No longer did she labor for words, but disclosed her infilling of God's love with ease and enthusiasm. When her final words had echoed between the trees, they were absorbed into the cushiony ground cover. Sven softly spoke.

Sven's words were flavored with sarcasm. "That's totally believable," he said. "I feel very special that you've confided this to me. As far as spiritual experiences go, I've had my share. Not that particular brand, however. I was never sure how to tell you about that part of me. You know, I love this river, these mountains, the oceans, stars; they are all part of God. Being aware and open to the spirit world enables us to participate in its existence."

"Now, Sven, you know I am not talking about the aesthetics of the universe. What do you think about the actual person of God and the resurrection of Jesus?"

"I believe that God is a concept, not a person or being. And the Jesus thing? Even though so many people subscribe to that doctrine, it's too limiting and can't be proven."

"Proven? What kind of proof do you want?"

"I'm saying, very simply, that when you accept the theory of Jesus being the Son of God, you choose to disbelieve all other theories of existence. Why limit yourself to one tiny piece of what the universe might be and risk missing what it is really about?"

"Gregory, by trying so hard to be open-minded and believing everything, you ultimately believe nothing."

"Now you are getting angry with me. You never call me Gregory. Maybe, as I suggested earlier, we just need to research further and become educated on the various doctrines and philosophies. Limiting every person on earth to acceptance of Christian philosophy automatically condemns the vast majority of earth dwellers. Quite drastic measures for a supposed loving God, wouldn't you agree?"

Rose felt the sarcasm clearly. Sven had always been cool, yet now seemed to have been put on the defensive. He no longer sounded like Sven, the calm, collected, free spirit. "But, Sven, I think if I could show you some scriptures. . . ."

"Ah, yes. The holy scriptures. From the Bible, I assume? A source that is *supposedly* the absolute word of your God?"

"I'm positive it is, though I didn't know I believed it until lately."

"Don't you feel there could be other peoples in other places, even other galaxies, with their own holy road maps?"

"No, I don't feel that."

"And why not?"

"Because the Bible says it is the word of God, and that is what we are to live by."

"No resource can be totally accepted as true, simply because of the human factor involved in getting it onto paper."

"I hear that, Sven. But what is revealed by God directly to our spirits is definitely unadulterated."

"Now you're making sense. So is the inspiration obtained by opening one's mind to allow communication with the spiritual world."

"Sven," said Rose, quickly removing the crystal from her neck, "you and I are attracted to one another. It's a mistake. There's no future. Only frustration. Once and for all, I think it's over between us." She dangled the stone before Sven. "In good conscience I can't accept your beliefs or your gifts."

"That's just it, Rusty. Can't you see? The fact that we both realize that insights can be gained by direct access to spirits, that theories, doctrines, and so-called holy books can be disregarded, that is the thread we can hold onto. They are mutual beliefs. We can agree on those things now and start our investigation and education together from this point. Please say you will try."

"I can't. Didn't you just hear what I said? There are other directions for me to take and my heart is breaking that my plans can't include you. I had honestly hoped . . ."

"That you and I could once again share our lives?"

"In some way, yes. But not investigating theology and philosophy," Rose snapped. "You have twisted what I've said."

"Take this crystal back. Hold it. Sleep with it under your pillow. Wear it near your heart. As you become accustomed to its feel and presence, you'll find you are more in tune to receive the insight it can reveal."

"No, Sven. It's not right. Too eerie. It goes against what I know in my spirit."

"That's because it's new to you. Give it, and me, a chance. Fair enough deal?"

"No. It's lovely, but take it back. I don't want any part of it. Or you, under the circumstances."

Sven sat very still and silent for several moments. Rose listened to the sounds of the trees and river as the two hummed out a strange, beautiful tune. Sven's voice joined into the song as he whispered, "I can't let you go. I'm used to having you around me. You are a part of me.

I love you, Rusty. That has to mean something. Tell me that means something, anything?"

"Of course it does. Just drive me home, though. While you're there, I'll give you the next couple of columns. That will cover us through next month, till I can think this through."

"You're not suggesting that you will be job hunting?"

"If need be. Just picture me trying to schedule my visits to the office around the times that you are away. Then there would be the discomfort of phone calls. Whether I stay with the *Avatar* or leave, it's a painful situation. It will be less awkward if I quit."

"Don't even think it. We can work this out. Never say die, and all that."

Sven's presence comforted Rose as he laughed a whimsical melody. He helped her to her feet, holding her hand much too long.

The airy atmosphere and liquidness of the moment gave Rose a sense that all really was well. This could be worked out, as Sven had put it. His absence would create a terrible void in her life. Had she given up on him too soon?

The drive home was taken with the convertible top in place and was much warmer and quieter. The mystical orchestra which played breathlessly romantic music flowed from the radio speakers as though the players were themselves present. But as Rose listened, the music was discomforting. The lyrics haunted her spirit, "The breath of God, I am the Wind, everchanging, always the same. I am and always have been." As the strange melody knitted in tinkling windchimes and rustling leaves, Rose knew her life with Sven was a musical presentation as disconcerting as the melody. The music continued and her thoughts blended, less clearly, until she could not distinguish between them and the lyrics of the song.

Waving a goodbye from the front porch, Rose watched the car descend the hill. She slipped her fingers into her jacket pocket where Sven had earlier warmed his hand as they drove down the mountain. There she found the crystal. Rose's fingertips brushed the smooth warm stone.

Folding her fingers around it, she remembered Sven's words, Carry it with you and sleep with it under the pillow, he had instructed. She lowered the sparkling holder-of-wisdom into the nightstand and closed the drawer on its radiance and on her relationship with Sven.

Chapter Eight

Paths Charted

Tracy peered through the opening forced between the venetian blind slats. "I see her leaving the yard; a couple of minutes it will take her to get here." She pivoted, visually checking floral arrangements, buffet table, and guests. "At the gate. Here she comes now."

The buzzing of the doorbell was met with shooshing from hiders. "It's open! We're in the den," Tracy called. Geneva twisted the knob and hesitantly pushed the door open. Unaccustomed to entering any residence without being greeted at the door, with one step over the doorjamb, she was hit with a blast of "Surprise!"

"Oh, I can't believe this. How exciting!" she exclaimed, meeting friends with hugs and kisses. "No one has ever given me a party, let alone a surprise party. I really can't believe it."

"Don't believe it, then. Sit down. Let the shock wear off," said Tracy, pushing a chair toward the honoree. "We've all been so anxious for you to get back from your honeymoon." Emerald carried packages wrapped in paper printed in bells and umbrellas, and spread them luxuriously across the coffee table top in front of Geneva.

"I still can't believe it. No wonder you told me to run over here without Duncan. He'll be so pleased."

"Speaking of Duncan, tell us, did he wine and dine

you or did you have to eat at Colonel Sander's the whole honeymoon?"

"Now Rose, don't tease the bride." Emerald snapped her fingers to get the attention of the partiers. "No discussion of the details until the gifts have been opened." So began the ritualistic unwrapping and folding of used paper. Each gift was oohed and ahhed as it was lifted from its box, lowered back down, and passed around to be inspected.

"Who is that from?" asked Tracy.

"Melba and Frank, it says on the card."

Melba grinned and nodded. "Frank picked it out. He even wrapped it."

"We can tell," giggled the ladies.

"I'm going to tell Frank you made fun of his efforts."

"Is that a blender or a can opener?"

"Both, actually," said Geneva, turning the item for the ladies to peruse. "Whoever heard of the like? Pass that around. You ladies will have to see this close up." Many other clever gifts were opened, then came Emerald's. The paper was a patchwork of fern leaves pressed between yellow cellophane.

"Now this is beautiful. Emerald, I can't open this. It's far too lovely."

"It's nothing, really. Undo it from the bottom and you won't damage it."

"You know, Emerald really is a clever person," Melba whispered to Rose, as she watched Geneva carefully untape the package.

"She certainly is, and she loves every minute of it," agreed Rose.

"She still has not remarried. What a shame."

"Not likely to, I'd say," said Rose.

"That is a shame. She's so talented and loves doing those chores that you and I dread. How does she keep up the inn alone?"

"Go ahead, Melba. Act as though I am no help," Rose defended herself.

"I didn't mean to insinuate that you do nothing. But aren't you still writing for that newspaper?"

"Yes, so far."

"You're gone a good deal of the time?"

"Not anymore. I've hardly left the house in weeks." Rose was already tired of Melba's probing and the wedding shower had just begun. "I believe I'll get a grocery sack to stash all that paper in. Geneva can save it if she wants to. She may want to reuse the larger pieces." Rose was rising from her seat when Melba's fingers touched her own.

Smiling as though she had not heard Rose's feeble attempt at escape, she patted the younger hand and advised, "I read in Sunday's paper that your editor is throwing his hat into the political arena."

"It's the first I've heard of it. What office is he running for?" Rose tried to hide her concern and surprise.

"Oh, he hasn't actually announced the candidacy, but he has been seen elbowing with the big boys at City Hall. There's even a rumor that he has backing from the governor and has political friends in D.C. So he may be one of our new city councilmen, easily. I'm surprised you didn't know. The two of you are pretty close."

"Sure, we're close. We've been friends for several years. But I sure don't know every single thing he does. He is, as you know, my editor."

"Oh, I don't mean *that* sort of close. The next

wedding shower could be for you."

"Melba, do you ever run out of things to speculate on?"

"Frank and I have friends living in Everett. Just up the street from Mr. Svenson, as a matter of fact. He walks to the *Avatar* office and lots of times my friends have seen him pass with this attractive lady. The way they've described her, you're a spitting image. And since you're in Everett alot. . . ."

"When you tire of this guessing game, look me up," said Rose in a second escape attempt.

"I simply think you'd make a lovely wife for the councilman. Oh, look! What's that she's just opened?" Melba motioned toward Geneva who was holding up a sheer lavender nightgown. Amid the laughter and squeals, Rose slipped away to the kitchen.

She spent the next half hour wondering why Sven hadn't mentioned his political intentions. If in fact those were his intentions, he should have made them known. Melba was predisposed to gossip. If she couldn't extract information from a conversation, she manufactured it. Rose had always been certain that whatever person Melba dissected in Rose's presence was, in turn, the spectator of Rose's dissection, sooner or later. Her ability to cast herself as the only living friend to whomever she was currently in the presence of was a characteristic Rose had long ago discovered. Evasion was the only tactic which could effectively be used to fight Melba's habitual gossip. The farther away, the better. However, her avoidance of the talebearer only added more speculative gossip to Melba's repertoire.

Tracy's voice startled Rose as she entered the

kitchen through the swinging door. "Hiding out?"

"You bet."

Tracy laughed and handed a serving tray to Rose. "Those glasses can be filled with punch from the 'fridge. I'll get the gossip stopped, temporarily at least, with these cream cheese sandwiches. They do it every time." She left with a mountain of snacks.

How Tracy always seemed to know what Rose was thinking was a puzzlement. Or maybe Melba affected everyone the same way. It must not be a mystery that when Melba was present, everyone must be on guard. Sixty tiny sandwiches and two gallons of punch later, the last of the guests bade Geneva their final well wishes and drove away.

"Can I walk you and your loot across the road, or shall we call Duncan to help his bride carry it home?" asked Emerald.

"I think you and I can handle it, if you don't mind helping."

"I don't mind, Geneva. I'll just say goodbye to Tracy and will be with you directly." Em stacked glasses and saucers as high as she dared and inched her way into the kitchen where Rose stood elbow-deep in dish suds.

"Just hand me those, Em. I'm on the clean-up crew. You and Tracy did a wonderful job planning the shower."

"It came off pretty well, don't you think?"

"Sure. Why don't you go on home from there? I'll see you in a bit," said Rose, making a last swipe at the table with the sponge.

"Fine. Oh, and Tracy, thanks for the use of your home today. I'd like to have been hostess at the inn, but guests are there this week," said Emerald, wiping her hands on her soggy apron.

"There's no problem, I've enjoyed it." Tracy waved at the ladies as Emerald and Geneva crossed the road, giggling and peering around their boxes.

When the dishes were dried and put away, Rose and Tracy walked onto the porch and inhaled the invigorating freshness of the air.

They stood beneath the plum red sky, Rose thinking she spied the twinkle of the first stars of evening. She had experienced sunsets so breathtaking they could never be duplicated. Yet she viewed this day's end with a new respect for its Creator. "Being born again," she said, "gives one a whole new outlook on everything, doesn't it?"

"Sure, because you're a new creation in Christ," answered Tracy, admiring the hues above.

"But, I mean the physical and all of nature seems to be different. Brighter maybe. As though it had been fine-tuned. Take the sky. It is the deepest scarlet I've seen."

Rose gazed full-face into the darkening canopy. She had counted fifty-nine stars when Tracy asked, "Have you told your sister-in-law, yet?"

"No, not all of it. And it's strange that you should mention it. Emerald has been avoiding me these past two weeks." Rose recounted the story of the note Emerald had penned that day. And when Emerald returned home, she acted as though she had never been gone. Rose knew that she had been depressed over Raylon's death. But, Emerald had refused to explain what she had meant by saying she was going to see a man who could help her locate Raylon. Emerald had insisted that she was feeling well, and Rose could not help disbelieving it.

"You don't suppose she's become involved in necromancy, do you?"

"Trying to communicate with the dead? I doubt it very much. She was devastated by Ray's death, but surely she realizes he's really gone."

"I don't know; she may be unable or unwilling to turn loose, even after all these years."

"But it's been so long. She is searching, spiritually, I mean. If I could only get her to listen to me for awhile."

"She will. We are all drawn to God by the Holy Spirit. Just continue praying for the right words and time. The best witness you have is to let your life speak for you."

"What if she *is* trying to contact Ray's spirit?"

"You stay in the word and watch her. If she's involved in anything so unnatural, you'll be able to tell."

"But what if she is? What will I do?"

"Don't worry about it. Pray about it and the Spirit will guide you regarding what to do. Trust Him."

"You're right. If we've gotten the party mess cleaned up, I'd better get home."

"If we missed anything, I'll see to it later. You run home. Or, I could drive you; the night has already fallen. It's too dark for you to see."

"Tracy, I've got my route memorized. There's not a hanging vine, soft spot in the soil, roots that could trip, or tree to crash into that I don't know by heart. I'll make it. See you later." Tracy waved till she could no longer see Rose, then went inside to survey the party area. All looked well.

It took only moments for Rose to maneuver her way through the dense, dark woods, reaching the steps to the inn. She closed the entryway door and caught a glimpse of Emerald replacing a settee cushion hastily. "Hi, Em. Beautiful party. You did a great job of coordinating. I love those little individual cheesecakes."

Emerald stood statuesque with her hands suspended awkwardly at her side. "If I didn't know better, Emerald Thorn," said Rose, "I'd say you were the cat that just ate the canary. Did I interrupt something?"

"Of course not. I just wasn't expecting you. After all, it is dark and I suspected maybe Tracy would drive you home."

"I needed the walk. She did offer to drive me, though."

"Well good. You're home. Can I get you something to eat or drink?"

"No, and if I need anything, I can help myself, Em. Why is it you are pampering me lately?"

"I'm accustomed to catering to our guests; it's a habit."

"Let's sit down and chat. We haven't really talked with each other for over a week."

Emerald's color returned to her face as she sat on the settee. "What shall we talk about, Rose?" She seemed relieved to hear a knock at the door. Rising quickly, she crossed the room mumbling, "Hold your thought, Rose."

"Mr. Disbrow. What a surprise. How can I help you? I thought you and Mrs. Disbrow had retired for the evening."

"We have been sitting out on the deck, enjoying this magnificent sky."

"It is lovely, you're right. Would you like to come in and visit with my sister-in-law and I?"

"Embarrassed as I am, I wonder if raiding the refrigerator is permitted? That supper was wonderful."

Emerald laughed with delight. "Flattery will get you fed around here. Follow me to the kitchen."

"Good evening," greeted the guest as he passed Rose in the parlor. The chattering in the kitchen threatened to continue endlessly. Rose walked toward the settee and arranged herself comfortably there to await Emerald's return.

Either this afternoon's partying had exhausted her or the night air had caused her to become drowsy. Rose drifted to sleep. It seemed like only moments, but Emerald told her she had slept nearly an hour.

"You should get up to your own bed. You'll have a crick in your neck, having curled up like that." Rose stood and slowly ascended the stairs. She turned to say goodnight, but stopped herself as she saw Emerald lift the settee cushion, retrieve a glossy red sack, and replace the cushion. She tucked the sack inside her robe and turned. Rose continued her ascent, quickly undressed, and was sleeping before she realized it.

The Disbrows were particularly cheerful guests and asked for a recommendation from Emerald as to a church they might attend that morning. "Phil and I haven't missed a Sunday at church in practically all our married life. We go even when we are on vacation."

"How commendable," said Emerald, placing a platter of croissants before the couple. "Coffee or tea?"

"Coffee is fine," came the answer from Mrs. Disbrow. It seemed to disappoint Emerald. She stirred around the kitchen, slightly disgruntled. How could she possibly become an expert tea leaf reader if nobody drank tea? Practice. Lots of practice was needed on reading the leaves of herself and unsuspecting Rose or guests. Maybe a party was in order. Yes, a tea party. She could plan a get-together and invite the ladies she had invited to Geneva's wedding shower. Her spirits lifted as she mentally began planning her practice tea leaf reading session.

"May I ask what denomination of church you attend?" inquired Rose, positioning herself before a plate of Quiche Lorraine. The Disbrows glanced quickly at each other. Mrs. Disbrow had a pale pastel countenance. Her blonde hair blended into a peachy forehead. Her cheeks, a little darker orange, lightened to a yellowish apricot at her chin. The spring palette was highlighted by two bright brown eyes. They seemed to coax her husband to speak, which he promptly did.

"We've discovered that no single church or denomination is going to arrive at Heaven based on their works, formalities, or rituals. So, we're sort of nondenominational. Lots of people from every faith will be part of Heaven's population."

A pang of recollection stirred Rose to think of the previous day's conversation with Sven. "Are you saying," Rose said, "that you believe that every belief is acceptable? They are all the truth?"

"No, and I hope I don't hurt your feelings if I speak my mind." Mr. Disbrow's voice grew somber. "We believe that salvation through the blood of our Lord Jesus Christ is the only way to heaven. Anybody who believes it can be saved."

Rose was relieved at those words. "Wonderful. I do, too. I've just recently been saved. But I'm excited to hear a confirmation of what I feel."

"Praise God," shouted the couple simultaneously. They both laughed at the outburst. As Emerald folded her napkin, she mustered the words to question just what church they'd like to be directed to. "Where do you ladies attend?"

Rose offered, "I haven't gone in such a long time, but I realize I need the fellowship now to strengthen my walk with God."

Emerald suddenly felt out of place in her own home. No great fuss had been made over the breakfast she had spent so much time preparing. The morning, which ordinarly would have been spent conversing with Rose over the newspaper in the parlor, was now a flurry of activity centered around Rose. Rose, who had something in common with these two guests, was flitting about like a schoolgirl.

Rose called Tracy and arranged for a ride to church. The guests and she would ride with Tracy, and they would all spend the afternoon in the aquarium in Seattle. They would be late this evening; don't fix supper, for they would all have dinner in the Space Needle. Instructions and plans were flying through the air like so much dust on a windy day.

"Are you sure you won't go with us, Em? It will be a great outing." Rose pleaded for her sister-in-law to join them. Not only did she need to get out of the house more often, but Rose knew Emerald should be in fellowship with Christian people.

But Emerald was never so glad to be rid of Rose. The inn was suddenly quiet in a frightening way. What would she do all day with no one to cook for? How unfair of Rose to have whisked the guests right out from under her nose. She felt a little remorse for having not gone bounding out the door with the happy group.

Tracy's car honked a pleasant goodbye as she drove out of the yard. The remorse evolved into relief that the flurry of insanity had ended. The dishes were washed and put away in record time. Stepping onto the front porch, she resolved to occupy herself and not to allow the loneliness to dominate this sunny day. A picnic. That was the solution.

A lunch was soon manufactured and her feet made their way down the path to the shore. The sun rays careened toward the ocean, exploding into millions of sparkling jewels on the ripples.

Squinting, Emerald's eyelids shielded her eyes from the brightness. Her senses filled with salty freshness. Several of the glistening ripples grew in size, being drawn to the shore. They drifted closer and became lovely swans, bobbing and gliding toward the foamy shore.

How sad, she thought, that something so beautiful as these swans would have remained unshared, had she not walked to the shore today. Had those religious fanatics not shown up, Rose might also have made this trek and seen these magnificent birds. Jealousy overcame her as she imagined Rose joining other new groups of friends, Christians at that.

She climbed onto a rocky point crusted with dried moss, and wondered why Rose had not mentioned her being-saved episode to her personally. Oh, she had been beating about the bush and dropping hints, but Emerald had painfully heard the news in the presence of strangers. Reading some scriptures and finding the truth, that's all Rose had said. Now she was saved. This was more serious. Why couldn't things have stayed the same?

Rose probably wouldn't marry Mr. Svenson now. Emerald was sure he didn't go to church; after all, he had spent all his Sundays, until recently, with Rose. And Emerald felt positive those Sundays hadn't been spent in church. She wondered if Rose had told Mr. Svenson she had become a Christian. If so, he probably wouldn't be seeing much of Rose. She would soon turn dull and lifeless.

Rose and Raylon's mother was still living in Oklahoma. Would Rose leave Port Orchard and go back home? After all, born again people usually think they have to quit associating with their old friends — friends who have stuck with them through good and bad times. If Rose did leave, she thought, could I live without her? Rose had always been the stronger of the two. Always practical and never fearful.

"Perhaps, I'll sell the inn and go to Oklahoma with Rose. But if she leaves, she won't want me with her. That's just the point. She won't want some non-Christian holding her back. If Ray were here, I would know what to do. Of course, if Ray were here, none of this would be happening now," she debated herself. Emerald's mind crowded with hellish confusion. She grew dizzy with the troublesome contemplation.

Opening her basket, she reached for a leftover croissant. Piece by piece, she threw the bread into the slowly approaching tide. The swans' heads disappeared from view as they scrimmaged for the soggy morsels.

"Ray," she said, "if you were here, none of this would be happening. Rose would not have lived here these past years. The inn would never have been the inn. The entire course of my life would have been different. It's not fair that one event could have changed the way my life has developed!"

The next hours passed swiftly as she troubled over how Raylon might look now, had he lived. Would his jet hair be salt-and-peppered? His sleek abdomen might reveal a slight spare tire. She had changed; she was sure Ray would have.

Life without ever having met or become close friends with Rose was her most troubling thought. Rose is my best friend, she thought. "Rose is my best friend." She had never told her of her love for her, nor could she now. The words sounded strange, for she'd never said them aloud. If she mentioned it at this point, it would appear to be an act to keep Rose at the inn.

Besides, she didn't trust her feelings. No. Life certainly is not fair in that it has no plan that can be known in advance. She envisioned masses of people being prodded by some unknown power. Rose called that the power God. If Emerald only knew the plan this unknown power had for her, she could take appropriate steps to accomplish the end. Too vague; it was all too vague. Each person has to decide how to manage these fragile lives.

She lay back upon the moss, trying not to think. But the Disbrows had been right about one thing. Even similar religions can cause conflict between couples. Ray had been of a different faith than Emerald. They resolved the problem by not proclaiming any faith at all. But they were young at that time and felt that life would never end.

Why plan for something that will never happen? By deciding how one feels about life after death, if it exists, one focuses too heavily on spiritual matters, missing out on the very real, important issues of this earth. But as it turned out for Ray, that commitment to enjoy life could not hold him to his commitment to forever care for Emerald. He was gone and Emerald now felt an urgency that her own death was inevitable. It was a never-ending cycle, ignoring death and worrying about death. It all frightened her.

Death for some. Birth for some. It was grossly irresponsible of a God to create people, yet not give them instructions on what to do next. If he loved them as much as she had heard he did, why didn't he just create a certain number of people — a cutoff point — and not let anymore be born? Those who had been created could just live on and on, never dying. But he could very possibly have set the cut-off point for a time before she had been born. She couldn't imagine having never been born. To avoid the sickening confusion in her mind, Emerald started back home.

The cliffs seemed steeper as Emerald proceeded toward the inn. Breezes blew the grasses ahead, revealing an opening in the rocks. She stepped around the cave's mouth, long since hidden by hanging vines and English ivy. The climb required her to pull her way up the slope, grasping the tall grass and ground cover. Breathlessly she trudged ahead, having not felt so old before. It must be my imagination, she thought. I'm just panicking.

She determined to develop her own plan. She couldn't rely on Rose any longer. Develop a plan and stick with it, Em dear, she thought. Stick with it at all costs.

The afternoon was almost over when she seated herself at the parlor desk. Where does one begin in the process of developing a plan for living one's life? Many thoughts ran through her mind as she stared at the blank paper. Mr. Sands had told her about Sanguine's ability to draw up a star chart. Maybe that was her plan for living. Did she dare to explore that avenue or consult with Mr. Sands about calling Ray's spirit?

No, she couldn't envision herself doing that. She

certainly could not conjure him up on her own. After all, she doubted if she was authoritative enough to command a spirit to make its presence known, even Ray's.

The tea. If she could develop that talent, it would give her an absolute plan. She might need consultations with Mr. Sands or some expert psychic from the Psychic Fair occasionally, but she now clearly felt she could become proficient at fortune telling.

It seemed that any of these plans involved staying in contact with Mr. Sands. She pulled the blank paper closer to herself, where it remained blank for several moments longer. Then, as she gained courage, she carefully wrote:

You are cordially invited to an afternoon tea at the Emerald Thorn Inn, given by . . .

Chapter Nine

Incensed

After a week, the guest list remained blank. Em was sure that Rose would not approve of her scheme. Every possible name had been carefully reviewed. Caroline Pritchett seemed a likely candidate, although she would possibly tell Rose about the party. It was common knowledge that Caroline frequented the home of a palm reader when important matters warranted it. So Caroline's name would have to stand alone until others could be screened.

Having overheard Rose make plans to meet Sven in Everett on Wednesday evening, Em determined that she would use that time to test her tea leaf reading skills. The empty page became a greater challenge now that a date had been selected. Em would have to invite guests by phone. Time was running out. So wrapped up was she in her planning, Em did not hear the phone ring.

"Em, good news. There are guests coming in the morning. Didn't you hear the phone?" said Rose, entering the parlor.

"No, I'm sorry, but I was thinking. Did you write the names in the reservation book?"

"I did. And surprise! They will take all three rooms." Knowing that would bring in three hundred dollars instead of the usual one hundred per evening, Em seemed drawn back into the world at hand. The bed-and-breakfast hostess character quickly returned.

"Rose, I haven't dusted those upstairs guest rooms in ages. Not since the Bloomfields last year."

"Well," replied Rose, "I'll help today. I've got business in Everett, but it's nothing so pressing that I can't do it Wednesday when I meet Sven for dinner."

"You go ahead. I'll clean after I finish working on the bills," Em said, shuffling the papers before her.

"Pay attention, Emerald. I'm offering to help. You start tidying the guest rooms. I'll finish the bills and mail them on my way out of town. That will help some."

A compromise was struck, and as Rose flipped through the stack of bills, she spied the red sack which, just a week ago, Em had so carefully concealed within her bathrobe. Beautifully inscribed onto its glossy finish were the words, "Answer In The Wind — A New Age Shopping Experience."

This sack was confirmation that the woman Rose had seen going inside the shop in Everett had indeed been Emerald. Here was the sack, still containing the purchase she had made. But why the secretism, Rose wondered? Opening the books onto the desk, she read, *Tea — The Key To Your Future* and *Fortunetelling The Delicious Way*. A door slammed and Rose's heart leapt. Returning the books to their original hiding place beneath the bills, she quickly finished preparing the payments for the post and left for her errands.

A few moments of sharing her fears with Tracy assured Rose that Emerald's odd and secretive behavior was cause for concern.

"It's definitely occultic," said Tracy. "Whether it's tea leaf reading or satanism, it's all poison to the soul. Do you know where this shop is?"

It took over an hour for Tracy and Rose to drive the long distance to Answer In The Wind. The smoky door boasted, A New Age Shopping Experience. The smell of incense was strong and immediately saturated their hair and clothing. First allowing their eyes to adjust to the darkness, they began investigating the contents of the store.

Neon lit the aisles at the floor and along the ceiling. The aroma of incense, mingling with the candle scents, coffees, and teas, created a thick mist which clung to greeting cards and posters. These paper products and stationary sported goddess figures amidst fantasy scenes of stars and moons. They rode on unicorns and sensuously stroked the mythical Pegasus. The mystical, cosmic music which played in the air created a sense of emotional freedom. Numerous shoppers browsed through books and video tapes.

The atmosphere reminded Rose of a party she had attended with Sven years ago. The air at that party was thick and intoxicating. And although the couple had not participated in the smoking of marijuana, as had other guests, they had left the place feeling drugged. The music advocated letting their minds go and loving one another in order to find one's self.

The words of today's gentle, soothing tune brought back the overwhelming sense of needing to know who she was. Only now the lyrics urged her to love herself in order to experience others. The feelings generated by both experiences were the same. She now recognized the feeling as the excitement of doing something forbidden. Not until the excitement of the deception subsides, she realized, does Satan reveal the ugliness of the entrapment. Rose doubted that had she not accepted Christ as her Lord, she would now be discerning this feeling to be the deception of Satan.

Books caught Rose's eye. She reviewed the many volumes; topics ranging from astrology to the study of Zen stood out to her. There were entire sections relating to psychology, hypnosis, reflexology, visualization, and trance-channeling. Positive thinking and meditation took their places on the shelves beside witchcraft and fortune-telling methods — I Ching, tarot cards, tea leaf reading, runes. The danger and evil of these individual studies became apparent as she connected them with the New Age movement. It was obvious that the movement encompassed every occultic, anti-Christian ideology ever conceived by man and devil. The New Age indicates a new awareness of man's potential; yet, in reality it represents the same deceptions Satan has always used to keep man from getting back to God.

Crystal jewelry, jeweled wands, talismans, and eagle feathers, among other power objects, decorated the display cases. Divinatory devices and elixirs for use in spells and curses were found alongside instruction booklets for their use.

Then a groaning, tortured voice caught Rose's attention. Overhead was a television monitor. A man, appearing to be the guest of a talk show, sat with his eyes shut. He spoke of changes which would soon occur throughout the earth.

"Only the pure shall survive. Heed my word. It is time to open your mind and realize that you are a god and have control over your destiny. Until you acknowledge your personal holiness, you cannot be counted among the pure. Thus sayeth the master." The man awakened from his trance and proceeded to explain to the show's host that he channels the spirit of a centuries-old holy man whose mission now is to enlighten today's men and women in the art of godhood. The host and audience applauded the demonstration and invited the channeler to join the show in the near future for a follow-up program.

Rose cringed and rounded the corner into another room. She was startled to find herself facing a tall, attractive woman. "Excuse me," the woman whispered, "I didn't mean to frighten you. May I help you find something?"

"No," said Rose, "just browsing."

"If you need anything, my name is Sanguine. I'll be glad to answer questions you have or to direct you to items of interest." The woman surveyed Rose's face briefly, then forced a smile as she crossed the room.

Tracy was soon at Rose's elbow saying, "I think it's a one-way mirror. Do you see?"

Rose realized, also, that she was viewing her image in a smoke-colored mirror. It shook slightly, giving Rose the eerie feeling that she was being watched from beyond.

"It's a door. No doubt there is more going on here than the obvious selling of tools of the occult," said Tracy. "They may actually have meetings of occultic practitioners or psychics here. Have you seen all you need to see?"

"Tracy," said Rose, "that music is familiar. Let me check out one last thing and I'll be ready to go." As she stepped to the music counter, she noticed a small placard which read, "The music you are hearing is from the album *Self To The Most High*." Rose perused the album cover, recognizing some selections Sven had played from a compact disc by the same orchestra. The song titles caused her heart to race to the carefree rhythm of flutes and natural wind and water sounds. She read slowly, "Doubt Not The Inner Light," "I Have Always Been," "Evolution Within The Universal Mind," "Cosmic Peace."

"Are you interested in seeing the transcripts?" spoke the counter attendant. "Of course, some would argue against the availability of the transcript, feeling that they get more out of a piece if they don't know what subliminal suggestions are being directed to the subconscious."

"I'd like to see them, please."

"Then, I'll be right back; they are filed separately."

Rose glanced at Tracy who shrugged. When the attendant returned, he continued. "Most New Age music utilizes subliminals, but the words are available only upon request. Then, there are individuals who are working on spiritual growth from the conscious and subconscious standpoints."

Rose silently read the transcript, Sven's face developing in her mind as she did.

The breath of god, I am the wind
everchanging, always the same.
I am and always have been
a snowflake with six yet endless sides
individually sculpted, yet not unlike
millions of others
I melt, mingling with new lives who rise
as the phoenix and return to the sky
to live again, to learn and relearn that

the windows of the soul are many,
allowing me access to the mind, the universal mind
that is god, that is I, the wind, the breath of god.
I am.

"This song exemplifies Sven's philosophy of life, Tracy. As long as he believes he is a god, he can't accept an external higher power God. And likewise, as long as he is evolving into perfection as a god, there is no need for a redeemer from sin, for to Sven, there is no sin."

"He's not the only one who has been deceived," said Tracy.

"Thanks for the help," said Rose to the attendant. "I'll pass. Let's go, Tracy." As the two ladies passed the jewelry counter, a glimmer of light caught Rose's eye. She recognized a crystal necklace much like the gift Sven had given her.

"Are you looking for a teacher?" said Sanguine from behind the counter.

"Pardon me?" replied Rose.

"It's a teacher stone you are admiring. A very effective tool in learning who you are and how to achieve the secrets of the universe. Of course, there are a number of power objects you could utilize to focus energy."

"Thanks, but I have one that is similar." As Rose and Tracy left the shop, they breathed the clean outside air. "I can't believe it," said Rose. "Everything in that place was geared to appeasing the senses and feelings. And I noticed there was no literature among all those books about Jesus Christ as the answer to the searching."

"No, everything was blatantly anti-Christian, or it presented Christ as just a teacher who had some good ideas, but never as the Redeemer. Even the name of the shop is deceptive, as though the answers to man's quest are blowing in the wind, to be captured by whatever method one chooses."

"Tracy, I'm worried about Emerald. It's not like her to entertain such eerie things as we have just seen. But I know it was Emerald I saw coming in here that day. I saw the books she purchased. They came from here," she said as they drove toward home. "So many people are being deceived, as you said earlier. How can we reach them?"

"It's imperative that the people close to you know how you believe. You can't compromise your beliefs; stand for Christ, at all cost. They will be won by your example."

"But, I feel this desperation to do something to rescue Em. And Sven, too. He's so wrapped up in his self-designed religion that he has closed his mind to the real truth."

"Rose, if you want me to, I'll come over and talk to Emerald with you."

"No, let me think about it. I know Emerald better than anyone. She doesn't like to be told what to do. If I try to influence her, she may go deeper into this tea thing and whatever else she may be involved in, for spite."

"Then let's pray right now." As the women prayed, Rose felt an assurance in her spirit that God had, indeed, heard them and would protect Emerald. But the question of Sven was a more complex one.

The beautiful music that began in her head grated against her spirit. She recalled the subliminal thought which would be instilled into those minds of unsuspecting listeners. I am, it had said. For the first time the terror which gripped her heart was not that of having lost the relationship she had once had with Sven, but knowing that whatever it was he believed was believed with a passion. Every pore of his body was convinced that he was living life in tune with some universal mind. There was no compromising and no slipping into what he called "the insecurity of needing a personal savior." Jesus was for people who didn't know where they were headed. And Sven definitely knew where he was headed. Except now, Rose knew that where Sven was headed was not where he really intended to go. His path was a straight one into the darkness and death of hell.

Emerald lifted the windows and dusted furniture, thinking of the guest list which was not being completed by itself. She still had to prepare supper and call the grocer before evening. Her mental *to do* list got longer when she looked at the guest register and realized the six guests would be staying a week. A phone call to the grocer, one last swipe of the dust mop, and she was ready to start supper.

Debating herself over cooking pork chops or meatloaf, Emerald was preoccupied when Rose entered the kitchen. She handed Em a sack and apologetically explained that she and Tracy had seen a drive-in burger stand on the way home. She had a sudden craving, and she hoped not to hurt Emerald's feelings, but if she didn't already have supper started, there were crab burgers and fries.

Never had Emerald been so glad to see fast-food. After eating and rechecking the guest rooms for occupant readiness, both ladies retired for the evening. Each knew that six guests for seven days would be work. Emerald would be spending much more time in the kitchen. Although the income would be welcomed, she knew it would be well-earned. Her party plans would have to be postponed and her search for answers put on hold.

Chapter Ten

The Great Commission

Rose had not anticipated a.m. to mean six o'clock when she had jotted down the reservation. She answered the parlor door in her robe.

"Sorry to disturb you so early, but we drove all night to get here. Is it too soon to check in?"

"Nope," said Rose, wondering what to do or say next.

"Great. We'll get our bags."

"Good idea," answered Rose, her eyes trying to focus on this woman whose hair hung stiffly to her shoulders. It was dyed blacker than any hair Rose had ever seen. The woman looked familiar to her.

When the six women and twenty pieces of luggage had collected on the front porch, Rose invited the ladies inside. Emerald, hearing the commotion, rushed into the kitchen to put the coffee on to brew before joining the chattering guests in the parlor. The chimney-broom haired woman presented the group's story.

They were from Los Angeles. At eight o'clock the conference they'd driven in to attend would begin registration. "Registration includes a continental breakfast," she went on. "If it's just the same to you, we'll get situated and get on to the meeting."

Rose set about collecting a week's worth of room

payments in advance and delivering two ladies and their luggage to the guest quarters around back. Emerald and the remainder of the group ascended the stairs. The upstairs guest rooms were positioned on each side of the far end of the long hallway and were relatively secluded. A guest bathroom at the extreme end of the hall, near the back landing, could be shared by both rooms. Next to the bathroom was a door which, at first glance, appeared to be a closet. But this door served as an entrance to a staircase leading to the outside back porch. Emerald explained that these stairs could be used by the guests to avoid entering the house through the parlor entrance. She and Rose simultaneously explained to their charges that all meals and room clean-up were included in the room rates. If they did not plan on taking a particular meal, leave a note or drop by the parlor to give them advance notice.

Like a whirlwind, the ladies unpacked, freshened up, and left the driveway in a van, blurred by speed.

Rose and Emerald stared at one another over their coffee. Under normal circumstances, they would just be rising. "They won't be here for lunch, but will make it back from Tacoma for supper at seven. That's twelve hours. I think I'll start my breads and desserts," said Emerald.

"But let's start the day over, Em," said Rose. "I'm still foggy. I'll cook breakfast while you shower. My years are beginning to show. I need my routine and rituals."

It was settled without discussion. The ladies restarted their day; by noon the kitchen smelled of hot bread, lemon custard, and pumpkin pie. With Emerald busily attending to details, Rose felt she was underfoot. A wave of approval from Em's hand and Rose left behind warm smells of the inn. The wet, thick air smelled heavily of pine. Rose was intent on appreciating each day for its uniqueness and beauty. The walk to Tracy's was taken at a slower-than-normal pace. Rose savored the clean breeze. She even thought she captured a whiff of Emerald's breads from Tracy's living room.

"I don't see how heaven can be any better than this," Rose told Tracy.

"Oh, it will be, though," Tracy said as she arranged books and cassette tapes on the coffee table. "I've collected this stuff over the years. You are welcome to take whatever you want. If you don't get them back to me for a while, that's fine."

" 'What To Do If You Miss The Rapture.' Is this a joke?"

"No. That tape was produced by a minister who is concerned about people who will not be saved by the time the Rapture of the church takes place. This tape might lead them to accept the Lord, after the fact. Thousands of people will be saved out of the Tribulation," said Tracy. "But it won't be as easy as if they'd given their lives to Jesus before that time."

"Sounds interesting. I don't know which books to take."

"Well, whatever else you take, take that tape," insisted Tracy. "It'll fill you in on the events of the end-times. Now, on these books, you'll want to get some information to help Emerald understand that what she's dabbling in is dangerous. After you asked what I knew about the New Age movement, and I'm ashamed to say it was very little at that time, I found there is mass information available from the points of view of actual practitioners, those who once involved themselves in various aspects of the movement, and from Christian authors seeking to expose the dangers of the movement. So these books are the tip of the iceberg. They don't include the volumes of information available only to those deeply involved in the deep darkness of the real intentions of the movement."

The ladies enjoyed the quietness of the afternoon. They browsed through titles, pamphlets, and books which Rose hoped would give her insight and confidence to witness to Emerald. She felt inadequate in her new-found faith. Since she, herself, had so recently been saved, she doubted her ability to convince Emerald to follow her example. But because of Emerald's unusual behavior lately, Rose felt an urgency to get Emerald safely into the kingdom of God. Although her own new life should be a positive witness to her sister-in-law, she felt there was no time to waste. Emerald would not be swayed, due to her stubborn nature, unless Rose could gather convincing evidence that salvation is in her best interest.

The phone rang and both women realized the evening was upon them. "Hello," answered Tracy. "Yes, she's here, Emerald. I'll send her right home." Tracy didn't have to relay the message. Rose had planned on staying only a few moments. When she and Tracy were talking about the Lord, time did not exist. "I'll get you a grocery bag; you'll never get all that home without a ride, either." So the ladies climbed into Tracy's car and, almost as quickly as they had boarded, they were at the inn.

Upstairs, Rose aligned the books and tapes across her bed. She wanted to hurry and read them all, or absorb them by osmosis. But the guests would be arriving soon and Emerald had met her at the door, making it clear she needed help with setting the table.

The guests were back by six-thirty and seated at the table by seven. Rose passed the bread and thought it strange that a group of women who had just arrived in the state would not be more talkative about the beautiful surroundings. Hardly a dozen words had passed among the members.

Rose began, "Is this your first trip to Washington State?" The eyes of the guests shifted back and forth as though mentally debating who would answer. Rose guessed correctly. The black-haired woman answered.

"Karen and I attended a holistic experience in Seattle in 1988. Each year it has grown and we've enjoyed it more. This year's large five-city conference is an outgrowth of that experience."

"We had such a good conference last year," added Karen, "that Sybil, Mora, Stacia, and Pamela decided they should attend this year."

"We're pleased to have you stay at the Emerald Thorn Inn," said Emerald in her most cordial hostess tone. "How did you come to hear of the inn?"

"Don't you remember? Karen and I stayed here during the Harmonic Convergence," said the spokesperson.

"Pardon us for not recalling you, Theta," apologized Rose. "Did I get the name right?"

"Yes, but I certainly didn't expect you to remember my name. Everyone changes over time, and you have so many guests. I'm sure you can't remember them all," Theta spoke softly and the other women continued eating.

"This is a very good meal," said Pamela. The conversation began to flow more easily. "The breakfast at the conference was good, but it didn't last long. We were busy in workshops all day and didn't take time for lunch." Pamela's face was pale. Her long, blonde hair had been pulled into a chic ponytail on one side of her head and was decorated with an unusual clip — a crescent moon with a star of black onyx perched on its tip.

"Emerald is quite a cook and prides herself in serving home-baked breads and quality meals," Rose bragged. "She is known for her generous breakfasts. Can we count on you to join us for biscuits and gravy tomorrow?"

"Theta is driving, so she'll have to decide what time we leave in the morning," offered Karen.

Theta was silent as she cleaned her plate. Her countenance was solemn and set the tone for the group. As she spoke, all eyes rested on her piercing blue eyes. "I might be driving," she announced, "but by no means should I have the final say on our plans." The others looked hopeful as she continued. "Since registration is required only on the first day of the conference, and taking into consideration that we've decided to attend the session being held right here in Port Orchard, I don't see why we can't get a good night's rest — sleep in, perhaps. We would all enjoy a hearty breakfast tomorrow."

The women seemed relieved and even smiled. During dessert, Rose thought she saw Theta smile. Rose studied Theta's face. Searching her memory for any detail which would spark her recollection of what it was about Theta and Karen's prior visit, Rose's spirit was disquieted.

Emerald chattered endlessly, her southern accent becoming more apparent with each statement. "And I baste the roast in applesauce and bayleaf. That's the secret," she said proudly. Karen agreed to try it upon her return home, giving Emerald credit, of course. Theta's authoritative presence released a chamber within Rose's mind and pictures of Theta floated to the surface.

Theta's previous visit had been to lecture to a group of Greek mythology students. Holistic medicine practitioners-to-be. She presented a paper on society's need for a goddess. Rose had been intrigued, at the time, by the goddess concept and had written parallel articles for Rose and Rusty. Since that time, Rose had not given one moment's thought to Theta, or the subject of the goddess.

"Do you ladies all work together? Does this conference relate to your occupation?" Rose asked suddenly. Theta glanced toward Karen, giving her permission to answer.

"No, we don't work together. In fact, we are really just friends on vacation. But we have a common interest in the conference."

"Does this have anything to do with your skill as a presentor on the subject of the goddess?" Rose continued. "I seem to remember that was the purpose of your last meeting."

"An accurate memory, indeed," Theta acknowledged. "Our week-long conference covers many areas. And the goddess is one subject. In fact, each day workshops are available at various locations throughout the Pacific Northwest. Participants are free to attend the workshops of their choice. We'll all come together again in a week to share our observations."

"Will you be presenting?" questioned Rose.

"Tomorrow at the Universal Church in Port Orchard I'll give another talk on the goddess concept," Theta said softly. "You're both welcome to attend as our guests."

The other women became still, fixing their gaze to the

table before them. Rose declined the invitation, explaining that she had a date. The women relaxed and Emerald cleared the table. "You all retire to the parlor and I'll prepare bedtime cups of tea," she said.

Rose, anxious to get to her research on the New Age movement, excused herself for the evening, and after showering, donned her robe and entered her bedroom. With all these books, she had no idea where to begin. Searching through her desk for a yellow highlighter pen, she came across her newspaper clipping book. Thumbing back through years, months, and days, she found the goddess articles. Slowing reading Rose Thorn's opinion, the words came back to her as though she had written them yesterday.

> *Since the feminist movement has entwined its long, tenacious fingers into every aspect of American women's lives, it stands to reason that its backers would want to have control of the way women exercise their spirituality as well. Additionally, since hard core feminists are men-haters at heart, they can't allow a male god to rule the universe.*
>
> *So the movement encourages women to exercise their freedom of religion (or be pushed in the proper direction if they don't willfully choose) by exploring the possibility that goddesses were worshipped before gods were. And further, because deities have changed and are changing still, is it surprising that the most high deity would be each individual woman, herself? Yes, the feminist movement encourages women*

to worship not only the goddess, but the goddess within the self. They can best fight the war against men if they realize they are supreme beings — goddesses.

— Rose Thorn

Rose's heart sank as she read the contrasting article.

So, now the conservative Ms. Rose Thorn thinks the feminist movement is responsible for the goddess concept. As women, we are becoming more aware of our personal situations and are simply taking charge of changing undesirable elements whenever they fail to support the spiritual harmony within ourselves. For this reason, it seems natural that women are turning to a more fair form of worship than traditional religions have offered.

We must stop depending, as little children, upon a parental deity and accept that we need only ourselves in order to make our destinies what we desire them to be. We must participate in the supernatural power of nature — physically, sexually, and spiritually — in order to translate the power to the development of our futures. And, if we must see ourselves in the role of goddess in order to tap into that source, so be it!

— Rusty Lively

Rose cringed. At this moment, she hated Rusty Lively. How those contrasting extremes could have crept from Rose's being, she could not imagine. Had she really felt at that time as Rusty did, or had her honest opinion of the subject been wedged somewhere between the two? She was definitely Rose Thorn. The side of her which was Rusty mirrored her rebellious self, running from God and the values she had been given as a child. Contrary to what Rusty had said, it is not childish to need God. She knew now that she could not make it without God. Left to his own devices, man will fail. She believed that with all her heart. Guilt overcame her. How many people had been swayed by Rusty's column? She wiped tears from the corners of her eyes.

Rose's research into the goddess concept had indicated that goddess worship walks hand-in-hand with witchcraft. Many covens of witches seriously study and practice the worship of the female deity. It was that element of her notes that caused Rose to be uncomfortable in Theta's presence. Theta must be a practicing witch. Rose would not be surprised to discover that all the ladies downstairs were veterans of the craft. Possibly new converts, she imagined, by their obvious submissiveness to Theta.

The next two hours Rose spent highlighting passages in a book she had borrowed from Tracy. The biblical case against the occult was overwhelming. As she leafed through the booklets and scriptures, she became adamant to divert Emerald's attention from the occult. Her main objective would be to keep Emerald from becoming aware of these women's real reason for being in Port Orchard.

Rose would keep an eye open for any attempt on their part to convert Emerald. She continued her methodical reading and highlighting until she fell asleep and presently began dreaming. She stood inside a bottle, the top of which she could not see for its height. Encircling her glass prison were six dark-hooded characters chanting her name. As she grew weak from attempts at escape, she quoted a scripture she had highlighted, although she couldn't remember from where. "For God hath not given us the spirit of fear; but of power, and of love, and of a sound mind; that's 2 Timothy 1:7," said Rose. "That's from the Word of God." The dark figures backed away, dissolving into the blackness.

Downstairs the women were just finishing their tea. Emerald watched them carefully, gathering her courage. "Excuse me, but would you all mind helping me with a little project I have going?" she asked. Before long each woman was swirling her cup and turning the contents into its saucer. She moved around the table, guessing each guest's fortune according to the first image conjured upon seeing the residue.

The predictions were all positive. Emerald wondered if she had actually seen into the future or would learn sometime in the future that she had merely made a spectacle of herself. Then, from within herself came an assurance that this new sideline was indeed her cup of tea.

Chapter Eleven

The God Within

Sven appeared unusually young and attractive, as he waved hello to Rose. "Love of my life," he said, pulling the chair out for Rose to be seated. "Are you wearing it?" He touched the back of Rose's neck, searching for the gold chain.

"No, Sven. I am not wearing the crystal. I did, however, bring it back to you. And may I commend you on your cleverness. How did you sneak it into my jacket pocket?"

"You certainly know how to set the mood for a dream date."

"I may as well get to the point. Did you purchase this at Answer In The Wind?"

Sven answered defensively, "What if I did? Would you have preferred me to have bought it at Bon Marche?"

"Having visited Answer In The Wind, I can't believe that, number one, a shop like that exists; and, number two, that you frequent it."

"Slap the cuffs on me, I confess." Sven held his wrists together and hung his head.

"Stop that nonsense," Rose insisted as the waiter approached their table. "Order us some lunch."

"Two gumbos and the fish-of-the-day." Sven smiled as he handed the menus to the waiter. "You aren't running away. Does this mean I'm back in your graces, Rusty?"

"Since I saw you last, I've done a lot of soul searching, and. . . .

"That's my girl. Back to the eternal soul search."

"No, I may as well say it all." Rose took a long drink of water and reluctantly continued, "Your girl is Rusty Lively; she's non-existent. Rusty was that part of me that was rebellious and stubborn. I've lost her, Sven. And with her, I've lost you."

"Rusty, I don't understand these mood swings. Have you seen a doctor? There are some good holistic practitioners out there. Rusty, I'm becoming concerned about you."

"See, you can't even bring yourself to call me Rose. You love that part of me which was in tune with your own free spirit. You can't admit that that's not really me. That's Rusty Lively. She's make believe. She gone. Dead!"

Sven, relieved at the waiter's interruption, stirred an ice cube into his gumbo and answered, "Now for my good news. I've decided to run for mayor of Everett and would be honored to do so with you at my elbow as Mrs. Mayor. I'll even call you Rose. Deal?"

Rose found herself laughing, asking Sven when he had made the decision to run for public office. The moments melted into an hour as Sven wove the story of his being ready to make a contribution to the community he had served as newspaper editor for so many years. He shared that the paper would be a good vehicle for his campaign and, if Rose would consent to being his wife, he would be sure to win the election. She had a powerful presence, he conveyed, that others couldn't resist.

Remaining noncommital as the couple strolled along the bench-lined boardwalk, Rose's mind raced with words she wanted to say. Yet, they'd all been said, at one time or another. Conscientiously screening the surging thoughts, she began, "Sven, I am concerned with different matters now that I have accepted Jesus Christ. I know it is a subect that nauseates you, but I am anxious about your soul. I won't give up praying for your salvation, but for the immediate future, I am focusing my energies on other things. Emerald for one. She has been dabbling in the occult. Oh, I don't know how extensively, but I believe she is involved somehow." Rose faced the splashing water of Puget Sound, avoiding Sven's searching eyes. "I feel the urgency to help her. With God's help, I know I can help her out of the evil she has begun."

"But, don't you see?" Sven interrupted, "you would be intervening in the natural process of her self-actualization."

"Sven, there really is only one right way to God. The Scriptures tell us that there is a way that seems right to man, but that path leads to death. That's Proverbs 16:25. You're on that way, and Emerald is on it. You won't listen, but maybe she will. I won't marry you, and I am quitting the *Avatar*. Don't ask me back, and don't ask me even once more to marry you. My life has been prioritized, and the job and marriage are not even on the list." She gazed with hurt into Sven's wondering face, delivering the last of her carefully selected words, "If I encouraged your separation from God by humoring you with my escapades as Rusty Lively, I apologize. Please forgive me." Rose lifted from her chair and walked back along the boardwalk to her car.

Sven didn't watch her retreat. He turned toward town, taking the long route back to his office. Past the hospital he walked, back through town, past the Bon Marche. The afternoon was gone when he opened the opaque glass door. Fred rushed toward him.

"Where have you been? The proofs are ready for you to approve. Our deadline was three o'clock, as always."

Sven sat atop his desk and looked at the photos. One of them would be used to kick off his campaign. "Get this," Fred suggested, "Svenson for Mayor. Or how about this? You've Waited Long Enough: It's Svenson Time. We could say, Svenson — New Blood for a New Age. By the way Greg, did you round up a campaign chairman yet? How about the lead you were working on over lunch?"

"It didn't pan out, Fred. You'll have to do as my manager."

"Have you given anymore thought to how we'll approach the problem of you being a bachelor?"

"The New York City mayor is single; there are others across the country who are single by choice, as I am. If the citizens can't accept that, I don't want to be their mayor. They don't deserve me. You'd think being single is some sort of disease."

"Don't take me wrong, Greg," said Fred timidly, "it could cast some doubts upon your sexuality."

"I've never been the shallow, plastic-type person, Fred. I don't have to justify my lifestyle to anyone. Maybe the mystery will help me win the gay vote."

"How about Rusty? Have you considered asking her to marry you? She's an intelligent, attractive woman. Also personable. She'd look great by your side at the election night watch party."

"Fred, don't you agree it would be slightly suspicious for me to suddenly marry? More of a P.R. stunt than anything. No, Fred. The citizens of Everett will take me as I am. That's it."

"I don't get it," puzzled Fred, throwing his papers on the desk before Greg. "That's what?"

"I'm a free spirit. I've spent too many years being who I am to change now for the sake of what someone else wants me to be. I'm going into this campaign on the premise that the traditional leader is a thing of the past. We've got to have men who aren't afraid to break with tradition. A mayor with vision. A mayor not afraid to bring about the kinds of changes necessary for the world to become what it should be. It's risky, but something tells me I'm destined to win."

"You speak as though you are running for position of world president."

"Today, Everett. Tomorrow, the world," Sven said with a laugh. His face became somber. "Let's run through those photos once again. The nineties are ready for someone who is self-actualized. A man who has observed the problems of this city through the eyes of a newspaper editor and is willing to solve those problems through spiritual insight. It will work, Fred. I feel it in my soul."

"Sounds spooky, sir."

"Don't *sir* me. Work up the headlines. I'll trust your judgment till I get a campaign manager."

"And what do I use as material in writing your biographical sketch?"

"That part I'll handle. If you can't see the significance in being a beatnik or hippie, you obviously can't grasp the importance of being self-actualized. Just do the teaser, Fred. I'll write the heavy stuff. I've got to speak at a workshop in Port Orchard. I'll be back here in time for the news conference."

Sven walked out the door and descended the steps at the rear of the building, wondering if he would ever see Rusty again. The Jeep, owned by the newspaper, was covered with dusty rain splotches.

"Well, boy. You are about to come out of retirement and give the next mayor of Everett a ride. But only because you are more rugged, not as sexy as the Jag. I'll be seeing more of you." He dusted off the seat and climbed in. "First stop, the carwash; next stop, spiritual enlightenment."

"Emerald," called Rose as she entered the parlor. She'd driven back from Everett in half the time normally required for the long distance along the peninsula. Wondering if she would ever see Sven again altered her state of mind. And what about her financial future, since she'd finally quit her job? Sven hadn't tried to talk her out of leaving the paper.

Suddenly she was free to focus on helping Emerald realize her need for Christ. Nothing else in her life seemed so urgent as that one desire. Now she had the time. Did she have the ability? She could only hope so.

"Em, where are you?" Rose looked in the kitchen and dining room. With so many guests to take care of, she should be cooking dinner. But instead of finding her sister-in-law, she found a messily scribbled note which read,

Have gone to a workshop with the guests. Supper is cold roast beef sandwiches. Help yourself. Be back late.

— Emerald

The first hour crept by as Rose sliced roast onto the thick bread. She ate in silence, counting each bite. After cleaning the small mess she'd made, she went upstairs. With Emerald gone, she was certain there was dusting and straightening to be done in the guest rooms. She had better get used to helping out more, she thought.

The dustmop left a shiny path on the hardwood floor as Rose rounded the corner into the room adjacent to her own. A day without rain had left the world dusty. She hoped it would rain and clear the air. Even the dresser and table appeared to have been neglected for an eternity. Rose's dustcloth followed the line of the cedar four-poster bed and rubbed nightstands clean. She turned to wipe the dresser. Her image in the mirror startled her.

The dresser top had been adorned with candles and a marble slab, upon which, in a brass bowl, charred piles of twigs and leaves appeared to have been burned slightly and extinguished before being totally consumed. The smell of stale incense hung faintly in the air. Her reflection stared back at her from between the candles.

If even one of these guests espoused witchcraft, it would be cause for concern, but Rose didn't like what she saw in this room. The chances were great that witchcraft was practiced by all the ladies.

Rose knew the Universal Church had been built a few years ago, just off the main highway to Manchester. Although she'd never seen it, she was sure she would have no trouble finding it. She closed the door behind her and hurried to her own room. Determined to clear her calendar in order to make tomorrow's conference, she perused the books and cassette tapes which lay on the bed, floor, and vanity table. Tracy had loaned her literature from various ministries. There was so much, Rose couldn't hope to sift through even a fraction of it. So eager had she been to fill her spirit, she had spent every spare moment reading her Bible. But now, several book titles stood out to her as *must read.* And all the tapes intrigued her.

Sleep learning. She had long been a believer in it. The spirit could listen as the body slept. If she could remember to do it, she would start a tape tonight. Taking great care and several minutes to choose, she selected those tapes sounding most exciting. "Faith — The Key To The Kingdom Of God," "Your Authority As An Heir With Jesus," and "What To Do If You Miss The Rapture." She stacked the tapes beside the tape player when a fourth tape stood out to her.

"Witchcraft, Demons, And The Occult," she read. "That's as good a place to start as any." Brushing the other selections into the nightstand drawer, she slipped the cassette tape into the tape player.

"Rose, we're home," Emerald called as she entered the room. "You missed it. You truly missed it. It was the most inspired day I've ever spent."

"Sit down. Are you alone?"

"No, the guests are back too. And I've had the best day today. Getting to know them and myself. It's just wonderful."

Rose had to admit she hadn't seen so much color in Emerald's face in a long time.

"Tell me about it, Emerald."

"We're all famished. Let's get the ladies some supper. We'll talk downstairs. You should come with us tomorrow instead of staying in this stuffy room listening to tapes. What is that anyway?" she asked, motioning toward the tape player.

"One of the tapes Tracy loaned me about witchcraft. Em, it bothers me to have those women here. I believe they're witches."

Emerald's face emptied of color. "You just have to ruin my day, don't you? Every time I get an interest of my own, you discourage me from pursuing it. I don't have a grand career like you do. So I stay cooped up here with no outlet for my creativity and self-expression."

Shocked at Emerald's hostility, Rose retorted, "You've always thrown yourself into this place by choice. And as for my career, I've spent the day setting my priorities straight. I've quit my job at the *Avatar*."

"You didn't! And if you did, who will keep a check on that spaced-out Rusty Lively?"

"That spaced-out Rusty Lively was really me. I wrote both columns."

"You don't mean it. How deceitful. Well, I can see right now that you haven't been a true friend to me at all. I can suddenly see very clearly. A friend would have shared that secret with her closest relative and friend. I'm appalled. But it does confirm what I learned today at the workshop. I am my own best friend. And what I do for myself is all that matters." Emerald was pacing the floor. She pivoted and stared Rose in the face. "And, on the subject of secrets. You didn't see fit to mention that Mr. Svenson was running for mayor of Everett."

Rose tried to hold back the surprise, but it showed as she tensed her body. Searching Rose's face, Emerald continued, "Don't tell me you didn't know."

"I truly did not know until noon today." Rose could feel her face heating with anger. "My surprise is only that you know about Sven's intentions. But how?"

"He made his official announcement at the workshop today," said Emerald with a smirk.

"Sven?"

"Yes. Didn't we tell you Gregory Svenson was the keynote speaker at the workshop? It was about three o'clock this afternoon. You had found out by then."

Shuddering, Rose thought, Sven? At a conference for witches? There could be no denying the women staying at the inn were witches. But the connection between them and Sven was just not clear. "Why was Sven there, Em?"

"You really don't know?" Emerald smugly answered, "He gave a lovely talk about the responsibility of each and every world citizen to seek self-actualization. It's for the good of the planet. It's for the good of the universe. And it can happen. We can bring about world peace with ease by recognizing the god within."

Chapter Twelve

Convergence Of Enlightenment

The evening hadn't gone well for Rose. Her last visit with Sven had tormented her mind throughout supper. She remembered him saying that she was interrupting the natural evolution of Emerald's self-actualization. Self-delusion was more like it.

Each time Rose mustered the nerve to question Theta about her world view, the words stuck in her throat. She had not the courage to speak before this woman about Jesus.

God forgive me, she thought. Today will be the day that is different. I won't forsake you again, Lord. If Theta is a witch, it's evident what her world view is. She doesn't believe in the redemptive power of Jesus' blood, and she isn't the influence Emerald needs. I'll have to speak up or risk losing ground with Emerald. Sven's lecture, Rose was certain, had not been in Emerald's best interest.

At breakfast, Theta seemed to read Rose's mind. "Rose and Emerald," she began, "the girls and I have decided we like you both. We think you'd benefit from the discussions on today's agenda. They will give you a grasp of our life philosophy."

"You don't believe you could put it in a nutshell here and now?" questioned Rose.

"We could talk all day and never scratch the surface.

A day at the Convergence of Enlightenment will be both, self-explanatory and rejuvenating," Theta insisted.

"This," said Pamela offering a program to Rose, "lists the times and places of all the experiences. Take a look. There is something for everyone."

Rose perused titles and presentors, suddenly spotting a familiar name. Gregory Svenson, the program read, will present "The Magick Of Sexuality In The New Age" at the Universal Church in Port Orchard. "What do you ladies suggest?" asked Rose, hoping the trembling voice was evident only to herself.

"We split up, take notes, and later share what we've learned," Stacia began. "It's like going to six workshops at once."

"Today I'll attend the session on cartomancy," said Pamela.

"Crystal powers is my interest," Karen said. "Stacia and Mora enjoy the New Age music concerts. I think they have a thing for the pianist," she laughed.

"Sybil," asked Theta, "which will you attend?"

"I'll stick to psychokinesis," she answered. "This piecemeal information isn't my style. You have to diligently focus your energies in an area to attain its full power. But you, Rose, surely have a specific area of interest you'd like to dabble in today."

"As a matter of fact, it's all fascinating. But is there anything that explains the New Age movement?"

The ladies glared at Rose for a painful moment. Then Theta seemed to call them off with her dark glance and they looked away.

"The entire Convergence of Enlightenment is related to the New Age. I wish you had attended the first day's seminars. There was a lengthy orientation on the techniques, practices, rituals, and doctrines of the New Age. It is really too much information for one workshop to handle. A single explanatory session would minimize the concept. Sorry. That's why," she continued, "the conference is divided into one-hour segments, runs for six days, and is spread out over dozens of locations throughout five cities."

"Don't apologize for my own ignorance. Emerald and I are new to all this," said Rose.

"Then just tag along," Theta announced, "and you can't go wrong. I'm going to the 'Magick Of Sexuality' session."

"And only because you like the speaker," giggled Pamela, "in more ways than one." The ladies laughed, except for Rose.

"The speaker?" Rose inquired.

"It's Gregory Svenson. Masters degree in journalism, extensive background in New Age issues, and probably the next mayor of Everett, Washington," answered Theta.

"Also," interrupted Stacia, "a luscious, towering, gray-eyed Scandinavian. The perfect presentor for such a subject as magic sex." Once again the room bulged in laughter.

"You'll see for yourself," said Theta. "Hurry now. We'll be late."

There is no real significance in letting Theta know I already know the Scandinavian, Mr. Svenson, thought Rose, as she tried to discern Theta's true interest in him. Her instant jealousy was quickly replaced by compassion for Sven, whose search for spiritual peace had him rollicking in the magic of sexuality. Once again, he had confused feelings with spirit fulfillment.

Rose couldn't believe her eyes. The parking lot of the Universal Church was full. Five blocks away, Theta steered the van into the parking lot of the foot ferry.

"I may get ticketed," said Theta, "but we've got to get to the workshop. The session has already started, but maybe we won't have missed too much."

"The girls and I are going to hurry ahead. We'll meet you in the welcoming center between sessions," Pamela said. She took off her pumps and ran. Sybil, Karen, Stacia, and Mora were fast behind her.

"They have energy that I lost years ago," said Emerald, watching the figures disappear down the hill.

Sven had just begun his talk when the ladies entered the main hall. The church pews were packed. Several people scooted together to make room for Theta and her guest.

"See what I mean? Cute, huh?" Theta asked Rose who just grunted in reply. Never had she seen so many people assembled in one place. Rose opened her yellow legal pad and began taking notes as Sven's charisma captured the audience comprised mainly of women.

After a typical Gregory Svenson joke, Sven began recitation of seductive prose. Either his body emitted a glow or microscopic particles mingled with white rays of light which streamed in the stained glass window, for his body radiated an iridescent aura, visually confirming the suggestive poetry's statement. So suggestive were the words that Rose, the woman who had been closest to Sven — his most intimate lover — was blushing with embarrassment. Throughout the reading of the prose, she was unable to look at Sven. Gazing about the room, she jealously witnessed the similar effects the words had on other women. Several of the listeners had folded their programs into fans with which to cool their ardor. None too soon, the reading was over and Sven awaited a reaction from his mesmerized audience.

"I see," he said, "you're in shock. Don't be. Each of you is capable of attaining a level of sexuality so high to thrust you into direct unison with the energy of the universe. Not me, you say. I'm just a housewife from Anacortes or a burger flipper from Barney's Burger Barn, you think. But I am here to testify that you each have the capacity to experience the entire universe through your senses. How? Glad you asked."

Rose jotted down most of Sven's talk as he articulated his way through "Steps To Accessing Your Aliveness And Sensuality."

In an attempt to elude Sven's eyes and to prevent further unwholesome brainwashing of Emerald, Rose was out of her seat as quickly as Sven stopped talking.

Surrounded by loud applause, Rose grabbed Emerald's sleeve and tugged for her to follow. Surprisingly, Theta also rose and left the great hall right behind them.

"Wasn't he wonderful?" asked Theta. "Look, here he comes."

Sven had exited the hall at a side door and was rapidly approaching the huddle of women. "Rose! Rose!" he called, waving to get her attention.

"I definitely know what you see in him," whispered Emerald as Sven's muscular frame strode toward them.

"Rose, I am so glad to see you here, a bit surprised however. Perhaps overwhelmed and elated are better describers." Sven looked down upon her with the same charismatic aura that had re-seduced Rose during the ardent recitation.

Theta and Emerald stood in amazement when Sven embraced and passionately kissed Rose. Rose felt as though she were in a dream. Drunken with the words of the prose and the pleasure of his presence, she submitted to the passion.

"Obviously, you two have met," softly insisted Theta.

"Excuse me?" said Sven, becoming aware of the women gathering about him.

"I'm Theta and," said Theta, motioning toward Emerald, "this is. . . ."

"Yes, Mrs. Thorn. Good to see you," he smiled as he spoke.

"And you already know Rose Thorn?" probed Theta jealously.

"Soon-to-be Rose Thorn-Svenson," he spoke firmly to Theta, giving Rose a hug.

Rose, still mesmerized, managed a faint objection. "Sven, stop this."

"Now, I know our marriage hasn't been officially announced, but let's not put it off any longer. I'm ecstatic! Ladies, may I steal her from you?" he asked the other two women. Emerald and Theta, astonished at this turn of the day's events, shrugged at each other.

"But Emerald is with me," objected Rose. "And I am with Theta."

"We can drop her off at home or get her a cab if she isn't ready to leave, yet. Let's grab some lunch." Sven was determined to get Rose to himself, and Rose felt compelled to stay and protect Emerald.

Theta spoke up, "We have other sessions to attend and Emerald is actually with me as my guest."

That fact alone frightened Rose more than being with Sven after his emotionally raping poetry session. "It's not a good idea," she objected.

"Go on with Mr. Svenson," insisted Emerald. "I'd like to check out the positive imaging workshop."

Instantly, Rose and Sven stood alone beside his red Jeep. He unlocked the door and firmly encouraged her onto the seat with a strong boost to her waist. In the sunlight, Rose felt the mental fog lift incrementally. Sven's words rang in her head, but were only vaguely translated to her understanding.

"I know the papers announced my candidacy as a bachelor — after all, you turned me down only yesterday. But we can hold another press conference and spring the news."

"The news, Sven, is that I'm still not going to marry you."

Sven reached for Rose's hand across the console. "I must have missed something. You came to hear my presentation. Was I dreaming to surmise that to be a step at reconciliation?" he said.

"No. I did it solely out of curiosity. I never intended for you to see me in the crowd."

"I did, though. And you love me. You're going to marry me, Rose."

When the Jeep halted at the next stop light, Rose struggled to release her seatbelt. "I want to go home this minute," she said. Rose opened the door, but was pulled in a powerful jerk toward Sven. The look of hurt in his eyes made Rose ashamed of her hysteria.

"Maybe if you'd attend more sessions this week," Sven whispered, "you could get a handle on what is really going on between us. I could get away from the paper to be with you."

"What would you suggest for starters?"

"Reincarnation would be a good place to begin."

"No way!"

"Listen to me for once," Sven insisted. "Our communication first began suffering when you decided to move out of my apartment. In case you didn't notice, that's also when our sexual involvement came to an abrupt halt."

Remembering Sven's steamy prose, Rose blushed deeply.

"That broke a spiritual bond we had. You and I are obviously soulmates. We've been together in another lifetime. We are destined to be together in future lifetimes. Face it. Let's get married and be Mr. and Mrs. Gregory Svenson, the new mayor and first lady of Everett."

"Suddenly, Sven, I am fatigued by this conversation. It's the only thing that is going full circle."

"But you don't understand the significance of being soulmates. I've seen it in my spirit. I've experienced you as the mother goddess and I as god of the cosmos in a sensual union where we become one. The electrical power of the universe grew within us. That poem was about you and me. I wrote it after we made love the first time. You have to remember that night as strongly as I do. It has controlled every breath I've breathed since then." Sven searched Rose's face and smiled sweetly, brushing her cheek with sensual fingers. "You did recognize the lovers in the poem, didn't you? Of course you did."

"I've got to get out of here." Rose jumped out of the vehicle and walked toward the inn. Sven drove beside her for a few yards. Rose refused to look at him. She watched the grass slip past, beneath her feet.

"Get in here!" Sven demanded, jamming his foot on the brake.

Rose obeyed, surprised at the urgency in Sven's voice.

"I'm taking you home, for now." Sven spoke through clenched teeth. "But listen to me carefully, Rose Thorn." Sven's facial expression became stern. His thick, white eyebrows knit closely together. "You'll pack a few things. I'll pick you up at seven o'clock tomorrow evening. While you are preparing your trousseau, I'll be in a press conference in Everett, announcing our wedding plans. Monday, after a short, yet romantic honeymoon cruise to Victoria on the *Princess Marguerite*, we'll return to Everett as Mr. and Mrs. Gregory Svenson. We'll hit the campaign trail immediately."

Rose was jolted against the door when Sven turned the Jeep into the inn's driveway. "You are going to marry me, against my will?" Rose screamed. "I won't have any part of it!"

"You will. And, in the long run, you'll know it was the right thing to do. One of us has to be rational and get things under control."

Sven pulled Rose to his side, kissed her in a passionate violence, then leaned over her to open the door. "Be ready on time. I have a lot to do before tomorrow evening. I love you. Now get out!"

Frightened by Sven's unusual belligerence, Rose crossed the parlor to the phone. She was confused and hurt. As Tracy's phone rang with no answer, Rose wept.

"Help. That's what I need, but where do I turn? The police?" She dialed the Port Orchard Police Department, then quickly replaced the receiver. Sven hadn't abducted her . . . yet. No crime had actually been committed.

Tracy did not answer the phone in Rose's numerous attempts. The newspaper, she thought. She could envision the headlines, "Mayoral Candidate Kidnaps Bride." But who would take the word of an author of rival columns over a well-known editor? That's it, she realized. A rival newspaper. Her story would hit the streets in the morning and suspicion would surround Sven.

The police would keep him under surveillance. He wouldn't dare try anything with his office and apartment being staked out. This is too crazy, she rebuked herself. You'd only ruin Sven's career. She knew she would be better off, but could she sabotage Sven's credibility by exposing his intentions to kidnap her? He might have been bluffing. Sven would probably call her later and apologize for his rudeness and beg her forgiveness. Her heart debated her mind. He had to be exposed.

The plan might backfire, on the other hand. What if, she wondered, I only expose his New Age involvement? He may have enough New Age supporters to usher him into the mayoral position by a landslide. Either way was a risk. She suddenly knew that prayer was her only help. I've got to pray, she comforted herself. God can help me out of this.

Rose knelt beside her bed and lifted her voice to God. "Heavenly Father, God. I thank you for your grace and infilling of the Holy Spirit. I know it's that guidance that has given me boldness to stand up for what I know to be the only true way back to you. But I feel powerless in this situation. I know you have the answer. Reveal that to me, Lord God. Keep me in your protection. I may not know what the future holds, but by faith, I rest in the peace that you do know the future and I am yours. Just help me through it, in Jesus' name I pray."

Endless moments passed. Rose sat in God's presence quietly, when almost audibly her thoughts screamed out, Henry Johnston. Startled, Rose went to the French doors and looked across the lawn. Nobody was there, neither had anyone entered the house. The parlor door was still deadbolted as Rose had left it.

Once again she heard the name. Realizing it to be inaudible, she contemplated the thought. Henry Johnston. She hadn't heard that name or seen the man in years. Henry had been the publishing editor of *Port Orchard Monitor* for several years. He and Rose had met years ago at a pro-life rally when she researched the issue which would launch her writing career into the Rusty Lively facade. If he really supported pro-life, and Rose knew he did from the definite anti-abortion stance taken by his paper, chances are that he is a Christian. Wouldn't a Christian editor be interested in knowing what is happening at the Convergence of Enlightenment right up the street from his paper?

Rose thumbed through the phone directory, dialed the number, then waited. The baritone voice sang out, "*Port Orchard Monitor*, Johnston speaking."

"Hello, Henry?" Rose felt it better to speak casually, reporter-to-reporter, lest she lose ground at the onset of the conversation. "This is Rose Thorn. Do you remember me?"

"Remember?" the man chuckled. "I read your column every single day, practically before I shave and brush my teeth."

"I'm glad and hope you enjoy it."

"I sure do. Keep them coming."

"That's just it, sir. I've given my notice to the *Everett Avatar*."

"And you need a job? I'd be delighted to visit with you."

"No, Mr. Johnston. I've decided to freelance for a while. But I do have an idea for a story. What do you know about the Convergence of Enlightenment that is occurring in Port Orchard this week?"

"They took out a full-page ad. That's the end of my familiarity with the event. What's the story?"

Rose wondered if she could trust this man. After all, she definitely needed more evidence to prove her speculation about his being a Christian. "I have reason to believe that just because the convergence is being held at a church, doesn't mean it has got anything to do with God."

"Yes, what else?"

"And even if it is related to a god, Mr. Johnston, which one?"

"Just a moment; you are stepping on toes here. I'm a believer in one God. This story isn't going to shoot my Christianity out of the water, is it?"

"No, sir. I just believe I can show you a link between what is going on in that New Age church and the occult."

"The occult in Port Orchard? No way. It's just a bunch of clergymen, business leaders, and positive-thinking normal people trying to get the world to stop fighting, end war, and save the environment. Right?"

"I've been there."

"And what did you find?"

"That the New Age movement is a conglomeration of every practice that is anti-Christian, occultic, and harmful to man's salvation. All this is presented in a passive-aggressive manner so that even its followers don't realize they are being deceived and destructively used by Satan."

"Anti-Christian? You don't mean just open-minded speculative religion?"

"No, Mr. Johnston, I mean they are a threat to real Christianity."

"I am interested. I'm giving you the go-ahead. How soon can you have a story to me?"

"Can I drop it by in the morning?"

"So soon? It's already written?"

"It will be tonight. I will be there early tomorrow, for it has to be in the morning edition. Otherwise, forget it."

The sleepy streets of Port Orchard were dark, except for the few neon-lit businesses open twenty-four hours.

"When you said early, you meant it," said Henry Johnston, wiping donut crumbs from his moustache.

"This needs to be released as soon as possible. And since we missed last night's edition," said Rose, "I thought we could catch the a.m."

"Makes sense, except the a.m. came off the press an hour ago. Route men will be trucking them out to delivery sights about now."

"Then I should have brought it over last night. I could have had it done by midnight."

"Don't worry. We'll get it in the evening edition."

Disturbed by falling tears, the cream solution swirled in Rose's coffee cup.

"Hey, don't take it so hard. We've got all day."

"Actually, Mr. Johnston, I don't have all day."

"Back up. I don't get it," said a concerned editor.

"My article links the New Age movement to the occult. I have overwhelming documentation that Gregory Svenson, who is running for mayor of Everett, is involved in the movement. I just wonder if his future constituents would vote for him if they knew his philosophy is anti-Christian."

"That's powerful talk. What evidence?"

"He is so entangled in New Age philosophy that he is about to abduct me."

"Are you sure? I still don't get it. Why you?"

"He believes we are soulmates from past lives. He's going to kidnap me and marry me to ensure that the soulmate status is maintained throughout eternity."

"Naw!"

"Would I make up something like this? I'm sorry for the tears. It's so unprofessional, but all night I researched the New Age. The truth is evident to me. It's urgent to expose the movement and to stop Sven." Rose sobbed uncontrollably. "Even though," she cried, "I love him, we just can't let men like that into public office. You know what scares me most, Mr. Johnston?"

Mr. Johnston wiped Rose's tears from her chin with his napkin. "Calm down," he said, "I'm sure it can't be so bad."

Rose continued, "There are already New Age practitioners in public office all over the nation, or the movement could not have gotten this far without being crushed. I brought along a conference program. Take a look at the topics that are being presented under the guise of spiritual enlightenment."

Mr. Johnston mumbled quietly in the donut shop

which was empty except for him, Rose, and a yawning baker. "Hm," said Mr. Johnston, "astral projection, UFO's, reincarnation, sacred sex, rebirthing, spirit channeling, holistic health. This is intriguing. Let me see that article of yours."

It seemed to Rose that it took Mr. Johnston too long to read the article. Although it was quite lengthy, Rose had it memorized. She watched the reader's face for a clue of approval. Soon, he looked up at her sheepishly. For several more minutes Mr. Johnston looked somber. He rolled the papers into a tube and thumped them nervously on the table. "Unless you are absolutely certain of this, it is considered slanderous. But your reputation as an ethical, experienced writer precedes you."

"Sven is about to become a public figure. He isn't protected by law, yet. But I'm not wrong, at any rate," assured Rose.

The editor finished his coffee. For endless more moments he glared out the window where the sun rose, reflecting orange streaks onto the water. "You'll take responsibility?"

"Naturally."

"Then you won't mind if I tack on a disclaimer?"

"You don't believe me?"

"I just have to cover the paper's interest. In any event, I'll help by printing it, but you get a byline and any flack. The main thing here is that I will help."

"Why?"

"Because I do believe you. We have enough problems in this world without letting people like that into government. It'll run in the editorials, without a word cut." Henry smiled at Rose, patting her hand. "Besides, it's the duty of Christians to expose sin. I only wish we could have gotten it in earlier. I'll get right to work on it. But do you think this will put you in any kind of danger?"

"I'm sure it will. The power that is driving Sven is evil. He has changed over the past months. He isn't the same man I have admired and loved for so many years." Rose shut her eyes to block the brightening sun. "I saw hate in his face yesterday. It was as though Sven had left the body, leaving no person, nothing human that is, beyond those threatening gray eyes. He was empty. Do you know what I mean?"

"Don't you worry. This will run tonight. If he gets rough with you, let me know. We can take this to the police. Until then, will you be safe?"

"I'm fine. Give me a call when the issue is released. I'd like to pick up one before a run on the newsstands," she laughed. "Mr. Johnston," she said, staring full-face into the blinding red sky, "deep within my spirit, I feel as though my life has changed. Things will never be the same, once that story hits the streets. Today is the day that is different that we writers are always talking about."

"For your sake," said Mr. Johnston, "let's hope things are different for the better."

Chapter Thirteen

I Am

Six o'clock. Too early to go to Tracy's house, Rose drove home. Her mind was clouded by fatigue. I've got to get some sleep, she thought. But an urgency in her spirit prodded her toward the work she knew must be done. This is the day that Sven would pick her up. This time tomorrow, if his plan is carried out, they will be on their honeymoon.

"God," she prayed, "I can't let that happen." Rose knew that if the wedding occurred, it would be just a matter of time before she would be totally brainwashed. He's too strong, she thought. I'm a baby Christian. "Lord, I don't believe I am strong enough to resist him. You know I have good intentions. I want everything pure and wonderful that comes from you. But if Sven gets me in his clutches, my soul will be lost."

Downstairs, Emerald prepared the dining table for breakfast. Rose heard glasses and china tinkling and the refrigerator door open and close several times. Emerald stopped outside Rose's door on her way to the guest rooms.

She quickly announced, "Breakfast," without awaiting an answer.

Rose wasn't sure she was hungry. Physically, she was too tired to eat. But her spirit cried out for nourishment. She arranged all the faith literature and tapes she had gotten from Tracy into one pile on her bed. Into another stack she put the occultic and New Age literature, both secular and the Christian exposés. Then she opened her Bible. The concordance in back she opened to the word *witchcraft*. Jotting hurriedly, she copied the scriptural references: Exodus 22:18; Leviticus 19:26,31; Leviticus 20:6,27; and Deuteronomy 18:10.

A knock at her door startled Rose. She arose and crossed the room to answer it. To her surprise, there stood Theta, looming threateningly in the doorway.

"Won't you be joining us for breakfast?" she asked. "You were whisked away too quickly yesterday; we hardly know what to think."

Rose wanted to tell Theta it was not her business, yet knew that her sudden departure with Sven must have been puzzling. She had studied in her room all evening, with no supper, working on the article for the *Monitor*. It had been early yesterday that Rose last saw Emerald. No doubt the reason for Emerald's curt breakfast call.

"I'll be down in a bit," she decided. Returning to her study, Rose looked up the last scripture she had noted. She transcribed what she read, "Deuteronomy 18:10-14, There shall not be found among you any one that maketh his son or his daughter to pass through the fire, or that useth divination, or an observer of times, or an enchanter, or a witch. Or a charmer, or a consulter with familiar spirits, or a wizard, or a necromancer. For all that do these things are an abomination unto the Lord: and because of these abominations the Lord thy God doth drive them out from before thee. Thou shalt be perfect with the Lord thy God. For these nations, which thou shalt possess, hearkened unto observers of times . . ."

Rose read, penning *astrologers* in the margin, ". . . and unto diviners: but as for thee, the Lord thy God hath not suffered thee to do so." Rose got a quickened confirmation in her spirit that what she felt about Sven and his beliefs was accurate. She also knew she had done the right thing in exposing him and the New Age movement to the *Monitor*.

She thanked God that he had led her to Henry Johnston. He seemed trustworthy. "Now God," she prayed, "deliver me from the hands of the devourer." Chatter from the dining room became louder as Rose descended the staircase, but as she stepped through the door, all voices stopped. The eyes of the women searched her face for a reaction as she immediately became aware of Sven's presence.

His comely face beamed with a childlike expression of joy, but Sven's eyes innocently evaded Rose's glare. He coyly ducked his head.

"I'm sorry for not calling first. But I was too excited to wait another moment. And when I got to the door, Emerald invited me in to breakfast. Are you angry?"

"The word angry is not apropos."

"Oh baby, let's not have a tiff in front of these ladies. I just had to bring over the morning paper. Right on the front page, our wedding announcement. Shall I read it to you?" Without waiting for an answer, Sven began, "Gregory Svenson and Rose Thorn to wed on mayoral campaign trail." Rose froze in silence. "May I have a moment alone with my fiancée?" asked Sven charmingly to the breakfast clutch.

"Why don't the two of you retire to the parlor and the ladies can finish their meal? Rose, take Mr. Svenson to the parlor like a good little hostess." The ladies tittered at Emerald's wit. Theta's countenance grew cloudy and she diverted her glance as Sven bid them goodbye. Congratulations and best wishes were bestowed by the remaining women, then they resumed their chatter over coffee and rolls.

Seated in the parlor, Rose refused to look at Sven. He mocked her silence, drawing his lower lip into a pucker. "Emerald tells me she foresaw this marriage while reading your teacup. I'm proud of her interest in the unknown. Everything is knowable, however. Wouldn't you agree?"

"Sven, I know that beyond any doubt, you and I will never be married. You can't force me. I simply will not cooperate."

"And why do you think I dropped by so early?"

"Weren't you honest about being elated over the newspaper announcement?"

"Indeed, and I wanted to arrive before you read it for yourself."

"What difference does it make when I read it?"

"Oh," Sven said rising to his feet, "alone, you may have panicked and done something drastic."

"Suicide-drastic or escape-drastic?"

"Oh sweetheart!" cried Svenson, rushing to Rose's side. He sat beside her, cradling her in his massive embrace and softly said, "I want to encourage you, that's all. To help you understand that this is your destiny. It's karma. Don't ruin it. You could affect future incarnations by refusing to work with me on this."

"Gregory Svenson," announced Rose in a stern, yet quiet voice, "you have only one minute to be in your car and gone from this property."

"I'll leave, but," he whispered fanning the newspaper in the air, "according to this announcement, we will be married in beautiful Victoria, British Columbia, where we will honeymoon and return via the *Princess Marguerite* steamship on Monday. Goodbye." He kissed at the air, "See you at seven."

Rose made sure Sven's Jeep was out of sight before coming back inside from the cool misty air.

"Emerald," she said, peeking into the dining room, "I'm walking over to Tracy's house."

"You aren't going to fill us in on the wedding details?" asked Theta.

"Read it in the paper!" she curtly said. "Emerald, will you be home all day?"

"No. I'm going back to the conference with Theta and the girls." Rose detected a near defiance in Emerald's voice.

"Then I'll see you tonight," Rose said slipping out the front door. She did not want to travel the road to Tracy's, for fear Sven was still looming about. She knew he wouldn't be, for he obviously had to attend to details of a wedding — a wedding which would never take place — a wedding of cosmic magnitude. The leaves underfoot were wet, sinking beneath Rose's weight. The dampness of the woods muffled the snapping of the twigs. Rose breathed in a long, cool breath and exhaled a cloudy wisp of fog. The burden of Rose's secret caused her to walk languidly. It was overwhelming and grew heavier as the darkness of the foliage canopy offered an aura of imminent doom. Her footsteps quickened, as she felt threatened by that heaviness.

She had to get out of the dimness and into the light. But as she approached the wood's edge, she noted the sky had grown cloudy. Rain slapped her face. A drop at first, then sudden torrents, careening into her body as though the precipitation had a mission to destroy her. A flash of red streaked toward her and Rose was airborne.

The pain was intense. Streams of rain raced over her body in the ravine. I have got to get up, she thought, or I'll drown. Her muscles wouldn't respond. Her imagination raced, then she realized she was in her rose garden. Oddly, she envisioned herself to be inside a rose bud with flourescent sunrays spotlighting her. Its warm, golden fingers stroked the single bud, glistening in cool, damp dew. As the radiance penetrated her tightly closed petals, she knew that she *was* the flower. She felt a part of the morning and lifted her orange face to the rejuvenating source. Rose swayed on a wobbly green leg with a dainty leaf-gown trailing in the breeze. Rays warmed and soothed the bud, which loosened her self-embrace and carefully, gracefully uncurled. Exposed to the yellow brightness of the day was her fullness. How carefree she felt, absorbing strength from this powerful source.

The breeze cooled suddenly, causing her to tremble with chill. Her face turned away from the frigid air. She was aware of herself being drawn by coldness into a stationary position, no longer bending in the draft. Her stony face would soon crack. Pain wrenched her body as she fell from her perch of green. The garden looked different from the deep, soft moss bed on which she lay. The stem from which she had fallen loomed high overhead. She was painfully aware that she had been flung from great heights. Her entire body ached in her immobility.

She peered upward at the stem and pleaded for the jutting thorn to have mercy on her.

Relentlessly she urged the thorn to lower itself and boost her to her previous station. Yet the thorn would not assist but turned, in arrogance, away from the pleading gaze of the rose. The thorn of opaque jade transformed into a glistening, flawless emerald. No movement. The thorn showed no life of its own, only statuesque beauty. The rose feared she would soon wilt into compost — to return to the earth from which she had sprung, to nourish future generations of coral roses.

She lay contemplating her last, lifeless thoughts, when there came a voice. "Would you like to meet your favorite singer?" She had always wanted to meet him. He was probably the only real heartthrob she had admired as a teenager. How distraught she had been at hearing the news that he had passed away.

"But where?" she asked. "He was given a celebrity's funeral. I saw it on television." Rumbling overhead, clouds darkened the rose garden into a blackberry-colored amphitheatre. Shadows of dusk followed her to the stage where she awaited the entrance of the star. But the faces in the audience caused her discomfort. They were grim, wearing grayish greasepaint. The faces melted in the dank stillness.

"Backstage you may get an autograph. Every American girl wants his autograph," came the voice. Rose followed the call down a concrete walkway to the back side of the stage. As the celebrity appeared, she gasped and her heart leapt. Her teen idol's face was ashen gray. Rose did not want to be there any longer. "You're dead. I remember now." Turning, she left the theatre grounds in haste. The further her progress, the more she was aware of bubbles. Millions of floating bubbles drifted toward her. She caught several in her hands; they did not break. Larger and larger they became. So much larger, they were, that when one finally did burst upon hitting her head, the escaping air blew so forcefully into her face, the blast attacked her ears, virtually rattling her brain. To steady herself, she sat on a park bench, holding her head in her hands.

"My head aches. Could my skull be fractured?" Someone had once told her that she took everything too seriously. All these bubbles were accomplishing their role in destiny. Things always happen the way they are supposed to happen. If she had only ducked, the bubble would have missed her head and she could be on her way. No, she knew it wasn't true. It was something Sven would have said. But who was Sven?

The pain worsened as she closed her eyes, hoping to speed her recovery. Her aching doubled as the bubbles continued in a swirling motion toward her. They made her dizzy. She avoided looking at them, but suddenly they were no longer coming near her. Had the wind shifted? Each tiny bubble appeared to zoom directly toward her, then veer instantly away.

Inches from her face, the iridescent airballs slapped into a shield and floated to either side of her nose. Lowering her hand from her head, she touched the invisible blockade. It was wet and cold. She walked in each direction, surveying the perimeters of this strange ball. Yet, it was as high as it was wide with no means of escape. The wall extended in a circle over and around her. She had been captured by a bubble. Kicking it only hurt her toe and sent pain reverberating through her skull. The bubble would not break.

"How can I get back to Emerald Thorn?" she asked. "I must tell Em where I am. She will worry, but won't wait supper. Mr. Higgins may eat my portion if I'm not back in time." She could not remember when she had last been home. But Mr. Higgins, she remembered, had checked out long ago. New guests needed her entertainment. Dark figures at Emerald Thorn troubled Rose, but she could not force her mind to sharpen the vision.

When she wished herself to float, she was transported, encompassed within the drifting bubble, back to the rose garden.

There the brilliant emerald thorn stood rigid on its stem. The setting sun shown blindingly upon the faceted surface of the jewel. It reflected an array of gold and coral light, too bright to look upon. Her eyes and head hurt worse now. Unable to escape the bubble, she seated herself near the stem from which she had fallen. If the thorn would just reach out a fraction of an inch, the bubble would be punctured.

Rose put her fingertips to the bubble's wet surface. If the bubble were to burst now, she might go sailing through the air — a passenger on the air of a deflating balloon released by a child. How fun those balloons had always appeared, twisting and squalling until safely crashed and devoid of propelling air. Oh, how her head would then ache. Already she hurt. Even her teeth were sore. She opted to snuggle down on the velvet moss until such time as her pain should cease.

"Rose, please answer me. Can't you hear me, Rose?" But the rose, listless on the comforting quilt of moss, heard not the voice urging her to awaken. Her eyelids were welded shut and her arms riveted to the floor of this bubble cage. She must be using up all the oxygen, for she now found it difficult to breathe. "I've got to rest, get back my strength. Maybe if I count to ten between breaths, I can make the air last until help arrives. Henry Johnston will help me."

The prison that enveloped her acted as protection until such time as her head ceased pulsing. She calculated a retreat, but no escape showed itself. As she dozed, she thought she heard a friend saying, "I am with you."

"Who is it?" She tried to speak, but only slurred, her lips pressed against the bubble."

"I am that I am."

A surge of warmth flowed over her body and she felt a peaceful calm as she drifted toward sleep. In the distance she heard music. Or was it singing? The words were not clear; she could not understand them, but she had heard them before. I am asleep, she thought, don't bother me now. She would search for the singers later, if she could wake up, if she weren't dead.

Chapter Fourteen

Karma Fulfilled

"You'll have to leave now, Mrs. Thorn. She can only have visitors for ten minutes each hour."

"But I just got here."

"I realize that. But Intensive Care has its rules. There are other patients to consider, and if we break the rules for one family, we must break them for everyone."

"Just one more minute?"

"Sorry, no exceptions. She doesn't even know you are here, anyway."

Reluctantly, Emerald let herself be guided through the swinging doors into the brightness of the corridor. She followed the yellow painted line on the floor to the ICU waiting room where she heard her name being spoken. Dozens of faces glared at her, but she recognized none of the people sitting quietly about the room, each mournfully awaiting the moments they may visit their loved ones.

Again a voice called to her. She determined it came from behind and she turned to face Tracy. "Oh, Tracy! It's just awful," Emerald released the tears she had held back for hours. "There's still no change. The doctors say they've done all they can do."

"Let's sit down. You just cry all you want. You're exhausted and have been through a lot. It's been a long day."

"I haven't been through anything," Emerald rebuked. "Think of poor Rose. She made it through surgery, but I know it is now out of their hands. I'm so glad you called me so quickly when you found her. I was getting ready to leave for the conference and wouldn't have been back until evening." Emerald dabbed at her eyes with her silky hankie. "These things are obviously just for looks; they don't absorb."

"Take some of my Kleenex," said Tracy, digging in her purse. "There now, that's better." She wiped Emerald's tear-streaked face and handed her a stack of tissues. "I knew when I found her crumpled in the ravine that it was serious."

"She hadn't been gone more than an hour. I had no idea she was hurt and needed me. Oh Tracy, if you hadn't found her when you did, she would have died. She still might."

"Rose is in God's hands, Emerald. The doctors have patched her and are doing their best. But God is the Great Physician. He can heal her and restore her body."

"Almost every bone was broken. Her skull was crushed. And, Tracy, I'll never get that horrible picture out of my mind. The moment I first saw the swirling red lights of the police cars and ambulances, her body already covered with that white sheet. The terror I felt nearly caused my heart to fail."

"Her pulse rate was so faint, they thought she was dead; the police officers told me it was impossible for anyone to have survived with such massive injuries," whispered Tracy.

"Then I watched," gasped Emerald, "as paramedics worked on her lifeless body in the ambulance. They radioed ahead to the hospital. They kept talking about her as though she were already gone. Then suddenly they said they had a pulse; she was shocky, but alive. Then they hooked up an IV They didn't even try to clean up the blood. Her hair was matted with blood and leaves, and that terrible rain just wouldn't stop pounding the ambulance windows. They weren't even cleaning her up. It's as though they were going to lose her anyway. As though she were already dead."

"Please, Emerald, don't put yourself through this. She is cleaned up now. She's dry and comfortable. They've got her medicated. She doesn't feel any pain."

"I know," she cried, "but I can't help thinking. . . ."

"Don't torture yourself. Let's just pray and leave it to the doctors and God."

"You're right, but it's like a dream. Why can't I wake up?"

"Let's just whisper a prayer right now, Emerald. I've been praying in my spirit all morning."

"Rose believed in God. Now this has happened. I'm not certain he even cares about her, or she wouldn't be in this condition." Emerald turned her back on Tracy, stood, and walked to the window.

The day was dark. It had been all day. Rain had melted one moment into another. Now dusk was turning to nightfall with no hopeful color on the Seattle horizon. Tracy joined Emerald at the window and stroked her shoulder. "God cares more than you realize. Had it not been for God, Rose might be dead instead of in a coma."

"She may not recover," said Emerald.

"Only God knows," said Tracy. "Remember that he had already worked a miracle in saving her life. He's working even now as she sleeps. Let's pray." Tracy led Emerald to the sectional sofa in the corner of the room. The ladies joined hands and Tracy began, "Lord God, you know this situation better than either of us. So we come to you, in agreement that you keep your hand on Rose. Heal her body and restore her to consciousness. We ask for your will, knowing that you are the Great Physician. We give you thanks for the work you're doing that we can't see. And, Heavenly Father, I ask that you give Emerald strength to endure this tragedy and that you show her your love through this situation that Satan meant as evil. We know you turn those things around, for the good, for your glory. In your Son Jesus' name we ask it. Amen."

From behind Emerald she heard a man clear his throat, then speak. "Excuse me, ladies." The man was tall and wore a uniform. Nervously fingering the stiff brim of his hat, he smiled. "I hate like everything to interrupt, but I'm looking for family of Rose Thorn. ICU nurses told me that you were the only relative. Is that you Mrs. Thorn?"

Emerald's face went pallid. "Oh no!" she cried.

"No, ma'am, it's not bad news. I mean, the doctors tell me she's holding her own. I just need to talk with you a bit." He motioned toward the seat beside Tracy, and she nodded as she nestled into the overstuffed chair. "I'm Officer Wainright of the State Police Department."

"I'm Tracy Wells, the neighbor who found Rose after the accident. This," she said, motioning to Emerald, "is Emerald Thorn, Rose's sister-in-law."

"Pleased to know you both," the officer cordially said. He grasped his kneecaps, as though to get down to business. "We still have not located the vehicle that ran Ms. Thorn down. We have no witnesses; we have no suspects; we have no clues. Local police have called off the on-site investigation until morning, due to darkness."

"Yes," said Emerald, "a Port Orchard officer dropped by an hour or so ago to tell me."

"Oh," Officer Wainright said, ducking his head.

"There's really something else you came to say, isn't there?" questioned Tracy.

"Well, ma'am, I would like to ask a question or two that the local police didn't get around to," said the officer in a soft, raspy voice.

"Emerald and I will be of all the help we can," assured Tracy.

"Good. I appreciate that," the officer said. But for several seconds the officer watched his own hands tightly clutching his knees. "Did your sister-in-law have any enemies?"

"Enemies?" asked Emerald, staring as though she were in a trance. "There were no enemies. Everyone loved her."

"Thank you, ma'am, but everyone has *someone* that hates them, for whatever reason. They tell me Ms. Thorn was a columnist who dealt with some pretty heavy issues."

"Sure, but nothing to make anyone angry enough to want to harm her." Emerald glared at Officer Wainright. "Do you think this was deliberate? Not a simple hit-and-run?"

"Not sure. We have to look at it from all angles. What about this rival columnist, Rusty Lively? There seems to have been some tension between the two. A little jealousy perhaps?"

Just then Tracy waved her hands in the air. "Over here! It's Gregory Svenson," she said. "Excuse me. I'll be back in a moment."

"I'll have a few questions for you also," said the officer. "Now, Mrs. Thorn, about this Rusty Lively?"

"Rusty Lively and Rose Thorn were the same person," said Emerald. She folded and refolded her tissues.

"How could that be? She was leading a double life?"

"Not a double life as though she had something to hide. Rose wrote rival columns."

"This sheds new light on all this. Rose Thorn didn't have any enemies, but did Rusty Lively?" asked the officer, cocking his head. He took out a cash register receipt. "I always forget to bring a scratch pad. This McDonald's slip will do," he laughed. "Rusty Lively," he said as he wrote.

"She never went by Rusty. It was always Rose. You won't find anyone who can tell you anything about Rusty. She didn't exist."

"Mrs. Thorn?" A doctor approached Emerald. She neatly wore a navy blue dress beneath her white jacket. "There is no change, but you may go in for ten minutes," she said sympathetically. Emerald did not excuse herself, but quickly arose and bolted toward the ICU door. Sven was at her side just as quickly.

"How is Rusty, really?" he asked.

"I've only got ten minutes, Mr. Svenson. I'll visit with you in a bit."

"Give her my love, please," Sven added. Tracy crossed the room and sat, once again, on the sofa beside the officer. Sven followed her and sat quietly, checking his wristwatch.

"Excuse me, sir. I'm Officer Wainright. Did I hear you call Rose Thorn *Rusty*?"

"Yes. It was a nickname, sort of. You know?" Sven said.

"Yes, I know. But Emerald Thorn didn't seem to think that many people knew about the alias. How well did you know her as Rusty?"

Sven squirmed, uncomfortably perched on the edge of his seat. "I was her editor at the newspaper. I'm Gregory Svenson."

"Then you were well aware of her double life?"

"Double life?" Sven asked, shaking his head.

"Yes, double life. It's the only reasonable answer. Did Rusty Lively have any enemies?"

"None."

"Don't answer so hastily, Mr. Svenson. Give it some thought."

Nervously, Sven arose. He paced before the sofa for several minutes. "No," he repeated, "no enemies. Why do you ask?"

"This could be a breakthrough. I believe we have more than an accident here. We'll find out. I'll be wanting copies of all her columns for the past several months."

At that moment Emerald came through the ICU door. She sat beside Tracy. For a few seconds the others watched her. Then tears slowly fell onto her cheeks.

"Well?" asked Sven. "Any news?" Emerald did not answer, but buried her face in her handkerchief. "May I go in and see for myself?"

"I've already gone in," explained Emerald. "Only one visitor is allowed per hour. Maybe you could go in next hour." Sven checked his watch again. "This must be especially rough on you, Mr. Svenson."

"How so?" asked Sven abruptly, as though he were being accused of something.

"Your marriage plans will have to be postponed. Or

cancelled." Then Emerald buried her face in Tracy's shoulder. "Perhaps she'll never live to become Mrs. Gregory Svenson."

"Marriage?" asked Tracy surprisedly. "What marriage?"

"Gregory and Rose were getting married. Hadn't she told you, Tracy?" asked Emerald. The look on Tracy's face was confirmation to all present that she was shocked. "And now she won't recover to become a blissful bride. The doctor suggests that we consider withdrawing life support. She's in very critical condition. If she pulls through, she will never be the same."

Sven continued pacing. "Do they expect her to pull through?"

"Mainly they are keeping her alive with all that equipment." Emerald bounded for the restroom and disappeared through its door, weeping.

"Don't worry, Gregory. God has this all under control. His will is going to prevail," assured Tracy. "Have a seat. I'd like to talk with you."

"And so would I," announced Officer Wainright. Sven's face flushed to white and he loosened his tie. "But I don't have time now. Will you make my apologies to Mrs. Thorn?" The officer swaggered down the hall past the public phones. Putting a quarter into the slot of the newspaper machine, he picked up an evening paper and entered the elevator.

"Gregory," Tracy began. Sven paced nervously. "Greg," Tracy's words developed slowly as she contemplated her question, "when did you and Rose become engaged?"

"Actually, we became engaged years ago. I've always

known she was the one for me."

"Yes, Rose had shared some thoughts along that line. But when I last talked to her, she was no longer thinking of the two of you in a romantic light." Instantly Sven stopped his hectic motion.

"Are you insinuating that Rose didn't care for me any longer?" he blurted. "Are you suggesting that the relationship was passé?"

"Not passé, but a bit one-sided. Rose indicated to me that her feelings for you had changed."

"I get the distinct feeling that you and she spent more time discussing me than I realized," Sven said worriedly. "Most of what you discussed was of a personal nature." Sven seated himself beside Tracy, picking up a newspaper which had been folded, dog-eared, and dismantled numerous times during the day. He turned to the women's section. "I guess you've had a chance to glance through today's paper. This item appeared in practically every newspaper along the coast. I wanted to make sure everyone saw it." Sven handed the notice to Tracy, then confidently sat back admiring the artwork on the wall beyond her. She read silently, shaking her head in disbelief.

"This is a marriage announcement."

"How perceptive of you. You're positive Rose didn't mention it to you?"

"She certainly did not. As a matter of fact, I'm confused. This had to have been a sudden decision."

"Sudden? Absolutely, if you consider a courtship of ten years sudden."

"Gregory, when I last talked to Rose, marrying you was the last thing on her mind."

"What precisely was the main thing on her mind?"

Sven probed.

"Your salvation and the souls of the people she loved."

"Were you a party," Sven glared as he rose to his feet, "to Rose becoming born again?"

"Yes, I am blessed to say that I was instrumental in that the Holy Spirit drew her and me together. She was obedient to the Spirit's convicting and I prayed with her." Instantly Sven knelt to the floor and grasped Tracy's hands. He looked directly into her eyes with his, which were empty beyond their beautiful color. His body trembled and his mouth grew taut. Tracy sought to console him through her confusion. Was he breaking down, realizing that he too needed Jesus? Or, she thought, was he grief-stricken over the tragedy of his fiancée? Quietly Tracy prayed, asking for discernment and the right words to speak.

Sven moved closer to Tracy and when his face was uncomfortably close to her, he broke the silence. "You haven't won," he whispered raspily. Tracy tried to free her hands from Sven's grasp, but he held to her wrists firmly. "You only think you've won. The victory is mine."

Sven's trancelike stare was broken by the noise of Emerald's clinking shoes nearing them. She approached Sven and hugged him as he knelt.

"Be strong, Mr. Svenson. She's going to make it. She has to. For all of us, she's got to make it," Emerald said softly. Sven's hand gave Tracy's a gentle pat, and he lifted himself into the chair across from Tracy, where he once again glared at her. Tracy closed her eyes and softly prayed.

When the top of the hour approached, Emerald allowed Sven to visit Rose, although she longed to visit once more. Emerald knew Rose's situation was hopeless, and they had spoken their last words to one another. Emerald dabbed at her eyes, discarded her hankie into her purse, and pulled a roll of toilet paper into view. She spun off a long section, meticulously folding it along its perforations. Tracy watched intently but did not speak. Emerald felt numb now. She was exhausted. As Tracy had told her earlier, it had been a long day. The night threatened to be even longer.

The ICU door swung open with such force it slapped the wall, then fanned several times before stopping. Sven stood, face white, staring at Emerald. "I think she's gone. She didn't make it."

"What!" Emerald shrieked, running to the door. Sven held her back, pushing against her shoulders with his strong hands.

"I was stroking her hair and talking to her when her heart monitor blasted a shrill squeal. Nurses and doctors were at her side immediately. They are working on her now, but I wouldn't get my hopes up." Sven embraced Emerald and rocked her gently, stroking her hair. Her tears rolled onto the front of her comforter's jacket.

"Did I hear correctly?" asked Tracy, approaching the pair.

"She's gone," whispered Sven. Once again the door opened and the doctor was quickly at Emerald's side.

"Mrs. Thorn," she said. All eyes watched as the doctor continued, "She's safe for now."

"Praise God!" said Tracy, watching Sven's surprised expression.

"You mean you've brought her back?" Emerald asked.

"It was a technical problem," the doctor announced.

"I don't understand." Emerald dabbed at her eyes

with the toilet paper stack.

"Somehow the respirator got unplugged. The heart monitor was on the same power strip, so naturally when the power was cut, the alarm rang at the desk. There is some good news, Mrs. Thorn. She seems to be breathing, although laboredly, on her own. We've checked all the plugs, making sure there isn't an overlap on any power strip. I don't know how the respirator got disconnected, but it all worked for the best. Now we know she can breathe on her own. We'll watch her closely, but I'd say there is a slight improvement over an hour ago."

"That's wonderful," said Emerald.

"There's still danger, Mrs. Thorn. We're watching her closely. I'll find a blanket for you. Why don't you rest on a sofa, and we'll know where you are, if we need you."

Sven, Tracy, and Emerald watched the doctor disappear through the swinging door.

"I guess I need to get back to Everett. It's a long drive home," he said, combing through his hair with his fingers.

Emerald spoke softly, "Mr. Svenson, you didn't take the good news so well. Rose is improving."

"I'm relieved, but don't want to be engulfed in false hope. As the doctor said, she's not out of danger. Her karma will be fulfilled. However tragic this is, it is all part of her destiny. Whatever is *supposed* to happen *will* happen," he said nodding to Tracy, then to Emerald. "I'll be back tomorrow. Keep me posted if things change."

Sven walked past the phones, to the newspaper machine, and perused the headlines as he awaited the elevator. He fumbled for a quarter, but before he could deposit the money the elevator bell dinged. Sven entered and the elevator rapidly descended. When the door opened, Officer Wainright greeted him.

"Mr. Svenson," he said, "I'm glad to see you again. I had hoped I wouldn't miss you. May I buy you a cup of coffee?" The two men walked down the corridor to the cafeteria. There were no other customers. Sven looked at his watch.

"It's late," he said, seating himself across from the officer.

"Yes, but I think you'd like to see this. I've just read the most interesting article written by your fiancée. It appeared in this evening's *Port Orchard Monitor*. Have you seen a copy?"

"No." Sven motioned upward with his quarter still in hand. "The elevator came too quickly."

"Save your money. This one is on me." Officer Wainright slid his arm across the back of the booth and handed the paper to Sven, whose face instantly faded to white.

Chapter Fifteen

Planetary Shift

Sven leaned far back in his chair, propping his feet up on his desk. "Then Officer Wainright and his bunch went over my Jaguar with a fine-toothed comb."

"You weren't formally charged with anything. They can't just search your car with no charges filed."

"Come on, Fred. It's a sensitive situation. I'm running for mayor. This article Rusty wrote put me under suspicion of attempted murder. Out of courtesy, and to show I had nothing to hide, I thought it the best thing to do."

"But they can't even suggest you did anything without probable cause."

"No harm done, Fred. I left a message on the answering machine of Gil Morley. He'll represent me if it comes down to it. What else could I have done? The man was waiting at the elevator with the blasted newspaper."

"I was shocked to see it myself," said Fred, unfolding the paper before him. "What a change of character. I thought you two were lovers, but this? Whew! She did everything but call you the devil, himself."

"So, of course, it drew suspicion, especially after the wedding announcement appeared in the same day's paper."

"Now that surprised me, too. I mean, day before yesterday our press release played up your being single, then yesterday your marriage plans were announced. Am

I missing something?"

"Not at all, Fred. It's all complicated. Even for me. I'll have to give it some thought. Catch the phones this morning, will you? The only person I want to talk to is Gil."

"By the way, how is Rusty?"

"She's hanging on, Fred. But it's just a matter of time."

"I'm sorry to hear that, Sven."

"Don't be. It's probably for the best. Narrow-minded attitudes like hers hinder the natural course of the universe."

"Hey, you're starting to sound like that bad guy she wrote about for the *Port Orchard Monitor*."

"Just kidding."

"You sounded serious."

"I guess I'll accept a call from Emerald Thorn if she happens to ring me up. I'd better get to work on my response to the media. It's inevitable that they'll want a reaction to the *Monitor* story. Blast it all! If I had only known about that article. Rusty Lively, even in a coma, you have managed to mess up my career and life."

"Having a little love spat over there?" The phone jingled, startling the pair.

"Mind your business, Fred, and answer the phone."

"*Everett Avatar*, Fred here. I'm sorry, Mr. Svenson hasn't come in yet. May I take a message?" Sven sat breathlessly, awaiting Fred's next words. "No. No, I don't know where he can be reached." Fred looked across at Sven who shook his head. "Who is calling, please?" Writing furiously, Fred continued, "Yes, I'll have him call you when he arrives." Fred hung up the phone and ripped the note from the scratchpad. "That's just the first of what I predict to be many. Johnston from the *Monitor* wants you to call him right away."

"I'll tell you what, Fred. I'm going home. If Gil calls, give him my home number. Keep up the message taking; I'll call in later."

"Hey! We have a newspaper to get out. You gonna leave me here to do it alone?"

"Snap out of it, Fred. You know the business as well as I do. You're the assistant editor. I've got to leave before the rest of the staff get here."

"How am I going to do it alone?"

"Delegate!" said Sven, jerking the glass door shut. He descended the stairs and looked up and down the street. Rain had just begun to fall. The sidewalks of Everett glistened, reflecting the streetlights which remained on, due to the morning's darkness. Sven walked quickly up the stairs to his apartment. As he turned the key, the apartment door across the hall opened slightly.

"Hey, Svenson, how's your girlfriend?" asked the robust man whose toweled body stepped into the hall.

"Excuse me?" Sven answered apprehensively.

"Your girlfriend, Ms. Lively. I heard it on the news that she had been hospitalized. Heard that she'd been put into a coma by a hit-and-run driver."

"Well, it's touch and go. But thanks for the concern, Suarez."

"Anything I can do?"

"No, but thanks again. Excuse me for rushing, but I'm on a tight schedule."

"Sure, Svenson. If things look up, give my best to Rusty. I sort of miss seeing her around here." The neighbor shut his door and Sven entered his apartment.

The article about the hit-and-run had named the

victim as Rose Thorn, proprietor of the Emerald Thorn Inn. Suarez must have made the connection between Rose and Rusty from the photo that accompanied the story. Blasted, Sven thought, if Suarez is onto the fact that they are the same woman, it's because he's read the *Monitor* story, too. Bolting the door behind him, Sven raced toward the phone, answering it before the first ring subsided. "Svenson . . . Gil, it's you. Glad you could get back to me. Have I ever got trouble."

The rain dripped through the pine canopy onto Emerald's head as she darted from her car to the front porch of the inn. No need to park in the car house, she knew. She would be home only for a few minutes. The newspapers from last night and this morning, both wrapped in plastic to keep them dry, dangled from the rose bush where the paperboy always threw them. She shook off the water and tossed them toward the coatrack.

The dawn had broken, yet the day remained dark. She switched on the lights in the kitchen, dining room, and parlor as she passed through the house. Because of Rose's accident, the house guests had checked out early. They planned on returning in a few weeks to months, their note had said. It instructed Emerald to keep their unused payment as a deposit on their next visit. They wished the best for Rose and thanked Emerald for her hospitality.

For the first time ever, Emerald was aware of a hollow echo which her shoes made as she descended the staircase. She paused briefly at Rose's door, but did not enter.

Searching her closet for her most comfortable dress, she realized there weren't many that were not jersey or silk.

Near the back hung a denim jumper which Rose had given her last Christmas. Something practical, she had told her, to garden in, since Emerald was opposed to ladies wearing pants. Rose had even given her a pair of navy flats that were supposed to be more comfortable than heels. She doubted it, but she'd give them a try.

After bathing and washing her hair, Emerald donned the casual clothing. She was surprised to find she still felt like a lady, in spite of the stiff denim. Quickly drying her hair, she plugged in her hot rollers to add some curl to the limp tresses — not that rolling it would have much success in light of the day's humidity. While the rollers heated, she descended the stairs. A sandwich would be good. She had not eaten since breakfast yesterday. Cold cuts she had planned to serve her guests today were folded into a single piece of bread with no mayonnaise or mustard. No time for extravagance, she thought. The hospital could call at any time. She had left the ICU waiting room after a fitful night of sleeping on the floor. The sofas had been saggy. She was accustomed to a firm mattress . . . not as firm as the floor, however.

Tracy brought a thermos of coffee from home about four o'clock. At that time, Rose's condition had not changed. Tracy would stay at the hospital in case the doctors had any news. Emerald gazed out the dining room window into darkness. This had been a worse day than yesterday for dreariness. The police had called off their investigation yesterday due to darkness. She was certain today would be no easier for an investigation to be conducted.

Emerald wondered randomly about Rose's condition, the driver of the hit-and-run vehicle, and Mr. Svenson's insistence that this had all happened because it was supposed to have occured as part of Rose's karma. How heartless. And to think that Rose would have married him. No chance of that now. At least not for a long while.

Gregory Svenson didn't appear to be the marrying type. Not that he wasn't masculine or attractive. In fact, Emerald often caught herself, while in his presence, shifting her gaze in order to avoid the lure of his deep gray eyes. She knew what Rose saw in him, for she saw it, too. But she must not let herself dwell on thoughts of Mr. Svenson's yellow hair that beckoned to be stroked, or his strong, firm arms which had embraced her earlier at the hospital. There was something out of sync with the incident at the hospital. Mr. Svenson hadn't behaved as a grieving fiancée should have.

Winding her hair around the rollers, Emerald scolded herself, "As though I'm an expert at recognizing true grief." The only thing that really bothered her was the image she had of him bursting through the ICU door when Rose's respirator became unplugged. His countenance was almost radiant, as though well pleased at the respirator's failure. Then when the doctor told Emerald that Rose didn't need the respirator, Mr. Svenson seemed to be disappointed. The transition must have been her imagination. Fatigue has its effects.

Emerald stretched out upon her bed, thinking of Rose. She should be at her side, but there was nothing she could do for her sister-in-law. Sure that Tracy would be there all day, Emerald knew that Rose was in good hands. Tracy had said Rose is in the hands of God. Maybe so. If there is only destiny, Gregory Svenson is correct in his suggestion that whatever is supposed to happen will happen. Emerald did not know whether to trust in God or fate. Too tired to work it out now, she rested her eyes for a moment.

Swiveling his chair, Gregory Svenson rocked slowly, deliberately, to convey his confidence. Lights were set up about the room. Fred tripped on cords as he maneuvered his way through the maze of cameramen and reporters.

"Yes," said Sven, "I intend to continue my mayoral race, without Rose Thorn by my side, in the hopes that she'll soon be able to join me."

"But Mr. Svenson," yelled a female reporter from the back of the room, "if you were concerned about her recovery, it would occur to the public that you would postpone your campaign plans to be at your fiancée's side."

"The city of Everett has a need for a mayor at this particular point in time, not after the recovery of my intended. When she recovers, we will be married. And I do believe she will recover soon. She has already made a slight improvement."

"Svenson!" shouted a voice from the front row. The lights blinded Sven. He squinted to see, but could not. "I'm Johnston from the *Port Orchard Monitor*." Sven unfolded a handkerchief, slapping it at the air, then wiped his forehead.

"Yes, Johnston," Sven said, sounding calm.

"Is there any correlation between Rose Thorn's article, which appeared in yesterday's *Monitor*, and her accident?"

"I don't see how the two could be related."

"Ms. Thorn did use some strong language in her exposé. And at the time she brought the item to me, she was fearful for her safety."

"Obviously there is a mistake. You may have even been dealing with an imposter."

"Actually, Mr. Svenson, Rose Thorn was exposing your true beliefs. Knowing the truth to be in the best interest of Christians within the city of Everett's purview, she made secrets of your life philosophy public knowledge."

"Get to the point, Johnston."

"Are you trying to indicate to the press that it doesn't bother you that the items in last evening's *Monitor* expose you as an advocate of the New Age movement?"

"Certainly it would bother me if the New Age held any public threat. Movement, as though it is a viable, organized organization or philosophy, is a misnomer. New Age simply implies a new way of life for this age."

"So, according to you, Mr. Svenson, the New Age movement doesn't plan for the destruction of Christianity to which Rose Thorn was a recent convert?"

"Rose was no more a Christian convert than I am. She and I are soulmates, a belief that Christianity doesn't encompass. Now, may I ask that you give others a chance to ask questions?"

From the center of the room an attractive man smiled and waved his hand. "Mr. Svenson," he said, "what do you intend to do about the problem of the homeless in Everett?"

"The plan is to work toward getting free shelters and rehabilitation centers opened. These are not throwaway people, but men, women, and children who could benefit from some training in positive thinking. Which they will get, along with food, shelter, and clothing."

"Thank you, Mr. Svenson." The comely man patted

a cameraman on the back and the crew left the crowded room.

"My question, sir," spoke an attractive brunette woman in a cream-colored woolen suit. "is about your talk at the Convergence of Enlightenment, which I attended to my utter enjoyment. Your presence there is an indication that you weren't hiding your New Age beliefs. That is encouraging to a great slice of the population. Is there any hope of getting some of these beliefs integrated into our city's policies?"

"Excuse me," Sven said, smiling at the handsome woman who stepped forward, "I didn't get your name."

"Beverly Hudson, sir. I represent Women for Planetary Unity."

"If the constituents want innovative policies that insure equitable treatment of all citizens, regardless of religion, race, sex or sexual lifestyle preference, or socio-economic status, Gregory Svenson is their man."

"Thank you," Beverly said. Smiling in satisfaction, she closed her notebook and folded her arms across her chest. Several other reporters seemed satisfied with the answers and packed away their equipment.

"Then, if that is all, I can get back to work," mused Sven. "I have a paper and a campaign to run."

"One last question, Svenson," said Johnston from the rear of the office. "I've checked with the other candidates. Summers, Blevins, and Parker are professing Christians. How will that affect the way you run your campaign?"

"In no way. I will run a fair and honest campaign, giving equal consideration to the desires of all religions, especially to Christians, since they are in the minority in this city and state. Let's face it, the Pacific Northwest is not exactly the Bible Belt." Chuckles from the crowded room encouraged Sven.

"You will be fair to Christian beliefs, even though Christians are targeted to be annihilated? Even though the New Age is an anti-Christian religion?"

"Johnston, you are out of line. These are issues I would gladly clear up with you, personally, over a cup of cappucino. New Age is not a religion, but a lifestyle."

"Then you are saying you are anti-religion, but not anti-Christian?"

Sven glared at Johnston, who now stood face-to-face with him. For the sake of the cameras, he smiled. "That sits a little easier with me. But what really describes my beliefs is the desire for freedom *from* religion. Let's run government with the unlimited human potential we all have. Let's discard the superstitions about a God before whom we must constantly watch our P's and Q's." Finally, the camera crews left. Johnston disappeared, and the office staff went back to their duties of answering phones and typesetting. Fred approached Sven and set a cup of coffee before him.

"You are as white as this cup, Sven."

"Do you think I said too much? Blasted! Why didn't I answer with *no comment* or something?"

"You handled it just fine, Boss. I've set up a speaking engagement with that lady from Women for Planetary Unity. Tonight at seven they are meeting in the back room of the China Doll for a dinner and planning session. She gave me a generous contribution toward your campaign."

Sven accepted the check and unfolded it. He blinked. "Wake me up, Fred."

"You aren't dreaming, Sven. It is made out for five thousand dollars."

"Better check with the city council again and make sure we know our contribution limit per organization." Sven stared at the check. "Fred, I may not have bombed as badly as I first thought. Maybe there really is a great slice of the population that is ready for me."

The Intensive Care Unit was dark, as usual. Tracy drew her chair beside Rose and took her hands, the backs of which were a network of IV tubes, giving Rose the appearance of a marionette. Tears came to Tracy's eyes as she sat down.

"Heavenly Father, God. We don't understand all this, but Rose and I stand in agreement that you are in control. Bless the Word as I read it today, and do your work in Jesus' Name. Amen." Tracy turned the pages of her Bible to Psalm 23 and began reading, "The Lord is my shepherd, I shall not want. He maketh me to lie down in green pastures." A nurse walked in and stood quietly behind Tracy as she read. When Tracy had finished the scripture, the nurse patted her on the shoulder.

"Your time is up. You have to go now," she said.

"Thank you," Tracy smiled up at her. "I'll be back from the snack bar in a few minutes. If you need me, please page me."

"I will," replied the nurse. "I noticed that you have been reading the Bible to Miss Thorn. She doesn't know you are here. She can't understand what you are saying."

"Her spirit does. She may not be able to respond, but her spirit hears me, and as long as she's alive, I'll encourage her with the positive words of God."

"Who is to say you aren't right? I'll call you if there is any change." The nurse ushered Tracy gently from the unit.

Tracy caught the elevator to the first floor. At a table, she quickly ate a hamburger and pushed the dishes to one side, leaving the last greasy fries. Opening her Bible once again to the Psalms, she mumbled the words, "He who dwelleth in the secret place of the most high shall abide under the shadow of the almighty. . . ."

The day had been long for Sven. It was about nine when he left the China Doll restaurant. His apartment was dark and the phone rang as he opened the door. Stumbling in the darkness, he reached the phone before the answering machine picked up the call. "Yes, this is Svenson. Mr. Johnston? Sure I remember you. I was indeed serious about the cup of cappucino, but I hardly know where we can get a cup in Port Orchard. . . . What are you doing at the hospital, man? . . . At this time of evening we'll be lucky to get a cup of instant from the snack bar's coffee machine. . . . Better give me longer than an hour. It's a long drive from Everett. Goodbye." Meeting with Mr. Johnston was the last thing Sven wanted to do, but to refuse would be an admission that he had something to hide. He should check on Rose anyway. The trip to the hospital wouldn't do him any harm. Had Emerald tried to phone him, he wondered? He listened to the messages on his machine, but none were from Emerald. Dialing her number, he loosened his necktie. The phone rang, but no answer.

Sven stretched the cord as he stepped to the

refrigerator. Looking inside he saw nothing appetizing. Leftovers and condiments stared him in the face. He wished, now, he hadn't been so preoccupied with his presentation to the Women for Planetary Unity to partake of the lovely buffet. Still no answer. He removed the phone from his ear and replaced it on the switchhook.

"Hello," answered a breathless Emerald. No response. She hung up the phone and looked at her watch. Nine-thirty! I've either overslept or been unconscious for hours. Tracy must be exhausted having been with Rose all day. Emerald yanked the curlers from her hair and ran her fingers quickly through. Barely stopping at the red light at the corner, she turned into the parking lot of the hospital. Glancing at her watch, she realized she had arrived ten minutes before the hour. She would have time to talk with Tracy and apologize for having slept all day.

The waiting room was empty. She peeked into the ICU door, but was motioned away by a nurse. "You can't come in," she whispered.

"I was just looking for my companion who has been sitting up with Rose Thorn."

"Oh. She stepped down for a bite to eat. She'll be back any time. There is no change in Miss Thorn's condition. Relax until the ten o'clock visiting time."

"Thank you," Emerald said. She took the stairs to the first floor. As she walked down the quiet corridors, she knew that regular visiting hours had been over for a while, for stragglers were just leaving. Nobody was in the snack bar. The sandwich line was closed and only vending machines offered nourishment. It had been hours since

Emerald had eaten the cold cut sandwich. She dug in her purse for loose change and inserted the money into the machine which groaned as it pushed a package of Fritos forward and dropped it to the delivery tray.

Emerald searched the room for Tracy, but saw her nowhere. Then she noticed some personal articles on a table across the room. Approaching the table, she recognized the purse and Bible to be Tracy's. A plate containing remnants of a hamburger bun and a couple of fries testified that Tracy had come down for a bite to eat. But where was she now? She could have stepped into the restroom. Emerald seated herself and began crunching corn chips. When Tracy had not returned in several minutes, Emerald crossed the room to the ladies restroom. Bending down, she surveyed the room for legs to verify the occupancy of the stalls. The room was vacant. It was a puzzlement, and Emerald knew that if she did not get back upstairs, she would miss the ten-minute visiting time with Rose. Tracy could have stepped out to her car or something. No time to worry about her now, though.

In the hallway, Emerald pushed the elevator button. What seemed like an eternity passed before she decided to take the stairs. On the second floor many people stood before the ICU door. "What's the problem? Isn't it ten, yet?" she asked a man. Standing on her tiptoes to see over the crowd, she peered through the glass window.

"Yep, but they've just come out and told us we can't go in," the man responded.

"What's going on?"

"I can't tell; everyone is literally flying from bed to bed, back and forth across the hall. It is as though they've all gone crazy."

"Some techincal problem again?" asked Emerald.

"I don't know. Oh! Here comes a doctor." The man cleared himself from the door's path as it swung open.

"Attention, please! May I see only the families of Smith, Taylor, and Snowbarger at this time?" The families stepped forward at the doctor's request and were admitted promptly to ICU. "Thorn, Jaworsky, Strongbear, and Lemmons." Emerald slipped in behind the family members called. Maybe Rose had improved and was being moved to a private room. "Follow me," instructed the sober-faced doctor.

The group was led to a conference room. The nurse had probably paged Tracy to tell her the news and Tracy had left the snack bar to phone her. She was certain to walk in at any moment. Into the room stepped a short, stocky man in a white jacket. "Good evening. My name is Hank Phelps, the hospital's administrator. I have been asked to advise you of a sensitive development." The group members looked at one another, puzzling over the statement. "Your loved ones aren't here." Several women burst into tears.

"The audacity!" shouted one man, "to call us together with a bunch of strangers to tell us our Penny has died."

"No, sir, Mr. Jaworsky, Penny has not died. Penny is missing."

"Missing? I don't understand. How could she be missing?"

"I'm afraid she is simply missing, as are the loved ones of each of you."

"What do you mean they are missing? Explain yourself. Do you mean missing, as in kidnapped?" screamed Emerald.

"No. I mean missing, as in vanished. Disappeared. Dissolved before the very eyes and out of the hands of our staff." Not one person spoke, but gazed in shock at the administrator. He continued, "At approximately nine fifty-one p.m. the patients named simply disappeared. All their hospital gowns, IV tubing, wiring, respirators, and other such tangible sundries are all the evidence that bodies were once there."

"But the other families," shrieked the woman beside Emerald, "you sent them in!"

"Those are the fortunate families of patients who did not vanish," explained the administrator.

"I want to see the authorities," demanded Mr. Jaworsky. "A fifteen-year-old girl does not simply vanish into thin air."

"We knew you would demand an explanation, and we want to give you one. I personally have contacted the police. They will be here soon. If it is any consolation, and I'm almost positive it won't be, about forty-three percent of the hospital's admissions are missing. That includes every single newborn baby and the entire pediatric unit."

"Not just our four loved ones?" squealed the woman next to Emerald.

The administrator continued, "At least one hundred twenty-nine of our three hundred beds are empty at this time, when they were full at nine forty-five."

"Lord God! What has happened?" she screamed, then the lady beside Emerald fainted. Emerald knelt beside her and fanned the victim with her handkerchief.

"Will someone ask a nurse to step in here?" asked Mr. Phelps. Emerald opened the door. The hallway appeared to be a Seattle freeway during rush hour.

Orderlies and nurses flew by with crash carts.

"Code Blue in ICU," announced a voice over the paging system. "Code Blue in 410B, Code Blue in 309A, Code Blue. . . ." Emerald proceeded across the hall when she found an opening in the traffic. She swung the ICU doors open and found a frenzy of hospital staff running to and fro, screaming and weeping.

"Excuse me, Mr. Phelps wants a nurse to come with me. A woman has fainted," said Emerald to the first uniformed person she managed to halt.

"You expect me to help someone who has fainted when I have a Code Blue on my unit and three more in the hospital? We've got a state of panic here. Fainting spells are not top priority. If she has a heart attack over all this, I'll see what I can do."

Emerald agreed that faints should not get immediate attention, when the idea occurred to her to check Rose's bed for herself. Just as Mr. Phelps had described, the heart monitor and IV monitor had been turned off, but the IV needles which had protruded from Rose's hands remained on the bed, still taped and blood soaked. Something awful was happening. Emerald was too frightened to think of what it could be and too frightened to ask anyone else. She walked back to the snack bar to find Tracy. No need to return to the conference room, with all those hysterical families demanding answers to this seemingly unanswerable situation.

In the snack bar, Tracy's things remained untouched. Outside the window, sirens screamed. Emerald walked to the doors. Stepping outside the hospital, she saw the same frenzied confusion as inside the medical facility. A car appeared to have slammed into a phone pole. Several others had crashed into it, and paramedics were lifting people onto stretchers. A police officer waved his arms, trying to get the attention of the survivors of one car, who were apparently upset that the driver of the first car was nowhere to be found.

Three wrecker trucks arrived about the same time. As the wreckage was pulled apart, Emerald thought she recognized a man talking to the last wrecker driver. She crossed the street and called out, "Gregory Svenson!"

"Emerald, it's you." Sven gave the wrecker driver his business card, a fifty dollar bill, and sounded off the address of his regular body shop. Emerald and Sven watched as the crushed Jaguar was towed around the corner. "It's like a dream," said Sven. "I keep expecting to awaken, but I can't think for the life of me what would put you in one of my dreams. I mean, that car was just moving along, not swerving or anything, when it cut in front of me, crashing into that pole. I tried to brake, but skidded right into him. You can see what it resulted in. A five-car pile-up. Blast it all! Then, to top it off, the driver must have sneaked away somehow, but I can't imagine how. I didn't see him step out of the car. He couldn't have. It's smashed like a discarded tin can."

"It's terrible," she said, "just terrible." Emerald didn't know if she was referring to Sven's accident or Rose's disappearance. But in any case, this was a terrible evening.

"Let's get inside. I could use a cup of coffee, even that snack bar slime." Sven led Emerald across the street to the hospital entrance. "What were you doing outside, Emerald? Did you just arrive?"

"I've been here awhile, but came out to see what all

the commotion was about."

"Well, pretty exciting, huh? The Jag is totalled."

"The sirens, Mr. Svenson, weren't sounding because of your accident. Listen. They are still screaming. They are everywhere. The whole city is shrieking."

Sven listened to the air as he inserted his quarters into the coffee machine and pressed the button marked *black with sugar*. "Don't hear a thing. Guess my ears are still ringing from the crash. Any change in Rose's condition?"

"Yes, Mr. Svenson. I don't know exactly how to say it, except that it is certainly a change. About one hundred twenty-nine patients are just gone."

"Gone? Gone where? You aren't making any sense. You should get home and get some sleep."

"I slept all day. The hospital administrator said he's notified the police, but he doesn't know where they've all gone."

"Where who have gone? You say you slept all day? I called you and there was no answer."

"You must have been the caller who hung up directly as I picked up the receiver. I was awakened by the call and came right over. I got here at nine forty-five and everything seemed fine. I came down to the snack bar to look for Tracy, whom I still have not located. When I returned upstairs at ten o'clock, the disappearance had taken place. The administrator said it happened at nine fifty-one. It was as though a nightmare began at that precise moment. I still can't believe it. We can't both be dreaming. Can we?" Sven looked distant. Emerald repeated, "Well, can we both be dreaming?"

"Just suddenly, you say?" Sven asked. "People just vanished? Poof?!"

"Yes. I know it's ridiculous."

"Not as ridiculous as you might think." Sven's eyes defocused and he took on an eerie aloofness. "I've heard for some time now that this was going to happen, but I never dreamed it could occur at a more opportune time."

"I don't know what you are referring to, but you are scaring me," said Emerald. Sven instantly grabbed Emerald's shoulders and pivoted her body to face him as they sat in the abandoned snack bar.

Looking at her full-face, eye-to-eye, Sven said, "You may not understand the occurrences of tonight, or the next few days, but soon you will discover that this is all happening as the result of a planetary shift."

"Planetary shift?"

"The cleansing we've awaited has happened."

"I still don't understand." Emerald began crying. Sven embraced her and rubbed her back.

"You will eventually," he said. "You may as well go home. You can't do any good here. They won't find Rose. She isn't on this planet any longer."

"Mr. Svenson, I'm scared. I'm confused! I'm dreaming."

"You'll be fine if you'll go home and sleep. Do you have a sedative to take when you get there?"

"I've slept all day. What about you? Your car is wrecked. You are an hour away from home. How will . . . ?"

"Don't worry about me. I'll get a ride home. I was expecting someone to meet me here. But," said Sven with the aloofness returning to his voice, "I have a strong feeling that I won't be seeing Mr. Johnston tonight or any other night."

At eleven o'clock Sven called AAA. Within moments a car picked him up. By midnight he was being dropped off at his apartment. He looked at the clock over the refrigerator. "A new day is dawning," he chuckled. "Today is a brand new, clean day on Planet Earth. My soul feels lighter." He poured himself a glass of milk. As he built a fire in the fireplace, he mentally noted necessary reforms for the city. When the flame's roar subsided to gentle beckoning lapping, he adjusted his legs into a lotus position before the hearth's warmth. Once again his eyes defocused and he stared, unblinking, into the fire. Relaxing his body, he softly spoke, "I am in harmony with your pulsing force, O universe, the breath of god, I am the wind, everchanging — always the same. I am and always have been a snowflake with six sides and millions of facets, individually sculpted, yet not unlike millions of others. I melt, mingling with new lives who rise as the phoenix and return to the sun to live again, to learn and relearn that the windows of thy soul are many, allowing me access to the mind, the universal mind that is god, that is I, the mind, the breath of god. I am." With palms turned up, Sven continued to soothingly chant toward the flame, "I am, I am, I am. . . ."

Chapter Sixteen

Millions Disappear

Morning dawned as gloomy as the past two days had been. She hadn't slept. Emerald found the evening paper in the clutches of the rose bush; tangerine petals dotted the porch where they had been scattered upon impact. The paper was soggy, but still readable. Emerald wondered why, with Port Orchard weather always so damp, the paperboy hadn't bothered to wrap the news in plastic sleeves. Her search for the morning paper proved futile.

No one at the *Port Orchard Monitor* answered the phone to receive her complaint. There has to be some news about the disappearance of the hospital patients, she thought. Opening the doors of the television cabinet, she reprimanded herself for the waste of time she was about to engage in. But, she mused, what else should she be doing? With Rose gone and no guests scheduled, her life had suddenly nose-dived into uncertainty.

"If you've been tuned in, already you know our lead story. Millions of people have disappeared. Reports have come in from around the world." The anchor woman looked disheveled. "We go now to our live report from Memorial Hospital. Ted Graziani is standing by."

"Thank you, Melissa. I am outside Memorial Hospital where last night, about nine fifty-one, the newborn babies in the nursery vanished from the cribs, incubators, out of the arms of ward nurses and even their mothers. This, according to hospital administrator, Hank Phelps. There are several mothers missing as well. I have the administrator with me now." Mr. Phelps appeared to Emerald not to have slept any better than she, herself, had. His white jacket was wrinkled and his coloring, pale.

"Tell me, Mr. Phelps, what was your first reaction to this occurrence?" asked Ted Graziani, holding the microphone in the direction of the profusely perspiring hospital spokesman.

"My first reaction was the same one that I have now — shock. I'm totally dismayed and have no idea what is going on."

"Just what was the first indication that something was wrong?" questioned Graziani.

"The phone calls. I mean, I began getting calls from every unit in the hospital. 'We have patients missing,' they told me. The final count is one hundred twenty-nine. As word spread throughout the hospital, the panic started. There were four heart attack victims last night."

"As a result of hearing about the disappearances?"

"Yes. As soon as patients received news. . . ."

"May I interrupt, Mr. Phelps? The media didn't receive news of your disappearance until the smoke had cleared regarding several other freak accidents."

"That's correct. But there are TV sets in each room, except ICU and the nursery. And the patients who panicked were watching your regular nightly news report. Their hysteria was a result of the frightening coverage of the plane crashes, suicides, automobile accidents, and other bizarre occurrences in the Seattle area."

"Thank you for joining us, Mr. Phelps. Let's now get

an update. Back to you, Melissa."

"We warn you," warned Melissa in a grave voice, "the tape you are about to see is of a graphic nature. If there are small children in your presence, parental discretion is advised. However, it occurs to me that earlier reports indicate that no children have been located. All are believed to have become victims of this tragedy. That being as it may, the tape is actual footage taken by cameraman Harley Heerwald as he taped an accident scene on the drawbridge north of Everett."

Emerald observed a pile-up of approximately one hundred cars, when instantly, screaming plane engines could be heard over the news team's voices and those of accident victims and bystanders. The camera zoomed in, focusing upward as a Boeing 747 glided overhead directly toward the cameraman, crashing onto the bridge, stopping short of the news team. "Oh my God! Did we get that on tape? Did you see that? Are we still broadcasting?" The voice-over became hysterical and the cameraman jerkily panned the wreckage.

"That, ladies and gentlemen, aired during our late evening newscast. Only five survived the crash. At least sixty of the cars were either abandoned after the pile-up on the bridge, or their drivers were among the victims of the mass disappearance at precisely nine fifty-one PST. At least forty-five people were reported injured, and all hospital beds in the Puget Sound area are full."

The ringing of the phone brought an astonished Emerald to the realization that she was not actually walking among the devastation. "Hello. Yes, Geneva, I'm safe. . . . Rose is missing. . . . Yes, Tracy was at the hospital and now is simply gone. I haven't tried calling her number this morning. There is a possibility that she is home. . . . Oh, I see, you've been over there. . . . I can't imagine what has happened. Yes, I have seen the news; it's on now. . . . Certainly, come on over. I don't know what I can do, but come on over."

Adjusting the volume of the TV set, the news cut to a distinguished man standing before the administration building on the University of Washington campus. He was obviously a professor by his attire of suit, lab jacket, and windblown hair. "As you know, there has been an unusually high level of UFO activity within the past week. Dozens of people have registered not only sightings, but visitations from our space brothers. It is my observation that all the disappearances, if you will, have taken place without the slightest trauma of those chosen to be lifted, *beamed up* for you Trekkies, to another dimension."

"Although those of us remaining seem to be suffering," the professor continued, "it is an encouragement to me, especially in light of the fact that our children have been selected, that all is well. Among the lifted millions are ten of my own grandchildren. This occurrence, which by some may be viewed as aggressive behavior on the part of the space brothers — perhaps even being perceived as kidnapping — is merely an attempt, by my deduction, to educate our narrow-minded earth dwellers in ways of the universe. It is my contention that soon, and what a wonderful experience that will be, we will receive our people back in the form of enlightened, perhaps even immortal beings. My only regret concerning this incident is that I was not deemed worthy of selection. That being as it may, the university has established a toll-free number, now appearing at the bottom of your screen. If you have further information regarding our space brothers call now. Or call to request our newsletter. . . ."

Emerald, being disturbed by a knock at the door, walked to the parlor, but Geneva burst in before Emerald could reach for the knob. Geneva's face was devoid of healthy color, and she sweated profusely. The dark hair was a matted mess of perspiration and natural oils. There appeared to be fuzzy globs clutching to the matted strands. Stumbling over the door facing, her feet tangled in the rug. Geneva's arms flailed as her feet slid uncontrollably across the parlor's slick hardwood, hitting the coatrack. It toppled, crashing squarely over Geneva's head. She lay in a shivering heap at Emerald's feet.

"I can trust you, Emerald. You've been my neighbor a long time. You won't betray me, will you? I've been hiding all night. As soon as I heard. They'll be coming for me. You too! But we have to hide. I've been under the bed, but they'll look there. I know they will. It's horrible." Emerald righted the coatrack and stared pityingly at Geneva. "I feel like screaming," Geneva continued in short, jerking bursts. "Like dying. My mother told me about this. My pastor. Every Sunday school teacher I ever had. Oh, God. What now? I can't make it. Seven years. No, I can't make it. It'll be too much for me . . . too horrible. Emerald, what are we to do?" She grabbed Emerald's ankles, causing her to lose her balance. She bent her knees and collapsed beside Geneva.

"I don't know what you're talking about, Geneva. You aren't making any sense."

"The Tribulation. The Rapture! The people are all gone, and we're still here. Don't you get it? Duncan was showering before bedtime. I saw him go into the bathroom, but he never came out. The water just kept running, running, running, till I went in . . . and he was gone." Geneva rubbed her head, further tangling the hair. Her jeans were covered with lint and dust. "As quickly as I turned on the ten o'clock news and saw those tragedies occurring, I knew it was the Rapture. I never felt so sick in all my life. They'll make us take the mark of the Beast. If we refuse, they'll torture us. I've been hiding under the bed all night."

"That would explain the lint and dirt," mused Emerald, picking at the hair. Geneva slapped at Emerald's hand.

"Stop! I have to think. Where can we go? They'll be here soon. Search our houses. Trick us into worshiping the Antichrist. Wait!" Geneva backed up quickly. With her back against the parlor wall, she screamed, then covered her mouth with her dirty hands. Fright in her eyes, she staggered to her feet. "The Revelation," she said, "friends will betray me. You're not my friend. You're too calm. One of them. I thought I was all alone, then I found you. But I'd be better off alone."

"Geneva, sit down. You need some rest. Something to eat, too." But Emerald's voice trailed behind Geneva, who shot out the door as suddenly as she had entered it. She was gone into the woods, across the road, and quickly vanished.

The television screen presented a montage of wrecks, rioting crowds, closed churches, and businesses being looted. She needed to calm down and collect her thoughts. First Rose. Then Tracy. Gone. Now Geneva was gone, too, though delirium was her exit. Emerald determined to put all this into perspective and get her life back to normal. A sickening pang of nausea made her realize, for the first time since this chaos began, that things would never be back to normal. The way in which she lived in normality no longer existed. Even if she later discovered that somehow she had been dreaming all this, the nightmare would haunt her forever. She would never forget the confusion and hopelessness she now felt. But the tortured words which Geneva had spoken disquieted Emerald more than anything. *Who* will be here? she wondered. What in the world was the mark of the Beast they will make us take? And what was the Antichrist Geneva insisted we would have to worship?

Glancing at the screen, Emerald saw a local clergyman smile consolingly. Occasionally on Sundays, Emerald had tuned-in to the program for company as she cleared the dining room table and did breakfast dishes. This man had such a kind, sincere voice that, although Emerald was agitated at the sight of his overly-gesturing hands and she rarely listened to his words, his voice was soothing. She now adjusted the volume and knelt beside the set.

"Peace be unto you, my friends. Many of you out there today are hurting. Many of you are confused. Much has happened in your lives and you think you can't cope. My beloved, I love you. God loves you. He wants to give you his peace during these chaotic times. For the next few weeks, my staff and I will offer around-the-clock counseling at our church located at the address listed on your screen. You also see our telephone number, manned by operators at this very moment. It is God's desire that you understand the events of the past several hours, and he would that you know his plan for your future, the future of the nation, and of our world. We are arriving at a New World Order, however confusing the onset may appear. Call for an appointment, or plan to visit one of our regularly scheduled fellowships. And remember, at the Universal Church, we care about you — you must do the same."

That was the first comforting discourse she had heard since last evening. Sven had told her everything would soon be all right. But somehow his smugness had conveyed to Emerald that he wasn't concerned that Rose was even missing. Perhaps she would go to a meeting at the Universal Church. They obviously cared about people. A ten-minute drive would put her in touch with this compassionate clergyman she had admired so often. And, hopefully, he could supply some answers.

For the immediate present, I should be doing something, she thought. I can't sit before this television all day. The faces, the cities, and the counties were different, but the events were the same. Devastation, suicide, panic, all results of millions of people disappearing. She couldn't tolerate another moment of it. As she reached for the knob to shut off the broadcast, Gregory Svenson's face appeared, along with the faces of dozens of other men and women. In the center of the group stood the governor. Each man and woman held right hands in the air. Emerald watched as the governor shook each hand in turn, and the camera flashes temporarily blinded the spectators who filled the Blue Room of the State Capitol.

"Mr. Governor, in this landmark event, tell us how you feel about breaking with the system of elections in order to directly appoint twenty-nine new mayors," asked a voice off camera.

"You said it yourself. It is a landmark event, due to the disappearance of twenty-nine incumbent mayors, statewide. We have no time for elections. The peace and safety of the public warrants an emergency situation. I trust these men and women will work closely with me to establish some semblence of normalcy for the cities they represent."

"Do you have a statement, as to exactly what has been the fate of our missing friends and family members?"

"The situation is being looked into very carefully. I have appointed a thirteen-member task force to collect information and they will give me an action plan."

"When can the citizens of Washington expect to know more?"

"As I said, our task force will work on it. But all over the state the Red Cross and other organizations and churches have set up crisis intervention centers. These CIC locations may be obtained by calling the Capitol Straightline."

He became mayor after all, thought Emerald. Congratulations, Mr. Svenson. Rose would be proud of you. If she were here, she would be Mrs. Gregory Svenson, First Lady of Everett, Washington, if there is such a title. She doubted if the mayor's wife is really called the first lady, but it was an impressive thought for her late sister-in-law's status.

The excitement of the political news diminished. Emerald stood in the center of the parlor, at a loss for what to do at this moment. Her life was on hold. Instantly she realized she hadn't thought of Raylon in a few days. The Convergence of Enlightenment had taken up her thoughts, then Rose's illness. Now the disappearances. Ray's face flashed before her now, yet she dismissed him from her mind. If he couldn't communicate to her what she should have done about keeping or selling the inn, she felt he surely couldn't lend insight into this obviously more serious situation. For the first time, she resented him for hanging about, filling her thoughts. You're dead, she thought. "You're dead," she spoke sharply. "Go to wherever it is you're supposed to be. You don't have any unfinished business at Emerald Thorn Inn!"

Emerald's eyes were drawn to the floor. Behind the coatrack in the corner, she caught sight of the newspaper she had tossed there when returning from the hospital that evening so long ago. It was the paper from the evening before the disappearances; there would be no chaos in that piece of journalism, she told herself as she rolled the rubber band into her hand. The paper had dried thoroughly in its rolled-up state and rebelled at being flattened. Several times it sprang shut against her efforts before Emerald forced it to remain flat. She spread the large sheets of print about the dining room table, as she carefully separated the pages to avoid tearing them.

She first read the grocer's ad. Tomatoes: a dollar and fifty-nine cents per pound. Down from last week, but still drastically more than the pre-Desert Storm days and subsequent aftermath. She failed to realize why everything from toothpicks to mouthwash had increased in price after the madman, Saddam Hussein, burned Iraqi oil fields. Emerald knew she could do without tomatoes, at that price. Perhaps she could make it back to Everett and find less expensive produce at that charming fruit stand. She wondered, in passing, what had happened to the flirtatious salesboy and the owners of the open-air market. The news section of the paper boasted of a new system of accounting which had been utilized successfully in several states. Cards which had previously been used only to access one's bank funds via automatic teller machines were now making grocery shopping simpler. Consumers were allowed to present their ATM cards, instantly being approved for payment of their purchases — the funds being directly transferred to their local grocer — and all with the wave of a laser scanner. The article continued that the concept had been adopted by the Washington State Ferry System to eliminate the long wait and inconvenience of payment at the ferry gates. Frequent ferry travelers may now purchase a decal for their front car bumper which will be read by cameras situated at strategic points along both the interstates and ferry ports. Not only will users have immediate access to the ferry system without flashing any cash, but the system will be instrumental in locating drug traffickers whose licenses, safety inspection stickers, and license plates have expired. Other lawbreakers, such as those driving without insurance, failing to buckle seatbelts, and anyone caught littering, could be more easily apprehended by the secretive cameras.

Another infringement on our freedom, steamed Emerald. Wasn't it enough that already the state police set up random checkpoints along the interstates to check for proof of insurance? Now cameras will document on tape the travelers who take the ferries and drivers on the highways. The motive being, according to the article, the safety and peace of the citizens of Washington State. Revenue enhancement was more likely, she thought. As well as control of the people. Emerald felt more of her freedom jerked from beneath her feet. Her choices would be to drive the interstate and be recorded on tape, or avoid driving to avoid being recorded. Either way, she will have lost freedom of movement. She would just have to consider what it all meant. Considering she was already a lawbreaker in her refusal to wear a seatbelt, one more offense, in the name of real freedom, wouldn't bother her conscience.

The editorial section was more than its usual tiny blurb. It covered nearly the entire page. The article, "Occultism Envelops Port Orchard," was subtitled "The Old New Age." Emerald began reading, the lead-in immediately grasping her attention.

> *There are as many philosophies for living life as there are people living it. Whatever direction you take, chances are you are not the only person taking that particular route to spiritual enlightenment. Paul Zuromski, editor of* Body, Mind, And Soul *magazine states, 'You are participating in a revolution of consciousness. The goal is an understanding of who you are, learning why you are here, and exercising your unlimited potential in this lifetime' (Paul Zuromski,* New Age Catalog, *1988, Foreword). His publication exists to help readers sort out and understand New Age trends and ideas. Product reviews, illustrations, and ordering instructions for services, products, literature, and music fill the 240-page resource book. Topics include channeling, crystal power, mind technology, and UFOs, to list a few. Weaving them tightly together, the New Age thread runs through each of these and sixty other listed philosophies, teachings, and techniques.*
>
> *Nestled in the city of Everett is a shop,*

Answer In The Wind, which boasts itself as a New Age Shopping Experience. This shop supplies occultic literature and paraphernalia necessary in the practice of witchcraft, satanism, and all other occultic activities addressed in the catalog.

Numerous church groups call themselves Christian, while encompassing New Age thought. They believe the Holy Bible to be only one book and source of inspiration among many. They contend that Jesus was just another teacher among many masters. The Apostle John said in 1 John 2:22, 'Who is a liar, but he that denieth that Jesus is the Christ? He is antichrist, that denieth the Father and the Son.'

This very week, thousands of New Age believers are gathered to celebrate the Convergence of Enlightenment. Port Orchard's own Universal Church is among the sponsors and locations of the statewide conference. Participants believe there is a power in the cosmos which is standing by to penetrate the earth and heal all environmental ailments. It will not only bring about peace, but will bestow immortality on the planet's occupants.

The New Age movement is a concerted effort to force changes on the earth which will bring about worldwide economic stability, feed the world's hungry, evoke a loving sense of brotherhood in the form of a One World Order; collectively man will link up with the consciousness of the universal mind and usher in the cosmic power that will change this planet forever.

But to devout New Agers, Christians are this planet's negative force which hinders planetary harmony. Christians, including this writer, have specific convictions and attitudes toward what we call sin and the need for all of humanity to be redeemed from that sin; thusly, Christians have created and continue to nurture a division of the planet, according to New Agers. And because unity is imperative for peace, a specific item on the New Age agenda involves eliminating the Christian population.

If killing these individuals is necessary, so be it. But the New Age believers trust that a planetary shift will occur, merely extricating Christian souls from the face of the earth. Those aware of the plan use various terms such as 'purify' or 'cleanse' the earth, or 'eradicate the problem individuals' to describe the main event of the New Age. I realize that 'to eliminate' seems like an uncivilized thing to do to people in the final decade of this modern century, but, '. . . The souls who helped bring the chaos of the present century will have passed into spirit to rethink their attitudes. . . . Millions will survive, millions won't. Those that won't will go into the spirit state, for there truly is no death' (Threshold To Tomorrow, *Ruth Montgomery, 1982, pp. 196-207).*

The fact that the New Age boasts 'there is truly no death,' indicates they are willing to condone murder in the name of planetary harmony. The New Age plan is authored by the teller of the original lie devised to separate man from God in the Garden of Eden over six thousand years ago. Even then, Satan was telling man he would not surely die, but would become like God. Men and women are still being deceived by the LIE.

The New Age lie is a threat to the souls of mankind. Each day the momentum of the New Age movement accelerates. It is at our doorstep. New Age advocates have infiltrated every occupation and seemingly harmless cause in existence. Even the area of religion, despite separation of church and state, has been polluted.

Gregory Svenson, currently a candidate for mayor of the city of Everett, was a recent speaker at the Convergence of Enlightenment, teaching on the 'Magick Of Sexuality In The New Age.' This exposé is a call to the Christian community and all those who believe in freedom of religion in this country. We must be aware of our politicians' world views. This is also a call to citizens of Everett to vote against Gregory Svenson, self-professing New Age practitioner. For according to the above biblical scriptures, Gregory Svenson, by embracing the New Age world view, is in possession of (or is possessed by) the spirit of antichrist. Can we afford to elect him at the risk of losing our freedom to practice Christianity?"

— Rose Thorn
Freelance Writer

Emerald quickly tore the article out of the paper. Mr. Sands and Sanguine, from Answer In The Wind, certainly didn't appear to be occultists. Occultists were secretive, black-clad, evil people. There couldn't be a correlation between them and the New Age. Emerald's hands trembled. I can't believe it, she thought. She wondered if Mr. Svenson had seen this article. If so, he hadn't mentioned it to her at the hospital. If he had not, it didn't matter now. Rose's call for the citizens of Everett to vote against Mr. Svenson had been in vain. He had been given the position, despite his world view.

Rose's attempt at exposure had probably worked in Gregory's behalf. It would have, if all she had said was true about him and the New Age. If it were accurate information, and she knew it was because of his involvement at the conference, he had been hand-picked *because* of his views. They had obviously come to light by some prominent circle before the running of the article. Hadn't Sven, himself, told Emerald that the disappearances were a result of a planetary shift? She hadn't understood it then; she didn't fully understand it now. But if the only people left are New Agers and those ignorant of their plan, the coming days and months will be a conglomeration of excited anticipation and fearful anxiety.

The question of what the world would be like without Christians was an interesting and frightening one. The contents of the article freshly caused her convulsively to shiver. Rose, Tracy, and other Christians were harmless people. Especially Rose. She had been a Christian barely long enough to qualify for the title. What real threat could they have posed to the New Age movement and people like Gregory Svenson?

No, it was impossible. This whole idea of people being drawn out of the planet by some cosmic force, so their negative attitudes could be rethought, was uncomprehensible. There had to be some better explanation. She only wished she knew what the explanation could be. Geneva's delirium could be contagious if this mystery were not solved soon.

Frightened and confused, Emerald didn't refold the paper, but left it scattered about the table. She folded Rose's article and placed it in the pocket of her skirt.

Each creak of the boards as she ascended the stairs echoed the realism that she was now alone. The nauseous emptiness she had first experienced when Hank Phelps explained that patients were missing had become a familiar symptom of her bewilderment. All of Geneva's panic over the Rapture, Tribulation, and Revelation brought back well-hidden memories of her youthful church days. Reaching the door to Rose's room, her stomach jumped. Compelled to open the door, yet frightened to do so, Emerald debated. If she opened the door, she would be forced to see the room empty of its occupant. Emerald would have to confront the truth, once and for all, that Rose was gone and would not occupy the room again. This had to be a dream. A terrible trick of her mind. Courage intensified in almost unnoticeable increments. With it, Emerald turned the knob. The door opened violently, startling Emerald. She gasped. Then, seeing the lacy curtains flutter about the French doors, she realized a draft had sucked the door open. She crossed the room and latched the doors.

The bed, cluttered with tapes, books, and papers looked as though Rose had merely taken a break from her research and would momentarily return to her tasks. Emerald knew she wouldn't. Not wanting to violate Rose's belongings, but feeling a compulsion to put things in order, which she admitted might help her work through her grief, she approached the clutter and began categorizing.

Papers were straightened into piles and placed on the highboy. She read the titles of the books. These are the last things Rose had read. She had studied them carefully in order to write her last article. Carefully, Emerald placed them on the bookshelf.

Gathering pencils and erasers, she opened the drawer to the nightstand. There, beside a crystal necklace, a tape caught her eye. *What To Do If You Miss The Rapture.* She read the label several times. Instinctively, she lowered herself to sit on the bed and grasped her stomach. "What to do if you miss the Rapture?" she whispered. Geneva wasn't off track with her panic. Emerald suddenly knew that she had missed this Rapture, whatever it was. Rose had known it would occur and had been ready for it. She had disappeared in the Rapture.

The tape grew moist with the perspiration of Emerald's palm. Snatches of torment had spewed from Geneva's mouth earlier today. Seven years of torture. They would be coming to get us. What had she meant? The tape might tell her. Emerald was drawn to listen to it. Right now, she thought. But fear of what she might hear held her back. She tucked the tape into her skirt pocket beside the news article.

Quickly she descended the stairs. Gathering her purse and sweater, she walked briskly, her shoes clinkily echoing across the floor. In the car, she turned the key, backed out of the car house, and proceeded to the

Universal Church.

No more speculation, she scolded herself. Quit putting yourself through this. Get some help. After all, she thought, this is crisis intervention. If this isn't a crisis, what is? With that, the car turned onto the street in front of the church. Hundreds of people were crowded onto its steps. A traffic policeman was directing her to bypass the parking lot. Emerald rolled down the window. The officer approached the car.

"If you don't have an appointment, go around, lady."

"But I've come to visit with a counselor," she pleaded.

"Yeah. You and the rest of the township. If you live around here, call for an appointment and walk over. There's no parking for miles. Just get out of here for now." He waved his arms and Emerald drove despondently home.

In her bedroom, she sat nervously fingering the play button of the cassette player. She had inserted new batteries. Twice she had checked to make sure the cassette was rewound to the lead tape. All set. For several moments she stared at the button. She stood and brushed the wrinkles from her skirt. Situating herself, once more, she sat on the end of the bed, but bounced up to reposition the cassette player on the nightstand. Emerald arranged her clothes about her as she now moved to the chaise lounge. Convincing herself that no furniture or bodily position upon it could relieve her tension, she felt faint at the thought of pushing that button.

When she could postpone it no longer, the button was depressed. A man's soothing, yet stern, voice announced, "What to do if you miss the Rapture." Emerald's worst fears were confirmed as she tearfully listened.

Chapter Seventeen

Deja Vu

"There is going to be a Rapture. Jesus Christ is coming back to this earth to catch away those people who are watching and waiting for him. In the Bible, which is the inspired Word of God, Jesus says in John 14:2-3: '. . . I go to prepare a place for you. And if I go and prepare a place for you, I will come again, and receive you unto myself; that where I am, there ye may be also.'

"First Thessalonians 4:16-17 reveals, 'For the Lord himself shall descend from heaven with a shout, with the voice of the archangel, and with the trump of God: and the dead in Christ shall rise first: Then we which are alive and remain shall be caught up together with them in the clouds, to meet the Lord in the air: and so shall we ever be with the Lord.'

"The apostles promised this thing called the Rapture. Not only did Jesus proclaim it, and the apostles predict it, the angels prophesied about it. In Acts chapter one, two angels appeared to the disciples just after Jesus ascended to heaven. And while they were yet looking at the place where they saw Jesus go away and disappear into the heavenlies, these two angels in shining apparel said unto them, 'Ye men of God, why gaze ye thus into the heavens? This same Jesus that you saw go away shall so come in like manner.' Even the angels preached this message and prophesied that Jesus would come back again and his people would be caught away to be with him.

"There *is* going to be a Rapture. It could occur at any moment. I believe that this momentous event is going to happen very soon. Anointed ministers are preaching it. Millions of Christians are looking for it. All the signs of the times point to it. The Holy Spirit, through his gifts to the church, is proclaiming it. You can believe it or not, but everything points to the fact that Jesus Christ is soon coming back in rapturing power. He's returning for those who look for him, those who are ready and waiting for his glorious appearing.

"Not only is Jesus Christ coming again, millions are going to disappear from earth in the twinkling of an eye. The most shocking event in human history is soon to take place. Nothing will create the stir that the return of Jesus to collect his Bride is going to create when those consecrated Christians have disappeared. First Corinthians 15:51-53 tells the story. 'Behold I show you a mystery. We shall not all sleep [die], but we shall all be changed, in a moment, in the twinkling of an eye at the last trump. For the trumpet shall sound and the dead shall be raised incorruptible and we shall be changed. For this corruptible must put on incorruption. This mortal must put on immortality.' Mark it down. It is going to happen.

"The Bible says the dead in Christ shall rise first. That means those whose bodies are in the graves will come out. Their spirits will be reunited with glorified bodies. And then we which are alive and remain, meaning you and me, will rise to meet Jesus in the clouds. If we should happen to be sitting in this church building, as I minister and make this tape, and the trumpet sounds,

Jesus would appear in the atmosphere above this earth. You would all notice that people from all over this congregation would suddenly disappear. And we're not going to leave a hole when we go through the ceiling. You may think this sounds weird, but it is the promise of God.

"Can you imagine the devastating effect that the disappearance of millions is going to have upon this earth? Planes will veer off their courses, because when Jesus calls away his chosen, the pilot who sits at the controls — if he is a believer — is going to leave that cockpit. These are realities I am speaking. Planes are going to crash. Trains will continue down the track without an engineer, because he has suddenly gone to be with the Lord. Cars, buses, and ships will collide as they are instantly unmanned.

"Wives will disappear from beside their husbands. Babies will vanish from their cribs. Every child and every born-again Christian on this earth will leave this planet and take a space trip with Jesus. Something *that* momentous cannot occur without causing devastating effects upon the thinking of those left behind. The governments of the world will be quickly reorganized in order to control the chaos and panic of the earth's occupants.

"Vast multitudes will be left upon this earth, because they were not spiritually ready to go with Jesus at the Rapture. Every sinner will be left behind with all the careless, sinning church members who did not have the blood of Jesus covering their transgressions. It is not everyone who cries, 'Lord, Lord,' that will go. Only those who are doing the will of the Heavenly Father. Believe me when I tell you this.

"You can be forgiven by God and be ready to go. Jesus *is* coming back after those who look for him and have on the pure wedding garment. No one on earth may know of your secret sin, but God knows. Such doers of sin will not enter the kingdom of God. They will not be taken in the Rapture.

"You must know that for a period of time after the Rapture there will be no born-again Christians on this earth. You think on that momentarily. That's why this taped message is so vitally important. There will be no preachers of God's Word to accurately tell the public what has happened.

"I've been told that the biggest headline print in the news business is known as 'Second Coming Print.' They are reserving this print in order to roll headlines bigger than world wars. This print will be larger than that boasting 'WAR ENDS' following the 1991 Persian Gulf conflict. Headlines will scream, 'MILLIONS DISAPPEAR.' If you are still on this earth when that news story breaks, you must now realize that you have missed the most important event of history. You have missed the Rapture of the Church. The millions of missing people are, in fact, with Jesus Christ in heaven, safe from what is to come for you during the seven-year Tribulation period. I tell you that very plainly, because for some of you listening to this tape right now, this event has already taken place. The governments of the world are going to be telling you all sorts of explanations about what has happened; none will be the truth, because no Christian broadcasters or journalists remain on the earth to write the truth. I don't tell you this to frighten you, but to warn you of the facts.

"The forces of evil are going to try to convince you of all kinds of things. They are going to tell you that the people went off in flying saucers or that they are hiding out. Others will tell you the planet has undergone a cleansing and can now become perfect. You may be nodding your head in confirmation, because you have already heard these New Age lies from Satan. Don't believe them. When you hear the story that millions of people have disappeared, then *know* that the Rapture of the Church has taken place, and you missed it."

Chapter Eighteen

What To Do If You Miss The Rapture

Emerald sank deeply into the chaise. She covered her head with her hands. All those who disappeared are in heaven with Jesus Christ? Oh, dear God, her soul cried. It must be true, for only God could be responsible for something so spectacular, yet tragic. She clutched her chest, aching with tension. She had missed the Rapture.

Her fingers reached to turn off the tape just as the man's voice pleaded, "Don't stop this tape out of desperation. There is still hope. Continue listening for instructions."

"Instructions?" Emerald questioned him. She depressed the stop button and found her pen in her purse. Opening a steno pad, she began writing the man's words. When he got too far ahead, she depressed the stop button to enable herself to catch up. At these times she wished she had passed high school shorthand. The tape finished playing side one. Eager to hear it all, she flipped to side two, frantically scratching her notes. At the tape's conclusion, she put a fresh ribbon in Rose's typewriter, typed the notes, and exhaustedly read her transcript:

Don't panic. *There is still hope. Though*

preachers have tried to scare people into the kingdom of God by telling them there is no hope if you miss the Rapture, that is not true, according to Scripture. However, if it is so difficult for people to live by God's will before the Rapture, the trials to follow will be unbelievably more difficult. But you CAN make it, by the grace of God. Satan capitalizes on fear, and if you get scared, he will attempt to cause you to commit suicide, or to hate and blaspheme God. Don't do it. Do not believe Satan's lie that it is too late for you to be saved.

Get your heart right with God. *Time is short. Act quickly. Salvation is your faith in Jesus Christ as the Son of God. You must have faith in your heart and confess Jesus Christ with your mouth, which may cost you your life. Following is a prayer, which when prayed with a sincere heart, will lead you to salvation. The words don't have to match exactly as I speak them; God knows your heart's intent.*

Heavenly Father, I believe that Jesus is the Son of God. He came to this earth and shed his blood on the cross for my sins. I know that he was put in a grave and on the third day he rose again. I believe that he is a resurrected Lord and that he lives forever. I ask you, Lord God, to forgive me of my sins. I confess that Jesus Christ is my Savior and Lord. I will live for him; if need be, I will die for him. I confess now that I am a child of God, a Christian. Amen.

Now, to assure yourself of the importance

of your salvation, and the fact that you are truly a Christian, and to verify that God has saved you — even though you have missed the Rapture — turn to Revelation chapter seven in the Bible. You will read that one hundred forty-four thousand (144,000) Israelites will be saved during the Tribulation period, but more importantly to you, you will learn that a multitude from all nations, all kindred, all people, and all languages washed their robes white in the blood of the Lamb and were saved. They will go to heaven out of the Great Tribulation. This multitude includes you! Believe it. You've accepted Jesus Christ as your Savior. You may not feel any differently, but don't let Satan tell you that you aren't saved. Hold onto Jesus, at all cost.

Pray without ceasing. *Live in an attitude of prayer. You will need all the strength you can receive from God. Nothing else matters anymore. The Tribulation lasts only seven years. Count backward to the Rapture, and you will know where you now stand in the seven-year period. The Bible promises that he that endures until the end will be saved.*

Round up all the Bibles you can find. *The Word of God will soon be confiscated and destroyed by government officials. So, gather up all you can find. Keep one for yourself, hide one away, and distribute the others quickly.*

Read carefully the Old Testament book of Daniel, the New Testament book of Revelation, and the remaining New Testament. *You may* *not be familiar with the Bible at all. All scripture was given by Divine inspiration and is the Word of God. You must take each word literally. In the New Testament carefully read Matthew chapter twenty-four and Luke chapter twenty-one. The things you read therein will help you understand the things that are going on in the world and give you further instructions. Read the New Testament every day, until you have read it through, underlining the things that impress you, for the Holy Spirit will help teach you what you must know. Keep reading the Bible every day. It is your source of spiritual food. Commit its verses to memory, as much as possible, especially verses that comfort you. They will be your source of strength during the terrible times ahead, and their memory will sustain you when Bibles have vanished from existence.*

Share this tape with your trusted friends, *leading them to become Christians, as you have done. Reproduce the tape, if possible. Hide some copies away and quickly distribute the remainder. Soon they will be confiscated and destroyed.*

Find other people who have become Christians, *so you may have mutual worship and encouragement. Worship in a secret place. Be wary of those you invite to your meetings. Screen them carefully, because government agents will infiltrate your group so that they may arrest and execute the undesirable Christian influence. Be as wise as a serpent and as harmless as a dove; pray the Holy Spirit's* *guidance in selecting companions.*

Be prepared to be betrayed by some who seem to be your friends. *Love your enemies, even those who take your life. Love them through Jesus, your Savior. Also, be prepared to be harrassed, hated, hunted, persecuted, imprisoned, tortured, beaten, and murdered. No matter how bad it gets, do not renounce Jesus Christ, for as bad as all this sounds, it is mild compared to the reward awaiting those who do not receive Jesus, or renounce their Christianity. Probably the sooner you are killed, the more quickly you will be with Jesus in heaven and be delivered out of the Tribulation.*

Expect great earthquakes, terrible famine, nuclear war, fearsome storms, and abnormal occurrences of nature. *Get out of the big cities into the countryside, for there will be nuclear war and half the people of earth will die, most of them in the cities. Stars will fall, the heavens will be shaken, the seas will roar with great tidal waves, the water of the earth will turn to blood. The Scriptures alert us to the signs in the heavens and the devastation of the earth. It will be the most fearsome time in all human history. It won't be easy to endure, but keep your faith in Jesus.*

The Antichrist will appear to bring about peace after the Rapture. *He will become the leading man of power in the entire world. You will know him when he arises. He will be influential, known worldwide for his intelligence and charismatic personality. He is Antichrist.*

He will make an alliance with Israel. He will have great military power. Antichrist will claim to be a man of peace, but he is your mortal enemy. The Scriptures tell us that he will set up his headquarters in Jerusalem at mid-Tribulation. Serving him will cost you not only your life, but your eternal soul. Read Daniel chapters seven, eight, and eleven, as well as Revelation chapters thirteen, fourteen, and seventeen. These chapters give information about this man called Antichrist.

The mark of the Beast. *Under no circumstances are you to receive the number of this world ruler, which is identified in the scriptures as 666. The mark will be administered in the hand or forehead of every individual. For reference, read Revelation 14:9-11. Get ready, for you will be told it is against the law for you not to receive the mark. You cannot buy or sell anything without it. Much speculation surrounds the mark's exact appearance; it could be a tattoo, a brand, an electronic under-the-skin implant, or another innovation not yet in existence at this taping. Its actual description and administration are mere technicalities, as the mark itself is an absolute. Its administration will be the inception of a method of monitoring all those bearing the mark, via a massive — beastly — computer system already in operation in Europe. To reject it will cost your life, but will save your soul. All those who receive the mark of the Beast will be tortured by hideous creatures who will be released, temporarily, from the pits of hell.*

One World Religion. *Do not join or trust the world religion that everyone is asked to join. Participation in it will result in everlasting hell. It is a conglomeration of Eastern philosophy, New Age thought, occultism, witchcraft, humanism, and satanism. It will involve worshiping the Antichrist and his image as though he is God. Failure to worship the image that the Antichrist will have made of himself will result in your execution. This image will have the ability to speak and he will require worship of all people. After this ruler breaks his alliance with Jerusalem, he will place his image in the temple at Jerusalem where it will be worshiped as God. When this takes place, you will be mid-way through the Tribulation. Jesus himself called this worship of the image the abomination of desolation.*

Don't be deceived by the miracles worked by the Antichrist or his false prophet. These will be the ministers of the one world religion. Great pressure will be put on you to accept this man as being God, and his miracles are intended to persuade the world of his godhood, but his power is from Satan.

Satanic power will be stronger on earth now than at any other time in history. *Sin and perversion will be rampant. Do not become part of the homosexuality, drug abuse, witchcraft, and demon worship (also known as spirit channeling) that will be widespread. Keep yourself pure in the presence of Jesus.*

Now that you are a Christian, expect the most terrible times of your life. *If you are to have eternal life, you must be true to Jesus Christ. You will be required to die for Christ, unless you elude the Antichrist until the end of the Tribulation. Losing one's life for Jesus will earn you eternal life in heaven. Revelation 20:4 says, ". . . and I [the Apostle John] saw the souls of them that were beheaded for the witness of Jesus, and for the word of God, and which had not worshipped the beast, neither his image, neither had received his mark upon their foreheads, or in their hands; and they lived and reigned with Christ a thousand years." This refers to the thousand years on earth following the Battle of Armageddon. Satan will be bound and cast into the bottomless pit of hell for this amount of time. For that thousand years there will be peace on this earth, under the reign of Jesus Christ, himself.*

The book of Revelation is specific about the events following the Tribulation. But a victory during the Tribulation will result in the description given in Revelation 15:2, "And I saw as it were a sea of glass mingled with fire: and them that had gotten the victory over the beast, and over his image, and over his mark, and over the number of his name, stand on the sea of glass, having harps of God." In this scene, the Apostle John sees the overcomers in heaven, for they have refused the mark of the Beast and have failed to worship the Antichrist and his image, although it cost them their lives. You, likewise, must stand in faith. Every possible pressure will be brought to bear upon you. You could be tortured to the point of insanity or death. But remain faithful; the grace of God will sustain you. Death will be a glorious release for you to be in the presence of Jesus.

Remember that we Christians, who have gone before you in the Rapture, love you and want you to succeed. *If we didn't believe that the Bible teaches there is a possibility of escape from the Tribulation, Christians would not have taken the time to duplicate this tape in order for it to find its way into your hands.*

In summary. *I realize that what you are hearing on this tape is frightening. It sounds bad, because it is bad. I can't express some of the horrors the world will be faced with. But I want you to be prepared for what is coming so you can withstand the evil one and receive everlasting life through faith in our Lord and Savior, Jesus Christ.*

Once more, if you are listening to this tape and you have missed the Rapture, you absolutely MUST accept Jesus Christ. If you have not done so, pray with me, right now, this sinner's prayer: Heavenly Father God. Holy is your name. I believe that Jesus is the Son of God; I believe in my heart that Jesus is the Christ and died for me. He shed his blood on the cross so that my sins could be forgiven. I repent of those sins. I turn away from them, and I hold to Jesus

Christ, only, as my source of forgiveness and salvation. So come into my heart, Jesus. Cleanse me of every sin, as I confess with my mouth that Jesus Christ is my Savior. He is my Lord. I'm going to live for Him the rest of my life. I confess that I am saved. I am now a Christian. Give me strength, Heavenly Father, to endure what I must and keep me by your power. In Jesus' name I pray, Amen.

Chapter Nineteen

The Beginning Of The End

The sinner's prayer haunted Emerald. She was compelled to turn the machine back on and repeat the prayer after the minister. But, a sinner? It was difficult for her to consider herself in that category she had reserved for such low-lifes as alcoholics, sexual deviants, murderers, and politicians. No, absolutely not. She had never actually asked Jesus into her life, but she had not committed any actual sin, either. She had debated the subject of sin with Rose recently, but had been insulted at her sister-in-law's insistance that there was a natural state of being a sinner.

Interrupting her thoughts, the phone rang. Emerald darted downstairs, grabbing the phone before the third ring.

"Hello," she announced, "Emerald Thorn Inn."

"Mrs. Thorn?" came the man's voice.

"Yes, this is Mrs. Thorn."

"Grant Sands, owner of Answer In The Wind." This was the one person Emerald did not anticipate hearing from. Since her desire to discern Raylon's plans had dissolved, she had not considered a return to the New Age shop.

"Yes, Mr. Sands. How can I help you?"

"I was going through my customer records, giving all

our clients a call."

"Well, I am hardly a client."

"But a valued customer. How are you, Mrs. Thorn?"

"I'm doing very well, Mr. Sands."

"Wonderful. I know it may sound odd, but in view of the recent earth evacuation, I was checking to see if you were among the missing."

"No, Mr. Sands."

"Good to hear that you are safe. While I have you on the line, I would like to tell you about a sale we are beginning. Forty percent off on everything in the store, this month only."

"And why this particular month?"

"Isn't it apparent? It has occurred to my staff and I that the planetary shift has taken place. Since spiritual activity is at its peak, we agreed it would benefit practitioners and novices, alike, for us to discount supplies and literature. That brings me to ask, how are you doing with your tea leaf reading?"

"I haven't given it much thought the last day or so."

"You must have lost a loved one in the shift?"

"Mr. Sands, this call is long distance. I'm sure you have others to call."

"Before I hang up, I'd like to invite you into the store. Just call for an appointment if a consultation becomes necessary. We would like to make sure everyone adjusts as quickly as possible. Our planet's peace and safety depends on it."

"Now that Christians are out of the way, peace is imminent?"

"Precisely! Now there are no holds barred. Our planet's occupants are free of narrow-minded insistance that we all experience spiritual fulfillment via a personal savior. Of course, you and I know *that* philosophy was a cop-out for those people too cowardly to pursue the cosmic force as it really is."

"Mr. Sands, you are long distance."

"Of course. I'll star your name on the mailing list to make sure you get information about future sales."

"Thank you, Mr. Sands. That won't be necessary. Goodbye." Surprising herself, Emerald slammed the receiver down. She returned quickly to her room and sat on the floor beside the chaise. Pushing the play button, Emerald repeated the prayer at the compassionate voice's leading. She played it twice more, awaiting some sort of emotional tidal wave to sweep her body. When nothing happened, she listened once again, saying the words with the minister and meaning each one with quiet intensity. This man, just as Rose had been, was personally concerned for her soul. Emerald's tears slipped softly onto her lap. Why else, she thought, would he have risked certain ridicule in making such a tape. A tape which, just one week earlier, she would have dismissed as either a joke or the work of a religious crackpot. Several times more she played the prayer, until she knew in her spirit that she was really a Christian.

Evening had crept silently about the inn. The emptiness of the rooms and the darkness sang loneliness to her soul. Emerald walked down the hall, wondering where to find a Bible. In Rose's abandoned room she found a King James Version among the books on the shelf. For several hours she reclined in the chaise, reading each scripture the tape's minister had quoted.

Morning found her resting peacefully. Routinely, she

called her grocer with a small order, then gathering her Bible and the typed notes, across the road she made her way. The walk through the woods to Geneva's house seemed longer as she anticipated her words to the friend who was on the verge of unavoidable collapse.

Geneva did not answer the knock on the door. She's probably hiding under the bed again, Emerald thought, knocking with greater force than her delicate knuckles had ever seen. Still the house appeared deserted. After checking the back and side doors, both locked, she returned to the front of the house.

"Geneva!" she shouted at the door knob. "It's Emerald. Let me in. I have some news to share with you!"

Still no answer from within. The garage was unlocked. Tracy's cat, Mickey, jumped from a rafter onto the hood of Geneva's car.

"Ooh, kitty, you scared me," she said, picking up the cat. "Did your mommy fly off and leave you to fend for yourself?"

The cat meowed and snuggled against Emerald.

"Is Geneva feeding you, sweetie, or have you been catching mice to eat?" Emerald already knew the answer; the cat's ribs protruded. "No one cares about the kitty, huh? You can go home with me. Let's go find Geneva. We'll take her home with us, too."

The ground was soft around the windows. Emerald's heels sank deeply into the wet dirt and moss. She let the cat jump from her arms and tiptoed to look into the high kitchen window. Geneva wasn't there. The draperies in the living room were separated slightly.

Emerald squinted to see through the crack in the drapes. Her eyes took several seconds to adjust to the darkness within the house. "Well, I don't see her anywhere. Let's go home." The cat followed Emerald, continually walking in front of her, winding its tail around her legs. "We will call Geneva after we have had some breakfast." Emerald entered the woods with a distinct feeling that God was going before her. The fear and panic she had felt yesterday were not present in the fresh new day's air.

Mickey lapped milk from a fruit jar lid. Emerald refilled it three times before the cat appeared satisfied. "Mr. Barker," Emerald explained, "said he would put a couple of cans of Fancy Feast onto my grocery order today. I called him just in time. He was about to bring it over. I don't know what we are going to do with you, Mickey. You're a pretty cat, but if you stay in the house, you'll rub hair all over this furniture. We may have to fix you a bed out in the car house."

Hearing a car drive up, Emerald got to her feet. At the kitchen porch Mr. Parker was struggling up the steps.

"Blamed kids!" he shouted, when he set the box on the countertop. "I had five delivery kids. You know the Nelson girl and Fred Henry's boy, Ted? They were both on this route. Them and the others haven't shown up for work since this planetary cleansing stuff began. Good for nothing goof-offs." Mr. Parker rubbed his bald head briskly. "That comes to fifty-four dollars and ninety-three cents, Mrs. Thorn; only a third of your regular order."

"Everything has been affected by this, what did you call it, planetary cleansing?"

"Yep. I went down to the Universal Church last night. Now, I was never a church-going man. All that doctrine and do-this-and-don't-do-that never did set well with me. But this church has been all right in my book since they loosened up the rules. You know, lightened up on us folks who believe there is really no devil out there waiting to stick us with his pitchfork if we mess up a little," he laughed. "They might as well not call that place a church, as far as I'm concerned. None of those tear-jerking hymns and hollering preachers. Just usable, sound information."

"But you called the disappearances a planetary cleansing."

"So I did. Father Pearman, that's the pastor, said that sometimes God, if there is one, has to do something drastic to get our attention. The father explained, last night, that this world has so much hatred toward homosexuals, people of other races, opposing church affiliations, and holders of different philosophical ideas, that there is no way we could ever have had peace. Take the question of whether there is a God. Pastor Pearman leaves that question up to each individual to decide. Anyway, he explained, even quoted from ancient prophecies, that narrow-minded people had been drawn out of the atmosphere because they were intolerant of other people's views."

"How intolerant could children and babies be?"

"Excuse me?"

"Mr. Parker, your delivery kids, all the children of this whole city, of the whole nation, the world's children, are gone. What views where they intolerant of?"

The grocer's palms grew sweaty; he wiped them on his white butcher apron. "I hadn't thought of it, exactly. I'll ask Father Pearman. Now, about your bill."

"Yes, I'll write you a check. Can I get you some coffee while you wait?"

"If you insist," he said. Emerald poured two cups of coffee. She remembered with a twinge of embarrassment that just last week she would have insisted that he drink tea in order that she might read his future in the leaves.

As Emerald wrote out the check, the dining room table vibrated as Mr. Parker tapped nervously. "I'll have to get back to the store before noon. I still have four stops to make. You wouldn't be looking for a part-time job, would you?" he asked.

"No, thank you."

"Just thought I would ask. My wife and I are handling the whole store, since the cleansing. At noon a representative of the cash register company is coming out to fit us for the new checkout system. You've seen the scanners that read the bar codes on packages?"

"Yes, I know what you mean."

"We're the only grocery story in Port Orchard that hasn't converted. Being a mom-and-pop set up, we just felt it was too impersonal to go to a computer system. But, we just can't keep up with business by ourselves. The system will inventory for us, do our ordering, and even do the ordering for our customers."

"How could it do my ordering?"

"Since the inn has an account with us, you'll be assigned a new system number. Each time you ring up with your order, the system will record your purchases. It will then average your first three month's purchases and from then on, we can fill your order without your even calling us up. Just like clockwork, your order will be filled and delivered."

"What if I don't want the same things each month?"

"Let me give you an example, Mrs. Thorn. If, over a

three month period you averaged twelve cans of Del Monte whole green beans in the sixteen ounce size, the system would record that automatically, and that's what your order would contain."

"But what if I needed twenty cans for some reason?"

"You could just call us and we would override the system and ring up a special order."

"I don't think I like a computer telling me how many cans of green beans to buy."

"Trust me, Mrs. Thorn, anything we can use to get things back to normal will be a blessing. You'll get used to it."

Emerald knew she wouldn't get used to it. But she also knew, from listening to the tape, that this was just the beginning of the end.

Chapter Twenty

Escape By Death

Last night Mickey had curled into a heap at Emerald's feet as Em read until nearly dawn. She didn't understand all she read; nevertheless, she found the books of Matthew through John in Rose's Bible to be comforting to her spirit. It was as though while she read she was not alone.

No Port Orchard newspaper had been delivered in over a week. She was unable to reach the paper's office by phone. Backing the car out of the car house, she determined to know the reason why; she drove toward town. Finding a parking meter in front of the *Port Orchard Monitor*, she tried the door. It was locked. A yellow sign taped to the outside of the window read: "This Business For Sale. Inquire At City Hall."

Driving up and down the city's streets, Emerald noticed numerous businesses with similar yellow signs. Out of curiosity she parked at City Hall and mounted the few steps to its doors. A yellow arrow labeled *Inquiries* pointed her down the hall. Being advised by the clerk that these businesses had been taken over by the city of Port Orchard, Emerald listened intently as the clerk explained. Their owners could not be located, thus they were assumed to be among the missing. If Emerald wanted to purchase a business, she was told, she would be allowed to fill out an application and submit a bid. The government, considering the prompt sale of all abandoned property an emergency, was granting loans. She'd be approved, most likely in thirty days. Emerald did not take the application, but thanked the clerk and walked out of the building.

Just like that, she thought. It has only been a week and the government is taking over.

"Emerald!" came a voice from behind her. She turned. Gregory Svenson bounded down the City Hall steps. "I was going to stop by and visit you today."

"Hello, Mr. Svenson. What are you doing in Port Orchard?"

"Just a little business to attend to," he laughed arrogantly, tossing his head back.

"I see."

"May I buy you a cup of coffee?"

"No, thank you. I was out looking for a newspaper. It seems the *Monitor* is closed up. I can't even locate a machine with the *Seattle Times*."

"In the Jeep I've got a week-old copy of the *Times*. If I had known you wanted a paper, I could have brought you today's and one of my own from Everett."

"I'm sure they all say about the same thing these days."

"You may be right, just presented from different slants. Hop in," said Sven, pointing to his vehicle which was parked in the fire lane.

"No. I don't think so, but it was good to see you."

"Mrs. Thorn, I know you don't like me, but if I didn't know different, I would say you were afraid of me."

"Afraid of you? Why ever would I be afraid of man of your flimsy character?"

"Clever. The donut shop is a block over. Meet me there," Sven insisted, then he drove into the light traffic.

Just as quickly he turned into the donut shop's parking lot. Emerald reluctantly steered her car, likewise, and parked beside the Jeep. Emerald could see through the window that Sven was pouring coffee. He held up two fingers to the cashier, who handed him two donuts.

Passing the Jeep, Emerald's heart leapt as she noticed a crack in its windshield. She followed the crack downward. The wiper blade was gone and a concave fender testified of an accident. No paint residue from another car was evident on the noticeable indention.

Inside the shop, Sven arranged coffee, donuts, napkins, and plasticware at a tiny table beside the window. "Creamer?" he asked.

"What?" Emerald was slapped by Sven's voice. "Oh, excuse me. No, I don't use creamer, Nutrasweet, or any other poison."

"You are your same charming self, but you appear to be somewhere else today."

"I don't know how I could be anywhere else. But millions of other people are, aren't they?"

"Oh yes," said Sven, with a forced sound of concern, "the disappearances." He placed a thick *Seattle Times* on the table. "Here's the edition that came off the press the first morning." Gregory pointed out the headlines — so large, they covered half the page — "MILLIONS DISAPPEAR." "Actually, this is old news now. All week the papers have been thicker and more positive," he said.

"Positive in what way?"

"People are getting their lives back in order. Some wonderful changes are in the wings."

"Like Gregory Svenson's appointment as mayor?"

"Yes," smiled Sven. "Since you mention it. I guess

you had to have heard that I was personally selected by the governor. I also was appointed to the task force to develop an action plan for the restoral of order."

Somehow, Emerald was not surprised by this announcement. "I didn't know you drive a Jeep," Emerald blurted out, not knowing why she had done so.

"Jeep? Oh yes. You knew my Jaguar was totalled. Until the insurance pays off, the Jeep is out of retirement. Seems there is a run on insurance claim offices. Did you hear that survivors are trying to claim death benefits on some of the people who disappeared? It's a circus down at AAA. I learned that some people, evidently far more advanced and enlightened than myself, made provision for the shift by adding a clause to their life insurance policies that enable them to leave their estates to surviving family in the event of a mass exodus of souls. Or as Christians used to call it, the Rapture. It's all driving the insurance companies crazy."

"When did you get that dent?" asked Emerald casually.

Sven's eyes searched Emerald's for a hint of her intentions. They scanned her face, her chest for breathing changes, and her hands for nervous twitches. But Emerald calmly continued, "The indentation on your right fender. Was the impact also the cause of the crack in the windshield?"

Sven sipped his coffee and brushed a napkin over his tie. "The Jeep has been in the garage at the paper office since I got the Jag. I was just trying to remember how that dent got there. It isn't really noticeable, is it? I never turned it in to the insurance company because it was so minor."

"You didn't turn it in because AAA would want to know what happened. Surely you haven't forgotten in little over a week the cause of the damage."

"You're right about my not wanting to tell the truth to AAA. I would have to admit to them that I had experienced astral projection while driving down from Mount Baker. When my spirit returned to my body, the Jeep had crashed into a huge aspen tree. Just think of the soaring premiums." Sven shook his head and laughed at his wit.

"I am not sure what Rose saw in you. Something about you, despite your physical attractiveness, is repulsive."

"Oops. I am sorry, Emerald. I apologize. It was a bad analogy. By the way, I recently ran into an acquaintance of yours."

"I don't know that many people who you could possibly know."

"But you do know Grant Sands? He owns a bookstore in Everett."

"Yes, I remember."

"Grant and I dodged the draft together. He made the long years in Canada bearable."

"I see."

"In seriousness, Grant dropped by the paper to have me print up an ad for his shop. Your name was on the mailing list. When I mentioned that I knew you, he shared with me the nature of your visit to him. I hope you don't mind?"

She minded, of course, but to let Gregory Svenson know she objected to his covert meddling would only be a satisfaction to him. "And your opinion of my visit,

Mr. Svenson?" Emerald cooly washed down the donut with the last bit of coffee.

"You are on the right track in my opinion. And since the shift has taken place, spiritual activity is at its peak. This would be an excellent time for you to take the plunge into TM or something more substantial than tea leaf reading."

"How about Christianity?"

Sven smiled coyly. "Now you are telling bad jokes. Christianity is passé. I urge you to take advantage of Grant's services. On the other hand, the Universal Church is offering seminars and counseling. In fact, a well-known channeler will be there tonight. She's great. I've met her on several occasions. Not only is she right on about current cosmic happenings, she predicted the shift, almost to the month. Until you learn how to tap into the universe for yourself, you could benefit from some expert advice."

"Thanks for your own expert advice. I've got to get back home now."

"Do you have guests at the inn?"

"No. Well, not human. I've sort of adopted Tracy's cat, Mickey."

"Tracy? Of course. So do you have any other neighbors left?"

"Geneva, the woman across the road is still here."

"Good. No chance of your becoming a hermit then. I encourage you to take advantage of this time of intense enlightenment. Get involved; the sooner we all get tuned in to our higher selves, the more rapidly we can be united into one peaceful nation under the guidance of one universal mind."

"One world government?"

"Sure. Sounds great, right?"

"There would be no need for mayors and governors if the world were to be run by one world leader."

"There is the slight possibility that my job could be phased out, but the resultant Utopia would negate the need for leaders."

"For your sake, I hope so. But don't count on it. I simply must leave. Get that fender checked out, won't you?" Emerald placed a dollar bill under her coffee cup, "I pay my own way." She felt the satisfaction of knowing that Sven's glare followed her out the door.

At the inn, she flipped the television switch on — more out of the need for noise than information. She was surprised to see a commercial instead of news bulletins or PSA's offering help. The clean-cut man on the screen waved violently as he advanced between the rows of cars.

"Ladies and gentlemen, the biggest sale of the century is taking place right now, here at Terrill's Used Cars," the man said. "Thousands of cars have been repossessed or abandoned as a result of last week's calamity. But bad news is good news at Terrill's. Their loss is your gain!" Holding up posters with prices, the man flung these in various directions as he continued, "New Camaros are selling for three thousand dollars. You heard me. Three thousand smackers. How about your choice of Dodge pickups for one thousand dollars. Any model. Any year. You're not dreaming. We have Buicks. Plymouths. Fords. Mercury. Cadillacs. You name it; we have it. All this year's models for as little as one thousand dollars or the loan payoff, if it is a repo. Our office staff has worked around the clock for a week now, getting these cars catalogued and computerized. Get down to any of our locations, while the selections are magnificent," the man said, smiling.

"Vulture," whispered Emerald, switching the set off. In the kitchen, she opened a can of cat food, snarling her nose at the pungent odor. "If I could get into Tracy's house," she told Mickey, scraping the chunky meat into the cat's dish, "I might find some more cat food. Something less offensive to the server. Besides," she said, "it is not doing you any good locked up in that house." When Mickey finished lunch and had licked himself clean, he stretched lazily and curled up at Emerald's feet. "No nap yet," Emerald scolded. "Let's get over to Tracy's."

The cat followed its new mistress through the woods. Mickey pounced on imaginary prey and rolled in fallen leaves. Approaching Tracy's yard, Mickey darted toward the house, escaping from Emerald's sight.

"Mickey, come back here!" yelled Emerald. "Kitty, kitty." But Mickey did not return. The cat door at the bottom of the front door swung violently as Emerald rounded the driveway. "I don't know how you expect to collect the cat food without my help," said Emerald, trying the doorknob, "unless you're more clever than most cats I know." She could hear Mickey squalling beyond the door. She went from window to window, hoping for an unsecured latch. Mickey followed from within, room to room, jumping onto the sills as Emerald tried each window. "Come on, Mickey. Help me."

Soon Mickey rejoined Emerald in the yard. He traveled in and out of the house through the cat door, as if to convince Emerald to follow. Reluctantly, she knelt before the tiny door. Poking her head inside, she rolled onto her back. Gazing up at the doorknob, she sighed.

There had to be two feet between the cat door and the doorknob. Backing out a bit, Emerald put her arm and shoulder through the hole. She could reach within a stroke of the knob. "What now?" she quizzed Mickey, who meowed from his perch on her hip.

Rethinking her plan, Emerald walked around the yard, looking carefully through the trash burning barrel, fruit house, and car house. When she found an old bicycle innertube, she grinned and ran back to the house. With arm and shoulder successfully through the cat door, Emerald tossed the rubber tube upward. It fell back to her several times, before the rubber finally gripped the slippery metal orb. She tugged on the innertube until she felt the knob turn and heard the lock release.

"Mickey. I think I did it."

Backing out of the hole, Emerald dusted dirt from her clothes and tried the door. Never would she have guessed herself capable of such ingenuity, ingenuity for the purpose of gaining illegal entrance to another person's home, at that. Life, she thought, certainly had changed in one week's time. Emerald knew Tracy wouldn't mind that she had committed her first crime. After all, who else was left to look after Mickey?

Inside the house, Mickey sprinted toward the pantry, rubbing against it with friendly remembrance. Emerald filled a grocery bag with tiny cans of Fancy Feast.

"Mmm. Salmon. Tuna. Chicken. Liver," said Emerald. "There's people food here, too. Vegetables. Mackeral. Red salmon; there is quite a stock of food, Mickey. But I can't carry it all home with me now."

Meowing at every threshold for Tracy, Mickey followed Emerald from room to room as she surveyed the contents. Dust had begun to collect on tables and books. Emerald found several Bibles among the titles.

"I'm sure Tracy won't mind me borrowing these." She placed the Bibles in the sack amid the cans. "Just in case I need something else, I'd better look around. Flashlights, good. Matches. Candles," she said, looking through drawers in the den. "This stuff is easy enough to take now, Mickey. But I've got to figure a way to get back in later. I could leave the door unlocked, but looters would get in," she laughed.

In the bathroom, Emerald climbed onto the toilet seat and stepped upon the tank. She unlatched the window lock and pulled the curtains shut. At the front door, she hoisted the heavy sack onto her hip. Taking one last look, Emerald got a sickening feeling. This could be my last time here, she thought. She didn't know if she would have time to scavenge supplies at a later date. She felt an urgency.

"Tomorrow, Mickey, we'll come back with the car for blankets and canned goods. I may have to drag out my old Girl Scout manual, too. We could be in for some rough times. Come on, kitty," she said, locking the door behind her. "Let's stop at Geneva's."

There was still no answer when Emerald knocked. "How about it, Mickey. Do you know of a secret cat door?" Emerald went to each window, tapping on each. I know she's scared to death, she thought. But together there is hope. The tape had instructed new believers to stick together, encouraging one another in the Lord. Geneva believed the Rapture, not some mysterious cleansing, had taken place. So it shouldn't be hard to convince her that the two of them could overcome the

Tribulation with God's help. Emerald knew that if Geneva was actually afraid of being forced to take the mark of the Beast, she wouldn't answer the door, even to a friend.

When no unlocked window presented itself, Emerald clutched her apron, wrapping it awkwardly around her fist. Then balancing herself on the rock wall that skirted the house she walked along its narrow ledge until she was behind the house, out of possible sight from the road. Gathering her courage and with one powerful blow, Emerald thrust her arm, up to the elbow, through the window.

The scream of shattering glass, the potent, putrid odor, and the realization of what she had done blasted Emerald as her body careened halfway into the house. Mickey meowed, running to the safety of a hollyhock bush. Emerald struggled to regain her footing on the rock wall. Her arm bled profusely and her sinuses rebelled against the stench of death. Rewrapping the apron, she applied pressure to the deep wounds. Covering her mouth and nose with her free hand, she poked her head carefully into the jagged hole. Several feet away, Geneva's lower torso was partially visible, crumpled upon the bathroom floor, from where Emerald viewed.

The body lay in a dark pool of dried blood, crusty patches of which at coagulated at the wrist wounds. Emerald grew nauseous. Jumping from her perch, she ran to the hollyhocks, frightening Mickey from his fortress. When her stomach heaved no more, Emerald sat trembling upon the ground.

Mickey softly padded toward her and curled into her lap. He smelled the blood on her arm and rubbed against her throbbing bosom. For the first time since the Rapture took place, Emerald cried uncontrollably. The tensions and anxiety of this permanent nightmare exploded into sobs, screams, and groanings.

Emerald was thankful she had not seen Geneva's face; she imagined, however, the fear and desperation it must have shown. Geneva had given up too soon. Now Emerald groaned for the lost soul of her friend and for her own total aloneness. God, her spirit cried out, show me your plan for me. Lead me to a safe place and give me the strength to endure.

Numbness was wearing off of her slashed arm. The apron could absorb no more; it dripped blood onto her patent shoes. Desperately and quickly, she scratched a trench into the soft flowerbed soil. "I doubt if I'll ever get that stain out," she told Mickey. "Might as well bury this and get it over with." Mickey scattered dirt as he helped Emerald fill in the hole. He sniffed the mound. When satisfied that the apron was indeed going nowhere, he licked his paws and groomed his fur. Crossing back and forth in front of Emerald — as she, laden with grocery sack and despair, inched toward home — Mickey nearly tripped her as he curiously sniffed her blood-speckled shoes.

Chapter Twenty-One

Visitation Of Evil

"What do you mean you can't sell me any more cat food?"

"Sorry, Mrs. Thorn. The new system that I told you about has been installed."

"I don't understand, Mr. Parker. It seems to work just fine. You scanned the cat food cans, you got a price, now I'll pay you two dollars and ninety-seven cents."

"It is not that simple."

"Simplification was the objective in buying this system. I am paying cash. What is the problem?"

"The system doesn't want cash."

"Mr. Parker, I am truly lost."

"Let me explain. Just a moment, Mrs. Thorn." Mr. Parker depressed a button and spoke over the intercom. "Open register two, please." His wife quickly opened the register and began scanning groceries for the impatient line of customers.

"Why can you sell groceries to those people?"

"These other customers have account numbers."

"I have had an account at your store for thirty years."

"Yes, but we can't take that into consideration any longer. Computers don't recognize your face or integrity. You have to possess a comprehensive account number issued by the city. Then," continued Mr. Parker, "the number placed in your palm or on your forehead and ATM card are exclusively your own and easily identifiable. But no card, no mark, no number, well. . . ."

"Mr. Parker, this is outrageous." Emerald watched as the woman at register two was given a total by a talking cash register.

"Please present your account number," it said. The woman passed her hand over the glass window on the counter. "Thank you. Your account has been adjusted seventy-four dollars and sixty-nine cents. Thank you for shopping at Parker's Mart."

"You see, Mrs. Thorn. Her account was automatically adjusted. No cash was necessary. No checks, no outdated ATM cards, no problems. Just automatic deductions. It's convenient. The system records her purchases and after three months, will average her shopping needs and our order department will pull her order, have it delivered to her home, and adjust her account, giving her more time to do other things."

"And less freedom. I don't want some computer knowing what I buy each month. What is going to happen to all that information? Some government agency will end up with my shopping list."

"You are overreacting, Mrs. Thorn. The government couldn't care less how much cat food you buy, or whether you buy it at all."

"Possibly. But they might be interested in my movement, whether or not I am still in the area, shopping or not."

"If you are worried about getting the account number permanently affixed to your body, I can easily sooth your fears. Look." Mr. Parker extended his palm.

Emerald saw nothing but the usual callouses of a man who had worked hard all his life.

"So?"

"So, there is the mark." He pointed to a bluish circle in the center of his hand. "It is a bar code that has my citizen account number. It is a painless procedure, and as you see, is almost invisible."

"But I don't understand how it is affixed to your skin."

"The process is simple. A set of thousands of tiny needles are arranged by computer into a configuration representing your account number and other statistics. The needles quickly penetrate the skin, inserting a small amount of dye which is picked up by a scanner. Many people like the way the mark looks and are requesting darker dye and in various colors. It's really quite trendy to wear the mark on the forehead. It correlates with the third eye, or some such thing. I'm not into all that. But, as far as pain goes, it amounts to little more than the old TB tine tests or insulin injection guns."

"You're wrong, Mr. Parker. It amounts to an invasion of privacy."

Mr. Parker sighed. He rubbed his bald head with his long butcher's apron. "No cash."

"I won't shop here any longer."

"Nor will you shop anywhere, I'm afraid," Mr. Parker grimaced. "Every store in town, in the state, has gone to the system. You cannot buy anything without the mark."

A pang of fear flooded her body as Emerald remembered the words from the tape. This had confirmed the minister's words of warning. "Good day, Mr. Parker," she resolved. "My animal doesn't need gourmet cat food that badly. He can eat what I eat." As Emerald left the store, she wondered if she could no longer buy groceries, what would she eat? She had listened to the tape several times and had planned to store food. She had even felt a desperate urgency to return to Tracy's house for the groceries she had found in the pantry. But she had no idea things would develop this quickly. Three months had lapsed since her initial intention to collect supplies at Tracy's. But the thought of having to pass Geneva's house had deterred her from even looking that direction when out in the car.

Geneva's freezer probably still had all those chickens, but with no room in her own freezer in which to store them, they would be of no use, she rationalized.

Since the mark was now mandatory, there would be many looters. She hated to put herself in that category, but Emerald had to plan for a personal famine. Quietly, Emerald stole through the bathroom window. She hurried through the house, flipping switches. No lights came on. When she opened the front door, an orange notice flitted off the doorknob which read: "We Regret That Your Electrical Service Has Been Cut Off For The Following Reason. . . . "A handwritten note was scribbled across the bottom of the notice saying there was an unpaid balance of fifty-eight dollars, dating back three months. Also, it cited failure to register by obtaining the new account mark. They would be pleased to reinstate service upon compliance with the new law and receipt of payment, by account deduction.

Emerald worked hastily, loading canned and boxed foods into her car. The perishable items had indeed perished, having had no electricity operating the refrigerator. The smell reminded her of Geneva's death. She worked even faster to change her thoughts. Room to room she hurried, confiscating everything she even remotely thought would be of future use.

There was no way to drive the car to the mouth of the cave to unload, so the trail leading down the hillside was wearing bare. Emerald stumbled under her load. The patent leather shoes, once shiny, were scratched and dull. One more thing to assemble, she thought, would be a workable ensemble. The shoes had seen better days.

She sat at the dining table, checking items off her list: Batteries. Matches. Candles. Canned goods. Blankets. Rain gear. Can opener. Bibles. Toilet paper. She wrote practical clothes at the bottom of the list as the phone rang.

"Hello. . . . Yes, Mr. Svenson, I remember you." Emerald did not laugh at Sven's cleverness, but rolled her eyes. She immediately took control of the conversation. "I am quite busy. What can I do for you? . . . No, Mr. Svenson, I am not booked up. . . . Well, yes, that means I have rooms vacant. . . . Tonight? You must be kidding. I haven't even thought of getting ready for guests since the Rapture took place. . . . Pardon me, the cleansing. It will be one hundred dollars per room. . . . For two rooms? Yes. . . . Eight o'clock. I suppose so. . . . No, I don't have a meeting room, but perhaps the parlor or dining room will suffice. . . . Yes, I see. . . . It's set then. Eight o'clock this evening. Goodbye, Mr. Svenson." Of all people, she thought, hanging up. Mr. Svenson wanting to rent a couple of rooms for the evening doesn't seem normal. I can't possibly get all these supplies stored in the cave and have the rooms ready and supper fixed by eight o'clock. Heavenly Father, she prayed, give me the energy to get this all done.

Her final trip down the hill was finished by six. Emerald put her last chuck roast on to bake and dashed upstairs to tidy the guest rooms. At eight forty-five Gregory Svenson knocked at the door. Emerald was thankful for his tardiness. She stepped aside as he and three guests entered the parlor.

"Let me make some introductions," Sven bellowed. "Grant Sands and Sanguine you already know. And may I also assume that you remember Theta?"

She looked the same — stiff, black hair, pale, sharp features. "Yes," remarked Emerald, "nice to see you again."

"And you. Although you are looking a little tired. Not enough rest?" Theta asked.

Had anyone rested any since the Tribulation began? Emerald wanted to turn these intruders around and escort them out the door.

"We are guest speakers at the Universal Church in the morning and thought how lovely it would be to stay here tonight," said Sven, smiling seductively at Theta.

"Yes, it's only ten minutes from here. How much more perfect could it all be?" asked Theta, blushing in response to Sven's glare.

"But you only reserved two rooms," noted Emerald.

"I believe we can work through that oversight. What's for supper?" Sven headed to the dining room and seated Theta, then himself. The other couple followed Sven's lead. "Will you expect payment in advance, Mrs. Thorn?" he asked in forced cordiality.

"I have never demanded advance payment," said

Emerald carving the roast beef.

"Aw, but these are new times," said Sven, kissing Theta's hand. "If you don't secure payment in advance, you may find that you have guests that are less than honest. You may put this to my account. We are paying customers."

The bluish imprint was faintly visible in the dim candlelight. "I'm not set up to accept payment by that nonsense of a mark," she retorted. "Just because it is all the rage, I'll not have it at the inn."

"That's just it," Sven smiled. "You have to or you'll go out of business. You see, part of my recommended plan to the governor was that the entire state population follow the precedent set by the nation's capital. No money is to be exchanged. At least not Federal Reserve notes. If you have the exchange mark, you can make cash withdrawals of rainbow-colored money. Got that idea from Canada. They've got the most beautiful money. All of Europe is using it. The U.S. has fallen behind. No more of those ugly greenbacks."

Theta laughed and asked Sanguine to pass the potatoes.

Sven continued, "You see, it's a way to determine who is a rebel and who is a supporter of the restoration of the earth in this New World Order."

"I knew my money was of no value, since all the stores went to the computerized banking system," said Emerald.

"If you have cash around, you may exchange it, and at the same rate of exchange for rainbow money," Sven informed. "But not without an account mark. So shall we clear this up now? But before you refuse to credit my account, let me advise you that under new Washington State law, if you are witnessed attempting to buy, sell, or even give anything to, or bartering with, those without the mark, it is an automatic misdemeanor. It's also a crime for a business to remain in operation without the owner being marked. It could be a few months before it catches on worldwide, but this system is the new wave."

Emerald frowned at Sven. He ignored the tightly knit eyebrows of his hostess and continued, "Therefore, either take this five hundred dollar rainbow bill, giving me three hundred dollars in colored change, or use a scanner to credit my account. The choice is yours."

The guests laughed and ate as Emerald squirmed in her chair. She rose from the table and walked to the parlor retrieving her guest book. Erasing Sven's reservation from the book, she slammed the book shut. "It was so nice of you and your friends to stop in for a visit. And what a coincidence that I had supper ready. I'm perfectly delighted that you could join me in this lonely house. You see, I have given up the bed-and-breakfast business. But since you have driven so far out of your way to visit me, it's the very least I can do to offer you supper."

Theta glared at Emerald and Emerald returned the cold stare. "You certainly have given up the business," said Sven, frowning. "I guarantee you'll never have another customer. But you haven't given up everything, have you?"

"Not only have I not given up," Emerald said, "I have just begun to fight you, Mr. Svenson."

"Oh please!" shouted Theta. "How did I guess you were going to say something so profound and southern? You can get off the Scarlett O'Hara trip, missy. I thought there was hope for you when you went to the Convergence with me. Then when Gregory told me you were left after the shift, I was encouraged. But I sense some real hostility here."

"Why not go to church with us tomorrow and hear some concrete reasons that you should join us lock, stock, and mark?" asked Sven.

"Never!" blasted Emerald. "And in the morning, get out. There will be no breakfast served."

"Where's the cordial hostess of the charming Emerald Thorn Inn?" asked Theta sarcastically.

"Gone with the wind. Cleansed with the shift. Redeemed by the blood of Jesus," Emerald announced. The dining room grew silent.

"It's impossible," insisted Sven. "The Christian element was taken from the earth. You can't be a Christian and still be here."

"The original Christians were taken, but I am a new convert, sir, and probably not the only one." For several moments the guests watched Emerald and Sven. Emerald surveyed Sven's gray eyes which seemed to dilate instantly as he began speaking.

"You can't win," he growled.

"I've already won, because Jesus has won," Emerald retorted, hiding her growing fear.

"I feel a spirit here," said Mr. Sands, sitting up straight in his chair. "Your husband is wanting to speak to you. Tell him to speak and he will do so. He awaits your command."

"If it is a command you are wanting, in Jesus' name, I command you to be quiet. Ray is dead! If you have a spirit wanting to speak through you, it's some demon. I have reconsidered my invitation to have you stay overnight. This is not a hotel. Out of here, all of you."

The guests, in surprised confusion, loaded into Sven's Jeep. Sven reached for Emerald's hand. She quickly withdrew from him. Sven winked. "You cannot win." The coldness of his smile matched the chill of the night.

Before retiring, Emerald checked all the window latches and prayed. All was secured against another visitation of evil.

Chapter Twenty-Two

The Jewel And The Lotus

It had been a month since Emerald had last seen Gregory Svenson. No news was a good sign. Her electric bill and payment by check had been returned to her with a brief explanation that payment could not be accepted without her immediate application, in person, at the main office. If she failed to appear within one week, bearing the state required account mark, her utility privilege would be discontinued. She knew she could not fight this system, but should prepare herself to quickly go into hiding.

Her phone, which had been disconnected for two weeks, suddenly rang. Chills ran up Emerald's spine as she stood watching the jingling instrument. It slightly shook the tiny table as it continued to sound. Slowly picking up the receiver, she listened.

"Mrs. Thorn?"

"Yes, this is Mrs. Thorn." Emerald listened with unbelief as the Pacific Bell representative explained that an individual had just left her office. The man applied for a telephone at the Emerald Thorn Inn, paying the delinquent bill.

"How could that be? I'm the owner of the inn."

The woman acknowledged Emerald's concern, yet stated that as long as the business owner has an account mark, services to that address must be restored.

"But what proof did this man offer that he was the owner? . . . A bill of sale from City Hall? . . . Yes, thank you." Emerald hung up and instantly dialed Sven's office number.

"*Everett Avatar*," came Sven's voice.

"Gregory Svenson, you snake."

"Yes, I wondered when you would be ringing me up."

"Just explain how you could buy my business without my knowledge or consent," squealed Emerald in fury.

"Your business? My darling Mrs. Thorn, you said yourself that you were out of business. And the city has the legal right, obligation actually, to seize and sell any property whose owner has disappeared or failed to accept the mark."

"You're a snake, Gregory."

"You are losing your sweet facade, Emerald. Can I talk you into having supper with me? Perhaps if you came to know me, you'd love me as much as your sister-in-law did."

"I don't know what hold you had over Rose, but I've read the article she wrote about you. I believe you had something to do with her accident, Gregory. I intend to prove it."

"You don't mean it?" Sven said surprisedly. "I had nothing but love for Rose. Will you please drive into town this evening? Allow me to persuade you of the good side of the man."

Emerald knew she shouldn't go, but Sven's voice was compelling. She jotted down the apartment address and hung up the phone. He couldn't just buy her home out from under her.

Meditation and prayer filled her drive to Everett. She

quoted the twenty-third Psalm several times to ease her fear of meeting Sven. Over the months since the Rapture, she had memorized many of the Psalms. They had been comfort to her soul.

Her food supply had lasted well, she had no guests to fuss over, and her time was filled with reading the Bible. This she had done for several hours each day, since she had first heard the tape urging her to do so. It was the only comfort in a sea of conflicting theories and solutions. But hadn't she read that Jesus Christ was the same yesterday, today, and forever? She wasn't surprised at his constant love and peace. The same peace the psalmist had felt in trusting God was also hers.

There were no parking spaces in front of Sven's building. Emerald drove down the alley and parked beside a dumpster. When she stepped out of the car, she kicked gravel onto a basement window pane. She thought, as she did so, that she saw a glimmer of light from within; but, as she stooped to look, could not see through the smoke-clouded pane.

Upstairs, Emerald straightened her dress and knocked at the door of apartment A.

"Just a moment!" shouted Sven. Emerald heard him talking within. When he opened the door, Emerald questioned him.

"Who else is here?"

"Nobody. I was on the phone. Come in, please."

Emerald was immediately impressed by the neatness and unique decor of the dwelling. A romantic, mystical melody flowed from the stereo. Sven took Emerald's purse and sweater and offered her a glass of wine in their place.

"No, thank you."

"Espresso, then?"

"Perhaps we should get right down to business."

"I disagree," said Sven, pulling Emerald by the hand toward the dining room. "I would like to apologize for my rudeness at our last meeting. My famous chicken cacciatore is the easiest way for me to beg your forgiveness."

Emerald had to admit that the aroma was heavenly. It had been several days since she had eaten meat of any kind. She did not divulge that secret as she smoothed her dress over her knees and covered them with her napkin.

"I had never noticed," said Sven, lighting candles at the center of the table, "the strong resemblance between you and Rusty."

"Her name wasn't Rusty. Why must you insist on it?"

Sven politely spooned sauce onto Emerald's plate and decorated it with rice and snowpeas. "Rusty fit her much better. I knew a side of her that you never did, obviously."

"And what name would you say befits me best?"

"Not having known you personally, I'd have to stick to the formal Mrs. Thorn. But after tonight, who knows?"

"Trust me, tonight will change nothing between the two of us. Tell me now, why did you buy the inn?"

"As a favor."

"A favor? I don't understand."

"The city of Port Orchard had your name listed as having disappeared, or at least being delinquent since your utilities have been unpaid. They would have sold your property sooner or later. I bought it, along with the other two on Inn Road, thinking you and I could strike a deal."

"Despite the lovely meal, I don't care for you, Mr. Svenson. What kind of deal could we possibly make?" They ate slowly, Emerald savoring each bite of her probable last gourmet meal.

Sven explained, "I would like for you to retain ownership of your property. Legally, of course, you can't. But you can have the property back under one of two conditions. Number one being that you would have to take the mark. Obviously you are opposed to that. And why, I don't fully understand."

"Never . . ." spoke Emerald, glaring through the candelight mist.

"Never say never," suggested Sven. "You see, the other alternative is that you marry me." Emerald's feelings surprised her. She felt a blush of color come to her face and Sven's eyes sparkled with encouragement. "I have come to the conclusion, quite suddenly, that you and I are soulmates."

"What?" asked Emerald awkwardly dabbing at her lips. She refolded her napkin, trying to remain unshaken.

"During intense times of meditation I have soared above the sky with an enchanting woman of beauty. She and I have become one through spiritual, sexual union."

"This conversation is out of line." Emerald rose from the table, searching for her purse and wrap.

"Don't leave, please. Let's move to the living room. It's more comfortable there," Sven insisted. He reclined on furry pillows before the fireplace while Emerald sat rigidly on the sofa behind him, facing the hearth. "The fact is that Rusty and I had an affair. You must have suspected that. At the time I thought she was the soulmate I was remembering from past lives. But she had such resistance to the idea, I can't help thinking now that I was wrong all along."

"This is too personal, Mr. Svenson. We should change the subject."

"Allow me to finish. In my visualizations I see this goddesslike woman. I finally realized that you, Emerald, are that woman. The resemblance between you and Rusty is so great it was an honest mistake. I could kick myself for the oversight."

"Really, Mr. Svenson." Emerald began to sweat before the roaring heat of the dancing flames.

"Don't argue. I'm convinced. And do you know what finally convinced me? Guess."

"I can't imagine."

"Your face is, without a doubt, the one in my past remembrance, but what settled it for me is your name. Emerald. It's gorgeous. The name of a jewel. Your eyes are almost the same green as emeralds. Your parents didn't name you Emerald by accident. There are no accidents, just ignorances. Listen to this."

Sven changed the CD in the stereo. A woman with soft, sensuous words chanted an eerie prose. Emerald could not make out all the lyrics. But the message was vaguely explicative of a jewel being in the lotus. They were worshipful words that built into an ecstatic crescendo, then near silence with a soft sound of ocean waves lapping the shore. At the end of the selection, Emerald reclined, embarrassed but impassioned against the sofa's embrace.

"What does it mean?"

"Simply that you and I are the jewel and the lotus. Our union will produce the highest possible spiritual experience. The interaction will link us with the ultimate cosmic power, transcending us to the status of god."

"You are way off track," whispered Emerald, fighting the excitement of the circumstances. "This is all a diversion. You would do anything to keep me from exposing you as the murderer of Rose."

"Murder? I'm shocked. Don't you feel the titillation and energy between us? And murder, you say. Where is the body? Any good detective will insist upon one before a crime is confirmed."

"Thank you for the evening. I'm leaving, Mr. Svenson. Don't contact me again. I'll be out of the inn as soon as possible."

"You will consider this, Emerald." Sven pulled Emerald roughly to the floor beside him. Startled and wondering if he were capable of committing rape, she faced his hot breath. "You will marry me. It'll be perfect for my career. You get the keys to the inn. And you get taken care of from now on without accepting the mark of the New Age messiah."

"Repeat that," insisted Emerald, struggling to her knees.

"The mark of the New Age messiah?"

"I hadn't heard it called that."

"Is this sudden interest in the messiah a diversionary measure or do you really want to know? He's been influential in Europe during the uniting of the nations, and has recently been nominated by the United Nations to become world chancellor. He has made tremendous strides in bringing about peace in Europe and the Middle East. In fact, he is slated to speak at the Pentagon tomorrow. I believe he is the messiah. What other time in history has one man single-handedly brought world peace?

The mark was his fabrication. But the world was ripe after the end of communism in the Soviet Union and the reuniting of Germany, not to mention the miraculous peace in the Middle East. Even the U.S. has become more socialistic than democratic as a result of the peace pact with the U.S.S.R. and the alliance with the individual states of the Soviet Union as they declared their independence. Everything has fallen into place. The man is a dynamic speaker, a charismatic leader, and a wise practitioner of Eastern religion. With no Christians left on earth, he's a shoo-in as the world messianic chancellor."

"But that's where you are mistaken. There are still Christians, Gregory."

"There can't be. But if there are, they won't be around for long. Don't you get it? They are the ones who caused chaos in the world. Now, without them, we can have peace, unrestrained freedom from religion — godhood within us all."

"You are scary. I've got to get out of here."

"Not before I show you something." Sven looked into Emerald's eyes. She trembled and looked away. "See, you find yourself attracted to me. You glance away when you feel yourself getting close. You've known me in the past. Kiss me and you'll remember the ecstasy."

Emerald struggled to her feet. Sven also rose and grasped her shoulders. He wrapped his arms around her and kissed her gently, then ardently. Too many years she had remained unkissed. Emerald grew dizzy and felt she would faint. She knew she must keep her senses. Then instantly, came the revelation that she was under satanic attack; she silently prayed for God's protection over her mind. The excitement subsided in as great a rush as it had arrived. Calmly she pushed Sven back and strolled toward the door.

"Something is wrong and evil about you, Gregory Svenson," she said, glaring at him from the doorway.

"You'll change your mind," he cooly retorted. "Soon you will run out of food. I've taken care of your other utilities, as well as the phone. When you get hungry for nourishment and begin to crave my embrace, my beautiful jewel, you will be back. Admit it. The kiss was drunkening."

When Sven had locked the door behind Emerald, he dialed the phone and spoke softly, "Hey, buddy, she just left. Just watch her. Nothing rough. I don't want that beauty spoiled. She may not know it, but she's about to become Emerald Thorn-Svenson. I need the total nice guy, family man image if I'm going to get this appointment as assistant world chancellor. Let me know that she makes it back to Port Orchard tonight. Oh, a little aside, get rid of the Jeep."

The alley had grown dark. When Emerald stepped into her car, she felt uneasy, as though one's eyes were focused upon her. Over her shoulder she saw a glimmer of light — a candle, a reflection of a passing car — escape from the basement window. As she turned from the alley, she felt certain that someone watched her. From the tiny ground level window? she wondered. She couldn't tell.

Pushing down on the stubborn door latches, she glanced over her shoulder again. At the corner a young man pulled his sweatshirt hood snugly about his face and directed his vehicle into the traffic behind her as she passed. Onto the interstate, Emerald noticed the lights following closely. The car was still there when she saw the lights of the Seattle Space Needle. If he's intending to abduct me, she thought trembling, he won't do it in a heavily trafficked area. But once I'm past Tacoma the roads aren't as heavily used. I'm sure it's only coincidence. He isn't following me at all, Emerald determined, but sweated, rolling down the window partially. What now? The old highway would never do. Too isolated. The airport!

Emerald exited at the SEA-TAC ramp. When she did, so did the trailing car. She drove around in the parking garage attempting to lose the pursuer amid the spiral staircase of ramps. Her tires screeched with each turn. But this was a skillful chase. When Emerald reached the open air, she recognized familiar signs. "Yes, the ferry!" she shouted. Even a person bent on abduction wouldn't be so obvious in his intentions as to follow her onto the ferry. The airport parking garage escapade had confirmed his determination, but the long wait for a ferry would discourage him, she thought.

Emerald knew the next ferry was scheduled to leave in little more than an hour. That's eleven forty-five. I won't be in Bremerton until twelve forty-five. Then the drive home. If he follows me onto the ferry, she thought, I could reboard at Bremerton, but that would put be back in Seattle about one forty-five. There was one more ferry leaving for Bremerton at two-ten. A lot of Puget Sound crossing, she thought, just to lose someone. Emerald grew exhausted, just thinking about arriving home after the one-hour ferry trip leaving Seattle at two-ten. It would be four o'clock before she was safe and sound in the inn.

What then? Would she then be alone or under surveillance?

Cautiously, yet speedily, Emerald followed the ferry system signs. The car which had followed so closely now fell back to a less conspicuous distance, yet weaved through traffic in constant pursuit. When Emerald pulled into the ferry parking lane marked *Bremerton-Kitsap County*, the pursuing car pulled to the curb. Other cars blocked Emerald in, momentarily giving her mind a peaceful relief. But in her mirror, she watched the driver step out of his car. He paced, observing Emerald's car and the approach landing. As more foot passengers filled the head of the dock, Emerald saw the young man in the sweatshirt depositing coins into a pay phone.

Once more she checked her door latches to comfort herself. The ferry arrived after countless agonizing moments. But a pang of panic struck her as she realized she was not in possession of rainbow money and bore no account mark. The police would arrest her, or at the very least, deny her access to the ferry. She smiled at the gate attendant shyly.

"Well?" he asked.

"Well, what do I owe you?" answered Emerald.

"This is your first trip on the ferry system?"

"My first time? Certainly not. My sister-in-law and I have traveled the system for years."

"I mean your first trip today?"

"Naturally," said Emerald, surprised at the curtness of the man's voice.

"Then you don't pay," said the man. "First trip is free, return trip you pay. Same policy we've had since nineteen eighty-six. Where have you been?"

Emerald hesitated, not knowing whether he meant

where she had been since nineteen eighty-six or this evening. She continued smiling as she sorted her panicked thoughts.

"Get on with it, please; you're holding up traffic." Emerald followed the direction of the traffic attendant, now waving her into the proper lane. As cars parked behind her and stopped their engines, many passengers got out of their cars. But Emerald felt safer sitting quietly in her locked Chevrolet. She mustn't worry about the driver of that other car. She had long since lost track of him in her mirror. Prayer was her only hope at this point, for she had no idea what to do when the ferry arrived at Bremerton. When the ferry set sail, Emerald breathed a little easier and reached into her purse for her Bible. Passengers in surrounding cars could not see her caressing the book low into her lap. She read silently at first, then softly whispered Psalm chapter ninety-one to provide herself company in her loneliness.

"He who dwelleth in the secret place of the most high, shall abide under the shadow of the almighty." Emerald had read the passage so many times she had memorized it. God had spoken to her spirit that the shadow of the Almighty has an underside. That underside is not the same as the darkness within the shadow, but is invisible and totally, secretly absorbed into the surface onto which the shadow is cast. Emerald now accepted and clung to that passage as a personal promise that God would hide and protect her from this man who was, for whatever reason, seeking to keep an eye on her.

Uneasy though, as if someone still watched her, Emerald drove from the off ramp when the ferry docked. She drove to Port Orchard and into the car house of the

Emerald Thorn Inn, still uttering the songs of praise she knew by heart.

The car rested deadly silent when she switched off the key. Collecting her purse, she turned to unlock the door. In the mirror her eye caught a dark figure rising from the back seat floorboard. The man's large hand loomed toward her. She could not move; her muscles froze. As the hand clutched Emerald's shoulder, she felt her breathing become shallow. She panted, trying to gain control of her hyperventilating lungs and racing thoughts. Her head whirled in dizziness, and when the man spoke, she slumped limply over the steering wheel.

"You are a Christian," he said in a firm voice. The words and honking of the horn mingled into deafening confusion as she sank into unconscious darkness.

Chapter Twenty-Three

Twinkies And Potato Chips

The coolness of the room awakened Emerald from her faint. She looked about the parlor and remembered the horror of the hidden man in her car. Her legs dangled from the end of the settee. The front door stood open. I must lock that door, she thought, and call the police. But as she stood, still dizzy and remembering that the police were no longer her friends, a towering man carrying an armload of firewood entered the room. Catching the edge of the door with his foot, he slung it shut.

"Good, you've come around," said a booming voice, characteristic of the lumberjack physique. Emerald opened her mouth to speak, but the man continued talking as he built a fire. "I didn't want to use the central heat, if you even have central in a house this old. Gotta conserve fuel and keep the utility bills low. Even if you did have central heat, most people have it turned off by this time of year. But there's a definite chill in here. And when I saw the fireplace, I located the woodpile and here I am. You can't begin to know how sorry I am for giving you such a fright."

"And a fright is mildly speaking. Who are you?"

He rose and shook hands with Emerald. "I'm Dan Suarez."

"The quarterback?" quivered Emerald's voice.

"I see my reputation precedes me again."

"Anyone who reads the paper, any paper, has heard of Dan Suarez."

"Fat lot of good that did me when it came down to what's really important. Which brings me to my original question. You are a Christian, aren't you?"

Emerald turned her back to him and silently prayed. She no longer felt threatened as she had in Sven's presence or while being stalked by the hooded man earlier in the evening. She knew a peace, although she was uncertain of the man's intentions.

"Yes, you could say that I am a Christian. And you?"

"The fact is that I used to think I was, but am now certain that I wasn't. As for the present, I am a Christian, but became one a day too late."

"I apologize, but I didn't understand any of that. May I prepare for you a bite to eat or something hot to drink?"

"That I am sure of. I'd like anything hot. I've been eating scraps from that dumpster for two days."

"The dumpster in the apartment alley?" asked Emerald, opening a can of corned beef hash. As she cracked eggs into a hot skillet, she learned of Dan's flight.

"I had just signed another contract with the Seahawks when the Rapture took place. You must identify with the hopelessness of being taught all your life that there would be a Rapture, thinking you were ready to meet the Lord, then not making it."

"No. Through my childhood I didn't know any of this." Emerald placed the plate of food before Dan and poured them both some coffee.

"Well, I knew, but shirked my responsibility to God. Football was my big love. I was recruited to the top university in my state, then left school, going pro before my senior year."

"I remember that. You became the highest paid quarterback in NFL history."

"Yeah. And where's the money now?"

"May I guess? Tied up in a bank account that you have no access to because you won't accept the new accounting mark."

"Mark of the Beast to be accurate. Let's be honest and call things as they are. There's no time left for playing games. Social Security, retirement funds, everything. I've checked into it all. And the answer is always the same. They tell me my contributions are safe with them and when I become eligible to withdraw, they will be credited to my bank account. But all provided, they say, that I have the mark."

Emerald felt the desperation in his voice. She had experienced the same emotions in the past few weeks. The two ate hungrily. Dan cleared the dishes, washed them under protest from Emerald, then poured the coffee, bringing it to his hostess in the parlor.

"What do you expect from a bachelor?" he asked. "I've had to pick up after myself for so long, it wouldn't be right allowing you to look after me, just because you are a woman. And a brave one, I might add. Please don't hold it against me that I scared you so badly earlier."

"You are forgiven, although I'm still confused over how you came to be in my particular car."

"Very simply, yours was the only car parked in the alley, right beside the window of the basement where I've been hiding for a week."

"How horrible! And eating from the dumpster?"

"For a couple of days. You'd be surprised how quickly a fellow can go through a bag of potato chips and a box of Twinkies. I didn't think I was going to be there for more than an hour or so."

"What drove you to the basement?" asked Emerald, knowing that she herself would soon be exiled from her own home.

"My neighbor, Greg Svenson," began Dan, "has a friend that he is evidently romantically involved with."

"Seems that several people are involved with Sven romantically," said Emerald, immediately thinking of Theta and Rose. She blushed that she herself could easily have fallen for him as the lust of the evening flooded her remembrance.

"Do you know Svenson?" asked Dan.

"I had been invited to his apartment; that's why my car was parked in the alley. You see, Mr. Svenson and my sister-in-law. . . ."

"Rose Thorn?" asked Dan surprisedly. "The Rose Thorn who was also Rusty Lively for the *Everett Avatar*? I always wondered if that Rose Thorn was a pen name. It's unusual."

"She was an unusual lady."

"And since you said *was* . . ." hesitated Dan, "you are saying she was Raptured?"

"She's gone."

"Well, praise God for that. I really liked her. We visited on several occasions when she was living at Svenson's. My apartment faces his. Not to be judgmental, but I wouldn't have thought she would have made it, knowing her lifestyle. But then I thought I would make it," laughed Dan. "I saw the article from the *Port Orchard*

Monitor that she wrote. Actually I read the reprint in the *Avatar*. I guess that was reprinted in every paper across the state. At Svenson's request, I might add. Did you know?"

"No," said Emerald. "But there's a lot I didn't know. It doesn't make sense. It was an exposé."

"Well, I suppose his purpose was to muster as much support among New Agers as he could. It worked. So as far as Rose's intentions, the article backfired. Svenson is rising quickly in the political world. I've seen limos drop dignitaries at his door. He's in tight with the governor, and it's rumored that he's got some intimate relationships going with some as high as the United Nations. He's got big plans."

Emerald shuddered. "How does Sven tie in with your hiding in the basement?"

"As bizarre as it sounds, Sven had checked into the status of several people at Everett City Hall. All records are public. He discovered that I am in default on my apartment. I've got over three million in the bank, but they won't transfer any of that to pay my mortgage payment."

"But didn't you pay cash?"

"I bought the apartment when I first moved to the Pacific Northwest. I'm not home that much and could have paid off the mortgage at any time. But you know how it is to let things slide? To get to the point, Svenson bought my apartment from the lender."

"And you were evicted?"

"Not immediately. Svenson told me I was welcome to stay indefinitely, since I was opposed to taking the mark, but then he began his attempts to convince me that taking the mark was the only moral, ethical thing to do. Eventually, he threatened to inform the police of my whereabouts. When I still wouldn't succumb to his insistence, he told me he had given my apartment to a friend and I must vacate."

"Just like that?"

"I dialed the police; they informed me that legally I had no recourse. Get out or be arrested. Sven stood laughing at my puzzlement. I knew I had to get out. And I knew I couldn't survive being cast into the street. But I also knew I had to. Do you understand? I mean, I knew from the Scriptures that all this was coming. But I didn't prepare. Sven handed me Twinkies and potato chips. I walked out of my home with no belongings; he yelled for me to eat hearty. He dialed the phone, said, 'Hello, police?' and that was that.

"Straight away I went to City Hall. They told me I had no claim to my own property. I could not buy, sell, own, vote; all my rights as a U.S. citizen were nullified because of my refusal to cooperate with the One World Order. They told me they would, likewise, call the police, so I left before I wore out my welcome."

Emerald grew faint, but fought the feeling. She rose quickly to her feet and announced, "I had anticipated trouble from Sven, but wasn't certain how quickly it would come. You see, Dan, Sven has bought my home also, along with the other two on this road. It's just a matter of time before they'll evict me. Tonight, in his apartment, Sven made an attempt at seduction in order to convert me to New age thought."

"Well, where do you keep the Twinkies?" Emerald swung around to see Dan's sparkling eyes. He smiled compassionately and her tensions eased. Sitting down once more, she composed herself.

"I have already begun taking things to a hiding place. It might be wise to go ahead and take refuge. I've rooted myself so firmly to this place that I didn't know if I could let go. But somehow, you've given me the encouragement to do so. Will you go into hiding with me?"

"It would be easier for two than for one."

"Settled. Soon it will be daybreak. I don't know who was following me last night, but I may be under surveillance even now. If we leave before dawn our chances of elusion are greater."

"What can I do to hasten this?"

"Take my car keys. I want my car to be found somewhere else. It may throw them off."

"But won't we need the car to get a good distance away from here?"

"Gregory Svenson and the evil he represents is all over this state. I'm going to hide right under his nose. From the road out front, take a left. That road leads straight to the main street of town. You'll see signs pointing to the foot ferry dock. Park the car at the dock and walk back here. It shouldn't take you more than half an hour. In the meantime, I'll change into something more practical and go over my checklist once again."

When Emerald heard the Chevrolet leave the driveway she ran water for a bath. She squirted lots of bubble bath into the pounding flow. The cascades became a billowing mountain of foam. "My last bubble bath," she said. Across the hall, in Rose's room, Emerald searched through the drawers for some jeans and a practical shirt. Socks, penny loafers — not at all her style — she carried back to the bathroom.

Ordinarily the bubble bath would have transformed her to a rapturiously relaxed state of mind, but as she soaked she was embarrassed at her foolishness. This seemingly innocent display of self-indulgence was robbing her of valuable time. She didn't know how many of these precious moments she could count on having in the future. Her guilt lifted when she stepped from the tub. Wrapping herself in a bathsheet, she sat on the toilet lid and slipped her legs into the jeans. Pulling them over her thighs and hips was a new sensation. They were foreign to her, but she realized that her journey may lead her to take on unladylike stances. She must be prepared for anything. The bobby socks and loafers were a drastic switch from patent pumps which she packed into her large silk purse beside the meticulously folded jersey dress.

Her overall look in the mirror was not as distasteful as she had imagined it would be. A flush of embarrassment overcame her as she considered removing the dressy clothes from her bag. She was too much a creature of habit; she may wear them again, under some bizarre circumstances.

Standing for several minutes trying to adjust to her new preppy look, her critical eyes finally gave approval, almost admiration, of the reflection, when a knock came at the front door. Downstairs she stood, hesitantly reaching for the crystal doorknob when a soft voice from behind whispered.

"Don't open it." Emerald turned to face Dan. He put his fingers to his lips and said, "Hush." He motioned for her to follow him. From the kitchen they heard the knocking get louder.

"Who could it be?" Emerald asked. "Shouldn't I answer the door?"

"He already knows your car isn't here. As I walked back from town I saw him investigating the car house. How would you explain if he asked why you are home and the car is gone."

"Rose's car is under the carport."

"Yes, but I have a feeling this man knows your car was in the car house last night."

"What makes you think so?"

"Didn't you tell me the man who tailed you was young and wore a hooded sweatshirt?"

"A dark color sweatshirt. I couldn't make out his face; it was shaded by the hood."

"I've been hiding in the bushes for a while, watching him. He walked the porch around the entire house, looking in each downstairs window. He tried the front door, and probably those on the other side. I darted in the side way when he was around on the south side. He tried the north door, just as I deadbolted it. Then I almost got lost in that passageway. It led me upstairs. I following the knocking sound down the hall and back down the main stairs."

"Yes, it's all quite a maze." Emerald remembered unlocking the outside north door so that Theta and her friends could visit with one another and avoid the main house. Rose's accident, the guests checking out so quickly, and the Rapture had all taken place so suddenly, Emerald had forgotten about it ever being unlocked.

"It's as though he knows you're in here and is determined to stay until he raises you," said Dan, as the knocking became urgent.

"But how does he know?"

"One dead giveaway is the smoke from the chimney."

Emerald felt a quickening in her stomach. "The bath," she said. "After you left, I drew a bath. He may have heard the water running. The plumbing is quite old and noisy. I'm afraid I was a fool to have craved one last luxury. That luxury could cost us both our freedom."

"Don't be so hard on yourself. You couldn't have known. It's nearly dawn anyway. Are you ready?" Dan whispered.

Emerald had imagined having time to walk through and bid goodbye to each of the rooms she had so lovingly pampered.

"Now?"

"Why not? You said you needed to change clothes and you would be ready."

"Yes, I am, but . . ." she hesitated.

"Then grab your purse. I don't know of any woman who could leave home without it. Follow me," said Dan, waddling across the floor. "I wonder if this is what they meant by squatters in the Old West?" he joked as he managed to get to the door jamb without toppling over. "Okay, Emerald, listen carefully. We've got to get upstairs and past the landing without him seeing us. Got it?"

Emerald nodded. She inhaled deeply and did not exhale until she and Dan sat on the bottom step at the passage door.

"Once outside, which way do we go?" asked Dan, charting their next steps.

"Left and over the hill. There's a path leading to a ledge overhanging a cave."

"Okay. On the count of three, get going. Don't look back. Don't stop until you're out of sight of the house."

Before Emerald could speak, the latch was unbolted and the door flung wide open. Emerald burst onto the porch, over the railing, and across the yard. She heard the door slam shut. Dan couldn't have made more noise if he had been trying.

Breathlessly she bounded over the hill and slipped, sliding down the mossy bank on her side. She found herself in a mass of tall fern and felt it the best place to stop. Anxiously she awaited Dan's arrival.

Dear God, she thought. Thank you for this stranger you've brought into my life to help me in my time of need. And keep your hand on him, hiding him from the enemy.

The sun rose. Emerald glanced at her watch in disbelief. She had left the house almost an hour ago and as of yet, Dan was nowhere to be seen.

Chapter Twenty-Four

Hideout

"When I heard the door slam, and you never showed up, I thought you'd been discovered." Emerald expressed her concern for Dan as she lit a candle.

"I intended for him to hear the door. When I heard his footsteps approaching I bolted for the woods north of the house, to keep him from seeing you."

"That could have been dangerous."

"Maybe. But I came out just fine. He followed me, but I lost him in the low hanging branches of those thick Monkey Puzzle trees. Then I climbed an evergreen and watched him. He almost lost his way. I think he was relieved to call off his search and get back to the house. I prayed that you would stay put and not come back over the hill to find me."

"I almost did."

"But you didn't. That's what matters. The guy sat on the back porch watching the woods for what seemed like an eternity. He gave up finally and walked back to his Jeep that was parked behind the car house. Seems he was prepared for another chase."

"Did you say Jeep? You know, it was a Jeep that followed me last night, and you said this guy wore a sweatshirt. I suppose it was the same guy. I think Gregory Svenson sent him. Svenson owns a Jeep, and it was on the corner by Sven's apartment that I first saw that guy."

"I only saw Svenson drive a Jaguar; are you sure about a Jeep?"

"Absolutely."

"This is a pretty nice hideout," said Dan directing candlelight into the deep cave. "You really have been stocking up. You could live on this stash a year or two. And it's great how all that ground cover drapes over the top of the cave, hiding the entrance."

"Tell me something Dan. How long do you think this Tribulation is going to last? Will it really be seven horrible years?"

"Mrs. Thorn, I think. . . ."

"Don't call me Mrs. Thorn. Emerald will do."

"Emerald," he smiled, "the Bible is specific that the Tribulation period lasts seven years. Some theologians believe that seven years started at the time of the Rapture. I'm inclined to that line of thought myself. Others feel the Rapture was to take place midway through the Tribulation, in such case persecution of Christians would have already been taking place for the past three and a half years. The Rapture would have delivered them out of Tribulation. Then on the other end of the spectrum, some believed the Rapture would not occur until after the seven-year period. Now you and I are both witnesses to the fact that up until the Rapture Christians were singled out as being fanatical and narrow-minded. But that's been so since Christ was on earth. Christians were never persecuted like we are about to see."

"What of the future?" asked Emerald with great concern. She stared at the stacks of blankets, gallon jugs of water, and boxes of canned foods.

"For me it's the mission field. I feel led, now that I have asked the Lord's forgiveness for my sins, to go to Russia. Don't ask why, but God is sending me to a missionary work in the midst of our nation's former enemy. There is great need there for the truth."

"Dan, you can't travel there. You haven't any money. You don't wear the mark of the Beast."

"When God gives you a job, he equips you with whatever you need and prepares the way. Some of us will be doing good to get through this without taking the mark. You realize that to take the mark condemns your soul to hell? I can't stress enough the urgency of refusing it. There are others of us who have been burdened with the souls of those who have remained after the Rapture, including the Jewish nation. There are Jews all over the world. Thousands in the Soviet Union romanced themselves into compromising positions somewhere between socialism and democracy in the name of global peace. In view of all the peace talk, thousands were slaughtered for failing to denounce the God of their fathers. They stood in the way of one world, under god. But the question is, whose god? Almost one hundred fifty thousand Jews are going to be saved out of this Tribulation, and I intend to help that come about.

"I don't know how I'll get there or what I'll do when I do arrive. But I won't let God down again."

A thundering rumble shook the cave. Mount St. Helen's is erupting, was Emerald's first thought. But the sound was too close, not a distant roar as she had heard when the volcano exploded in nineteen eighty. She stared at Dan with silent fright. When the rumbling stopped for a moment, she held her breath. Soon an explosion on the shore below shook the puzzled pair. Dan crawled to the entrance and lay on his belly, trying to see through the thick moss and English ivy veil.

He motioned for Emerald, who joined him at the cave's mouth. "Do you think he's still in it?" whispered Emerald.

"It's totally engulfed. If he survived that plunge over the cliff, he couldn't have survived the explosion."

Not daring to leave the safety of their shelter in the side of the cliff, Dan and Emerald watched silently as the Jeep was consumed into a charred heap of metal. It burned quickly, but smoked for hours. At evening the tide would cautiously approach the wreckage and in a soft sizzle, cool the skeleton and its passenger.

Chapter Twenty-Five

Abandoned Resting Place

Emerald awoke with a start as Mickey's soft fur brushed her face. "I was worried about you, kitty cat. Dan, I'd like to introduce you to Mickey. Mickey, Dan."

"Hello, Mickey. I'm relieved to meet you. This would explain all these cans of cat food. I thought you were planning on becoming desperate for food at the end, Emerald."

"No, no, no," said Emerald, rubbing Mickey's fur and speaking in a baby's voice. "Mickey and I have gone through quite a lot together already. How did you find us? Were you tailed?" Emerald laughed. "Mickey has been at my heels every day as I stocked the cave. I knew she would know where to find me. And you did, didn't you?"

"I was never much of a cat person. But since I'm an intruder myself, I can hardly object," said Dan smiling. "Welcome aboard."

"I think it is very odd," began Emerald as she lit the small coleman stove, "that after two days nobody has been down to the beach to check on that burned out Jeep."

"It crossed my mind, too. It could be that it hasn't been spotted from the bay, yet. But that's unlikely. There have been fishing boats and sailboats by here at least every hour or so since the crash. And there are a dozen houseboats across the bay. My idea is that it's been reported to the police."

"Perhaps they are too busy to investigate?"

"It's more than that," Dan smiled at Emerald as she handed him a paper plate of corned beef hash and scrambled eggs.

"Coffee is almost ready."

"Thanks," replied Dan, "but they're holding off on purpose."

"But why?" asked Emerald. "Why wouldn't they investigate? Wouldn't they be anxious to identify the body?"

"And if there were no body?"

"You mean the Jeep went over the cliff with no driver?"

"Exactly."

"I can't imagine how or for what reason."

"Me neither. Yet. But I am determined to find out. This is your property. The driver had no reason for being near the cliff. There's not even a road to the shore. It was intentional, that's all I know. I'm going into Port Orchard this evening. Care to join me?"

"Do we dare leave the cave?"

"Aside from beginning to feel like one of the Flintstones, I think we should keep in touch with the outside world. Cautiously, of course, but we have to see a newspaper once in a while and talk to people."

"Shouldn't one of us stay here?"

"Emmy, this is a great place of refuge, but there are people out there who need us. It's dangerous business, but we have to witness Jesus to as many people as possible, while we can. There will come a time when the Holy Spirit will be withdrawn from the earth and no more souls will be saved. Pretty final, huh? I've committed my life, what there is left of it, to winning souls. It's all or nothing. It won't be easy. If I couldn't serve the Lord one hundred percent before the Rapture, how much harder will it be now?"

Emerald knew he was right. She remembered the words from the tape and from her own reading in the Scriptures. She looked at the box of Bibles and Christian books she had collected from Tracy and Rose's belongings. She knew that it was by God's grace that she had found that tape. She was obligated to share Jesus with others.

"If we do go out at the same time, we should split up. We have less chance of being approached that way," said Dan, rising and stretching into a bent position. "I've got to get out of here and stand upright for a bit. Be careful. And, by the way, don't go near your car at the ferry dock. They may be expecting you to return."

"Sure," said Emerald. "I've relied on you these past two days, as though I'd known you all my life. Be on guard yourself. Where do you plan on going?"

"The Universal Church for starters. It's the biggest disseminator of information, or disinformation, since this mess began. And you?"

Emerald stretched from side to side. "Alleys, wharfs, anywhere I might find survivors who are in need of help."

"Good girl," said Dan. As he reached for the ivy curtain he turned slowly back toward Emerald. "Oh yes," he said, "in the event that we don't meet again, thank you for your help and companionship."

"Don't say that. We have to stick together."

"As long as possible, yes. But there will come a time when we will be separated. Keep up the faith, and *do not* accept the mark of the Beast. When it's all over, we'll reign victorious in heaven along with our blessed Savior."

Emerald could not look into Dan's face. Tears clouded her eyes. When she cleared the tears with a blink, he was gone.

Emerald opened her silk purse. Why she hadn't exchanged it for a more practical one she couldn't guess. A Bible and the tape that had led her to salvation were all that would fit into the purse. She smoothed the wrinkles on the jersey dress and draped it over the boxes. Placing the patent pumps beside the dress, she sighed, wondering when she would wear them again.

Cautiously she left the sanctuary of the cave, the bright sunlight blinding her momentarily. Mickey stretched and scampered down the hillside to the ocean. Through the woods Emerald ventured toward town on spongy moss that absorbed all sound. She was awed at how in the midst of calamity God's beauty was still refreshing and evident in his creation. At the main road she turned away from town, drawn toward the cemetery. Reaching the treelined drive, she heard hoarse sobs wafting across the lawn.

Emerald stared at dozens of open graves. What had happened here, she wondered. Caskets lay at the bottom of gaping holes with their charges gone. She surveyed the yard. At least half, maybe more, of the graves appeared to have burst open in an explosion that had scattered dirt in all directions, toppling tombstones, and expelling the bodily remains into thin air. Had the Rapture created this eerie devastation? Following the sobs, Emerald approached a figure slumped over into an open hole.

A woman sat upright and turned to watch Emerald's approach. "They are gone," screamed the wild-eyed woman rising to face the visitor. "All of them. My kids, my husband. My mom and dad were over there. The twins right here and Paul lay next to them. Grave robbers have stolen my family. The shift took the living and some cruel prankster stole the rest."

"I'm so sorry," Emerald embraced the crying woman. "Pranksters didn't do this and the shift didn't take your living. They have been gathered into heaven to be with Jesus."

"Aliens didn't take them? They told me at the Universal Church that UFOs had collected my loved ones and they'd be returned after they'd been perfected. They were all innocent Christians. What perfection did they need to go through? They were all good people."

"And you can be encouraged by that. They are in heaven. I promise you that."

"How can you be sure? I'm not certain of anything. I just want to die. I don't know what to believe. I've been told so many things."

"Jesus loves you. Will you let me help you find him?"

"I don't know if I should. The church said not to have anything to do with people who talked about Jesus. You're troublemakers." The woman's voice suddenly rose and she broke away from Emerald. She stood quickly and jumped into the grave at Emerald's feet.

Emerald dropped to her knees and peered over into the dark casket. The woman had stretched herself upon the satin coffin lining.

"I'll just stay put until I die."

"How long has it been since you had anything to eat?"

"I don't remember. Go away," said the woman weeping. "I just have to die. I can't make it anymore. Too tired, too hungry. So confused. Go away."

"I can't. Let me help you. Give me your hand." Emerald, on her stomach, stretched as far into the grave as she dared, but she could not reach the desperate woman. "It's going to be dark soon. Come with me and I'll give you a place to sleep and some hot supper. You'll get a chill down in that grave." But into the night the woman remained, zombie-like, in the cold darkness of her husband's casket.

Emerald, without understanding her own actions, began pushing dirt into the grave. She flung every loose clump she could grope in the night atop the casket's occupant. Momentarily the woman screamed.

"What are you doing? You could suffocate me."

"That's what you want, isn't it? Death? To escape this world?" Emerald yelled into the hole and knocked more dirt onto her subject. I must be crazy, she thought. The stress of the Tribulation has driven me to do this irrational act. I must be insane. Yet she felt no malice in her actions. There, instead, was a satisfaction that she had raised an emotion other than despair in this distraught stranger.

"Help me out of here," came the cry as the woman stood extending her arms. Emerald pulled on the hands, and the woman dug into the sides of the grave with her sandaled feet. As she did so, the ground collapsed. Dirt piled in upon her.

Emerald slid partially into the hole, clawing and

shoveling the ground with her manicured nails. When the woman was finally freed from the trap, she and Emerald walked slowly, arm in arm, through the woods to the cave.

Emerald hoped Dan would be there. Carefully the women stepped along the ledge and slipped behind the thick green veil into the cave. Candlelight reflected onto the startled faces of a handful of strangers. Emerald felt her heart race. Her first instinct was to faint, but as she swooned with dizziness, she leaned against the cave wall and breathed deeply, quickly recovering. From out of the crowd walked a robust man in a police uniform.

"You," he said, extending his hand toward her, "must be Emerald Thorn."

Chapter Twenty-Six

Fugitives

"Dan told us you'd be back in a while," said the officer, grasping Emerald's hand, pumping it in a wild handshake. "He said to make ourselves at home."

Emerald smiled hesitantly and looked around the cave at the wild-eyed, fearful faces. "Yes, I'm pleased to meet you, Officer. . . ."

"Officer Roger Franklin. If you don't mind, I'll sit down. This hunching over is rough on the lower back."

"Yes. Make yourselves comfortable. All of you. I feel further introductions are in order. My name is Emerald Thorn. My friend here is. . . ."

"Alisha," said the woman, wiping dirt from her face with dirtier hands.

"And I'm Chase Wilbanks."

"Tammy Talmadge."

"Perry. Do you remember me, Mrs. Thorn, from the fruit market in Everett?"

"Of course I do. It's so good to see you. But you're far away from Everett."

"Yes, ma'am. You were so kind to me that day last spring, and I had nowhere else to turn. I had hoped I could depend on your generosity and kindness."

"Of course you may," assured Emerald. "Now, let's get one question out of the way. Are you all here because you have refused to be labeled with the one world accounting mark, the mark of the Beast, or the New Age messiah's mark? It's been called many things. It is plainly a symbol representing the Antichrist. All those against taking it, step forward."

Each stranger stepped, in slumped posture, to meet Emerald face-to-face. "The authorities are insisting upon it," Emerald continued. "According to scriptures in the Bible, it is going to be rough going for those who refuse it. But if you are determined not to take it, you're welcome to stay." Not a single person appeared to be anxious about staying. "Then I guess the next step is dinner. Let me at that coleman; I'll heat up something edible."

Opening several cans of Spam, Emerald listened to each of her guests recount their personal experiences during the past months. Chase had been an industrial hygienist for the department of the Navy when his life took a bizarre turn. Several times he had assisted in conducting safety inspections aboard nuclear submarines. He knew the routine points of operating the subs, and fortunately for him, he noted, was able to recall them when midway to the Alaska coast from Seattle, his supervisor vanished.

"It was similar to an episode from the *Twilight Zone*," said Chase. "Out of thirty crew members on board that day, only five were still on board when we reached Alaska. Not only did I have to complete the inspection alone, I got a crash course in navigation, k.p., and every other duty on that boat. When you're eight hundred miles out in the Pacific, and some freak event takes place, survival becomes your number one objective."

"I'm sure that has become the number one priority of

each of us here," interjected Emerald. "My husband was killed in a submarine mishap years ago. Lieutenant Raylon Thorn. Did you know him?"

"I'm sorry to say that was before my time. The Navy just took me on as a replacement for a fella who took an assignment to the Philippine Islands when Mt. Pinatubo blew."

"Oh, I see," said Emerald. "I'm usually a better hostess, serving dinner on china as opposed to paper, but under the circumstances, Spam sandwiches on throwaway plates seems apropos." She saw that each guest was served before sitting in a corner on a folded quilt.

So quickly and deeply into her thoughts did she sink that she barely heard Officer Franklin mention something about his wife and baby disappearing from her mother's house while on a visit back to Joplin, Missouri. He had accused his mother-in-law, by phone, of harboring his wife under some unknown pretext. But, deep within himself, he knew her commitment to God had always been greater than his own. As he told of a whirlwind marriage and happy life together, Emerald thought of Raylon.

Somehow, during this ordeal, she had been able to admit he was dead and to bury him in her mind. That confirmation of her changing mental state came as she realized she had been capable of telling Chase that Raylon had been killed. It was only by God's grace that she had been able to accept and put behind her that portion of her life. If God could work that great a miracle, he could sustain her through anything she had yet to face.

Emerald uncomfortably waited for Dan to join them. When he had not returned to the cave by midnight, and conversation had waned to an occasional, "so how long do you think we'll have to hide out?" and a shrug in reply, Emerald distributed Bibles and began her first Bible study session. Reviewing her notes transcribed from the Rapture tape, she informed the group about the events which had led up to the Rapture and the events to come, stressing the importance of rejecting the mark of the Beast.

"But what if we are forced?" asked Perry.

"We will all be pressured; most already have been, for example, losing our homes. But we are warned in the Bible that we must avoid the mark." Emerald read the passage to them, "Revelation 13:16-17 says, 'And he — the Antichrist — causeth all, both small and great, rich and poor, free and bond, to receive a mark in their right hand, or in their foreheads: And that no man might buy or sell, save he that had the mark, or the name of the beast, or the number of his name.' 'And the third angel followed them, saying with a loud voice, If any man worship the beast and his image, and receive his mark in his forehead, or in his hand, The same shall drink of the wine of the wrath of God, which is poured out without mixture into the cup of his indignation; and he shall be tormented with the fire and brimstone in the presence of the holy angels, and in the presence of the Lamb; And the smoke of their torment ascendeth up for ever and ever; and they have no rest day nor night, who worship the beast and his image, and whosoever receiveth the mark of his name. Here is the patience of the saints; here are they that keep the commandments of God, and the faith of Jesus.' That's found in Revelation 14:9-12."

"That's pretty clear," stated Chase.

"But what if," began Perry, "you were apprehended,

literally held down, and the mark was administered to you by force. And you were kicking and screaming. . . ."

"Perry," said Emerald, patting the young man on the shoulder. "The Antichrist will deceive people. He wants followers who are willing, loyal participants in his plan for world rule. And besides, God knows your heart. If you are truly saved, God will work in your behalf so that you would not be placed in that position."

"Besides that," interjected Chase, "if it came down to it, you'd be better off being killed by your persecutors. Death is but for an instant. Eternal damnation, like Emerald just read, is the reward of those taking the mark."

"But I'm saying if I don't want to take the mark, and God knows that, won't he honor my heart's desire and not punish me if I'm forced to take the mark?" Perry was sweating now. He wiped his forehead with his sleeve. "You see, I can't hide out forever. I've gotta get air, talk to people. Live again. But I don't want to take the mark if it means losing my soul."

"Sounds like you want your cake and yet you want to eat it," snapped Tammy. "You aren't saved, are you? There are a lot of people who will not take the mark, but they won't be saved, so they are going to suffer hell, anyway."

"Being saved was for people before the Rapture. All that is passed away. The only thing that will get us through now is refusal of the mark," insisted Perry.

"A fence rider, even now." Tammy crossed the cave and sat beside Perry. "Back before all this, I was a good person. I didn't smoke or drink. I said *no* to drugs. Was celibate. Abstinence was practically my middle name. But look where I am. I never made a commitment to God. I never asked Jesus to fill that void left by all that abstinence. I believe what Emerald and Chase are saying is that when you make that decision for Christ Jesus, he puts his seal of protection on you and you won't have to worry about being forced to take the mark of the Beast. To lose your soul is a choice. Your soul can't be stolen by these servants of Satan. Your physical life may be required, but not your soul. That choice is yours. It has been your choice all along, even before the Rapture. Just think, if you had died somehow before the Rapture, your soul would already be in hell."

"This would be a good time," said Emerald, "to take the steps to salvation."

"But then I'll have to give up some things, won't I?" asked Perry.

"Remember, I gave up everything except my heart?" questioned Tammy. "Unless you give your heart to Jesus, nothing else matters."

"You don't seem to understand. I'm gay," said Perry, looking into Emerald's eyes for approval.

"The blood of Jesus covers all sins," said Emerald, taking Perry's hands in her own. "Let's pray and ask Jesus to forgive you and. . . ."

"But I don't need forgiveness, don't you see?" said Perry, jerking away from Emerald's touch. "You homophobics are all alike. You don't understand that we are gay, not by choice, but as a result of our God-bestowed personalities. Are we required to seek forgiveness for a wrong we haven't committed? God is love. God loves me just as I am. And he accepts me as I am."

"He loves you, Perry," said Chase, "not the sin."

"May we pray for you? I believe God will save you

through Jesus' blood, and change your heart."

"Oh, I see. Change me so I won't want to be homosexual, Chase? It can't be done. Even now, I feel a tendency to get to know you a little better. I love loving men. But you say I either have to change and ask forgiveness or ask forgiveness, then get changed by God, automatically? If those are my options, I pass." Perry rose to a slumped position in the dimly lit cave. "I'll give it some thought. If I decide I'm in the wrong, I'll look you up. If I have to hide, I'd rather do it with a more liberal group of people. I thought all the Christians were gone. So much for wishful thinking."

Perry escaped Emerald's reach and stood at the cave's entrance. In an instant he was gone and the group stared silently.

"Alisha, there is a washpan in the box behind you, and jugs of water along the rear wall so you can wash up. I don't have a change of clothes, except for this jersey dress. It'll do till we can wash out your own clothing. Your own sandals will suffice for footwear. They're more practical than the pumps I brought along. It's not like we're fashion show candidates at this point. You can slip behind those boxes to dress," she sternly suggested, still disappointed in losing Perry.

She hoped a seed had been planted in his heart. She had learned that to God, all sinners are equal. No sin is greater than any other. All must be forgiven. Perhaps he would give it some thought, as he had suggested, and would return to the safety of the cave, ready to submit to the protection of God.

Dan appeared in the cave sometime during the night. He awoke Emerald with a nudge and motioned her outside. In the darkness the moon appeared red. Its scarlet iridescence frightened Emerald. The tide lapped the shore with fevered intensity. Below the cliff she saw men working to clear the wreckage from shore.

"Why at night?" she whispered.

"Shh. Listen," Dan said, pointing toward the ridge in the direction of the inn. "It's a diversion," he continued, "to cover the noise that those guys might make."

"I don't hear anything," said Emerald, still whispering.

"They know we are here. For over an hour they've streamed light across the cliffs in search of this place. They know we are here. I watched them set up camp. When we leave here, either singly or as a group, we'll be arrested, or ambushed on our return."

"How did they find us?" Emerald crouched low and crept back into the cave.

"My guess is that either they've watched us from the beginning or we have an informer among us."

"Officer Franklin, do you suppose?"

"No," said Dan, rubbing the back of his neck, "too obvious. Besides, I checked him out pretty carefully."

"Then who? I brought Alisha here, but she didn't know anything about the cave until we arrived." Emerald explained the state of desperation she'd discovered Alisha in. The others had offered a repentance prayer, acknowledging Jesus as Lord and accepting him as Savior, before retiring for the evening. She couldn't imagine a spy going that far to blend in.

"Who else is here?" said Dan, "I feel I could use some rest. My muscles are tied in knots."

"Tammy, Chase, and Perry. But he left already. I'm disturbed about him. Where did you find Perry, Dan?"

"Emerald," said Dan, looking with horror into her face, "when I brought the others to the cave, I found Perry here. He told me he was a friend of yours. I should have questioned him further."

"Don't worry. You haven't done anything wrong. Perry is confused and I don't think we'll see him again. He wants to avoid the mark, but doesn't want Jesus."

"It just occurred to me that a lot of people are hiding out. The Mormons have always prepared to meet in Salt Lake City to await the Messiah. Then there was that Wyoming New Age cult that went into underground shelters in the spring of nineteen ninety to wait out a nuclear holocaust and world catastrophes."

"Yes," said Emerald, "I heard that on CBS news. It was led by that prophetess. But whatever happened? Do you suppose they are still there?"

"The relevance to all that is the fact that not only new Christians are hiding. Not everyone eluding officials is a friend. It would be better to break up into groups of three, two, or even individually for the sake of safety."

"But isn't there strength in numbers? We have to stay together." Emerald was growing shaky. She sat and stared at the cold rock walls. She couldn't make it on her own.

"It would be better to be alone with Jesus guiding you than to befriend a Christian imposter. If there is a traitor here, we wouldn't be able to tell by the absense of the mark in his forehead or hand. Not if the government felt that a few unmarked personnel would be benefit to the cause of capturing Christians. Anyway, I have a plan. Chase has a plan, actually. He and I discussed this before he joined the others in the cave. I'll explain arrangements to the others in a few minutes. For now, they are sleeping like babies. They'll need their rest."

Emerald knew Dan was thinking in behalf of all these and future new converts. She had been independent so long, but somehow felt a satisfaction in trusting this new friend. He would be a lifelong friend; she knew it in her spirit.

"You," began Dan in a whisper, "will go to Everett with Alisha. She'll need a stronger person with her."

"Me, strong? Why, I'm as weak as a kitten. I should stay with you."

"Emerald, you are as strong a rock as your name indicates. And you are a jewel in God's eyes. Trust him. Go to Everett. God will lead you from there. We have to get you across the Sound before movement onto or off the peninsula becomes more closely monitored."

"And the others?"

"Officer Franklin has been printing underground newspapers using the equipment at the *Monitor*. He'll continue that as well as distributing Bibles."

"But, Gregory Svenson owns the *Monitor* now," cried Emerald.

"Yes. And he's too busy to do anything with it at this moment. Franklin will be a good contact in Port Orchard. He'll find a hiding place easily. He still has friends on the force. Although it is illegal to help a rebel, there are those who will do it anyway. There have always been crooked cops. Now it's to our advantage."

"Tammy Talmadge is a foreign language student at the University of Washington, majoring in, of all things, Russian."

"So what?"

"So, it just proves that God knows what he is doing. He has matched up this little group perfectly. Chase is a veteran in submarine travel; Tammy speaks Russian; and I am called to minister to Jews in the Soviet Union."

"I don't understand," said Emerald, lying, for she secretly knew what Dan was alluding to. She had just met a wonderful friend — life-long, she had hoped — but was losing him just as quickly as he had entered her life.

"I think you understand all too well. Now, for the plan. Your car is still parked at the foot ferry dock. I noticed it today. When dawn breaks, officials will observe your car leaving for Bremerton and boarding the ferry to Seattle. But, once underway, you won't be found when they search the ferry."

"Where will I be?" she asked perplexedly.

Without answering, Dan smiled and went from person to person awakening them for the pre-dawn briefing. As the dawn approached and the small group exited the cave for the last time, each followed different routes to the center of town. Knowing that one or all were being tailed, Emerald reflected that just a few months ago she had never worn jeans, did not believe in God, hopelessly awaited, in frustration, her husband to contact her from beyond his watery grave, and wouldn't have believed that she was soon to become an accomplice in the hijacking of a nuclear submarine.

Chapter Twenty-Seven

The Informant

"But officer," cried the young voice. "They were here. Just two hours ago. I swear!"

"Your job was simple, son. You muffed it. Step aside," whispered the raspy voice. The state police officer stooped within the cave, clutching his knees. "You say there were boxes of food and jugs of water along that wall?"

"Yes, sir."

"And sleeping bags, lanterns, a campstove, and a box of Bibles?"

"Yes. I promise I saw it all."

"Mind telling me where it all went? And all the people? How many did you say there were?"

"Six in all, sir."

"Quit *sirring* me and get out of my face."

"Yes, sir. I did just as Mr. Svenson said. I followed Mrs. Thorn back from Everett. I stashed the Jeep up the road and walked to the house so she wouldn't hear the engine. When I got to the house, she was already inside. I saw lights and everything."

"Yeah, yeah. You said all this."

"But officer, I did just as I was told. She didn't leave that house, at least I never saw her. Then when the door slammed, I went around back to check it out. I never saw her leave. I looked all day. I knew she couldn't go far."

"Then how did you find this place?"

"The cat, sir, led me right to this cave. From the shore I never did spot it."

"Then the crash was a waste of a perfectly good Jeep."

"Yes, sir, as it turns out. But I felt since Mr. Svenson told me to get rid of the Jeep, I could kill two birds with one stone."

"But all you accomplished was the murder of a Jeep. The rebels have escaped. You'd better hope that Mr. Svenson has a good sense of humor, or you'll have that lovely little laser tattoo you dread so much."

"Sir, it really wasn't my fault. I don't know where they've gone or how they got out of here so quickly."

"Well, you'll have plenty of time to think about it on the ferry back to Seattle."

"No, sir. I can stay and help with the investigation."

"Seems that the boss wants to see you."

"But, officer. . . ."

"Don't *officer* me. And get out of my face."

"You don't understand. He'll make me take the mark."

"Stop crying. It's painless. I have the mark. Nothing to it. Beats starving."

"But if it's true about sealing my eternal damnation, I don't want it."

"Snap out of it and knock off the Christian propaganda."

"That's what we said about the Rapture and it happened!"

"Perry," said the officer, grabbing the young man by the collar, "you sniveling wimp. I don't know how the likes of you survived the shift, but I guarantee, I'm going to drag you down to the station and personally administer the mark if you don't get your act together. Now you get out my face and out of this cave. You be on that five-forty ferry."

"But, sir, the foot ferry has already left for Bremerton."

"Out of the cave, Perry. My back will never be the same."

"Wainright here," said the officer into the radio transmitter of the patrol car. "Suspect has eluded us once again. This time she has five accomplices. I'm sending our man, Perry, back to Everett; the locals can keep an eye out for the fugitive. I'm on my way back to Olympia to organize security for next week's Soviet visit to Everett. He arrives Saturday for the dedication of the joint U.S.-Soviet nuclear sub. Anything you want me to tell the Russians? . . . Later then."

"Hey, Perry," he said replacing the transmitter, "ever hotwire a car?"

The figures stood stealthily on the foggy shore. "You can't just tell me goodbye like this, Dan," said Emerald, crying.

"There is nothing certain now that the Tribulation has begun. You're needed here to evangelize while there's still time. I know God caused our paths to cross, but I have work to do in the Soviet Union. The apparent breakup of the Communist Party and the states being allowed to declare their independence was a deceptive trick of the Party to gain the confidence of democratic nations. It has worked, more easily perhaps than even staunch Party leaders had expected. The U.S. and the Soviets have joined in an unholy alliance that will be instrumental in ushering in the Antichrist. When the U.S. issued the Soviet nation credits in the form of vouchers to be tracked through the European computer system known as the Beast, they made it easier for the world to accept the notion of trading, buying, and selling without the exchange of money. Which leads us right to where we are today. The only positive result of *perestroika* is the facade of religious freedom. Even that was meant as a deception to gain the trust of the commonwealth.

"Until the confusion of the Rapture dies down," Dan continued, "I still have a chance to get into the country to minister."

"But why can't I come with you?"

"America as a nation has bought into every heresy possible. It's vital that someone preach the Word. Quickly, Emerald, while there is still time. You can do it. Alisha will help."

The frail woman stood on the amber shore, her borrowed dress fluttering in the dawn's misty air. As Emerald watched her from beside the dock, she said, "All Alisha wants to do is die. She accepted the Lord, but she wants it all to end quickly. She has lost so much and is fearful that she won't be able to stand against the enemy for long."

"She will make it with your help. Listen to me. We only have forty-five minutes to get to Bremerton to catch the ferry. The supplies we loaded onto the boat that Chase checked out from the naval shipyard are already on their way to Bremerton. Chase will meet me at the ferry landing."

"But you are driving Alisha and I onto the ferry!"

"And as soon as we board, I'll deboard on foot, rendezvous with Chase and get on our way to Everett to the new shipyard. By seven a.m., at the shift change, we stow away. Saturday will find us headed for Vlodivostok, the San Francisco of the Far East, in a brand-spanking-new Typhoon."

"I'm scared. I don't think we can get off the ferry in Seattle and get to safety without someone seeing us."

"What is it you don't understand? You know how to push the back seat forward to get from the trunk into the car's interior?" asked Dan.

"Yes, but. . . ."

"The two of you will ditch the car, split up, get lost in the crowd, and deboard on foot as soon as the ferry docks."

"But, Dan . . ." interrupted Emerald.

"No arguments. You'll meet again at the aquarium."

"That's just it, Dan. What then?"

"Interstate Five takes you to any number of cities. Granted, you'll be on foot and traveling at night, but stay out of the city of Everett, Gregory Svenson's territory."

"Interstate Five doesn't lead to Vlodivostok."

"Once and for all, Emerald, I've loved coming to know you. It's by God's grace that I met you. But now our ways part. Had this been another time before the Rapture, I know beyond any doubt we would have been lifelong friends. But the entire world has changed. At this point, only Jesus matters." Dan dabbed at Emerald's tear-streaked eyes with his thumb. "This will be over in a few short years," he continued. "I'll see you on the other side where we'll never be parted but will reign forever with our blessed Savior."

Dan unlocked the car trunk and helped the ladies inside. The closing lid sent chills through Emerald's body. What if something goes wrong? She and Alisha would certainly die in this dark, smothering deathtrap. The backseat could jam. Dan might be apprehended. The car would be their tomb.

Emerald listened for the car door's slam and almost instantly imagined she heard voices. Straining intently over the engine's purr, she heard them again.

"Mr. Suarez, isn't it?"

"Yes, Perry, good to see you," answered Dan.

"I bet you are. What are you doing in Mrs. Thorn's Chevy?" Emerald listened for a reply from Dan, but heard none. "I thought so," continued Perry, "this is grand theft auto, you know?" Had Perry stood silently by, watching the women stow away in the trunk? Would they be captives until the police arrived? Emerald panted, then slowed her breathing to calm herself. Listen, she thought. Pay attention.

"I suppose I could forget all about this little incident if you could give me a lift into Everett," insisted Perry.

"Hop in," said Dan, "the ferry leaves in half an hour."

Emerald heard no conversation between the two men, even after the car was parked on the car deck. Then suddenly Dan laughed, "Guess I have to be your nursemaid until we get to Everett, or may I get out and stretch my legs?"

"Don't smart off to me, Suarez. I'm holding the advantage here. I could very easily alert security that you are a fugitive."

"Take it easy, Perry. I'll grab us a couple of coffees

and some Danish rolls on the way back from the men's room."

"Make it snappy," insisted Perry. "By the way," he added, "leave the keys. I might be able to pick up some tunes on the radio."

"I guess I can trust you," said Dan's voice, trailing into the distance. At five-forty sharp, Emerald heard the ferry's departure horn sound. She knew Dan had safely deboarded when an eternity later Perry began cursing.

"Who cares?" he shouted suddenly. "So you skipped out on me. I've got the wheels. Emerald Thorn's wheels. This could be the vintage offering to patch things up with Sven." he said.

The ferry crossing and subsequent ride to Everett culminated in exhaustion; Emerald struggled for enough oxygen to keep her awake, hidden in the deep darkness of the trunk. Each muscle of her back and limbs screamed to be stretched. Wanting to enquire about Alisha's condition, she feared that the slightest whisper would draw attention from the unsuspecting chauffeur. She remained silent, predicting that Alisha was in the exact state of discomfort as herself. She closed her eyes and tried to relax.

Perry carefully wedged the car in between Sven's Jaguar and the concrete garage wall. Emerald listened to diminishing footsteps, and when the sound had totally receded, she nudged Alisha indicating the time for escape was now. We must get out of here and into hiding before our discovery, she thought, working quickly to slide the car seat forward. Through the revealed opening, the women crawled stiffly. When their feet hit solid ground, they stretched and briefly shook their arms. Debating their next move, Emerald stood with her hands uplifted in an attempt to restore feeling to her fingers which had become numb from having been rested on for three hours. they tingled, then a surge of feeling pulsed. She remembered Dan having eluded Sven and local officials in the basement of his apartment building. Sven's apartment building. The thought of being this close to Sven sent a rush of fear through her body.

"But what better place to hide than under his very nose?" she said.

"What?" asked Alisha, stopping her windmill twists.

"Follow me, quickly." Emerald held a finger to her lips. Alisha sheepishly mimicked Emerald's tiptoe retreat into the alley. Past the dumpster they crept, knelt at a small smoked window, and entered the dankness of the cellar.

"How long do you think we can hide out in this place? It smells musty and decaying. And what's all that trash? It must be a mouse nest. I can't stay in a place like this. It's terrible."

"Not much worse than the grave you would have buried yourself in."

"You're right," said Alisha, ducking her head in shame. "I could have died and gone into eternity in hell. I'm better off here."

"We'll do fine. God is with us in this desolate place. More refined people than ourselves have faced worse circumstances."

"You're right, Emerald. Thank you for saving my life and taking me under your wing."

"Thank God, not me," said Emerald digging around in her handbag. I didn't even bring a hairbrush. My hair must look like a wombat's. "What's this?" she asked, straightening a wadded piece of paper. "Alisha," she said as she creased the paper, placing it in her jeans pocket, "do you like Chinese food?"

Spooning apricot sauce onto her eggroll, Emerald said, "Imagine that voucher for free meals still being in my purse. I had completely forgotten about it. A lifesaver it was. We can eat at the China Doll indefinitely. They didn't ask to see our marks, simply looked at the voucher as though it were gold. And at the time, I didn't consider a foreign object in my food a Godsend."

"May we have doggie bags?" asked Alisha, as their waitress began clearing the table.

"A dragon bag?" giggled the waitress.

"Whatever you call those little cardboard cartons," replied Alisha. Beyond the waitress she spied several tables at which sat a dozen uniformed sailors. "What are those naval personnel doing here in hordes? Do you typically have that much Navy business?"

"We have regulars from the new shipyard, but," answered the waitress' reverent voice, "many military in town for Saturday dedication of new naval base and peace submarine."

"Really?" quizzed Emerald. "Do you know what time the dedication is?"

"I hear officers yesterday say they shove off nineteen hundred hours, but they not say what time. I get you dragon bag, please." The waitress bowed and disappeared into the kitchen.

"They leave at seven p.m. That means the dedication will be earlier," said Emerald, calculating.

"How much earlier?"

"I'm prepared to guess the pomp and circumstance could last a couple of hours. If I could get one last glimpse of Dan. . . ."

"But," interrupted Alisha, "you don't know where he will be. Even if you did spot him in the crowd, you'd give him away, maybe spoil his plan, by recognizing him."

"Not if I'm careful. I think I feel a plan of my own coming on, as we speak. See that attractive redhead at the back table?"

"You can't be thinking," whispered Alisha slyly, "of impersonating an officer of the U.S. Navy."

"Why not? Anything is worth a try at this point, even abduction and impersonation. We're already in trouble, for doing nothing. We're traitors to the new global system; one more offense won't heighten our punishment if caught."

"Not me," objected Alisha. "I can't hold a straight face. My nervousness would disclose us immediately. But I'll help in any way I can so that you can get your final glimpse of Dan Suarez."

The waitress was back, and the ladies remained silent as she scraped chow mein and sweet and sour pork into the boxes. "The manager say this meal on the house. Could I get you something else?"

"Nothing else, thank you." Emerald smiled at the petite woman, watching her delicate fingers close the carton tabs, then Emerald noticed the universal mark on the hand. The enchantment of the evening had momentarily diverted Emerald's attention from the hideous circumstances the world now faced. Above everything else, she must proclaim Jesus to others before they are coerced into accepting the mark. She was saddened and could look no longer at the emblem of Satan on the tender palm of this lost waitress.

When the red-haired officer and her comrades rose to leave, Emerald motioned with a glance for Alisha to follow them to the door.

"One last thing," said Emerald as her waitress passed by with a tray of eggrolls, "do you know where all these officers are staying?"

"I sorry, but I not know."

"Thank you. I'll see you again soon."

"Yes, you have voucher. Manager say you welcome all time. . . ."

"Excuse me," interrupted Emerald, seeing the party leave the restaurant, "goodbye."

For several blocks Emerald and Alisha trailed far behind the laughing party of sailors. Emerald sized up the female officer, wondering how she and Alisha could cut the redhead out of the crowd. More difficult yet, could these two pampered women subdue her, steal her clothes, and tie her securely enough to safely effect a final, brief meeting with Dan? She would be risking her life for this man; she suddenly blushed. She was in love, she mused. Jesus — the only pressing matter — had to be proclaimed. She couldn't be in love. Not now.

The redhead broke from the crowd, stepped into the door of a dry cleaning shop, and just as quickly returned with a beautifully pressed suit of Navy blues. There must be other dry cleaning left by these visiting Navy personnel, she thought. I just have to get at them without drawing suspicion.

Emerald flinched as a man called, "Lieutenant

Adams!" Incuriously, she and Alisha window browsed at an antique shop as the dry cleaner explained that, with the Navy in town en masse, a backlog had formed. Would Saturday evening be too late for her to pick up her other uniform? The lieutenant smiled and assured the man that Saturday she'd make it in before closing to pick up the uniform. If her plans changed, one of her mates would drop by. In such case, advance payment would be expected, she realized. She handed the man a five dollar bill; he frowned.

"Oh yes," she said, "the scanner." As Lt. Adams stepped back into the shop to be scanned for advance payment of the cleaning bill, Emerald beamed as a stroke of enlightenment occurred to her. The Lord had just provided a means of her obtaining her disguise. Borrowing a uniform was certainly less distasteful than committing abduction.

"I'm glad we brought the leftovers with us," said Alisha, licking the last bit of sauce from the disposable fork.

"Right. We don't know when we'll eat again," agreed Emerald. "The restaurant manager's kindness could have been a set up. It's my guess that anyone — voucher or no — without the mark is reported to authorities. They may be expecting us to try it again and be waiting for us flies to return to the web?"

"Those sweet little Chinese people, spiders?"

"Sweet spiders who sport the mark. I don't think we can trust anyone. They may have alerted the police when we left. For all we know, we may have been followed here."

"We'll starve if we can't leave the basement," sighed Alisha. "Maybe that's the best thing. The sooner I die, the better off I'll be. I know I can't elude the law for seven years or hold up under torture if I'm captured. I just pray if they do apprehend me, my death will be swift."

"Stop it, Alisha," Emerald whispered, "we can make it. We have to. Other people's salvation depends on our staying alive to tell them of Jesus' sacrifice for them."

"Yes, that's the most important thing now. There's nothing other than that to live for."

"When night falls, I'll go through the dumpster for something at least edible. And, although it's a little damp, we'll sleep in the corner here. By Saturday the heat may be off and we'll seek better shelter."

When the sun's light no longer shone through the cloudy basement window, Emerald searched through the dumpster adjacent the building. Collection had already been made. Only a well-worn windbreaker jacket, a tarnished silverplate fork, and an empty pork 'n beans can remained in the bottom. She slipped on the jacket, dusting coffee grounds from the sleeve. As she prepared herself to escape the gloomy stench, voices came through the night toward her. She crouched low.

"I know they came this way. The Chink phoned while they were still at the restaurant. We watched them the whole way, but lost them when they turned into the alley. They must have caught on and made a break for it."

Emerald hoped Alisha had hidden herself, as flashlights lit the side of the apartment building, streaming a beam along the terraces, reflecting off the mist shorebound from the Sound. When the voices subsided, Emerald hoisted herself over the trash bin's rim. She found Alisha trembling in the cold darkness of the cellar.

"I know I can't stay in hiding. I know I can't. Tomorrow I'm leaving."

"Alisha, let's give it a chance. That was a close call, but we weren't detected. That's proof that we can make it."

On Friday evening, Alisha grew apprehensive at the suggestion that she would be alone while Emerald went to pick up Lt. Adam's uniform at the cleaners, but she agreed that when the time came, she would stay in the safety of the basement until Emerald's return.

Since the Oriental feast, hunger had been constant. On Thursday the women had captured a dozen snails and brewed them into a putrid stew in the pork 'n beans can filled with water extracted from a neighbor's outside faucet. On a small fire, kindled from trash from the mouse's nest and lit from matches that one of the police officers had dropped, they simmered the foul-smelling dinner.

Police had been only steps away both night and day. Gloom had settled over the building and in the minds of the women. A slug inched its way up the side of the cellar wall. Emerald scraped it into the can and bent the ragged lid closed to prevent its escape. Saturday she would look for more appetizing fare in trash cans in the alleyway behind businesses lining Broadway.

Alisha slept fitfully, exchanging tortures of realism for the magnification of it in her dreams. The Rapture had taken place. Emerald had accepted it. Soon it would be winter. It must not find her cowering in an apartment building basement. She knew Alisha would eat no more of the snail stew, so Emerald determined not to awaken her.

"The last match," Emerald spoke to herself as she struck the sulphured tip against the cement wall. Torn paper and rags, resembling petticoat ruffles, ignited in brilliant coral. The flash subsided as quickly as it appeared, leaving a struggling glimmer of fire. For what seemed like hours, she relived the loss of Ray, her fairytale existence as a southern belle imposter, and the events leading her to this place in time. Anger unexpectedly arose within her. If millions of people had vanished, where were those same millions before the Rapture? In her entire lifetime, not even a handful of acquaintances had presented themselves to her as Christians. And when they did, it was more apologetic than with boldness. They spoke elusively of being saved. From what? she had always wondered.

When the subject arose, there was the insinuation that something horrible would come down on her if she refused to be saved. It was as though she were being threatened, forced under condemnation by some holier-than-herself well-intender. Where was the love of God in those few who had attempted to minister to her? Attempted. Attempted in a crude way, she supposed, but at least attempted. The rest were too busy being religious to share Jesus with her, or were fearful of her possible rejection. It was Rose who had first urged her to consider her soul's standing with God. Everything Rose had said had been presented in love. Then later, too late for being caught away with Rose, the Holy Spirit himself drew her to the Lord Jesus through His love. Her entire life would have been different had she only known Jesus sooner.

The only real blame, she knew, had to be put on herself. With churches, televangelists, books, and endless resources available to her, she had dismissed the invitation to become part of God's kingdom. She had freely chosen to disregard the compelling of the Holy Spirit.

Now she sat humbly before God in this desolate place, realizing that if she were to escape the Antichrist, avoid taking the mark of the Beast, it would be by the grace of God.

Chapter Twenty-Eight

The Surrender

The smoke from last night's cookfire had added a welcome layer of smoke to the basement window. Had the police tried to peer through, it would have been impossible. Emerald scratched a slit in the grime with a fork. Surveying the small area in her visibility, the alley appeared free of police, apartment residents, and vagrants.

"I'll pick up the uniform, try to collect a decent meal for us, and be back soon. Please stay put until I get back."

"Yes, Emerald. But I'm so hungry."

"So am I. Our lives depend on staying out of sight, though."

"Then don't go out at all."

"We have to eat something. You refuse to eat what little I've accomplished to cook," said Emerald.

"But slugs?" interrupted Alisha.

"Exactly why I have to find something else. We were correct that the Chinese man turned us in. So that's out of the question. I simply must get to that uniform before Lt. Adams. And unless I get out of here before the sunrise, I may be discovered."

"Emerald, I want to know . . ." began Alisha.

"Don't start, Alisha. Keep my purse with you. Silk is gauche with jeans and loafers. Besides, my Bible is in it. Read it while I'm away. It will keep you company and comfort you. Bye now. Stay put!" Emerald lifted herself through the narrow window onto the rock alleyway.

The uniform fit perfectly, Emerald discovered, but she continued to be concerned about the loafers which, although they were navy blue, were a clear giveaway that she was not truly a Navy officer. And no hat, she thought, this is not going to work.

Alisha stood to a stoop and peered through the slit in the dark windowpane. The sunrise was scarlet and mist rose eerily from the ground. The seasons are changing, she thought. It will soon be winter. We'll starve in the winter. They'll find us, victims of hypothermia, huddled together in a corner of this hideous place.

A tall, thin man rounded the corner into the alley. He tossed a large trash bag into the dumpster, whistling as he walked to the parking garage. When he had driven away, Alisha unlatched the basement window. Awkwardly she lifted her leg to the ground above and scooted through the open window. Just as she dusted gravel from her palms, a voice above her spoke.

"May I help you up, ma'am?"

In terror, Alisha searched the face of the man. "We've been waiting for you. Considering you might be hungry, we arranged for the trash deposit, a little bait to lure you from your hiding place. Nice touch, don't you think? Now don't be scared, little lady," said the man, pulling her to her feet.

He continued, "I'm an officer of the law, and the law is your friend." Alisha quivered with fear. Her throat tightened, and she was unable to utter even a squeak. "I need a unit to the alley. Subject has been apprehended," he spoke into a radio transmitter. Immediately a police van rolled around the corner, stopping just short of Alisha. *The United City of Everett,* she read on the van's side. The rear doors opened from within and out stepped a female police officer.

"Hi," she said confidently. "Are you the woman that is causing the stir?" Unable to speak, Alisha remained silent, her heart racing. "You must be. We have a description," continued the officer, "frail, fair, wearing an elegant jersey dress. Yes, I can see you have class. Which is exactly why I trust you will cooperate today."

"Cooperate?" whispered Alisha.

"Yes. I've been dispatched to administer the symbol of the New Age messiah to you, or. . . ."

"Or what?" Alisha's voice trembled.

"Or you won't see tomorrow. Cut and dried, you'll be killed by Officer Helms, there." The indicated officer ducked his head; at his side hung a machete that glimmered in the morning light.

"I'd rather not, ma'am. I know of your reputation in the state. You've been a fine citizen. I can't see why that can't continue. Do you?"

"I won't," Alisha whispered. "I won't. You can kill me now." She instantly knelt at the officer's feet. He stared at the woman offering her neck to his blade. To the female officer he glanced, then upward to an overhanging terrace his eyes darted. The sound of the French doors opening caused Alisha to flinch.

"How noble!" shouted the voice from overhead. "The lady is determined to be a martyr. I assure you it isn't necessary. I've set out the guidelines for your redemption.

Are you sure you won't be spared?"

"Mr. Svenson?" the officer called, "She insists on holding out."

"No matter then; do it."

"But, Mr. Svenson . . ." opposed the officer.

"I haven't the time for this. I have breakfast to eat, business to see to, and a submarine dedication to attend. Get it over with."

Officer Helms and the administrator proceeded, methodically lining the ground before Alisha with newspaper. She glimpsed a headline as Officer Helms bound her hands behind her. "Heads Of Hundreds Required For Civil Disobedience." Alisha closed her eyes and prayed it would be over quickly.

"God, I thank you for your Son, Jesus, and your strength in my hour of need," she murmured.

"What did she say? Is she begging for her life?" laughed Gregory Svenson.

"No, sir," called Officer Helms, "she's praying."

"I assure you that praying will do you no good," Sven said, nodding to the officer.

One slicing blow. The officer wrapped the head in the newspaper. "Officer Helms to dispatch. Pick-up unit needed immediately." He gave the location of the body and waited in silence for the unit's arrival. Gregory Svenson supervised the process from the terrace. When the pick-up unit and administration van had left, Svenson called down to the officer.

"Good work, Helms. Did you find her cohorts?"

"No, Mayor Svenson. She was alone."

"Check again, Helms." The officer's flashlight beam fell on Emerald's purse as he perused the interior of the basement. He squeezed through the window, then back out.

"She left some personal property, sir."

"Toss it up, Helms." Sven caught the handbag and motioned that Helms was dismissed. Inside the apartment, Perry walked into the living room.

"What's the commotion?" he asked, tying his robe.

"We've just captured and beheaded Mrs. Emerald Thorn. And I'm delighted to say the Thorns are no longer thorns in our sides," laughed Sven.

"Then we should celebrate. Is it too early for champagne?" asked Perry.

"I'm afraid there is none."

"Espresso then. You relax. I'll fix us a brunch and join you in a flash."

"Perry, you spoil me. How about a little mood music?" asked Sven, dropping the silk purse on the sofa. The flap opened and the contents spilled onto the floor. "A tape," he announced. "Let's just listen to a little of whatever Emerald Thorn found entertaining."

He inserted the tape into the player, adjusted the volume, and stepped into the atrium. Dropping his robe to the floor, he climbed into the hot tub. Perry joined him in the churning liquid with a floating tray of breakfast delicacies. Boisterously he recounted his investigative work in pursuit of Emerald, and Sven poured two espressos as the compassionate voice on the tape began, "What to do if you miss the Rapture."

Chapter Twenty-Nine

World Peace

The breeze from the Sound slapped Emerald squarely in the face and eventually dislodged the mist from the water's surface. Brightly colored pennants fluttered impatiently, extending from the hydroplane of the black submarine to the dock. At seven p.m., the dedication of the new Ohio submarine, with its U.S. and Soviet flags displayed proudly on the conning tower, would begin. If Dan was at the port, he was nowhere to be found. For two hours she had stood, feeling dangerously out of place amid the shipyard employees and occasional passerby. There were no uniformed personnel among those spectators slowly gathering in order to get a bird's-eye view of the dedication.

Emerald knew that Dan was smart enough to have boarded before crowds developed. But she now faced the dilemma of locating him in order to bid him one last farewell. She became obsessed, without knowing why, with telling him she felt the work he planned to do with the Soviet people was admirable. When she thought of the plagues that would soon befall all nations, she knew that determined, unstoppable evangelists led by God were essential in delivering the message before God's Holy Spirit would be withdrawn and nobody else would be saved.

Alisha must be frantic with worry by now. A pang of guilt flooded her being as Emerald realized she hadn't attempted to obtain anything for Alisha and herself to eat. Smells of vendor booths were wafting her way. The sensation which had been barely noticeable moments ago now gnawed unmercifully at her stomach.

"Lieutenant," cried a voice from the submarine deck, "enjoy your leave. Blue team is on in two hours." The neatly clad officer saluted to Emerald. She mimicked the gesture, relieved that she had passed the first test as an imposter.

"Thought for a second that you'd been discovered, didn't you?"

"Dan!" Emerald whirled about in surprise. "Where did you come from? How did you . . . ?"

"Know it was you? I've been stalking you since you strolled across the wharf this morning. A little suspicious, I'd say."

"How so?"

"A beautiful woman, even in Navy regalia, loitering aimlessly at the site of a celebration that won't begin for a couple of hours."

"I did feel a little like a sore thumb," said Emerald, "but I didn't know where to begin in my search for you."

"Is there something wrong?"

"Not a thing," Emerald assured Dan. "I just felt an urgency to see you off." She blushed slightly, wishing she could retract the urgency part of that statement. But Dan wrapped his arms around her and squeezed her shoulders gently.

"We have to get off this wharf; it's dangerous."

Emerald followed Dan the length of the boardwalk and into a small breezeway beside a sandwich stand and smoke shop. In the shadows Dan turned to Emerald. "How did you come by that uniform, Lieutenant. . . ."

"Adams," finished Emerald, smiling. "It seems the dry cleaners just handed it over." Laughing, she recounted the story of her plot to abduct the redhead in order to obtain her uniform.

"And what do you hope to accomplish in a Navy uniform that you couldn't have accomplished in the clothes of Emerald?"

"Eluding the police long enough to find you."

"I see," smiled Dan. "I'm glad you found me."

"And I am *very* glad I found you." Emerald blushed again. "Excuse me," she said, "I'm acting like a school girl with a man young enough to be my. . . ."

"Don't hold my age against me. Dan Suarez isn't quite so young anymore. This whole thing has aged me considerably. Ever since we parted in Port Orchard, I've wondered how you've been, wondered if you had made it to safety. But I didn't want you to end up back in Everett. It's too risky. Anywhere Gregory Svenson is can be perilous."

"We're staying in Sven's apartment building."

"Risky, Emerald," he said in surprise.

"He'd never think of looking for me in his own back yard."

"Perhaps not," said Dan comtemplatively. He dusted a plank of the wooden steps which led to the shore and motioned for Emerald to sit with him. "I think you should get out as soon as you can. You'll have to be leery of people, but somewhere there are Christians you can trust."

"I trust you," whispered Emerald.

"And I am flattered, but that's hardly what I meant," reproved Dan. The two sat silently for several minutes.

"Chase has it all figured out; we'll leave here at five. Figuring at thirty knots speed, and if all goes well, we'll dock in Vlodivostok in about. . . ."

"How can you steal a sub at five p.m. when it is scheduled to sail at seven o'clock. People are already gathering for the christening. You'll never get away with it. This joint U.S.-Soviet dedication of the new Ohio sub has been publicized worldwide and hundreds of crew members, foreign dignitaries, and U.S. government officials will be present. I heard the news on the radio at the cleaners. An important diplomat, whose identity has been concealed until now, will do the dedication as honorable peace consulate. How can you hope to sneak it right out of the Sound with a thousand spectators staring at it?"

"Simple," answered Dan. He stood and descended the steps. At the shore he turned the opposite direction of the Ohio.

"With the U.S. Navy's newest and largest class of nuclear submarine berthed at the country's most recently built Navy base, the fact that a Soviet Typhoon is floating a half mile down shore has been completely overlooked. The confusion of the crowd is just the diversion needed to glide silently into the Pacific. With a two-hour leadtime and separate points of destination, we're home free." The two gazed downshore at the monstrous dark shape.

"Dan, that's an ingenious plan."

"Don't praise me. It was God's idea. He gave me the idea and he just worked it out before my eyes. Chase knew the Ohio would be sailing, but it hadn't occurred to him that one hundred fifty Soviet crew members were twice as many as needed, after adding the seventy-five U.S. sailors that would join them on this peace mission. In other words, seventy-five Russians need a ride home. That ride would have been the Typhoon, except the carpool is leaving early."

"But how? You don't have enough of a crew."

"Piloting the world's largest sub with a handful of crew members will take a miracle. But since God gave me the mission, he'll work out the details."

"I admire your efforts, Dan. Can't I come with you? One more hand won't help too much, but I'd like to offer my assistance."

"You're needed here in America. Alisha needs you. Have you thought of her?"

"Oddly enough, I hadn't thought of her. She can come with us. That's one more hand to help out."

"No way. It's too dangerous."

"Dan Suarez. You just told me that God's hand is on you. That wouldn't change if we came along. Besides, you once said you wanted me as far away from Gregory Svenson as possible. How much farther could I get than Vlodivostok? Sounds distant to me."

"Your charm and wit I'll miss." Dan spoke softly. "I only wish we had met sooner."

Emerald thought she saw tears glisten on Dan's eyelashes. He quickly turned toward the Typhoon. "Then the answer is *emphatically* no?" Emerald's heart wrenched. She searched for the handkerchief she knew was not there, and followed Dan up the steps to the wharf, listening for his reply. Her thoughts grew noisy. Leaving for the Soviet Union on a hijacked submarine is risky. But no more so than staying in America. My native country teams with agents of the Antichrist, ending the lives of all who refuse the mark of spiritual death. The time is at hand when Gregory Svenson will find me. My life will be required, unless I escape. Escape is my deliverance, she concluded.

"There you are!" came a voice from behind her. A man in a dark suit took Emerald by the arm. She could not see his eyes through the black glasses, but she felt his stare penetrate her. "I've found her, sir," the man spoke into the air. "No, I won't let her get away."

Emerald's heart raced. Cocking his head, the man spoke again, cupping his ear with his free hand. Emerald realized that instructions for her future were being transmitted to her captor by way of a receiver. He must also be wearing a transmitter, but Emerald saw no visible wires. Nervously she watched Dan, whose calculating expression indicated he was devising a plan for overtaking her captor. The captor had obviously not correlated Dan's stature and features with any description having been issued by the authorities; he ignored him as he continued gazing complacently past him. Emerald wished she knew what the person transmitting was saying. It mattered very little; she had been caught. Only a matter of time stood between her and doom.

Heavenly Father, she bravely prayed to herself, this looks like the end here on earth. I thank you for the grace you've shown in saving me. I pray that the end be swift. Give me strength to withstand. I'll soon see you and my precious Rose. And about Dan, Emerald closed her eyes, visualizing his safe escape across the ocean. Peace settled upon her, and she knew without further petition that God had already answered her prayer.

She was perplexed that at the same time the captor

relaxed his grip on her arm. She wriggled her tingling fingers.

"Sorry about that," he began. "I've been looking for you for nearly an hour. Except they told me I was looking for a redhead. Until I read your name pin, Lieutenant, I wouldn't have recognized you by their description."

He must believe I'm Lt. Adams, she thought. Emerald grew uncomfortable as the man stared at her loafers and said, "Long night, huh?" He grimaced and then winked at Dan. "They'll never be noticed in the confusion we expect today. So your secret is safe with me, as long as you do me a good job at crowd control." He turned his back to Emerald and pointed south. "The route starts on Broadway at Main Street, over to the wharf, and up this way to the docked Ohio. Keep the folks on the other side of the street. Got it?" Emerald nodded. "Good girl. Just look pretty unless someone crosses to the boardwalk. Then get fierce. Don't leave here. The new world prime minister will be leading the parade and I can't locate the rest of security. It seems the entire Navy had a long night." The man briskly walked in the direction of the dock. "Oh, and Lieutenant," he said calling over his shoulder, "tell your boyfriend to get lost."

But Dan was still standing beside Emerald when the grand marshall's car turned the corner. "This is too dangerous," he said. "We should have gotten out of sight before the parade started."

"I'm safe here, as safe as anywhere."

"Sure," Dan mused, "you in your penny loafers. Any Navy officer wandering by wouldn't think it so humorous that you were out late and misplaced your government issued footwear!" he yelled over the shouts of the crowd.

With the approach of the motorcade, the cheers grew louder. Emerald strained to see the faces behind the windshield. The passenger on the side nearest her waved in robotic gesture.

"The new world prime minister," cried Emerald. "That's him!"

"What? I can't hear you," said Dan at her elbow.

"That's him. The Antichrist."

"How can you be sure?" Dan mouthed the words that were lost in the roar. There was nothing sinister about this man who, although seated, appeared tall in stature, with distinctive masculine features. He held his determined chin up and displayed his teeth in a charismatic smile.

As the convertible advanced, his powerful presence caused spectators to clap and shout uncontrollably. They closed in around the motorcade, reaching out to touch him. So much for crowd control, thought Emerald, as uniformed security officers forced their way through the crowd, pushing people back onto the sidewalk. But as quickly as they were reprimanded, the crowds surrounded the car again. It slowed to a near stop while officers pulled at weeping, screaming spectators, apparently in worship of this handsome leader. The crowd now crossed the street, and Emerald was overcome by pushing and shoving of the hysterical entourage.

Startled, she searched the crowd for Dan. Nowhere. She had lost him. The passing of the motorcade played in slow motion. Screams of worshippers deafened her.

"Master!" they cried. "Holy one. God bless you, peacemaker!"

Emerald cried with pain as her feet and legs were stepped upon. She fought with every ounce of strength to avoid being swept away in the current of this human sea. In despair she gave up and let herself be pushed alongside the car bearing the man of perdition. Only inches away from him, she cast her gaze upon him once. His hypnotic glare captivated her. She almost saw a tranquility in the center of the tempestuous dark eyes. Movement from the man sitting beyond the prime minister broke her trance. Just as instantly, Sven recognized her. He stood in the motorcade and lunged at her.

His intention, misinterpreted as an invitation, was mirrored by the crowd. They pressed even closer, crushing Emerald into the side of the black vehicle. She found herself face-to-face with the prime minister, held by the shirt nap by Gregory Svenson's strong hand.

The motorcade stopped. The prime minister stood. The crowd was exultant; security men were frantic. Not one person knew the significance of the scenario, but all eyes looked with envy upon Emerald who was being lifted into the car by the most important man in Everett, Washington, and the world's most influential and holy man.

From behind, the mass of spectators pulled at Emerald, that they might replace her in getting a seat of honor beside the parade's honorees. Suddenly cast upon the ground by the crowd, pain shot through her body as feet of worshippers trampled her. It seemed an eternity before she fought her way to the sea's surface.

A hand grabbed her elbow, pulling her resistant body against the tide. Running, running. Her legs would not stop. Down steps and along the rocky shore she felt herself coaxed. The salty air revived her and she struggled, weakly, following Dan's lead into the hull of the Typhoon submarine.

"Open main vents," Chase ordered. A startled Emerald sat bolt upright, hitting her head on the bunk overhead. She searched the crew quarters for the origin of the voice, but found she was alone. Again, over a loudspeaker she heard, "Come on crew; open main vents. Let's get this baby sunk." Stepping through hatchway after hatchway, Emerald followed narrow passageways to the control room. As she entered, Chase, positioned at his command post, rotated the periscope. "It appears," he said, "that we have made our getaway."

"You mean we are underway?" asked Emerald. "Who are all these people?"

"Let me make the introductions," announced Dan from behind. "How are you feeling?" He took Emerald in his arms. "You were roughed up quite a bit back there. You'll be sore for a few days."

"I'm fine. Are we really underway to the U.S.S.R.?"

"Under the expertise of our able crew we'll be there in less than a week," explained Dan. "Tammy is assisting Planesman Kuznetsov, a capable driver." He nodded toward the electronic screen on which the two drivers watched the watery roadway straight ahead. "There is Senior Officer Soboleva and Radar Operator Norilsk." Dan continued, "Chase is captain, since we couldn't get the actual Russian captain to volunteer the post. The engine room and reactor room have another twenty U.S. and Soviet Navy volunteers; although that's a skeleton crew, we'll make it. We have to."

"How did you get these Russians to volunteer?" asked Emerald.

"Don't forget," answered Dan, "the Tribulation affects the entire world population. When Tammy explained the situation to these Soviets, they not only accepted Jesus as their Savior, they volunteered to take us to their country to minister to their people. They're anxious to intervene in the administering of the mark of the Beast to their people."

"I guess the Soviets are so conditioned by government control that accepting the mark to insure they don't starve will be a natural reaction to this crisis," said Emerald. "What does the future hold for us, once we reach Vlodivostok, Dan?"

"The Scriptures paint a dismal portrait of things to come. Water turning to blood, plagues of horrible beasts that will prey upon those who have taken the mark of the Beast, and death to those who refuse it. The only optimism at this point is the eternal reward in heaven for refusing the mark."

"Now that I'm here," said Emerald, "what can I do to help?"

"What previous experience do you have?" Dan laughed, patting his stomach over his shirt.

"I can run a galley and dust circles around anyone else."

"You've got the job," said Dan, leading Emerald back to the crew's quarters. Cooking for twenty-seven shouldn't be that difficult, thought Emerald. The completely stocked food storage area set Emerald's heart dancing. There was enough food here for a year. Although Dan said they would reach Vlodivostok in less than one week, Emerald found peace in knowing if the worst happened, and they couldn't actually dock in the Soviet Union, they would be safe in the Typhoon for some time. That next year could pass quickly or stretch into a hideous eternal nightmare. She could not bring herself to think on that future, uncertain increment of time.

"What does the future hold?" the man behind the podium began. The crowd hushed. All eyes were directed toward the tall man. The PA system amplified the genteel voice, causing it to echo between buildings several blocks away. "You've tasted my plan. As new world prime minister, I've brought every nation together under one leadership. From the time of my appointment, I have restored the economy, implementing the one world banking system. I've eliminated the currency that was a hindrance to unification. Under my administration, one religion has been established, dissolving religious walls that have separated us as spiritual beings, and I've invalidated any elusive borders dividing countries. From henceforth, there are no plural nationalities, and no religions. There is one religion alone, or non-religion, I'd like to call it, and one nationality. We are all citizens of Planet Earth, citizens of the cosmos, and worshippers of that same cosmos." The crowd cheered. The dark-suited security man looked about nervously.

"I'm sorry, sir. I haven't located Lieutenant Adams since that incident on the parade route."

"It would be worth your while to find her," said Gregory Svenson.

"It is with great honor," continued the prime minister, "that I dedicate this newest U.S. Ohio class submarine today. It has been manned with one hundred fifty crew members from each of the globe's hemispheres as a statement of my sincerity to bring all peoples together, regardless of race, color, creed, or sexual preference."

Another deafening cheer from the crowd distracted Svenson from his perusal of the crowd for Emerald's face.

"I, myself, will be traveling on this maiden voyage up the coast of North America and under the pole. For most of the next several weeks I will be making stops in Canada, Norway, the United Kingdom, France, and Spain. Ultimately the city of Jerusalem will be my headquarters." The noise from the crowd echoed sudden disapproval. "Don't panic. I will be as close as your television sets," the prime minister said with a wave of consolation. "Satellite links will make me accessible from anywhere I may travel. I love you all." The prime minister blew a kiss, and with a marionette-like wave stood for several minutes letting the crowd drink in his arrogant beauty.

Finally, he held a champagne bottle by its neck. High into the air he held it. "The only official vessel of the world's New Age, you will not be called the U.S.S. or any such nationally inclusive label, since you belong to the Planet Earth," announced the prime minister to the submarine, "I name you the *World Peace*." Crashing the bottle against the fin, the world prime minister dedicated the submarine.

"Peace! Peace! Peace!" chanted the crowd. The smiling leader disappeared into the hull of the vessel. Soon the *World Peace* was underway and out of sight of the cheering, waving crowd. After several minutes, it vanished completely from a radar screen, watched carefully by the crew of a Soviet Typhoon which, itself, slipped quietly undetected into international waters. Its crew members ate a southern-style meal in anxious anticipation of orders from the only higher power, God.